# THE FIFTH KNIGHT

# THE FIFTH KNIGHT

E. M. Powell

THOMAS & MERCER

Text copyright © 2013 E. M. Powell
Originally released as a Kindle Serial, November, 2012.

Published by Thomas & Mercer
P.O. Box 400818
Las Vegas, NV 89140

ISBN-13: 9781611099331
ISBN-10: 1611099331
Library of Congress Control Number: 2012921112

For Jon and Angela

*Remember the sufferings of Christ, the storms that were weathered: the crown that came from those sufferings…All saints give testimony to the truth that without real effort, no one ever wins the crown.*

*Saint Thomas Becket*

# CHAPTER I

*The English Channel, December 27, 1170*

For all his twenty-three years, Sir Benedict Palmer had heard priests preach that hell was hot. But he knew they were wrong. Hell was towering, smashing water. And he was near in it. He and his four fellow knights fought alongside the crew to bail out their small craft. The flat-bottomed sailing cog pitched under his feet as it crashed into another deep trough.

"Someone grab the sheet!"

He tipped his head back at the thin shout from above. Icy rain and spray slashed his dark hair across his face. He could scarce make out where the young sailor clung halfway up the wooden mast, the rescued rope dangling from one hand. Palmer stretched to his full height as the dark snake of rope thrashed above him. A fresh howl from the gale spun it out over the foaming waves.

"Pass it again!" said Palmer. The loose heavy canvas sail hammered, battered, drowned out his call to the boy. He swallowed deep as he went to call again. Though he'd emptied his stomach five minutes after he'd stepped aboard, his guts still churned up choking bile. "Pass it." Bitter spittle cracked his voice.

The sailor swung the rope back again. Palmer's fingers stung as he got a hold with his right hand.

"Look out, look out!"

Palmer looked over his left shoulder at the lad's shrill scream. A giant storm wave surged toward the ship, grew above him to the height of the mast. The cog began to climb the steep gray sides of the mountain of water, the bow rising higher and higher. Men shouted, yelled, cursed as Palmer too tried to keep his footing. The wooden hull squealed and protested as the ship tilted up on its stern. Palmer crashed onto his back on the deck, rope still in one hand. The wave broke above him and tons of white foaming water roared down, washing the boy from the mast before striking Palmer in a freezing, pounding wall. Sightless, suffocating, he slid across the listing planks, sheet still in his grip.

His palm ripped and burned as the ship heeled harder beneath him. Water poured from the decks, sweeping him with it. His shoulder slammed into the wooden deck rail, and he jolted to a stop. With his numbed free hand, he grabbed for it. Palmer hauled himself out of the emptying torrent and into the salt-filled gale. He coughed and spat as he clambered onto his knees and let go the rail to grasp the rope with both hands. Then the world dipped beneath him as the cog swept down the other side of the wave, righted again now that he had control of the sheet. The ship hit the trough in another shuddering blow, but kept upright, drawing its balance from the set sail. He bit down hard against the pain and held the sheet firm. If he loosed it, they'd all be lost. As he tightened his grip, the wind howled harder and the rope tore deeper into his injured flesh. "Succor!"

"Are you a maid at a maypole, Palmer?" A soaked Sir Reginald Fitzurse scrambled to his side and grabbed onto the rope too, breath jagged, fine features drawn in a deep scowl.

"Sorry, my lord. My hand's bad."

Fitzurse hauled hard alongside him, palms safe in his leather gauntlets. "This thing pulls like the devil." The scowl disappeared. "You've the strength of three, man."

Relieved at his leader's praise, Palmer still held tight, the sodden cord staining with his seeping blood. "That sailor lad. We need to start a search."

"In these seas?" Fitzurse's unmoved blue eyes could have been wax.

"But couldn't we—" Another wave sluiced over the deck and rocked the ship hard. Pain sparked through Palmer's hand, and his grip threatened to give.

"Hell's teeth." Fitzurse looked toward the rear of the ship. "Le Bret! We need you, sir!"

Richard le Bret's huge, hulking frame straightened up from his work at the stern. He handed the swinging tiller to two crewmen, who grabbed it between them. "Aye." He stumbled across the deck and landed next to Fitzurse and Palmer.

"Relieve Sir Palmer," Fitzurse said to le Bret, "and make that sail secure."

Le Bret took hold of the sheet in his massive fists.

Fitzurse nodded to Palmer. "Get yourself below, fix up your hand."

"It won't hold me back, my lord." Palmer let go with his good hand, but his injured one stayed stuck to the soaked thick hemp. Bracing himself, he yanked it free without a blink, aware of Fitzurse's sharp-eyed appraisal.

Bent low to keep his balance, Palmer went to step to the hatch that led below decks. His boot met something soft on the rough wooden planks, and he picked it up. It was the boy's red wool cap, swept from his head as the wave washed him to his death. The poor wretch had joked to Palmer as they set sail, *Me mam made it special, thinks it'll keep me from catching a chill.*

"Good cap." Le Bret hooked it from his grasp and stuffed it in his own pocket.

Palmer squared up to le Bret, injured hand or no. "But not yours." He staggered as the cog pitched again. "The lad's mother should have it."

Le Bret lowered his face to Palmer's. A fleshy scar bloated one cheek and thickened the side of his mouth. "Then try and take it."

Palmer forced his cut right hand into a fist, ready to land a blow.

"Palmer." Fitzurse rapped out his name. "Stop carrying on like an idiot. Fix yourself. Now."

Dismissed like a slack-breeched page. Palmer forced a curt nod at Fitzurse's response. "Yes, my lord." He made his unsteady way across the deck to the ladder below.

"Don't fall, Palmer." Le Bret smirked with the undamaged side of his mouth and busied himself with the sail.

Palmer itched to rub that smile out. Knighted a year early for his battle skills, he knew he could easily take le Bret. But he ignored the big lug as he lowered himself to the first rungs, careful to use his good hand. He had no estate, no lands to inherit. He made his living as a fighter, traveling to wherever he'd be paid, selling his hard-won skills for the best price. This mission to Canterbury could make him one of the greatest knights, one of King Henry's most faithful servants. And with that would come great rewards, huge riches. All rested on how he performed. He would not, could not, risk any of that.

He had to succeed.

"I confess that my mind wandered during this morning's Mass." Kneeling on her wooden faldstool, Sister Theodosia Bertrand kept her mouth close to the small, barred cell window that opened out onto the back wall of Canterbury Cathedral. Secure across it, the embroidered white linen curtain kept her screened from her confessor, Brother Edward Grim.

"When the holy sacrament was being said by Archbishop Becket himself?" came the monk's low-voiced reply. "I cannot believe your openness to distraction, Sister. You are nineteen, preparing to take your final vows, yet you are tricked by the devil like a peasant girl daydreaming at her loom."

Her cheeks warmed at his sharp words. "I am so ashamed of my lack of control, Brother. It should not happen, I know that."

"Have you more to trouble my spirit with your besieged vocation, or have you cleared your conscience?"

"Not yet, Brother. There is more."

"Go on."

Her enclosure meant she had not had sight of a man, nor indeed woman or child, for over two years. But she could picture Brother Edward's tall imposing presence, his immaculately tonsured black hair. The stern disapproval in his green eyes. She squeezed her clasped hands tight as she sought the right words.

"Brother Edward, I...I had a wicked dream last night. I dreamt I was dancing. At a feast day, the kind of dancing I saw when the lay sisters would take me out visiting the sick, when Mama was at prayer."

"Mama?"

She crossed herself at the slip. "I mean Sister Amélie."

"You do. But we do not speak of her or that time."

"No. Forgive me, Brother."

"Tell me of this sinful dream of dancing."

"I was part of a group, with other girls. We had dresses of bright reds and yellows and straw bonnets, decked with flowers. We danced before an audience who clapped and sang."

5

A sniff from Brother Edward. "Such brazen displays are most impious."

"I know, my dear brother. I used to think so too when I saw it. I could hardly believe women could disport themselves so. But there is more."

"More."

"In my dream, a man joined the group and danced with me. H-he put his arms around my waist, linked my hands, spun me round. Put his cheek to mine. I made no attempt to stop him." She paused, summoning her courage to reveal the depths of her repulsive imaginings. "Not even when he went to kiss me. But before he could, I woke. Woke in a frightful state at such a terrible lapse."

"Oh, Sister." Brother Edward exhaled a long breath. "It is no mere lapse. You know you have been visited by Satan himself, don't you?"

"It was a man, not—"

"Satan is as cunning as he is cowardly, and takes many forms. He waited until you lay in bed and sleep overcame you, waited until you were defenseless and vulnerable. When you were dead to the world, Sister, you were dead to God."

"But I am alive to God. I am private in here with Him, I am away from all temptation."

"Indeed you are away from the world. Behind locked doors and surrounded by thick stone walls. So how do you think Satan got his chance to uncurl the vile tentacles of lechery within you?"

She clasped her hands tighter. "I let him." She dropped her head to the sound of another long breath from Brother Edward, this time of satisfaction.

"Yes, Sister. Let him in with a weak mind, a weak body. A weak soul. Your confirmation as a bride of Christ is still a long way off."

Theodosia dipped her head to fight down mortified tears, her veil brushing against her cheeks. Its gray cloth might never be replaced by black. "I am so sorry, Brother," she whispered.

"It's not I you have to repent to." His tone softened. "Sister Theodosia, you still have much to do in your quest to achieve holiness. Yes, you have put aside many luxuries. But sleep is also a luxury. To stay awake, to watch and pray, is a weapon against evil that you must master. Is there anything else you need to confess?"

"No, I have cleared my conscience."

"Good. As you have freed your mind from guilt, so you have armed yourself afresh against the onslaught of sin. For your penance, a full rosary after Vigils."

She flinched and lowered her forehead to her hands. A further hour of prayer after the midnight office, when her cell would be as cold and still as the grave and her whole body would cry out for rest.

As if reading her thoughts, Brother Edward said, "Hardship, Sister: that is what will bring you to God." He sniffed again. "And it will be fewer hours for you to be at Lucifer's pleasure. Now make your act of contrition."

She began the oft-repeated Latin prayers, and Brother Edward murmured her absolution in a quiet harmony.

"*Et Spiritus Sancti.* Amen." The monk finished his blessing and his silhouette rose before the screen. "Good night, Sister. God be with you." The swish of his robes and his fading footsteps confirmed his departure.

Readying herself for the next recitation of the Divine Office, Theodosia opened her Book of Hours and Psalter on the sloped reading shelf. The words crystallized into instant meaning, but she could draw no comfort from her reading. She still did not have the nobility, the purity, the containment she needed to make her final vows. She stood up from her faldstool, heartsick at her continued weakness.

She tucked her chilled hands into the covering outer sleeves of her black woolen habit and paced the floor of her tiny stone cell. The cell that kept her from the world, that should keep her soul safe. Three short paces brought her to the far wall and her wooden pallet bed. She stared at it with a wave of loathing. For all its hardness under her bones, for all its prickly straw-filled pillow, for all its rough sackcloth cover, when she lay in it and closed her eyes, she might as well be a whore on a silken couch, calling to Lucifer in her wanton dreams. He would stand right here, on this spot, looking down at her as she slept. He was tall—she knew that from her illuminated manuscripts. Tall, with the muscle and hair of an animal across his near-naked body. A face of sharp, pointed features and a ravenous mouth, and feet and hands that twisted into yellow-nailed claws, and the stench of decay as he breathed on her cheek…

"Oh, Saint Christina, help me." She called aloud for the intercession of her beloved virginal saint. The vision of Satan faded in the chilly air, with only the racing of her pulse to remind her of his presence.

Theodosia turned from the bed to resume her pacing, knees weak. Two long steps to the left wall, where her supper awaited on a simple table: the usual coarse maslin loaf and jug of cold spring water. She kept a frugal diet to suppress her physical desires, but even so, her innards growled at the sight. She turned from it with disgusted resolve. She would not eat tonight, not risk inflaming her lust.

With her remorse a dead weight in her heart, she finally focused her gaze on the large wooden crucifix nailed on the wall opposite. Hanging from it, painted in colors so lifelike He looked alive, was her Savior. Despite her failings, His outstretched arms looked ready to embrace her, His bowed head lowered for her kiss. He had forgiven her, though she did not deserve it. Tears pooled in her eyes, blurred her sight. The words of Aelred of Rievaulx, whose great teachings she studied, echoed through her soul: *Touch Him with as much love as you would feel for a man.* She loosed her hands from her sleeves and stepped over to the carving as her tears spilled over. She reached her hands out and caressed the stretched sinews of her tortured God with trembling fingers. How could she, as His waiting bride, have added to His suffering through her pathetic sinfulness?

Her hands showed pale against her Lord's bleeding wounds, lilies of purity against His royal roses. But that was a wrongful pride—she should not admire them so. She palmed her eyes dry and turned from her Lord.

Squatting to the ground, she started her daily task of scraping the earth from her cell floor. She rubbed harder and harder at the cold stone until her skin rent. With furious satisfaction, she examined her filthy, damaged palms. *Not lilies now.* But the ritual was her proof, her reminder, of her true vocation as an anchoress: she would die, be buried, and rot in here. That was her sacred calling.

◆  ◆  ◆

The narrow slats of the ladder that led belowdecks were slick with rain and seawater. Palmer climbed down with care, as the ship's bounce and roll could have him off at any minute. The wooden hull juddered in the deep thud of every wave, the planks groaning and squeaking like a creature lived in them.

"Oi! Watch your feet."

Palmer looked down past his wet boots at the sudden call. A crewman of around his own age sat on the damp floor of the hold, propped up against a pile of full grain sacks. The man clutched a small covered lamp, which cast a dim glow.

*The slacker.* Palmer got to the bottom of the ladder, ready to send him up above. But now that he was closer, he saw the sailor had a deep cut down one cheek, deep enough to see the white of bone in the bloody gash.

"Excuse my rude tongue, sir knight."

"It's I who should seek excuses, fellow." Palmer hauled his drenched surcoat up over his head and flung it over another pile of sacks to dry. He nodded at the man's injury. "That's a belter."

"Deck plank came loose and caught me smack on." Forehead pebbled with sweat, the man shifted his eyes to Palmer's hand. "Yours isn't bad either, sir."

Palmer looked down. Scarlet drips swirled through the small puddles of seawater around his wet boots. He examined his jagged cut. "Can't feel much at the minute; my hands are that cold."

"That'll pass," said the man, "and it'll hurt like the devil then." He swallowed and tried to smile. "Like me face."

Palmer looked around the swaying, cramped space. A large jug of wine with a cork stopper sat wedged between two sacks. He reached down, uncorked it with a flick of his thumb, and bent down to pass it to the man, hanging on to the sacks for balance. "Get some of that down you. My squire master swore by drink to help lay the pain. And even if it doesn't, at least you won't care so much."

The man murmured his thanks and drank.

As he did so, Palmer ripped a strip from the top of one of the sacks with his knife. He tore the rough cloth in two with his teeth, then wound it around his injured hand. The man was right. In the warmer air, the open flesh throbbed with new life. He took the offered jug from the sailor and downed several large mouthfuls himself.

A clatter came from the ladder. The scrawny calves of Sir Hugh de Morville appeared, scrabbling for a hold on the wet rungs.

"Hold this thing steady, can't you, Palmer?" The whined request was thin as the man himself.

Palmer moved over and propped it with his foot while he drank another draught of wine.

De Morville slid from the ladder and gave the injured man a disinterested glance. Like a hungry bird, he eyed the jug Palmer held. "Share it, can't you? I'm piss-wet through and half-frozen besides." He clicked his fingers as he held out his hand.

Palmer wiped his mouth with the back of his bandaged hand and passed the jug over. He no longer wanted any. The movement of the cabin in the storm stopped his thirst. Soon he'd have to spew the alcohol out to the fishes. At least he had its warmth and numbness—that would last a while. He took another section of torn sack and tried to wipe down his wet chain mail.

Two loud thumps came from the ladder. Sir William de Tracy jumped from the middle rungs and landed with a bang on the floor, narrowly missing the injured crewman. "Saints alive, man. Don't get underfoot."

The man murmured a low apology and tried to shift.

"Leave him be," said Palmer. "He's caught a bad blow."

"Bugger him," said de Tracy. "I smell Gascony, don't I?"

De Tracy hadn't much on de Morville in height, but with his barrel chest he made two of de Morville crossways. It was the same with his hair: de Morville's sat like a thin, dead rat on his head, while de Tracy's curled red and thick till it met under his chin in a heavy beard.

De Morville hung on to the jug. "Do you have to arrive everywhere like a battering ram, de Tracy?"

"That's because I've nowt to hide." He signaled for the wine. "You don't have to look like a widow who's going to be ravished. I'll give you the bloody thing back."

De Morville handed it over and watched de Tracy's supping with greedy eyes.

De Tracy pulled the vessel's rim from his lips with a loud smack and held it out to Palmer. "You did a right special job up there, boy. I'll warrant Fitzurse chose well when he asked you to join us on our quest."

Palmer wordlessly waved it back to de Morville. His head rocked in time with the tossing boat.

"You're white as a corpse, Palmer. What's the matter with you?" said de Morville. "Fainting because you lost a finger of blood?"

Palmer shook his head in reply. He stepped past the injured man over to the ladder, hand firm over his mouth.

"Can't hold your drink? Thought so, with a wench face like yours." De Tracy laughed hard. "And a sap with no sea legs too."

Palmer scrambled up the ladder to the deck, willing his stomach to hold on. He made it out on deck and ran to the edge. He leaned out over the thunderous waves and retched himself empty, same as the day he'd been sent away to become a page. Seven years old, his landless cottar father dead from a terrible growth that filled his stomach and ate the rest of him away. His four small sisters clustered in a mute group, as his weeping mother pushed him from her to the rough clutch of the earl's steward. The bewildering journey by cart, which ended at a busy port, where a ship waited to wrench him from his family, his home, his childhood. The green and gray curves of land had shrunk fast as the vessel tossed up, then down. His insides had coiled in loss so hard he thought his heart would stop. But he wouldn't cry, not in front of the hard-eyed men who sailed the ship and mocked him for a fearful whelp. Yet he couldn't keep his grief and loss in: he'd gone to the side of the ship and vomited and vomited.

As Palmer straightened up, he used his tongue to clean off his coated teeth. Fitzurse stood by the mast, deep in conversation with the hulk le Bret. Neither seemed to notice that, though quieter than before, the world tossed and bounced beneath them. The ocean raced past, the set sail making quick work of the many miles' journey to England.

Palmer would prove his worth as a professional soldier once they were on dry land, once they got to Canterbury and its mighty cathedral. Within its walls, they would find Thomas Becket, its archbishop and leader of all the souls in the kingdom. A leader locked in bitter conflict with King Henry himself.

The King had ordered action, action that Palmer could scarce believe he'd been hired to execute. Oh, he'd rise to the challenge, serve his king, demonstrate his loyalty, his fealty. 'Course he would. He'd be paid handsomely for it. His jaw had dropped of its own accord when Fitzurse had named the price.

His stomach and throat drew together in a fresh sour spasm, and he leaned over the side yet again with a stifled oath. He'd do anything at all. Long as he could do it on dry land.

# CHAPTER 2

"How much longer till we get there?" Palmer asked le Bret, the driver of their small tarpaulin-covered cart.

Ahead, down a long, straight, featureless highway, with winter-empty ploughed fields on either side, lay the town of Canterbury. The storms of two days ago had been replaced by clear skies and ice on the air, making for easier progress along the mud-churned road. Plumes of grayish-white smoke rose from hundreds of hearths and hung above the distant roofs, shrouding the cathedral's huge towers.

Le Bret shrugged. "Hour. Two, maybe."

"Good," said Palmer. "My backside's sick of this seat." He shifted to stretch his deadened legs and nodded to where the other three knights led the way on horseback. "I'd rather ride any day. Keeps you moving. And warm." He pulled his thick woolen necker-chief tighter to keep the afternoon's deepening chill at bay.

Le Bret shrugged again. "Need the cart. Fitzurse says so."

"What for?"

"Don't know."

Palmer shook his head to himself. Le Bret didn't know much.

"You there!" De Tracy's shout carried across the frozen fields. "Make haste and stand aside."

Palmer leaned to one side to see past his mounted companions. Shortly ahead on the roadway on the left side were two men, ragged laborers mending a wide gap in the hedge by laying new pleachers.

Piles of dead branches and shorn evergreens spilled partly onto the road. Both men looked up at the order and dropped their billhooks at once. They bent to scoop the trimmings back into the ditch, scrabbling low in their haste.

As the knights on horseback went past, the men snatched their coarse dark woolen caps off and bowed their heads.

Palmer's rumbling cart drew level. One of the ragged men risked a glance up, then dropped his gaze abruptly again.

"Sorry, sirs," he muttered, eyes fixed low on the muddy wheels.

Neither Palmer nor le Bret acknowledged him.

"Stupid peasant," said le Bret as they carried on.

Palmer glanced back around the canvas cover. The men had replaced their hats and were reordering their work, gesturing angrily to each other. He faced forward again. "He should have better manners. But they've a job to do with that hedge."

Le Bret smirked. "You a clod-grubber, Palmer?"

"Better that than the son of a gargoyle and a whore. Go grab yourself, le Bret." But Palmer was born a clod-grubber, with no land, no money. He'd hedged, ditched, picked stones from behind a plough, pitching them into a basket on his back until his five-year-old knees would near give way. Unblocked privies, carried hay on his shoulders. Always following behind his weak, meek father, trying to earn enough to feed them as well as his mother and his sisters. And never succeeding. Like the men on the side of the road, he'd lived in rags, feet numb and frostbitten in split, useless tatters of boots. He too had snatched off his cap a thousand times to his betters.

Palmer took a last look back at the two men bent low at their backbreaking task. There would come a day when they couldn't do it anymore, when illness or old age or a slipped billhook would rob them of their pitiful livelihood. He settled himself onto the hard seat again. He wouldn't have to face that fate, not anymore. Once he'd finished his work for Fitzurse, he'd never know poverty again.

◆    ◆    ◆

Dusk sucked the last of the daylight from the sky as they made steady progress through Canterbury's muddy, narrow cobbled streets. A hoarfrost white-edged the steeply pitched red roofs. Above them, the gray stone arches and towers of the cathedral rose to five, six times the height of the tightly packed half-timbered houses. Palmer had to lean right back to see how far they reached. "Happen they tried to build all the way to heaven, eh, le Bret?"

He got a grunt in reply.

The few people out and about hurried to their hearths, with their noses buried in cloaks and shawls. By the time Palmer and his companions arrived at the neat grassy area next to the huge church, they were alone. Leafless tall oaks and sycamores surrounding the cathedral patterned the sky in the fading light to the west. Dark-feathered crows filled the branches, settling for the night.

"Dismount." Fitzurse's rapped order sent the birds calling and fussing into the air. As he swung himself from his horse, he turned to address his men. "Our first task is to track down the Archbishop." He nodded toward the Episcopal Palace, with its brightly lit mullioned windows. "I have been told we will find him there."

Palmer secured the cart's pair to a post alongside the others. Excitement surged within him. Here he was, a workaday mercenary knight, about to deliver the King's displeasure firsthand. About to arrest the Archbishop himself.

"Forward, men," said Fitzurse. He pulled a double-headed axe from his belt in a swift movement. "Let valor be your watchword."

Palmer tightened his hand on his sword. He was used to fighting. But being part of this group was true power. Something new, something special. The quick thump of his blood through his veins told him how much he liked it.

Fitzurse arrived first at the closed heavy wooden door of the palace. He pounded hard on it with his fist. "Open up, in the name of King Henry!"

Silence but for more cawing from the crows.

"Open up, I say!" Fitzurse hammered again on the door. It remained unopened. He turned to le Bret. "Break it down. Now."

◆　◆　◆

Theodosia knelt in prayer in her cell as the choir of monks in the cathedral sang their way through Vespers. It used to be her favorite Hour, the one that closed the day, with scores of candles lit to defeat the gloom. Now it signaled the start of the night, and its long, dark hours where she would be at her weakest and wide open to temptation.

At least she had remained unmolested last night. Brother Edward had been full of praise when she made her confession earlier. While she'd been grateful for his encouraging words, she couldn't claim a purer heart or stronger resolve. Her repose had been a deep, dreamless sleep, so exhausted she had been from her penitential rosary on top of Vigils. But now another night faced her, a night where Satan could slide in and tempt her with sunshine and flowers and music and men. How could she fight against him?

As if God heard her fears, the monks' voices echoed in reverence in the sung psalm: "Domine, clamavi ad te: exaudi me; intende voci meae, cum clamavero ad te." (I have cried to thee, O Lord: hear me; hearken to my voice, when I cry to thee.)

17

She rested her hands on her open Book of Hours, not needing to read the familiar text. The words could be sung for her ears only. She closed her eyes and lost herself in the powerful message, her lips in silent echo. *Incline not my heart to evil words; to make excuses in sins.*

A faint thud interrupted her contemplation. She opened her eyes.

The monks sang on to the next psalm, but she was behind now. Refusing to indulge her irritation, she traced a finger along the sacred phrasing to try and catch up.

Another thud. She rose and pressed her ear against her curtain, lit from beyond by the candles in the cathedral. Nothing.

A louder bang came this time. Again, the choir prayed undisturbed. It must be from outside. She heard a male shout through the tiny outside circular window that gave her cell some air and daylight. Was a soul in distress, desperate to seek help from Mother Church? A further call sounded.

She got to her feet, but what help could she be? If she looked out, she might be seen, a grave offence, the graver if seen by a man.

A third loud thump decided her. Her beloved cathedral, her sacred shelter, might be being desecrated. She could not stand by and allow such sacrilege. Most of the daylight would be gone; no one would see her at the rounded opening in the dark stone. She pulled her little table below it and climbed up to have a look out. All seemed quiet. Whatever was afoot, it ceased and so would be of no further distraction to her.

As she prepared to climb back down, a sudden movement at the doorway to the Episcopal Palace caught her eye. With the loudest bang yet, the door caved in and light spilled out, illuminating a group of knights who stood there with weapons drawn.

One of the young monks stood in the doorway, gesturing to the strangers that they could not enter. Then the biggest stranger pulled back his massive broadsword and ran the young brother through. The monk doubled over the blade that pierced him, then fell to the ground as the knight yanked it back out.

Theodosia stifled her scream of horror with her sleeve.

The first four knights surged in through the door, stepping on the lifeless brother. Only one of the group hesitated, the last broad-shouldered one. He paused and looked down at the murdered man, but then stepped through after the others.

*A raid.* Every man and woman of God knew of such terror, where men intent on murder, rape, plundering, descended on houses of God and destroyed everyone and everything within. Her vow of silence could be broken in a dire emergency—she had to warn the monks. She stepped over to her internal cell window and wrenched the curtain back. Yellow light pierced the gloom.

"Brothers!" Her voice, quiet for so long, made a feeble plea. "Brothers!" Louder, but still unheard. She knocked against the metal bars, but the dull clinks were no match for the choir in full worship. "Listen! I beseech you. The cathedral is under attack."

The monks' voices soared into the next psalm of the service, and it echoed back from the vaulted ceiling. They sang that God would hear them, that He would help those in distress.

"Can anybody hear me?" She hit her balled fists harder on the rusty bars, hammering as loudly as she could, though her knuckles split and tore. "Brothers!"

The monks sang on, as if mocking her pleas.

Theodosia shrank back from the window and slid to her knees, the strength gone from her legs. Her fate, all of their fates, were in God's hands now. Her bloodied fingers fumbled for the crucifix tucked beneath the neck of her habit as she tried to join the prayer.

But the sacred words deserted her, her dry mouth unable to form a single one. She knelt in frozen terror, listening out for the next shout.

◆　◆　◆

Palmer stepped over the young monk's body into the high-ceilinged hallway of the Archbishop's palace. He brought up the rear of the group with rapid steps, his footsteps echoing with the other knights' on the red-and-black tiled floor. These rules of engagement surprised him. The monk had been defenseless, unarmed. A hard shove with a shoulder would have got past him.

"You there!" Fitzurse broke into a run.

Another brother peered out past a partially opened door in the far corner of the hallway.

Fitzurse stopped before him. "Take us to the Archbishop. At once."

This monk was old but did not try to flee. He stepped out into the hallway, staring at Fitzurse's raised axe, his drooping chins quivering. His horrified gaze went to the crumpled body at the front door, and he crossed himself. "What errand of the devil are you on? We are all men of God in here. No one will fight you, sir knight."

To Palmer's unease, Fitzurse brought the edge of his axe blade to the old man's throat. "Take us to Thomas Becket. Now. Or you can join your young friend in Paradise."

The monk shook as if gripped by fever. "He is that way." He raised a cautious pointed finger to a shadowed passageway to the left.

Fitzurse lowered his weapon and jerked his head for the knights to follow him. The monk sagged against the wall, his breath a terrified rattle in his thin chest.

The red-bearded de Tracy gave a shout of laughter and hauled at the front of the old man's robe, lifting him to the tips of his toes. "Paradise is not so appealing when you think you're going there, eh?"

"Please, have mercy," said the monk.

"Put him down," said Fitzurse. "We have a task to finish."

De Tracy flung the monk to the ground and dealt him a savage kick to his ribs as he moved on. "All yours, Palmer."

Palmer ignored de Tracy and went past the old man, shamed to see him flinch when he met his eye.

Fitzurse stopped before a paneled closed door, hand on the metal-ringed handle. "I'll wager our prize is close by, gentlemen."

Agreement rippled through them, and Palmer added his.

His prize. This was a task ordered by the King, with a purse to match. He tightened his grip on his sword.

Fitzurse kicked the door open to reveal a simply furnished study, lit by a lively fire in a carved stone fireplace. Archbishop Thomas Becket stood before it, dressed in a gold-edged, dark-green cassock. A tall monk stood beside him, wearing the workaday black of the rest of the monastery.

"Fitzurse," said Becket. "I might have known." His glance met the monk's. "See, Brother Edward? Send the worst to do the worst."

Palmer's every instinct was to bow before this revered man of the church. Though Becket was well into middle age, he stood almost as tall as Palmer himself, with his hair still dark. His finely featured face held a well-humored look, while his eyes burned with a fierce intelligence. But none of the other knights so much as nodded his head as they entered the room, weapons ready.

Fitzurse strode up to Becket. "Strange, then, that the monarch thinks I am the best." He leveled his axe directly at Becket. "Now tell me: Where is the whore and her bitch?"

The question flummoxed Palmer. Not so the other knights. Nor Becket.

"Do you really expect me to answer that?" Only the Archbishop's slight stutter betrayed his dismay.

"I do." Fitzurse's voice was ice.

The monk stepped between Becket and the raised blade. "Sir knight, you cannot threaten the Archbishop of Canterbury. Please leave this place in peace."

"Or?" said Fitzurse.

"Or we will defend his lordship to our last man." The monk's green eyes showed surprising valor for an unarmed man of the cloth.

Becket put a hand on his shoulder and moved him to one side. "Brother Edward, please do not endanger yourself on my account. These knights' quarrel is with me only. I can promise you that."

The clink of weaponry underscored how that fight would be conducted.

"Now, Becket," said Fitzurse, "I will ask you only one more time: Where are the women?"

Becket crossed himself slowly.

De Morville's nasal whine rose in protest. "Have we time for prayers now?"

"Maybe you should." Becket dropped to his haunches and grabbed the unlit end of a large burning log from the hearth. He turned and swung the flames at Fitzurse, who ducked out of the way.

"Get him!"

Palmer rushed forward with de Morville. Becket swung the log again and caught de Morville on one shoulder. Palmer dodged to one side as sparks flew up and showered across the room.

"Help me, I'm afire!"

Palmer moved to beat out the lines of flame flicking along de Morville's cloak and hair, de Tracy helping him.

"Quick, my lord," the monk called from an open door behind the wide desk at the back of the study.

Becket swiped, then thrust the log at an advancing le Bret and Fitzurse, halting them for a stride. Then he dashed the log to the floor with another burst of sparks and heat. Making for the door, he stumbled against the desk and half tipped it, scattering papers and rolls of parchment. Edward shot out a long arm and pulled him through the doorway.

Fitzurse rushed it, but it slammed shut. The clunk of a stout bolt engaging brought a string of oaths from him.

"Forcurse it, we'll be fried." Palmer kicked the red-hot log away from a charring bunch of papers. Le Bret ground the broken-off chunks of glowing wood into smoking black across the polished floor tiles.

Fitzurse's nostrils pinched in fury. "They've headed for the cathedral," he said. "We'll get him there. By the time I've finished with him, he'll tell me everything I want to know. Palmer, le Bret. Break that door down. I want Becket, and I want him now."

Palmer stepped up to the secured door as ordered. He raised his weapon for his turn as le Bret landed the first blow to the old waxed wood.

Nothing made sense. Becket's disagreements with the King were power struggles, politics. Had been for years.

Palmer struck at the panels, but the blow bounced off a rusted hinge to a snort from le Bret. He struck again. The door stood firm as le Bret landed another blow, still without success. Becket was to be arrested, to be brought to account before Henry. But instead Fitzurse was demanding to know where two unknown women were, and threatening Becket with his very life to get the answer.

No matter. His reward would be the same, and he had to make sure he earned it. Summoning every pound of strength,

Palmer raised his sword and brought it down in a double-handed blow. The door's planks split in two. "We're through, my lord Fitzurse."

♦   ♦   ♦

Male shouts came from the other side of the shut door that led to the cloisters. Theodosia's breath came faster, in noisy gasps. The marauders had found a way in.

Out in the cathedral, the choir faded to a questioning halt as the calls got louder.

The crash of the door bouncing back on its hinges shot through her bones. She tucked her crucifix out of sight beneath her vest and gabbled out a last confession, words half-formed.

"My dear brethren! We are under attack!"

*God be praised.* The shout came from Archbishop Becket, warning the monks where she'd failed.

"Leave now, Brothers. Make all haste." The familiar voice of Brother Edward came too, along with the snap of metal on metal as bolts were shot home. "The Archbishop and I will deal with the intruders."

Puzzled exclamations from the monks in the choir matched her confusion.

"You should come with us, Archbishop," said one. "And if not, our place is with you."

"Indeed." The chorus came from several others.

"Thank you from the bottom of my heart." Becket's voice deepened in his emotion. "But you must leave. I order you. Hide yourselves as you know how to do. Make for the crypt, the lofts, the cellars."

Still the muted clamor of hesitation continued.

"You haven't much time. I've bolted the doors from the Archbishop's study and the cloisters, but they won't hold for long. Now leave, Brothers." Brother Edward's order allowed for no disagreement.

She heard the rapid clops of leather sandals along the wooden choir stalls, then fading across the stone floor as the monks made their way out through the northeast transept. The door boomed closed, the sound vibrating through the cathedral. As the golden light visible through her barred window faded, the sweet smell of the extinguished beeswax candles wafted in.

Becket's head and shoulders appeared as a dark silhouette at the window. "Sister Theodosia?" His usual measured tone had an urgent edge.

She ducked her head to her knees and folded her veil across her cheeks, the better to hide her face. "Here, my lord. But pray step away—I have to draw the curtain. I am sorry I left it open, but I—"

"It is of no consequence."

She kept her face averted and carried on. "My lord, I saw one of our brothers murdered only minutes ago, God have mercy on him. Is it a raid?"

"It is a time of great danger," he said, "and you must conceal yourself."

"I am concealed."

"Not well enough, I'm afraid. You must come out. At once." The rattle of Becket's fitting a key in the lock came from her door.

She looked up in shocked disbelief as Becket pulled the door open. But his appearance shocked her as much as his breaking of her vows. High spots of color shadowed his cheekbones, and a smear of what looked like black ash marked his temple and the front of his robes. He gestured to her with a hand covered in yet more ash.

25

"Have they set the cathedral on fire?" she asked, her veil still tight to her face.

"No. But they will be in here soon. You have to come out."

Behind him lay the vast shadows of the cathedral's long, straight nave. The start of the world, an endless, impossible world where she would be open to sin, to death. To step out there would be a step to hell for her soul. She shook her head wordlessly.

Two of Becket's long strides brought him to her side. "Fear not. Now come."

Theodosia climbed to her feet, her gaze fixed on the lines of gray stone pillars and high shadowed arches beyond. Demons lurked there, she was sure of it, waiting to swoop for her spirit. "But I am not allowed to leave. My lord, you order me to commit a great offence."

"That offence will be on my soul. I order you to leave."

He carried the scent of fresh smoke, a reminder that Lucifer did too. Her legs would not comply.

Becket raised pleading hands. "Obedience, Sister. One of your vows. I beg you."

His humility spurred her to action, but she could manage only slow, unsure steps. Her heart beat so hard she could hear it. "I leave the place of my eternal rest, my lord."

"I know. Forgive me." He followed her out as she passed the threshold.

The immense space pressed in on her like the confines of her cell never had, robbing her of the air in her lungs. She let go her veil to clutch at her chest and took fast, shallow, useless breaths. Her terrified wheezes bounced back at her, a hundred tiny echoes from the darkness, as if the demons had found a voice to mock her fear.

"Steady your resolve," said Becket.

She met his gaze with her own and felt the blood rise in her face. She should not expose herself so.

But Becket seemed not to notice. "There is a better place for you to hide from the knights. Go with Brother Edward."

The monk waited by a pillar, his face a mask of fear that surely mirrored her own.

"But what about your safety, my lord Becket?" she said, breathless still. "You cannot face those men. Hide with Brother Edward and me. My cell could easily fit all three of us."

Becket gave her a tired, gentle smile. "I dearly wish I could, but I have my duty to perform." The faint shouts of the strangers came from the cloisters beyond. He raised his hand in a swift blessing. "Lead the way, Brother Edward."

Edward gave an urgent gesture. "Come, Sister Theodosia."

With her chest straining, he hurried her up the long stone nave as yells and thumps came from the cloister door that opened onto the northwest transept. "Brother Edward, we are going toward the intruders, not away from them."

He stopped before the altar of Our Lady, tendrils of smoke trailing from the quenched candles.

"Step over the rail," said Edward.

"They will see us immediately," she gasped. "These shadows make weak concealment." Sweat dampened her whole body. "My cell, I should go back to my cell. Please, Brother."

A crescendo of thuds echoed from the door.

"Edward," said Becket, "you have but moments left." He walked past them up the nave.

"My lord Becket, where are you going?" she asked.

He did not turn his head.

She looked back at Brother Edward. "Where is he going?"

The monk responded by clearing the low metal rail in one high step. "No time to argue. Please trust me." He dropped to his knees before Mary's statue on its high plinth.

27

Bewildered, Theodosia looked from his bowed shoulders to the benign stone face of the Queen of Heaven, surrounded by a crown of stars. Was the monk hoping Mary would grant a miracle? Theodosia turned at the sound of splintering wood, and her throat tightened again. A split ran the length of the door, and an axehead gleamed through.

"Stop where you are!"

"They're coming in." She appealed to Brother Edward: "My cell, Brother. We have to hide. Quickly!"

The monk ignored her. His fingers beat out a sharp tattoo as he rapped the base of the carved wooden altar.

"Hurry, Edward," came Becket's steady order, steady as his stride as he neared the transept steps.

"I have it, my lord," said Edward.

With a sharp click, a large section of the altar front opened out, revealing a space underneath.

Edward moved quickly inside and gestured for her to follow him.

The cloister door's planks squealed in protest as the axe wrenched free for another blow.

Theodosia hitched herself up onto the altar rails and swung her legs over. She scrambled into the confined space with Brother Edward.

He swung the wooden panel shut. "Forgive my unseemly closeness, Sister," he said, his whisper close to her ear. "I do not touch against you with any intent."

She nodded, subduing her ragged breathing with her palms folded across her mouth. The altar front had several small holes that formed the leaves and flowers of its intricate carving. Her view was of the transept, the only pool of light that remained in the dark cathedral.

Becket climbed the short flight of wide stone steps up onto it and faced where the crashes at the door had quickened, grown louder. His stately figure radiated calm as he clasped his hands before him.

Then he raised his voice over the din. "Away, you cowards. A church is not a castle."

The lofty stone arches resounded with the final collapse of the door, followed by a terrible roar.

"Where is Thomas the traitor?"

# CHAPTER 3

Palmer and his fellow knights joined Fitzurse's charge through to the cathedral. A solitary tall figure stood at the far side of the transept. Becket. Two yard-long church candles in waist-high carved holders lit the stone-floored space and made curved shadows of the large pillars behind the Archbishop. The rest of the huge church was in darkness.

Palmer had his sword raised and ready, and a quick glance told him the other knights' weapons were ready too.

Hands joined in front of him, Becket addressed Fitzurse without a flinch. "Here I am. No traitor, but archbishop and priest of God."

Fitzurse motioned that his knights should fan out around the transept, form a circle from which Becket could not break free. Palmer followed the order, watching the Archbishop for any sudden moves after his agile speed with the fire.

Fitzurse stood directly opposite Becket. "Priest of God, eh? You must be aware, then, that it is a sin to tell a lie."

De Morville snickered.

Becket did not dignify Fitzurse with a reply.

The knight shifted his grip on his axe. "I have asked you once. Where are they?"

Becket spread his hands. "You see me here alone. Alone I am. They're gone, Fitzurse. Gone where you will never find them." He joined his hands together again.

"That's not what I've heard," said Fitzurse. He looked around. "Palmer, go to the back left corner, along from the main doors. The anchoress's cell is there. Get her out of it by any means you can."

◆　◆　◆

*The anchoress?* Theodosia crushed her hands harder against her mouth and bit down on her fingers to stop her scream. She shot a stunned glance at Edward in the shadows of their flimsy hiding place.

The horror in his green eyes affirmed hers.

Her whole body weakened, shook. They came for her. *For her.* But why?

Edward's raised a hand as a wordless message of comfort, even as he gave an imperceptible shake of his head.

Then he did not know either. She watched the broad-shouldered knight called Palmer take one of the candles from the transept holder and descend the steps. The stone floor echoed under his metal-booted tread. He walked swiftly past their hiding place down the nave, toward her cell, bearing the light aloft.

Her cell. Her precious cell. Her refuge, her protection. Or so she'd believed in her weak foolishness. Somehow her lord Becket had known, had been told by God to make her leave. But she'd tried to resist. Had she succeeded in her sinful disobedience, she would still be in there. Her innards twisted to sickness.

Palmer's surprised voice called back up the nave. "The cell door's open. There's no one here, my lord."

"What?" Fitzurse ground out the word.

"It looks as if there has been," continued Palmer. "And recently. There's a bed. A half-eaten loaf of bread, and it's not that stale. Water. And some holy-looking books."

With a suppressed oath, Fitzurse stepped closer to Becket, axe raised. "What have you done with her?"

"Sh-she's gone."

Theodosia's heart fell at Becket's trip on the word. It always happened when his well-checked emotions ran high, when he spoke from his heart. Every soul in the kingdom knew it.

Fitzurse knew it too. He gave a slow smile. "Methinks Thomas has sung for his supper. Palmer, de Morville, de Tracy: search this cathedral. I want that nun found. Le Bret, you stay here."

"Courage," came Brother Edward's tiny whisper in her ear.

But she had none. A search was on for her, a search by men who'd sliced a sword through another in the blink of an eye. But why her? What had she done to be hunted like this?

The thinnest of the knights and the red-bearded stocky one made their way down the steps. The thin one headed for the confessionals that lined the walls, the other made for the choir stalls. The one who was near giant stayed with Fitzurse, looming above Becket in the transept.

Becket, his composure restored, looked straight ahead, as if the strangers' presence in his church was beneath contempt.

"You'll need lights." Palmer's call floated up from the back of the church, where he continued his search.

"Bugger those," came the reply from the red-bearded one. "The point of my sword will find her far quicker than your peering about."

The loud rattle of his steel blade on the wooden choir stalls made Theodosia start, bite back a scream. The sound of confessional doors being slammed open joined the din. A glow of light from the left showed Palmer was on his way back up the nave.

"Check the altars, Palmer. De Morville and de Tracy can deal with the rest."

The altars. Like the one she hid beneath. She risked a glance at Edward. A trickle of sweat at his temple showed he shared her terror. A sword thrust through the front of the carved altar would pierce their faces, rupture their eyes.

As the crashing from the other two continued, Palmer came into her sight across the nave at the altar of Saint Joseph. Candle aloft, he looked behind columns, beneath altar cloths, using his sword to prod and pry.

"We haven't got all night, gentlemen," said Fitzurse. But his gaze was on Becket.

"I'm almost done, my lord." Palmer turned and approached the altar of Our Lady.

They were surely lost. She clamped her jaws more tightly on her fingers to keep her silence.

He stopped in front of the altar and seemed to look right into Theodosia's eyes. She lowered her hands as she moved to give herself up, before the steel, the pain. Edward's warning grip stopped her.

The knight's gaze traveled away from her and over the altar. Even holding the light, he could not have seen her through the tiny holes. Despite Fitzurse's order to use his sword, he continued his perusal of the tableau before him, dark eyes searching for anything out of place, a subtler approach that could yet find them out.

To her horror, he stepped over the altar rail and approached the statue above them. His tanned skin showed rugged from a life outdoors. Thick, dark hair escaped the hood of his chain mail, and his angled cheekbones were shadowed from lack of shaving. Broad, mud-stained hands, one with a dirty bandage, circled the handle of his sword and the candle. His long, chain-mailed legs were now inches from her and Brother Edward's faces. It was as if Satan stood over her again, but this was no dream. The stone statue above them rang out as he tested it with his sword. Then, dear God, no. He raised a boot and gave the altar front an almighty kick. She shot back, knocking her head against Edward's jawbone. The altar front held firm, gave nothing to suggest it could be opened.

An age passed. The knight must surely be able to hear them breathing.

Finally, he stepped away and out over the rail. "Nothing, my lord Fitzurse." He walked back up the aisle to the transept.

Complete silence fell as Palmer replaced the candle in the transept holder.

"We have nowt either." De Tracy too returned to Fitzurse, along with de Morville, who shook his head.

Even from this distance, Theodosia saw the frustration burn in Fitzurse's ice-blue eyes.

"You have no more business here, Fitzurse," said Becket. "Now go, and take your shameful crew with you."

Theodosia's lungs filled with relief. They were saved.

"I have plenty business here." Fitzurse turned his axe and struck Becket across the face with the handle.

The Archbishop stumbled back with a suppressed cry, hand to his injured cheek.

Edward recoiled in horror beside her as she stifled her own reaction.

Fitzurse nodded to le Bret and de Tracy. They stepped in and grabbed Becket by either arm. Dragging him to one of the transept pillars, they pulled him tight against it, with his hands flat and wrists pinned.

Fitzurse handed his axe to de Morville and drew his sword. "I know you of old, Becket, and I know you are lying. I can't find the anchoress, I can't find her mother. But you will tell me."

*Mama too?* Theodosia went rigid.

Fitzurse brought his face close to Becket. "You will tell me because de Morville and I will remove your fingers, digit by digit.

And if you persist in not telling me, I will carry on: your tongue, your eyes, your genitals."

Theodosia's sight shadowed, and she shook her head to keep from collapse. She could not hide while her beloved, blessed Thomas was hacked to pieces for her. She had to act. She went to push the panel open, but Edward's hand tightened on her shoulder. "Hold, Sister."

Becket met Fitzurse's gaze with no fear. "Do what you will. My body is of no consequence. God wants only my soul."

Fitzurse laid the edge of his sword across the joint of Becket's right thumb, the better to position his blow. "By the time I have finished with you, you will doubt if there is a God." He raised his sword.

"Stop it! Leave him be!" Theodosia broke from Edward and flung open the carved door of their hiding place.

◆　◆　◆

Palmer raised his weapon at the sudden female cries. He looked around to see a slightly built young nun scramble over the altar rail of the Lady Chapel, the tall monk called Edward behind her. Where in devildom had they sprung from?

The monk called out too. "Stop, sirs, I beseech you."

"Theodosia, no!" shouted Becket.

"Hold him, damn you."

Palmer turned back at Fitzurse's order to see Becket break de Tracy's grip, but de Morville moved in whip-fast with Fitzurse.

Palmer swiveled as the girl reached the bottom of the steps.

"Don't hurt him, for the love of God," she said.

"Stop there." He raised his sword and she halted, one foot on the steps, gray eyes wide on his blade as shouts and oaths came from the struggling group behind him.

35

"It's her," came Fitzurse's call. "Take her, Palmer."

"You will not."

Palmer glanced to his left.

"But I will." Brother Edward lunged for him from farther along the wide steps.

Palmer swung his sword and the monk jerked away, overbalancing onto one hip and hand. The nun sprinted up the steps and ducked past Palmer as he went to grab her. *Forcurse her.*

She flung herself at de Morville, who still tried to pin Becket down. She pulled at the knight's bony forearm with both hands. "Let him go. You must, you must."

"Off, whore." De Morville kneed her in the stomach, but she kept her hold.

Palmer was on her in three strides. "Enough." He flung his forearm across her throat and lifted his sword against her neck. She shrieked and let go of de Morville.

"Please, have mercy on us." She choked her words out and raised both arms in a plea as he flexed his grip tight round her neck.

Becket stopped writhing in the knights' hold and glared at Palmer. "Leave her be, you churl. I command you."

"I'm afraid Palmer's not yours to command," said Fitzurse.

Palmer had to will himself not to respond to Becket. But he relaxed his grip enough to let the nun breathe as he pulled her well back from the group. He kept his sword raised.

Fitzurse stepped away from Becket, with a quick glance to make sure the others held him firm against the pillar once more. He observed Palmer's captive with a thin smile. "I do believe we've found one." He reached out and slapped Becket hard across the face, making him gasp in pain. "Where is the other one?"

"There is no other, Fitzurse."

Fitzurse raised his sword over Becket's hand once more. "Dear me. Back to where we started."

"Stop it, I beg you," said the nun.

Palmer clamped the girl hard to him again, in case she made another attempt at Becket's captors.

She tugged at his forearm as she fought for breath. "You must believe him. As God is my witness, there is only me here, I swear to you."

With a wary eye on Palmer's sword, Brother Edward hovered at the edge of the circle, face drawn in torment. "It's true what Sister Theodosia says. I beg you also, sir knight. Leave his lordship be. There is no one else to be found. No one."

"Then our work here is almost done." Fitzurse stepped away from Becket, sword by his hip once more. "Palmer?"

"Yes, my lord?"

"Take the girl outside and put her in the cart."

"No." The nun backheeled Palmer's legs, clawed at his arm as he started to haul her across the transept.

"Unhand me!" Becket struggled like a man possessed against the three who held him, pulling de Tracy and de Morville near off their feet and making le Bret grunt with effort. He dragged his head from the pillar and looked directly at Palmer. "Let her go, sir. Don't let Reginald Fitzurse make you a pander."

Fitzurse's nostrils pinched in fury at the insult. "Wait, Palmer. I'd like her to see something." Fitzurse moved back to Becket as Palmer halted. "Leave him." He nodded to his other three knights. Surprise writ on their faces, they loosed their hold on Becket. The Archbishop stepped away from the pillar to face Fitzurse.

"Oh, thank you, sweet Jesus." With her murmured prayer, the nun sagged against Palmer in relief.

Fitzurse pointed a finger at Becket and jabbed him hard in the chest. "Kneel before me."

The nun gasped, echoed by the watching Edward.

Becket regarded him with rage. "Do not dare to touch me, you who owes me faith and obedience. Leave this place, you and your fellow fools."

Fitzurse's punch was a blur, and Becket was on his knees to a scream from the girl. "I don't owe faith or obedience to you," said Fitzurse. "Only to the monarch." He pulled his sword up and swung.

Palmer flung his other arm across the girl's face as he saw the blow's arc.

Becket ducked, but Fitzurse's blade caught him at his crown and crunched through the bone. A shard of Becket's skull flew off and splintered on the stone floor to a roar from the knights.

"Help us! The Archbishop is being murdered!" Edward rushed forward as Fitzurse gave the sprawled Becket another blow to his head that glanced off and caught the monk on one arm, sending him yelling against a pillar.

The girl in Palmer's hold screamed and screamed as if she voiced a banshee. He kept his hold rigid; she couldn't see such sights.

"He's up, Lord Fitzurse," said le Bret, as the mortally wounded Becket attempted to rise, watery blood soaking his face and neck.

"In the name of Jesus and in defense of the church, I am willing to die," gasped Becket. "But leave the girl alone."

"Willing or not, you're dead." Fitzurse's breath too came fast and deep. "Finish him, le Bret."

Le Bret took his sword grip in both hands. Blade pointed down, he lifted his weapon high, then brought it down on Becket's skull. His savage thrust went clear through to the floor beneath, smashing the Archbishop's skull in two and shattering his sword.

Palmer's captive's screams turned to wild sobs, and she scratched helplessly at his hands to try and loose his hold.

Edward cowered by the pillar, face pallid, fist to his mouth.

"Devil take it." Le Bret cast the ruined handle aside.

"Don't know your own strength." De Morville grinned and raised his sword to a cowering Edward.

A chorus of shouts built from outside.

"Leave him. The other monks must have summoned help," said Fitzurse. "We need to make our escape." He looked over at Palmer. "But first, let Sister Theodosia see what happens to those who cross me."

Palmer reluctantly lowered his arm from in front of the anchoress's eyes, steeling himself for a fresh struggle. But she stopped her cries, went completely still. He felt her give a huge gulp and knew she fought her vomit.

Fitzurse watched her face intently. Then, still watching, he placed a boot on Becket's mangled head, crushing out the whiteness of the brains to mix with the growing puddle of the Archbishop's dark-red blood.

Still she didn't make a sound.

With a shrug, Fitzurse gestured to the others. "Away, knights. Becket will not get up again." He looked at Palmer. "Bring the girl." He set off toward the transept steps as the others acted on his command.

She remained fixed on the sight of Becket on the altar but started to pull against Palmer once more as he hauled her to the steps. A long, low moan escaped her. "No. No. No." Her gaze was locked on the floor as she began to cry, her body racked with silent sobs.

He followed her line of sight and saw Fitzurse's boot had left a trail of bloody footprints down the nave. "Do as you're bid," said Palmer. "And be thankful it's not your blood spilt."

He hurried her down the darkened nave, her struggles feeble against his tight grip.

"Murderers!" The venomous cry came from the transept. Palmer looked back to see the injured Brother Edward Grim kneeling beside the dead Archbishop in the flickering candlelight.

The monk leveled an accusatory finger as le Bret wrenched open the front door of the cathedral and led the way out into the cold, black night.

Edward's voice followed them. "I bear witness to this savagery and to your abduction of the Church's holy anchoress. Mark my words, your sins will find you out."

The slain Archbishop, the sobbing girl he held prisoner, the monk's shouted warning. This mission was not a noble one, Palmer didn't need his battle sense to tell him that. But, noble or not, he would see it through to its end. His payment was on completion, and complete it he would.

# CHAPTER 4

Palmer sat in the back of the cart, the thin roof and sides of stained tarpaulin swaying in its steady progress through the night. Dim light shone from the guide lamp hung over the driver's seat. Le Bret sat up there, hunched forward in his job of keeping them on the icy roadway. The wooden wheels crunched and scraped on the frost-hardened mud road below.

Opposite Palmer, his prisoner huddled away from him on the rough floor planks, head down over her bent knees. His prisoner? Faith, she was a young nun, a small bird of a girl. She didn't need guarding. He could be sat up next to le Bret, or better still on horseback like the others. Not cooped up like a dunderpate. But Fitzurse had ordered him in here as they'd made their escape from Canterbury, with a look that let no argument.

He couldn't even use his sword; he'd not got the room in the tight space. He'd pulled his dagger from his belt and held that ready instead. It was likely his own fault he was in here—Fitzurse's punishment for his poor work in the cathedral. The altar of Our Lady, where the nun and that monk had hid, touching distance away from him. And he'd not found them. If it hadn't been for this girl and her foolhardy attempt to save Becket, they might have remained hidden. Fitzurse's mission, whatever that might be turning out to be, could have failed, and the money not been paid out. A quiver of anger passed through him. He, Palmer, would have stayed penniless. And it would have been her fault.

He watched as the nun moved her black rosary beads through her cut and dirty fingers, head bent over her joined hands. *Where are the whore and her bitch?* Fitzurse had asked Becket. Well, it looked like they had the bitch. But at what cost? The King had ordered Becket's arrest, wanted the Archbishop to account for his meddling. Not have his head taken off his shoulders. Palmer tapped his dagger blade against his knee. No mind. He wasn't paid to make sense of things; he was paid to do as he was told.

A set of hooves sounded loud beside the cart, and the tarpaulin lifted partway to reveal Fitzurse astride his stallion.

The girl sat bolt upright, face pale in terror.

"Is Sister Theodosia giving any trouble, Palmer?"

"None, my lord," said Palmer.

"Good." Fitzurse rapped on the wooden side of the cart. "We have no further need of this. It slows us too much. Even at a hard ride, it's five days to de Morville's castle in Knaresborough. De Tracy has ridden ahead to an inn to secure a couple of fresh horses. You'll ride with Palmer, missy." He dropped the tarp again.

Theodosia stared set-faced at Palmer.

"That's me." He pointed at his chest. "Sir Benedict Palmer."

Her expression didn't alter.

"And don't think that you can struggle and jump off. It's a long way down from the back of an animal. You'll likely break your neck. You hear me?"

"Yes."

The look she gave him matched the one she had given Fitzurse. Good.

The cart ground to a halt, the unseen horses blowing long snorts in relief. Le Bret looked back from the driver's seat as he secured the brake. "Get her out the back, Palmer."

Palmer undid the tight-laced opening in the canvas at the rear of their cart. "This way."

Her hands trembled as she tidied her rosary onto a loop on her belt.

Sticking his dagger back in his belt, he climbed out first, his breath cloudy in the frozen air. The hour would be close on the middle of the night but was well lit by the still-large Yule moon. The low-roofed inn lay silent and dark. The only sign of life was a yawning groom in the cobbled yard at the front, a couple of saddled horses held by him holding a couple of saddled horses on a short rein. De Tracy stood checking them over, his ruddy beard and hair lit by the lantern he held.

As Fitzurse led his stallion to a pile of fresh hay, Palmer turned back to the cart.

Theodosia climbed out and down with the aid of the wooden step. She scanned the yard without looking at him, and he recognized the set of an animal about to bolt.

He circled her right wrist with one hand, and she stiffened under his hold.

"Palmer."

He glanced around to see Fitzurse leave his horse to its repast and walk over to them.

Fitzurse continued. "A task for you while we get our mounts refreshed. News of Becket will travel fast, and I don't want us hindered on our way." He pointed at Theodosia. "With her appearance, the girl could draw attention to us. Take her round the back of the stable block and get rid of her veil and habit. Do what else you like—I don't care." Fitzurse returned to his horse's side.

Her sharp intake of breath gave away her intent to call to the groom for help.

"No, you don't." Palmer yanked her to him and choked off her cry. His bandaged hand stifled her screams as he dragged her to where Fitzurse had ordered.

The back of the stable block had no windows. A couple of piles of firewood and the inn's frozen, heaped midden hid them from sight. She kicked harder at his shins through her long skirts, struggled to break from him.

A sharp heel to his kneecap almost made him lose his hold. "Curse you, lady." Hand tight on her mouth, he loosed her arm and grabbed for his knife. He raised it to her line of vision, and she froze. "I'm warning you," he said, his voice low, "you set about de Morville in the cathedral, but don't think you can try me in the same way. One move, one shout, and I'll cut you." He released her to turn to face him. "Take your clothes off."

Theodosia shook her head as she kept her terrified gaze on his blade. "I have vowed my chastity to God. By taking it from me, you commit mortal sin."

"Your chastity?" He snorted. "No wonder you fought me so hard. I'm not interested in your chastity, just your clothes. Take them off."

Still she trembled. "Then you despoil my modesty, another grave sin."

"Off." He gestured with his knife. "And hurry up."

She loosed the leather belt that held her rosary and slipped it from her waist. "At least let me have my rosary. Please."

"I said to hurry." Palmer shook his head as he took the belt from her. The softest of good leather, the dark, shiny beads that hung from it made of jet. Holy folk never changed. Disgusted, he threw the belt onto the clumps of yellowed grass, grinding it underfoot onto the frozen churned mud.

Her black wool dress hung loose about her waist. With a stifled sob, she crossed her arms and began to pull it off over her veiled head, for all the world the same way he pulled off his own surcoat. But where he wore chain mail, she wore a cream wool shift that fitted tight to high, firm breasts and a narrow waist.

His groin tightened. Mouth dry, he took the dress from her. Its heavy weight and fine quality put down his urge. "Take off that black skirt too."

"It's my undersk—"

"Take it." With his blade steady, he cut down hard through the thick black wool he held, strip by strip, to the sound of her sobs. He watched her disrobe further as he flung the cloth on the ground.

She wore another underskirt—cream, this one. That could stay. He snatched the black undergarment from her. "Leave those pale clothes on." He shredded the skirt as he spoke.

Theodosia watched him, hands to her face, tears streaming from her eyes.

One last thing remained. "Your veil, Sister."

"You cannot. It is my life."

He itched to slap her for her whining. "Forcurse it, it's cloth." He dropped the last of her torn skirt to his feet and stepped over to her. "On your knees." He grasped her shoulder with his free hand and forced her to the frozen ground.

"You take my life."

"It's only a head cover, not your skull." Palmer slashed down with his blade, and she caught back a scream. His expert cut went through the close-fitting white wimple that fitted round her face and covered her hair. One hard pull cast it off with her veil. A white linen band secured her hair cap beneath. He made a quick slash and it fell away too. "See? Not a scratch."

But she gave him no thanks for his skill, scrabbling across the black earth for her torn clothing and raking it into her arms. A long, low keening broke from her as she clutched it to her chest. "These were my modesty, my wedding dress for Christ." She rocked in open grief. "My humility. My poverty."

Her prating riled him to his boots. "Poverty, is it?"

The anger in his voice stopped her noise, and she looked up at him in fear.

"You God-botherers, you're all the same, with your playacting at being poor," he said. "Your belt, your beads, your precious habit: most folk could work for a lifetime and still not afford them. Weep and wail over a dress if you like. Folk in the real world save their tears for death and disaster. You should be thanking God you're still in one piece."

"Have you gone asleep, Palmer?" Fitzurse appeared around the corner of the stable block.

"No, my lord. Just finishing," said Palmer, blood still quick from his anger.

Fitzurse stopped in front of the huddled Theodosia. He reached down and roughly raked her short, combed-down hair into dark-blonde tangles around her face. He pushed her from him and she stayed crouched, still hanging on to her holy garments.

"Nicely done, Palmer," said Fitzurse. "She looks common enough now."

"Thank you, my lord."

"Now bring her round; the horses are ready." Fitzurse left them, calling for his own animal.

Palmer looked down at Theodosia. She clung to her clothes, head bent over them, crying and murmuring into them as if they were a dead child. He gave an impatient click and bent to her.

"No," she cried out as he yanked the bundle from her and threw it behind him.

He pulled her to her feet and jerked his head toward the yard. "Get moving," he said. "Our horse is waiting."

Shoulders down, she went past him, stumbling as if she took steps in sleep. With her bowed head, tangled hair, and thin wool clothing, she could be any luckless peasant.

Palmer cared not. What happened to her was no concern of his. His task was to get her to Knaresborough Castle, keep her secure there. And do whatever else Fitzurse asked of him.

◆   ◆   ◆

"We'll pause here for respite." Fitzurse's call came from the front of the group of mounted knights.

"Aye, my lord." Sir Palmer's response came loud in Theodosia's ear, and she flinched.

Seated before him on this wide-backed horse, his sinful hold secure on her, she shared every breath he took, every word he spoke.

Fitzurse had called their halt in the midst of thick, deserted woods. Dead leaves surrounded the bases of bare-branched trees, and not even a bird broke the quiet.

Sir Palmer loosed his unwelcome grip on her waist. He dismounted, as did the other knights, landing with a rustle in the thick leaf cover underfoot.

"That stream's a sight for sore eyes," De Tracy's voice bellowed out, as loud as ever. He made his way over to a quiet brook, icy clear in its mossy bed.

"Horses need it." The huge le Bret led his animal over to join him.

Sir Palmer held his horse steady and jerked his head for Theodosia to climb off. She dropped awkwardly to the ground, where she struggled to balance on deadened legs.

The knight didn't acknowledge her difficulty, merely waited for her to straighten.

"We all need it," came Fitzurse's clear tone as he and de Morville lined up at the water's edge too.

Theodosia walked beside Palmer as he led his animal to the brook's edge.

He nodded at the water. "You need to drink something."

Theodosia bent low and scooped up a palmful of moss-tasting water. She watched the line of the knights' reflected faces in the water's surface while they drank their fill and bantered with each other. Her insides coiled afresh. It was as if they were sin made flesh, as if evil itself had taken bodily forms.

The massive le Bret was like the bear of dead sloth, slow and menacing, with a sword as sharp as claws. The red-bearded one, de Tracy, with his bellow of a voice, always blaspheming, for all the world the lion of arrogance. De Morville, whose castle she was being taken to, his spare frame and flaking, horrid skin a reminder of what death would bring. But his eyes were bright like those of the fox of covetousness, always peering, poking, weighing up what everyone else had. Fitzurse, of the blue, blue eyes. Eyes as dead as a snake's, and a coldness about him that oozed the poison of evil.

She straightened up and folded her arms across her chest to keep from trembling.

Palmer glanced over at her. "Take some more. You'll need it."

She shook her head.

"Please yourself." He helped himself to more.

And Benedict Palmer, the last one of this horrific menagerie. He would be the unicorn of anger, with his heated temper, his quickness of mood, his angry dismissal of her and her sacred calling.

Her calling. She had hidden herself from the world to keep her soul safe. As her beloved Thomas had said to her, "You do not carry a brittle container in an unruly mob. You have to keep a precious vial safe." But she hadn't kept her soul safe. Her own uncontrolled emotions had swept in, had her run from her safe hiding place to his side. To what end? For him to be hacked to pieces and for her to deliver herself into the hands of those who killed him. She'd taken that vial and shattered it with her own hands, and all through her sinful disobedience.

"Remount, men," called Fitzurse. "If we press on, we'll be there before nightfall."

Theodosia stood by Sir Palmer's horse, bracing herself for his hand at her leg to boost her up. Here it came again. She grasped for the saddle pommel and pulled herself up. With a swift movement, he was behind her once again, arm tight about her waist.

She offered up yet another confession. Being touched by him, over and over, as she had over these last interminable days brought her sin after repeated sin. Her purity, her holy noble vows, were in shreds from him, as surely as her precious clothes had been from his cruel knife.

"Forward," said Fitzurse. He led off and the line of mounted horses fell in behind him, one after another. Palmer's place was in the middle, with two before and two after, as if she were being guarded from harm instead of being delivered to it.

On the horse immediately in front, de Morville looked around. "We'll soon be at my castle, Palmer." He gave Palmer a hideous wink. "I'll have to find you another maid to hold to your crotch."

"That would be pleasure," came the quick reply. "This one's only work. But I thank you."

Theodosia's face burned at their base talk.

De Morville grinned. "She's near the same color as you now. It's not just her blushes, neither. A few days on horseback and the air has her fine skin as rough as a peasant's."

Palmer leaned over her shoulder to look at her face.

She stared resolutely ahead.

"Nah, de Morville. It's only travel dirt. She's still indoors-pale." He settled back.

"Well, she'll be paler. I have a cell ready for her, and it's properly underground, not like at Canterbury. Sister, you'll never see another soul. Or light. Or anything at all. Ever." He smiled, his gapped teeth green-tinged and revolting.

Her insides turned over.

"See how I look after her, Palmer, and yet she gives me no thanks?"

"I'm sure that will come in time, de Morville," came the deep-voiced reply behind her. "As lord of Knaresborough, you're due it."

"Time is something she'll have plenty of." De Morville faced forward again with a coarse laugh.

Theodosia clutched at the saddle pommel for support as de Morville's words sank into her soul. *Take me, dear Lord. Take me. Before this horror comes to pass.*

No. She had started to pray for her own death. She clutched still harder at the saddle pommel to contain her anguish, her disbelief.

Satan was surely close by.

# CHAPTER 5

"It wobbles like a whore's titty. That it may taste as good!"

Seated with the other knights in Knaresborough Castle's great hall, Palmer joined in the roar of laughter at de Tracy's loud jest.

Dressed in red-and-yellow livery, the sewer and his two grooms carried the quivering blancmange before them on a wide platter. They took careful steps as they made their way from the screened-off kitchen door toward the top table on the raised stone platform.

"Are your whore's teats usually striped, de Tracy?" Palmer raised his full goblet to the red-bearded knight sat to his right, to more roars and hoots.

The servers climbed the steps to the raised stone platform. At the center of the long table, de Morville sat in his place as lord of Knaresborough, Fitzurse to his right. The servers placed the huge domed pudding before de Morville, and he nodded, then raised his hands and applauded. At his signal, a group of four minstrels struck up in the gallery set high in the wall at the opposite end of the hall.

Along with de Tracy and le Bret up the table beyond Fitzurse, Palmer joined in with the applause. The pudding, with its layers of white, pink, and yellow topped off with a nub of rich pale green, made his mouth water, full as he was.

Though the feast had been for the five knights only, Palmer had never eaten so well in his life. Broiled venison, each thick steak coated in rich gravy and sweetened with cinnamon. Wine-stewed mutton, the tender meat and its yellowed fat melted into the savory sauce. Roasted chicken stuffed with eggs, lard, and spices, its skin crispy and glistening fresh from the spit. Fluffy white bread, the first he'd tasted, easy to chew as a cloud compared with the tough rye bread he was used to. Spiced hot fruits cooked in honey. He stifled a hiccup.

The sewer used a curved spoon to divide the pudding up with swift, neat movements while his assistants laid fresh trenchers and spoons before each of the knights.

Palmer caught the slight tremor in the hand of the younger server and smiled inside. He'd hated this duty as a squire, waiting on lords and knights, carving fine meat with all noble eyes on him, while getting only the scraps and leavings to eat. Worse had been the ladies, many old enough to be his mam, who'd run their glance over him as he bent to serve them. He'd had more than one whisper about his strong fingers and his well-filled breeches.

He took a scoop of pudding and put it on his trencher. The serving lad refilled his goblet as he did so. Palmer helped himself to another mouthful of wine, then tried some of the pudding. Sweet, smooth, creamy, with flavors he didn't even recognize.

"An excellent end to an excellent meal," said Fitzurse, helping himself. He raised his eyebrows as he tasted it. "You have the finest of saffron in there, de Morville."

*The finest of saffron.* Palmer noted it to himself. He would have to have this in his own dishes when he had his own great hall. He scooped another mouthful and peered at the brightly colored contents of his spoon to see what it looked like.

Fitzurse cleared his throat. "The yellow layer, Palmer. The taste, man. The scent."

Now everyone roared their laugh they all roared their laughter at Palmer. Heat rose in his face.

"Fire too hot for you, boy?" De Tracy grinned at him, face shiny with drink.

Palmer showed the knight his middle finger and took another deep draught of wine. He wasn't bothered at the ribbing. Once he had his fortune, he'd employ flocks of servants, same as de Morville. They'd know all about the best herbs. He drank again. The best wine.

"Speaking of fires," said Fitzurse, "I must compliment you on a magnificent hearth, de Morville. The stone is very fine."

Palmer looked at the stone fireplace set into the wall halfway down the great room. A man could stand up in it, save for the huge logs that burned in it and sent out waves of heat that warmed the vast space of the hall. He'd have one of those too.

"Is that your motto?" continued Fitzurse. "'Ipsa quidem pretium virtus sibi.'—Virtue is indeed its own reward?' Virtue is indeed its own reward?"

Palmer squinted down the hall, sight blurry from wine. There were letters carved in the mantel, but he couldn't read them in a thousand years. He'd have to pay a clerk too.

"Not mine." De Morville belched. "Brought it back from one of my campaigns. Some monastery we burnt down in Castile."

Fitzurse nodded. "Well collected."

Palmer drained his beaker again. He wouldn't want an old one, especially not with writing on it. And definitely not church writing. He thought of that nun, that Theodosia, and how she'd nearly foiled him. Well, she hadn't. She was off in de Morville's dungeon now, and good riddance. No, he'd buy a new one, have it done specially. He couldn't wait.

"Clear this." De Morville didn't bother to turn round to address the servers who waited for orders, backs to the wall, arms folded behind them.

The men reacted as one to their lord's demand and set to clearing the dishes and spoons scattered across the stained white linen tablecloth.

"Refill all these goblets before you go," said de Morville to the sewer, "and leave the jugs of drink."

The two grooms left for the kitchens with stacked plates and dishes. The sewer topped up every drink as ordered, folded the cloth, and gathered it into his arms.

"Now get out. All of you," said de Morville. "I'll call if we need anything."

"Yes, my lord." The man gave a low bow, and the minstrels drew their tune to a quick, final piping note. They clattered from the gallery as the sewer hurried away to the kitchens.

"Gentlemen, a toast." Fitzurse rose from his seat, full pewter goblet in hand. "Raise your glasses to our success in the first stage of our mission."

"I'll drink to that." De Morville hit his vessel against Fitzurse's.

"I'll drink to owt," said de Tracy.

A silent le Bret grasped his drink to join the toast, his goblet like a youngling's in his huge hand.

Palmer raised his own goblet and joined in, adding to the warm fuzziness of the numberless glassfuls he'd drunk.

Fitzurse sat down again. "You have all played a valiant part in our success so far. I'm sure you'll be tested more before we're done."

A rumble of agreement came from the other knights.

"And when will we be done?" said Palmer.

"When I say so," said Fitzurse with a thin smile.

"And what does our king say?"

The company went silent, the crackle from the fire the only sound.

"I beg your pardon?" said Fitzurse.

"My apologies, my lord. I meant only, do we know what His Grace has said about Archbishop Becket? We were supposed to arrest him, now he's dead, and instead we have this nun—"

"My, my, Sir Palmer is a curious soul." Fitzurse exchanged glances with de Morville. He looked again at Palmer. "Yes, Becket is dead, devil take him for the traitor he was. The anchoress, who is also involved in treachery, is safely locked away." His voice hardened. "Now, are you impertinent enough to further question me and my actions, or have you finished?"

In spite of the fire, the hair rose on the back of Palmer's neck. With Fitzurse's blue gaze still fixed on him, he heard the unmistakable clink of someone loosen a sword from its sheath. "Sorry, my lord, sorry." Palmer plastered a wide grin on his face and held his glass aloft. "The Knaresborough wine is far too good. It loosens my tongue and makes it wag like a fool."

"Don't need wine for that, Palmer," said le Bret.

Laughter broke the tension.

To Palmer's relief, Fitzurse joined in, then looked in his goblet. "I've run dry again, de Morville."

As de Morville reached for a jug and filled Fitzurse's vessel, Palmer steadied his breathing. Forcurse the drink, it had pushed him to try and find out when he'd get his payment. Worse, it had made him prate out the questions he'd had since the murder in Canterbury. But he shouldn't bother with them. Fitzurse was in charge, and Fitzurse held the purse strings. Asking questions wouldn't bring Palmer his money any sooner. He had to remember that.

◆　◆　◆

The darkness pressed against and around Theodosia, seemed to suck the air from her prison and make it hard to breathe. She opened her eyes as wide as she could, as if such action would let in some light. But the blackness remained impenetrable, with tiny flashes of light the cruel invention of her own mind.

The dank stone and soggy straw on which she sat chilled her to constant shivering. Her feet had lost all sensation, and damp crawled through her skirts to soak her skin. A rusted iron collar fastened tight around her neck, so heavy she could hardly keep her head up, and chafing her neck raw with every slight movement.

A thick chain attached the collar to a stout column of wood embedded in the filthy cobbled floor. That had been her last sight as de Morville's guards had walked out, before they slammed the door shut and cut her vision as sure as if they'd pierced her eyes. Trying to rise to her feet to explore her surroundings by feel, she'd found the chain was too short and she could at best kneel.

Trapped on the floor, she had tried to rejoice in the torment of complete darkness, embrace it in prayer. *A dungeon is the same as a cell. It is a solitary place, far from temptations. I can serve God in its harshness. I can be private with Him in here and see His bright face more clearly.*

She'd called to God for hours in this foul place, with its stale, dank air and sour stench of rotting straw. But He hadn't come. She'd been cast into the darkness like the Bible had warned all sinners would.

She swallowed down the hard lump of misery in her throat as she adjusted her position on the floor, back and shoulders knotted in pain. She was still alone in here, alone for when those terrible men came for her, and come for her they would. It could be in a minute, it could be in days. But all she could do was wait, was listen out, for those metal boots on stone, for the bang at the door, for the swords, the knives.

Her chest heaved as she fought for air. She had to bring her mind elsewhere, take it away from this place. Otherwise she would lose her reason. She fumbled with numb fingers for her crucifix, tucked into the top of her woolen undergarments.

The familiar embellished metal was warm from her flesh, as it had been from Mama's skin the day she'd hung it round her neck. Mama's parting gift as she'd left her daughter, left Canterbury. *Mama.* Her noble, holy mama.

The murdering knights sought her too. Fitzurse's questions to Becket in the cathedral. *I can't find the anchoress, I can't find her mother. But you will tell me.*

But Becket did not tell them, and they killed him. Now they would get her, Theodosia, to tell them. She would bring death to Mama's door as surely as she had to her lord Thomas's. Hot tears ran down her cheeks and splashed onto her clasped hands. How could she do that to Mama?

Not Mama. Brother Edward had admonished her in confession. Sister Amélie. Not to be spoken of. Ever.

She scrubbed at her face with her fingers, gulped the tears back. "Stop it." Theodosia's command to herself in the sightless cell was angry, fierce. "Stop it now. You're not a child anymore. You are a woman of God, an anchoress."

But how could she claim such things? She had disobeyed, rushed in to the sight of men. Called forth the evil of murder.

Her teachings from Aelred flooded back. *"From sight comes all the misery that there now is and ever yet was and ever shall be."*

With a low moan of despair at her foolishness, she bowed her head against the rough collar. God had been with her in here all along. By removing her sight, He was trying to show her where she had gone so wrong, to remind her of her true vocation of staying hidden from the world.

She had to repent, and repent quickly, for her sins before those knights, those brutal men, came for her, bringing whatever torments they had to find out what she knew. But she would resist them. Resist them to the end, even if that end meant death.

◆ ◆ ◆

*The early sun warmed Palmer's face and neck as he ran down the rough track to his tumbledown home. He clasped the dish in both hands, unable to believe his luck. A quick glance down told him it was true. He had a pudding for his father, a rich, sweet pudding, all the colors of the rainbow. This would do it, would make Father eat, would make him well. Palmer pushed open the sagging door, his eyes still blinded from the light outside. "Father, Father! Look what I've got you." No answer. He squinted hard.*

*His father lay on the earth floor, silent and still.*

*Palmer put the dish down and went to his side. "Father?"*

*Father's eyes opened, and he forced a small smile. "You're a good boy, Benedict. But 'tis too late for me. Bring the pudding to your mother; she needs it or all will be lost."*

*"But Father—"*

*His father groaned and arched his back in sudden agony. "I'm full, boy, full. Can't you see that?"*

*Palmer gaped as his father's ragged tunic fell open. He backed away. He could count his father's ribs in his thin, thin chest, see them move up and down with fast breaths. And he looked like he was about to birth a child. A lump the size of a baby's head stuck from the paleness of his stomach.*

*"Full," his father gasped. "Now go."*

*Palmer snatched up the bowl and ran from the cottage, haring past it to the meadow beyond. Mother and his sisters walked right at the top of a steep, steep slope, specks against the blue sky. "Mother!" He called, he ran, but the field seemed to rise up under his feet. His mother and sis-*

*ters walked on, backs to him, not hearing him. He stumbled on a thick grass root, and the pudding flew from his hands and splattered across the grass. He struggled to his feet to set off again but fell over another root. A buzzing came from it. It was covered in flies. As was another and another. Palmer stood in the tipping meadow, flies all around him. It wasn't grass roots, it was the arms and legs of dead soldiers, cut down not by battle but by the bloody flux. A fly buzzed into his face. He swatted at it with a yell and turned to run, to flee from this meadow full of disease and death. Another fly hit his other cheek. And another and another, filling the air with blackness and noise.*

Palmer awoke to darkness on his narrow rush bed. Sweat coated his whole body. He'd no idea how long he'd slept, but the night was still pitch.

The loud buzz carried on. De Tracy made even more noise asleep than when he was awake. His snores fair echoed off the walls in this room. Le Bret slept in the other corner. What he lacked in noise, he made up for in stink.

Palmer looked into the darkness, rubbing his face dry. When death came knocking, give him a straight fight any day. Disease and sickness were no way to be taken, silent enemies that got you without your seeing them come. The dream was still crystal, but the terror faded. A miracle pudding, eh? He rolled his eyes at his own foolishness. He must have had a real skinful. He tested the inside of his mouth with his tongue. Tasty as the bottom of a birdcage and twice as dry. He had to find some water. The upside of going to bed so drunk was he was still fully dressed. He roused himself from the rumpled bed and made his way over to the door, careful not to wake the other two.

Out in the corridor, a number of small sconce lights lit the way. He went down a couple of flights of the stone spiral staircase. He'd try the hall first. The servants had left jugs of water with the wine. Not that he'd drunk any water. He'd been too busy emptying de Morville's fine cellar. If there were no water left, he'd go to the kitchens below.

Palmer spotted a door ajar through which dim light shone. This must lead to the hall. He stepped through. No, he'd gone in one too soon. This led to the empty minstrel gallery. He looked down at the quiet hall, the table cleared, the lights quenched, and the fire burning low. No chance of water there; he'd carry on down to the kitchens.

As he went to retrace his steps, he stopped in surprise as a voice floated up to him.

"I don't agree. Palmer wasn't a mistake."

Fitzurse. He was being discussed. Had he fallen short? With a silent oath, Palmer crouched down behind the low, tapestry-hung wall of the gallery. He couldn't be about to be dismissed. Could he?

"I bloody think he is." De Morville's familiar whine slurred at the edges from drink.

Palmer took a cautious look over.

The two knights sat on the stone hearth of the low fire to catch its glowing heat, a large pitcher of wine between them.

"He does as he's told. He's a good fighter—nay, a great one," said Fitzurse.

"Or so we've heard. I've not seen that yet. He couldn't even find the anchoress and the monk in the cathedral."

Palmer's jaw clenched at the sneer, though he knew de Morville was right.

"Neither could you, de Morville. Nor anyone else."

"Well, he worries me," said de Morville. "Like at dinner, with questions he'd no business asking. Blathering on like a simpleton, he was. Especially about Becket." He spat into the hearth. "Not that he'd laid a hand on the Archbishop. Left that to us."

Palmer tensed more. De Morville was right again.

"Yet look at him on the ship," said Fitzurse. "If it hadn't been for his quickness, his strength, we'd all be wet corpses." He jabbed a finger at de Morville. "Achieved nothing."

De Morville grunted. "I suppose. Still, he bothers me. I don't know why."

Palmer relaxed a mite but stayed where he was. He needed to be sure he was still on this mission.

"Palmer's perfectly safe," said Fitzurse. "He's a mercenary, and mercenaries are like whores. They'll do anything if you pay them enough."

*My battle prowess scorned as a putain's tricks.* Palmer forced himself not to rise and shout Fitzurse down. He went to leave, hear no more.

"Speaking of paying enough, he needs to earn his purse." Fitzurse took a drink.

His words halted Palmer.

Fitzurse continued. "I agree with you that he has been found wanting on a couple of things. But he can still be of use with what I have planned for the girl. What's more, it will be a useful test of his backbone."

A test? Palmer squatted low again, peering over the edge. To hell with their test. He wouldn't be found wanting.

"What plan?" De Morville hiccupped. "What test?"

"You've heard of Phalaris, the great Sicilian ruler?" said Fitzurse.

"Oh, balls to you and your high-minded carry-on," said de Morville. "'Course I haven't."

Fitzurse filled their glasses again. "An ancient Greek. He is mentioned in great writings."

"Greeks? I've killed 'em. Not read 'em."

Both men laughed, de Morville with his wheeze, Fitzurse with his clipped sound.

Fitzurse said, "He is credited with overseeing the invention of one of these." He reached into the ashes of the hearth and pulled out a stick of black charcoal. He drew something on the pale stone.

Palmer squinted hard, barely able to make it out in the dim light. It looked like an animal.

"A cow?" said de Morville, mystified.

"No, a bull." Fitzurse tapped a finger on his drawing. "A Brazen Bull, to be precise."

De Morville's shake of his head matched Palmer's own confusion. "How's a Brazing—"

"Brazen."

"Brazen Bull going to test Palmer?"

"A Brazen Bull is made of metal," said Fitzurse. "Traditionally bronze, but any will do. It is hollow, and there is a door, or a hatch, on the back here." He squiggled on his drawing.

De Morville shook his head again.

Fitzurse went on. "The fire is lit beneath here." He made another mark. "Of course, the victim is usually placed inside before the fire is lit."

De Morville gave a stunned gasp as Palmer's limbs locked rigid.

"I want your blacksmiths to fashion one of these, de Morville."

"Fitzurse, you're going to put Palmer into this thing? Fine by me, but—"

"Not Palmer, you dolt. The girl. Stripped naked and bound. By him, and he will put her in."

Palmer's fists curled.

De Morville gasped again. "A good test, by my life. But is it worth killing her just to see what he's made of? We need information from her, remember? We still don't know where the mother is."

"The bull will serve both purposes, de Morville. Palmer can put her in, give her a taste of it. Promise her release if she tells us what we want to know."

De Morville coughed suddenly and Palmer started, knocking one knee against the gallery wall. His pulse tripped for action. Had they heard him?

"Here, have another drink, man," said Fitzurse.

Thank Jesu, they hadn't.

"You have one too."

"I've used this thing before. No one can stand the pain. So he can haul her out, find out what we need."

"She'll be a bit raw, but no matter. As I've got her here, I want to try my cock in her. She'll be pure, and I like that."

"Sorry to disappoint you, my friend. Palmer will put her straight back in and roast her till she's dead."

"Where's the pleasure in that, Fitzurse?"

"Oh, I forgot the best bit. I will show the blacksmiths how to fashion a set of pipes here, leading to the nose. You can't really hear the screams through the metal; instead the sound comes through these pipes and out the nose. Because of their shape, they change the human voice so that it sounds exactly like a bull."

"I ask again, where's the pleasure in that?"

Fitzurse looked at de Morville askance. "It's very, very amusing, of course. As the Greeks wrote, 'The screams will come through to you through the pipes as the tenderest, most pathetic, most melodious of bellowings.'" He smiled at de Morville. "You see?"

Palmer's pulse pounded in his ears. De Morville stared at Fitzurse. "You and me laugh at different things, Fitzurse. But as a test for Palmer, it's a good 'un."

"He can clean up afterward, of course. Get rid of the body."

De Morville nodded. "He'll earn his purse with that job. Don't think I'd fancy it much."

"My thoughts exactly." Fitzurse drained his cup. "We'll make a start on the morrow. Early. I'll meet you at the forge at dawn. Now, how about a drink for me before it all goes down your neck?"

Their talk shifted to blacksmiths, with de Morville whining about the time it took to train them.

Palmer's temples hammered as if they'd burst. He'd sworn to pass any test. But this? His hands tightened more. Hands that would seize the small-boned Sister Theodosia. Strip her. Put her into some metal beast from a nightmare. Reach back into it, take hold of her while she was half burned to death. From his own mouth would have to come the lie of a promise that she could live. He'd see her hope in eyes blistered half shut. Eyes that would then know his lie as he placed her back inside, onto red-hot metal that would make her skin bubble and melt. Palmer fought his bile. And last, lift out her cooked remains and bury them. This was Fitzurse's test. So sure he'd sounded that he, Palmer, was as low as a whore and would do all of this for his money.

Well, he wasn't that low. He was a sworn knight. A fighter, yes, a killer, yes. He'd done plenty of both. But he'd done them against other men, men armed and ready to kill him in return. Not this. He'd failed the test. And lost the money. No matter. Right now, he needed to get out of this castle, cut his losses, and go back to the life he knew. *But the money.* No matter, he told himself again. He could have all the riches in the world, but no one would respect him for such a deed—he least of all. And every time he used his hands, every time he so much as looked at them, he would have a reminder of what he had done. His wealth would be fouled with shame, with dishonor of the worst kind. He went to rise, and his gaze lit on the sketch of the terrible bull again, as the pair below rambled on.

Still sick to his stomach, he crouched back down. He was still being tested again, but not in the way Fitzurse intended. Even if Palmer succeeded in leaving Knaresborough, Fitzurse would easily find another sap to torture and kill the anchoress. It wouldn't take him long—the money was simply too good. Fitzurse would just do it himself, forcurse him.

That meant only one thing. He'd have to try and get her away from here. Go against Reginald Fitzurse and suffer the effects of his actions. It would probably mean his certain death. Palmer knuckled the side of his head with his fist as Lullworth, his squire master, used to do. *Think, lad. Think. Use what's in that skull, not just your strength. Think it through, before you rush in like a ninny.*

But Fitzurse's words came back to him. *"The screams will come through to you through the pipes as the tenderest, most pathetic, most melodious of bellowings."* No matter if he never actually heard them. If he did nothing, those sounds would haunt his dreams till the day he died.

Bent low behind the gallery's edge, Palmer took silent steps back out to the corridor. He drew his dagger from his belt and hastened down the dark stairwell, heading for the dungeon below, where he knew the woman of the church was held. Palmer paused. Wait. The church. Wealthy as the King. Wealthier. They'd pay to get her back. Pay a fine ransom. A ransom he could name, as he'd have saved her life.

Palmer allowed himself a wide, wide grin. Low as a whore, eh? But one that was keeping all the rewards. Lullworth would have been proud of him.

◆    ◆    ◆

The steps led down past floor after floor. Palmer hurried, taking the steps two at a time on the curved staircase, careful to make no noise.

Finally he reached the bottom and stepped off the last stair into a poorly lit stone corridor. The last flight of steps had been far older than the rest, worn in the middle to a smooth curve. The changed air told him he was underground: stale, damp, a mushroom-like smell. He must be near the dungeon now. Or dungeons. In a castle this size, de Morville could have any number of people locked away. And any number of guards to watch them.

He put his hand to his belt and drew his dagger, cursing he didn't have his sword. But that lay beside his bed. He couldn't risk going back for it. He might wake the sleeping le Bret or de Tracy, or, worse, meet Fitzurse and de Morville on the stairwell.

Palmer took cautious, quiet treads. The corridor sloped down to take him deeper underground. Black mold spread thick on the flags under his feet, and close on either side the walls oozed damp. Ahead, the wall curved to the left and orange light flickered from beyond. He halted. That would be the guards. He cursed his lack of sword again.

He couldn't rush in blind, not as badly armed as he was. He needed to judge his foe first. Sticking his dagger back in his belt, he raised his chain mail hood and straightened his surcoat. He stepped forward with definite strides and rounded the corner.

"Stop right there." The bulky guard who stood outside the iron-hinged wooden door held a hefty axe. But there was only one of him. And only one door.

The man raised his weapon, and the blade caught the torch-light, a large *K* for de Morville's Knaresborough engraved on the shiny metal.

Palmer held up a hand. "Hold, soldier. I'm Sir Benedict Palmer, sent by Sir Hugh. A disturbance has been heard upstairs. We're checking the whole castle."

The guard kept his weapon up. "Why haven't they sent the regular watch?"

"Because in that cell behind you is no regular prisoner, is it?" Palmer kept his look firm.

"No. De Morville usually keeps his girls upstairs."

He'd found her. "Exactly. This one must be kept secure. That is Sir Hugh de Morville's direct order. I hope you're not questioning your lord, fellow."

"My apologies, sir knight," said the man, lowering his axe. "All has been quiet down here."

"Good. Make sure it stays that way." Palmer gave him a stiff nod and went to retrace his steps back around the bend in the corridor. "Stay alert. You understand?"

"Yes, sir." The guard gave him a sharp salute.

Palmer went back the way he had come, with loudly echoing steps. He gave a quick look back. The man hadn't followed. Palmer bent to the floor and scooped up two handfuls of the mildewed rubble and mortar that lay scattered there. Rising to his feet, he stepped silently back to the curved corner.

He flung the debris hard at the ceiling. It clattered against it and fell back down.

"What's to do?" The guard came round the corner, eyes up to the source of the noise.

Palmer drove his fisted knuckles into the man's face, and he went down, palms to his nose. The axe fell to one side and Palmer was on it. Handle grasped in both hands, he pointed the weapon at the writhing guard. "Open the cell. Now."

Blood seeping from his nose, the guard got to his feet, his sight only for the axe. "You sapless cur. I knew you was off." He sought out by touch the bunch of keys that hung from an iron loop on his belt.

"Another word and I'll have your head," said Palmer.

The guard glared but nodded. With Palmer close behind, he retraced his steps to the cell, where he unlocked the door, then twisted the rusty handle. The door opened to a scuffling sound inside, but darkness so complete Palmer could see nothing.

"Take down the wall light," Palmer said. "Enter before me. Slowly."

Again, the guard did as he was told. As he followed the man into the cell, the torch's flare lit the blackness.

"Oh, please have mercy, I beg you, I beg you." Theodosia's voice, below him. The clink of a chain.

Palmer looked down.

She was on her hands and knees on the filthy floor, scrambling away from him and the guard, pulling a chain with her. It stopped taut from her neck to the wooden post that secured it. She gasped hard.

"Unlock her," said Palmer.

The guard bent and yanked the chain to him with his free hand.

Theodosia gave a strangled cry and fell onto one hip. Her hands went to her throat as the guard hauled her back to the post like a dog. A rusted collar was tight round her neck, and she clawed at it to ease her breathing, gray eyes wide in panic as she sprawled on the floor.

"I don't want her throttled." Palmer showed his axe to the guard, and Theodosia ducked from it with a scream, arm across her face. "Sister, I've come to free you. But stay quiet." She lowered her arm and looked at him as if she'd not heard right.

Palmer nodded to the guard. "Do it."

The man went to carry out the order, hauling her up into a seated position. The torchlight lit her tear-flushed face as he struggled with the rusted lock on the collar.

Her eyes flicked from Palmer to the guard. "Please don't let him take me, please."

"Wench, he's already broken my nose." The guard's voice came thick from his injury. "He'd have my head too. Far as I'm concerned, he can do what he likes to you." He straightened up and dangled the open collar from one hand. "Sir." He gave Palmer a surly glare.

"Thank you, soldier." Palmer spun the axe and hit the man on the side of his head with the handle. He folded at the knees and slumped to the floor, torch clattering beside him.

Palmer picked it up. "Hold this."

Sitting stock-still, Theodosia stared at him, hands to her throat where the collar had been.

He looked at the unconscious guard. "He won't be out for long." He thrust the torch at her. "Hold it. We haven't much time."

She held out one trembling hand as she stood up and took it from him.

Palmer laid down the axe so he could grab the guard's legs and maneuver him nearer to the wooden post. His shoulders knotted with effort, it took him two or three hauls. He knelt down and fitted the iron loop around the man's neck. He locked it swiftly, then hooked the door key from the loop on the guard's belt. "That's him done. Let's go." He looked up at Theodosia. And a sheet of flame hit his face.

Theodosia flinched back and almost dropped the torch as the knight dodged away from her with a yell of pain.

"You'll not take me." She screwed up her nose at the acrid smell of his burned hair and swiped again.

Sir Palmer slapped at the side of his cheek. "What are you doing?"

She moved between him and the axe, heart pounding. If he reached it, she was dead. "Stay away from me." Her voice shook almost as much as her hands as she held the flaring torch close to the knight's face. "God has given me this weapon against the darkness of your sin. Hand me the door key. This will be your prison while I make my escape from here. If you don't, I shall, I shall burn you again. You mark my words." She braced herself for his quick lunge, for his powerful hands to knock away her defense.

To her surprise, Palmer lowered his head with a snort of contained laughter, then looked up at her again. "Oh, then I surrender, Sister." He held up both hands but got to his feet and took a step toward her. "Or maybe not."

"Stop where you are." Theodosia shook the torch at him, but he kept coming, his height a head and a half above her.

She backed away, kicking at the axe handle with her heels to keep it from him, praying it was hidden under her skirt.

Palmer stepped again. "Sister, you're being as foolhardy as you were with de Morville in the cathedral. I might get a bit singed if I were to go for that axe, but believe me, I'd get it." He glanced down at the guard and around at the doorway. "We haven't much time. You must come with me."

She backed again, and her shoulders hit the wall. "So that you can kill me, like you did my lord Becket?" Arms straight out, she waved the flames again. "Give me the key."

"I'm not going to hurt you."

"Liar!" She lunged with the flame at his face.

He swerved aside with an oath. "Would you shut up? I'm trying to save your life, and your noise will call down the whole place." The knight looked around at the doorway yet again and, with a hand up, went quickly over to it to listen out.

His claims to save her made no sense, and he seemed nervous. She'd seen his quick moods, his shift to anger. Maybe he also shifted to madness.

But now she had a chance as he stood in the doorway. If she delivered a hard swipe with the torch, she could get past him. Then run. The axe still lay on the floor and would be in darkness. Theodosia adjusted her grip on the torch and moved forward with small steps. She brought it round to slash at the knight, teeth gritted for his howl of pain, the stench of burned flesh.

He turned back as she hit out. He shot out a long arm and grabbed the torch's shaft. "Forcurse you, woman."

She'd lost her chance. Now he'd have her. She tried to wrench the torch free.

Palmer swore again. "Listen to me. For one minute. Your life depends on it."

"I am sure it does, for you have been sent here to kill me."

"Not this time." His dark eyes bored into hers through the quivers of heat from the torch.

She saw no madness there. Her throat tightened. "What do you mean?"

"Have you ever heard of a Brazen Bull?"

Pictures in her illuminated manuscripts. Saint Antipas, Saint Pelagia, Saint Eustace. Martyrs all, roasted alive inside terrible metal contraptions. "Yes." The word stuck in her throat.

Palmer leaned closer to her and lowered his voice. "Fitzurse is having one worked at the forge on the morrow. Within a day, two at most, he'll have you put in it to make you tell what you know."

Theodosia's mouth could barely form her words. "Know about what?"

"They want to know where your mother is. And once you've told them, Sister, he'll finish you off in there."

71

She'd sworn to resist the knights, not to tell what she knew. The torch prickled raw heat onto the backs of her hands, mocking her vow. To have burning metal against her face, her breasts, her arms, her legs, have it secured there, with no release. Resist that? She let go of the torch with a stifled cry.

Palmer held the flame aloft. "I'm glad you see sense."

"But why are you suddenly my savior?"

"Because he wants me to do it to you."

He'd tricked her. Theodosia whirled round. The axe, she had to get to the axe.

Palmer was quicker than she. With two long strides, he jammed his foot on its handle as she flung herself to the floor to grab it.

"You sinful, evil liar." She hauled at the axe handle but could not budge it.

"I'm not lying."

Theodosia stood up and shook her head. "Do not make it worse. At least have the courage to speak the truth."

"Sister, I know you don't trust me, but believe me when I say I can't carry out Fitzurse's order."

She gave him her most distasteful look. "You carried them out in the cathedral. At the inn. Yet now you tell me you have reformed. Repented. Seen the evil of your ways, so you would rescue a helpless nun. I do not know what you are up to, but I am not a complete fool, Sir Palmer."

The knight took a deep breath. "I worked for Fitzurse for his money. But I can't do what he asked to you." His look hardened. "But neither am I about to risk my life for naught. You, Sister Theodosia, are worth a pretty penny to me. If I save you, I'll ransom you back to the Church. That way, I can still collect. See?"

She summoned another look. "But by the way of the cross, you are truly an ignoble soul."

The man on the floor groaned and stirred.

"Our friend is about to wake up, Sister. Ignoble as I am, I am your only hope. Are you coming with me?" He jingled the key. "Or do you want to stay in here with him and wait for Fitzurse to come to you?"

# CHAPTER 6

Theodosia clambered up the narrow staircase with her skirt clutched to keep from tripping, the muscles in her legs weak from effort. But she carried on as fast as if Fitzurse were two steps behind her, ready to roast her alive.

Ahead, Sir Palmer's long legs made easy work of the climb up many stairs.

What if he lied? What if she were running toward an even worse fate? The pictures from her manuscripts flashed before her again. Her prayers as she'd read of the martyrs' deaths imagining their agony, their hell. No. There could be no worse.

The next flight had an iron handrail to one side. She reached for it with sweated palms and used it to lever herself up, grasp by grasp. Palmer could have easily killed her in the dungeon, if that was his plan. But he hadn't, not even when she'd burned him with the torch, horrifying herself. His story of ransom must be true. An ignoble, base act, but one that would keep Mama alive. Would keep her, Theodosia, alive and deliver her back to the safety of her beloved church.

He halted on the landing above and looked back down at her, finger to his lips.

Theodosia nodded her comprehension as she steadied her breath.

He gestured toward a half-open door as she climbed from the top step.

They went through the doorway.

A stone open range, banked for the night, gave poor light to a large shadow-filled room. The castle kitchen.

Theodosia scanned the room for another door. The walls held only the range and wide shelves with earthenware and copper pots of every size and shape. "There's no way out of here," she whispered.

Palmer pushed past her and went to a large wooden table on which half a dozen pottery pitchers stood. He peered into the pitchers and gestured to her. "Go and look on that back wall." He kept his voice low. "There's some aprons on there. Get one and put it round you. Hurry."

He made little sense. Theodosia looked at him as she crossed the wide kitchen. Now he poured dregs of wine into his hand and rubbed it on his face and neck.

To trust this man may have been a huge mistake. She rummaged amongst the hanging clothes covers, the cloth sticky and foul with grease. She looped one on over her head as she went to his side.

Palmer continued to search the pitchers. He glanced at her. "No, not like that. Put it around your head and shoulders, make a cloak."

She did as he said, the stained cloth reeking with splashes and stains of a hundred meals.

He thrust a jug patterned with glazed green leaves into her hands. "Drink some of that. Wet your clothes with it too." He moved quickly over to the range.

Theodosia stared at it. A sheep's face fashioned into the clay as a spout stared back. "Wine is a pleasure of the flesh. I cannot sip a drop."

He hurried back to her with a deep scowl. "You won't have any flesh left if Fitzurse gets hold of you."

She took a deep breath and raised it to her lips. The sharp liquid flooded her mouth, and she spewed it from her lips in disgust.

Palmer made an impatient sound. "Put some of it on your clothes."

Splashing it across her, she wrinkled her nose at the foul fumes. She was as foolish as the animal on the jug to carry on like this. She'd agreed to follow a madman. Replacing the beaker on the table, she looked up at him in trepidation.

He brought his hands to her cheeks, and she twisted in his hold as he rubbed her skin hard.

"What are you doing?"

He let go of her and showed her his hands, filthy with ash from the range. "You look as dirty as these, Sister."

Theodosia brought a hand to her face and looked at her fingertips. She was indeed smeared with new filth. "Sir knight, you have no intention of saving me. You only want to play some horrid jest. I was a fool to follow you." She looked toward the door, waiting for the dread figures to show there.

"I thank you for your trust in me." He grasped her by the elbow.

"Why should I trust you?" She shook him off. "I am not doing anything else until you tell me what your plan is."

"It's simple." Palmer gave her a humorless smile. "We walk out the front door."

No bloody drink left. Sir Hugh de Morville shoved at the dead ashes of the hall's fire with the heel of his boot. No bloody heat, neither.

He was supposed to be lord of this castle. Instead he sat here like a turnip-headed peasant, without sup nor warmth. At least bed would bring one of those. Rising to his feet, he swayed to balance.

Fitzurse had not long since retired, with his stuck-up "Go easy, my friend" as he'd gone abed.

De Morville hawked on the floor in disgust. He was in charge here, it was his castle, his land. Not Fitzurse's. Who did Fitzurse think he was, issuing orders all the time? *We'll have Palmer, we'll do this, we'll do that. You'll not do the girl.*

De Morville went toward the door with careful steps. He cursed Fitzurse for the arrangement to meet at dawn in the forge. Up with the bloody cockerel, and nothing to do except watch Fitzurse take up the castle blacksmiths' expensive time with some metal bull.

"Some bullshit would be more like," he muttered to himself. His own joke set him off into a long wheeze of a laugh, and he clutched the doorjamb for support.

He finished in a spasm of coughing as he considered Fitzurse's plan. It would get the information they needed from the girl, no question. Fitzurse would get his pleasure too. The gleam in his pale eyes as he'd described the workings of the bull meant only one thing.

De Morville shook his head. His own pleasures were much more straightforward. He liked a virgin more than anything, especially one who fought her taking. The girl wouldn't be up to much fighting if she was half-cooked. He belched long and hard. Then why not do her now, eh? Pissed as he was, his cock warmed in his breeches. It might take her mouth first to get him fully up, but he'd have no problem with that.

He staggered toward the stairs. It was all his: his castle, his dungeon, his prisoner. He could do what he bloody well liked.

◆　◆　◆

The door that opened out from the deserted corridor squeaked loud on rusty hinges as Sir Palmer pushed it open, revealing a covered porch. Despite the dirty cloth that muffled her face and neck, Theodosia's flesh pimpled with cold in the frigid night air.

She looked across the courtyard. Mercifully empty though it was, the high walls surrounding it linked even higher towers of forbidding yellowed stone, enclosing it completely. The main doors stood at the opposite end, the dark, metal-studded wood three times the height of Sir Palmer and shut tight.

"How can we get out this way?" she asked, voice low.

Palmer pointed to the gates. "Like I said. Out the front door." He reached a long arm around her waist and tugged her to him, hip to hip.

"Do not hold me so." Her sharp whisper had no effect, and she squirmed. "What you do is sinful."

He held her tight. "It might be shameful for a nun," he said, "but not for a whore."

Now she understood his actions, the lecherous caitiff. "You had no plan at all. That you would trick me so for my virtue." She pulled against him, to no avail. "Then I would rather die."

Palmer hauled her round to face him. "Not to be a whore, Sister. Only to act like one. For the next few minutes." He gripped her arms tight. "And we've no more time for questions. You do as I say. Or I'll leave you here."

His glower told her he meant it.

She gave a stiff nod.

He pulled her to his side again and descended the steps from the porch. They set off across the icy courtyard, the knight's boots echoing against the stone flags.

"Come on, wench." He said it with full voice.

He made such a noise, he'd wake the whole castle. Theodosia pulled at his surcoat. "Quiet!" she hissed. "Someone will hear you."

Instead, he took a hefty stagger almost to one knee and pulled her down with him. "Bollocks to this ice."

As she struggled to keep her foothold, a voice rang out from the shadows by the main gate.

"Who's there? Show yourselves in the name of de Morville!"

The call shot through her soul. Palmer had roused the guards.

◆   ◆   ◆

"Guard! Open up the bloody door." Sir Hugh de Morville shouted his order as he rounded the last corner of the passageway that led to the dungeon.

He stopped in surprise as the door came into view. All in order, closed tight. But no one stood watch. The torch flickered on an empty post.

De Morville made the last few steps and tried the door. Locked, of course. He swore and spat richly on the damp floor. Where could the knave be? Doubtless sat on the privy, or other such time wasting. Worse, the man might be curled up in a warm corner, using the deserted castle and late hour to sleep off his watch.

Wherever he was, it meant de Morville's pleasure was thwarted, leastways for the time being. He dealt the door a hefty kick. "Raise yourself, Sister. Once I have the key, you'll be at my bidding."

A muffled voice came from within.

De Morville halted his next kick in surprise. That were no maid's voice. He put his right ear to the door. "What are you up to, you mangy dog? Unlock this bloody door and come out. You've no business in there."

"I can't, sir. He's locked me in, took the key. Chained me up too. Can hardly breathe."

"Who has?"

79

"One of the knights, sir. He went with the prisoner."

"Which bastard knight?"

"Called himself Palmer, sir."

Rage sobered de Morville as quick as a bucket of icy water over his head. "I knew it." He kicked the door so hard he near broke his foot, but the wood remained solid. "You fool, soldier. I'll deal with you later."

"Very sorry, sir."

"Don't worry. You will be. Sorrier than a gelded goat if I have anything to do with it." De Morville gave the door the punch he wanted to give to this oaf's face.

Then he turned and sprinted back toward the stairwell.

◆  ◆  ◆

"Show ourselves? Have you no eyes, man?" Sir Palmer slurred his words as he lurched toward the gate.

Theodosia staggered too, half pulled off her feet by the knight's tight hold on her waist.

The thickly clothed sentry looked askance at them as they approached and drew his sword in readiness. "Stop where you are."

Theodosia tried to respond to the clipped command, but Sir Palmer paid no heed. "I'll thank you to have some manners, soldier."

"Stop. Now." The sentry held his sword in readiness.

Theodosia grasped at Palmer's arm as hard as she could. They would be cut down.

The knight carried on, halting only a couple of steps away from de Morville's man and his sharp metal blade.

Her heart pounded in her chest, and she feared her knees would give way.

"I'll thank you to open that gate, soldier," said Palmer.

The sentry's unimpressed look swept over them both. She could strike Palmer for his foolishness. Had he stayed quiet, they might have had a chance.

"And I'll thank you to explain yourself, you insolent swillbelly." The sentry gave a loud sniff. "I can smell the drink from here. Sir de Morville will want to know how you and your trollop got hold of his supplies."

Palmer drew himself up and took a step toward the sentry. "I am Sir Benedict Palmer, returned with Sir Hugh from his recent mission. He poured his supplies into my glass with his own hand. How does that make me a swillbelly?"

The sentry paled and lowered his weapon. "My lord, apologies—"

Palmer cut him off with a wave of his free hand. "Enough of your blubbing. I care not. And you were right about one thing." He made a clumsy lunge at Theodosia's chest, crushing her lips with his. She held in her cry of disgust. He broke from her with a coarse laugh and addressed the sentry. "You're right, she is a trollop. A bit dirty, but very willing."

He jabbed his unseen fingers against her ribs to prompt her enthusiastic nod.

"So willing that she wants me to meet her friends at a bawdy house in the town. Are you going to keep me from my pleasure, soldier?"

"No indeed, Sir Palmer." The sentry turned and hurried to the massive main gate, where he busied himself raising the heavy wooden bars.

Palmer glanced down at her. "Keep it up," he whispered through clenched teeth.

Stomach turning at her own base actions, she flung a hand to the knight's neck and stroked it.

The gate opened with a deep creak, the gap enough to allow them through. "As you required, Sir Palmer."

81

"Good man." Palmer leaned Theodosia against him and made his way to the gate.

"Good night to you, sir. What's left of it." The sentry gave a brief salute as they passed through.

The road ahead dipped steeply toward the straggle of the town of Knaresborough lining the river along the narrow valley.

"Carry on with our slow stagger," came Palmer's low murmur. "And once the gate's closed, we run."

◆　◆　◆

The sentry slid the bolts in place and made the gates secure once more. It was tricky work in his thick leather gloves, but he wouldn't remove them for a gallon of hippocras, not on a night as cold as this. At least his work on the gate had made his blood move round a bit more. Guard duty in winter could lead to black fingers and toes if you weren't careful.

He stamped his feet a couple of times for good measure.

Across the courtyard, the door from the porch at the bottom of the main keep flew open. A flushed-looking de Morville dashed out.

The sentry snapped to attention as his lord ran over to him, slipping and sliding on the icy stones.

"Have you seen Palmer and the prisoner?" said de Morville.

"I've seen Sir Palmer. But he had no prisoner, my lord. Only a harlot."

"A woman?"

"Yes, my lord. I allowed them passage to the town. He wanted to go to her brothel."

"Fool!"

The sentry ducked from his lord's furious swipe. "I'm sorry, my lord. He said he'd been feasting with you tonight. He had great authority."

"And you have a tiny helping of sense."

"I will get the gates open at once, my lord. We can give chase—they must only be at the bottom of the hill."

"Forget that." De Morville heeled round to return to the castle. "I'll take the sally port. Going down the tunnel will give me the surprise of being ahead of them, when they expect me to come after." He held out a hand. "Give me your sword."

The sentry complied. "Please excuse my foolishness, my lord. Whatever you want, I will do it to put it right."

"Then take yourself up to wake Lord Fitzurse. Tell him to follow me down the tunnel. Armed."

The sentry breathed a sigh of relief as de Morville hurried off and he hastened behind. His apology had been accepted.

De Morville paused and gave the sentry a sour look. "And on the morrow, you'll get your flogging. Six for each prisoner and six for your stupidity."

"Yes, my lord." His bowels knotted tight but cramped at his lord's next words.

"And if I don't find them, I'll hang you."

# CHAPTER 7

Palmer's breath clouded before his face as he and Theodosia ran through the unlit narrow streets of Knaresborough, his arm locked tight through hers to keep her speed up. Dark houses and shuttered shops meant no one would see them pass but might easily hear them. The brown, smooth ice that coated the mud road snapped and cracked under his boots, her shoes.

Theodosia's feet went from under her, but he blocked her fall and pulled her on.

"Hold, sir knight." She panted so hard she could scarce speak. "It feels like a knife in my side."

"That'll pass. We can't stop." He hurried her along the slippery surface. "Keep going, and faster."

Her brow creased as she fought for breath.

He knew how much it hurt when you couldn't get air in your lungs and still had to run. Yet she tried to match him, even with her shorter legs. "That's it." He took more of her weight to help her.

They neared a row of wretched cottages, the wattle-and-daub walls splintered and crumbling. A dog barked as they passed, scrabbling against a warped door.

Theodosia clutched at him hard. "What if it gets out?"

"Keep moving." He forced her past.

The animal fell quiet and she relaxed her hold.

"We've nothing to defend ourselves with. Nothing." Her gray eyes shone with fear.

"I've got my dagger."

"There was an axe in the cell." Her look judged him as a fool.

"And what would the sentry have done if I'd come into the courtyard carrying a weapon with the Knaresborough crest?" He fixed her with a scathing glance. "Leave the fighting to me, Sister."

Beneath the filth on her face, the flush rose at her mistake. "With pleasure." She gasped. "What's that noise?"

Palmer paused to listen out. The ceaseless rumble of turbulent water. Knaresborough's river, the Nidd. "Our guide from this place." He headed down the steeply sloped road toward the loudening roar of the river, Theodosia still in his grasp.

As the land flattened out, he released her, scanning for the best route. The buildings and streets petered out to a broad swath of thick shrubs, patches of grass, and a few moisture-loving willows. It might be a waste of land, but one look at the river beyond told him only a fool would build a house this low down.

Palmer signaled to Theodosia. "We need to find the towpath. But mind, the river's very high."

She followed him with a wordless nod.

As they drew close, the noise grew. The wide Nidd battered against the frozen banks, churning the brown, soil-filled water to yellow foam. The recent rainstorms had swollen it right up to the top of its normal channel, threatening a breach. Its fierce current bit out chunks of the riverbank, carrying more soil, weeds, and pieces of grass with it. A few hundred paces downstream, it thundered over a high natural weir, throwing up spray and more foam.

"At least no one will hear us now," said Palmer. "Keep behind me on the towpath and stay away from the edge. And while we need to make haste, don't run."

"But we have to run—you made me on those icy streets."

"It's too dangerous on here."

"Then if it's perilous, we should find another way."

The axe. His route. His judgment. His jaw clenched at her picking. "I don't know this countryside. If we strike out, we'll get lost. We only have a couple of hours till the alarm is raised." Palmer pointed ahead, past the weir. "We'll track the river's course till we come to another town." His boot slipped in a patch of mud made liquid by river water, and he fought for balance. "Watch this bit." He looked back to check she obeyed.

She trod with short rapid steps, focused on the path. "I don't see how a town will help us. We could hide better in the woods."

*Questioning me again.* "There'll either be a church, a monastery, or folk will know of one. Once we find it, we're safe. I can state my case for ransom. It won't take them long to arrange payment. Then you and I are done." *Thank the Almighty.*

"I suppose I owe you thanks. Though your methods are not honorable." She inclined her head stiffly.

Palmer ignored the goad. "I don't need your thanks, only your value." He set off again, taking long strides on the drier patches, shorter ones where mud and water pooled.

Then stopped dead as a familiar voice floated over the thrum of the river.

"Goodness, what have we here?"

His gaze shot to the opposite bank.

Fitzurse stood there, drawn sword in hand. "I do believe that's my prisoner, Palmer. How did she get there?" He didn't sound angry, merely curious. But his curiosity was backed up by a ready broadsword.

Palmer glanced back at Theodosia. She stood rooted to the spot in terror. He took a half step to shield her from a thrown weapon.

"I'm waiting, Palmer."

He had nothing. No weapon. No defense. All he had was the truth. "I released her, Fitzurse."

"Indeed. May I ask why?"

"I overheard your conversation. With de Morville."

"How did you do that, Palmer?" Again, the tone even, measured.

Again, he had nothing. "Earlier tonight, I went to the minstrel gallery by mistake. I heard what you said. About not being sure of me, testing me. About the Brazen Bull. I freed her because I couldn't do that."

"He will kill us both now." Theodosia's anguished whisper came to his left ear, but he didn't respond. Fitzurse had one sword, and he couldn't get them both, not from this distance across the rough river.

"Then we were right to question you, were we not?" said Fitzurse, eyebrows raised. "You ran away, like a yellow-breeched knave. Not able to see a job through."

Palmer boiled inside, but he kept it down. He had a chance at getting a weapon. "Not a bit of it. I'm going to ransom her back to the church. I'll still be paid." He adjusted his stance, ready to pull Theodosia to the ground when Fitzurse's sword flew.

Fitzurse shook his head slowly, then, to Palmer's astonishment, lowered his sword. "Well done, boy. You've passed the test."

"Test? Your test for me was to roast the anchoress alive."

"I'd already seen your strength, saw it on the ship. But I had to ask questions about what you carried between your ears. You missed the girl and the monk in the cathedral, Palmer."

Another whisper. "Don't listen to him."

Palmer opened his mouth to respond, then closed it again. Fitzurse was right.

Fitzurse nodded. "There was also the question of your mettle. You didn't land a single blow on Becket."

"I didn't—"

"No, you didn't." Fitzurse shook his head. "A quest ordered by the monarch allows no room for doubt, Palmer."

"Stop filling his head with your poison!"

Palmer started at Theodosia's sudden cry above the river's noise. Fitzurse merely smiled. "Don't take on, Sister." He didn't move his gaze from Palmer. "Hence your test. De Morville and I invented a terrible fate for the anchoress. Planned for you to hear of it on the morrow, see how you'd react. As it happened, you came clattering into the gallery and gave us a ready-made opportunity." Fitzurse gave his clipped laugh. "We were obviously convincing. I must say, you acted far faster, far more effectively, than we thought possible. And making sure you'd be paid as well? You'll go far, Benedict Palmer."

"Th-thank you, my lord." All wasn't lost. In fact, nothing was. He'd been tested and found true.

Another cry. "You lie!"

Fitzurse brought his sword across his body and slowly sheathed it, shaking his head. "It's a royal mission, my girl. Why would I lie?"

A wave of relief swept through Palmer. "What he says is true, Sister. And he's withdrawn his weapon. We have our proof."

"Palmer!" Fitzurse reached beneath his surcoat and pulled out a bulging leather pouch. "Here's your reward. I know waiting for it plagues you." He threw it high across the water, and Palmer caught it in one hand with a loud *clink*.

He unknotted the looped tie at the top and looked inside to see the unmistakable glow of gold. He opened it up fully. Fabulous yellow discs, too many to count as they lay atop each other against the red silk lining. A fortune. Forever. He raised his gaze to see a smiling Fitzurse. "You're most generous, my lord Fitzurse."

"Half of it is for the girl. She can take it back to Canterbury. Use it to build a shrine to Becket, or whatever the monks want to do with it," said Fitzurse. "I truly regret frightening her, but it had to be done. We only have to ask her a few questions. If she knows nothing, we'll release her."

Palmer turned to Theodosia and thrust the open bag before her. "Now do you believe him?"

"No. More fool you if you do." She swung up her right hand and hit the bag hard.

It flew open wide, and the coins showered onto the frozen ground.

He bent to pick them up with a loud oath.

"Palmer!"

He looked up at Fitzurse's shout. Theodosia fled back up the towpath as if chased by dogs.

"Stop her!"

Palmer took off after her. "Theodosia! No!" She couldn't ruin things for him now. He'd show her the back of his hand when he caught her.

"Palmer! If she gets away, you'll get nothing. Our mission depends on what she knows."

Palmer lengthened his strides, but panic seemed to give the girl wings. "Theodosia!" For God's sake, why wouldn't she listen? As she ran, she ran with all his hopes. The gold, his fortune. All right for her, with the comfort of the religious life, no fear for her old age. Not like him, going from battle to battle, each one harder as he grew older and the other knights got younger. Old age was a begging bowl and destitution. He'd been raised with that—he couldn't do it again.

Ahead, she slipped on the wet path and went down on her hands and knees with a cry.

He'd take her now.

She looked back as he gained on her, then scrambled into a dense thicket of shrubs and bushes next to the path.

Palmer's rapid steps brought him there in moments. "Sister." He bent low and peered in through the dense evergreen foliage, his breath fast and hard. "Listen to me. You must give yourself up. You'll come to no harm. You must see that."

A faint rustle sounded from within. Palmer thought he saw a glimmer of cream wool amongst the shiny dark-green leaves.

"Sister? Answer me. I order you."

Complete silence.

"Any luck?" Fitzurse's call came nearer as he picked his careful way along the opposite riverbank.

"Not yet, my lord." As Palmer forced his way in through the branches, brambles and ivy tangled round his legs. With such a small moon, the darkness in here made his sight of little use. He would have to rely on his ears. A rustle by his boots came from a mouse or water rat in the muss of dry, dead leaves. The constant roar of the water at the weir. Nothing else. He went forward, progress slow through the tough tendrils that laced the bushes. A twig snapped close ahead. He made for the sound, face and hands ripped by sharp branches and hooked thorns. The bushes thinned. Bent double, he propelled himself forward toward the weak moonlight and out from the thicket.

"Looking for aught?" De Morville stood above him to his left, sword drawn. Pointed at his head.

Palmer raised his hands. "Drop your sword. It's only me. The sister is still hiding."

De Morville didn't move. "I know she is, Palmer. And I'll find her. Soon as I've finished with you, you traitor." He swung his sword in a deadly arc.

"No!" Palmer's forearm shot up by instinct to parry it. His eyes closed unbidden at his last thought. *Killed by your own greed. You fool.*

The blade thumped into its target. No pain.

"Drop it, you mare!"

Palmer opened his eyes to de Morville's shrill yell of rage.

The knight's sword was buried in a stout dead branch, held fast by Theodosia. "You killed my lord Becket. You will kill no more."

"When I have my blade, you'll lose those pretty eyes." De Morville yanked hard to free it.

"Leave her." Palmer unsheathed his dagger and leapt for de Morville.

The knight's ready boot cracked into his jaw, and Palmer fell to one side over the gnarled roots of a dead tree.

A thick holly bush broke his fall. He pushed back from the spiny leaves onto his feet, dagger firm in one hand.

Theodosia still grasped the branch as de Morville shook her from side to side. "No!" Her feet slid beneath her on the slippery mud.

Palmer closed in on them again, dagger ready. "Let go of her."

"A sound instruction." With a vicious shove of his sword, de Morville pushed Theodosia closer to the foaming river's edge. He punched his free left fist onto her clasped grip. She cried out but didn't let go.

"Curse you, you bitch." De Morville drew back his fist for another blow.

As Palmer surged forward to sink his dagger into the knight's scrawny neck, the sodden mud path quivered beneath his driving step.

"Forcurse it. The path. Save yourself, Theodosia!"

Her panicked gaze flew to his. "I can't."

The ground gave a tremendous shudder. Palmer flung an arm around a thick branch and made a desperate lunge for her.

Too late. The towpath burst into the river in a wave of useless soil. De Morville and Theodosia plunged into the racing water and disappeared beneath the surface.

# CHAPTER 8

The sudden cold bit like an animal. Theodosia sank through the mud-filled water as bubbles boiled around her, robbed her of hearing, direction. The river rolled her over and over, in a pull she couldn't stop. Water forced itself up her nose, down her throat. She had to open her mouth. Earthy liquid rushed in and she gagged. More followed. Her whole body convulsed as she tried to stop it. She could not. God was taking her.

Then the water fell away and her head was out in the air. She coughed, snorted, gulped for precious breath. The racing torrent churned yellowed foam high all around her, sucked hard at her skirts, her legs. But she didn't sink back, not yet. She gasped and gasped with cold, couldn't shout for help.

Another pale head floated in the thick froth next to her.

"Get away from me, don't touch me!" She thrashed at it with her hands as it bounced against her chest. Harmlessly. The thing was her woolen chemise, stretched in an air bubble by the current. It couldn't last long, and her limbs numbed fast. The banks—she had to get to one side.

Icy water splashed up through the foam and over her face again. Coughing hard, she twisted her neck around. Her stomach fell.

Fitzurse. No more than a few yards away, across the boil of yellow and brown water. He stood on an old tree stump that jutted into the channel. The river swept her straight toward him.

"Come on, Sister." He gestured to her with an outstretched hand. "I've got just the thing to dry you out."

Theodosia tried to kick out, change her course, but her long skirt wound around her legs, trapping them. She flailed her dead arms in useless splashes. Her course continued. She had one hope left. "Sir Palmer!" Her scream was a thin echo, hidden beneath the water's roar. Nothing. He'd gone.

"Try and get to this side."

Her heart leapt at his call. She turned her head, and a clump of floating dead leaves washed into her face. She raked them away with a cry.

On the bank opposite Fitzurse, Palmer dangled from a willow tree's long branch, one arm extended to her. "I can't reach you."

"A shame, some would call it," came Fitzurse's mock.

Theodosia hauled her sight back to her tormentor.

He squatted now on the stump, low over the racing water, to pluck her from the Nidd, blue eyes fixed and unblinking.

She beat at the water with numb hands, tried to twist, turn, haul her woolen float to change direction. To no avail. The water carried her to within his grasp.

"Stay away from me!" The current spun hard beneath her, and her skirt untangled. She kicked out, and her feet met the stump's submerged roots.

Fitzurse reached out and grabbed a handful of her hair. She flung a hand up and dug her nails into the back of his hand.

"You little shrew." He let go for an instant, and she pushed at the root with both feet. It was enough. The current pulled her back out of his reach and swept her away.

Fitzurse's shout echoed after her. "De Morville! Get her, man!"

"I will, my lord."

As she bounced and spun in the freezing, choking torrent, she held her head as high as she could. The water's surface broke on the weir only yards ahead, before arcing over and down. Thunderous rumbling and a haze of spray told her how long the drop was. Worse, clung to the weir was a soaked de Morville, his thin face rapt in anticipation of where she would be swept to.

Theodosia scanned the banks, the bushes opposite, her head full of the water's roar. She couldn't see Sir Palmer anymore. With a huge boom, the river surged against the weir and smacked her against its thick rock. Blood tasted iron in her mouth from her bit tongue. The water battered her, kept her pinned tight. Yet she felt nothing now.

De Morville gave her a slow nod and started to maneuver his way across to her, hand over hand.

The only escape was down, to let the river take her. Theodosia shook her wet hair from her face and looked over the edge of the weir. Her stomach seemed to fall with it. Tons of water hammered down, roiling in lumps of foam as it set off faster than ever.

De Morville called to her. "You don't want to go down there, Sister. Very dangerous."

She looked back up.

He was almost able to reach her, but he kept his movements small and cautious as the flow of the torrent increased at the center.

"Theodosia!" Another voice.

She tore her gaze from de Morville and looked down once more.

Sir Palmer stood on the riverbank below, waiting by the bottom of the weir. "Jump! You must."

"I can't, I'll drown!" She looked back.

De Morville was inches away.

"I won't let you." Palmer's call floated up to her.

"Don't worry. I'll soon warm you up. Start between your thighs." De Morville's few teeth had the green patina of old bronze, and the putrid scent of decay wafted with his words.

She'd rather drown. She took a deep breath and flipped her senseless limbs over the weir.

The roaring water pummeled her body, her head, drove her down and down into total darkness. She felt something give and put a frantic hand to her front. The bubble in her undershirt had burst. Her only hope now was Sir Palmer. Her chest ached, then burned for release. *My God, please take me quickly.*

A knock to her ribs. She clutched hard for the object, and her deadened hands found something solid. As she took a clumsy hold, it tugged upward, then, with a sudden pull, her face broke free of the water again.

"I've got you." Sir Palmer stood above her on the bank, pulling her to him with the broken-off sapling he held. She took shuddering breaths, coughed up mouthfuls of soil-tasting water. But she could breathe, thank the Lord, she could breathe.

He hauled her up to him, her chest, stomach, then legs bumping against the stone-filled muddy bank. With a final drag, she was out.

Theodosia collapsed on the ground at his feet, chest searing, soaked clothing plastered to her. She was cold no longer. Strange. But very nice. "God be praised. Thank you." She looked up at Sir Palmer and recoiled. "Behind you."

De Morville stood there, leather strap in hand.

Palmer dropped the sapling, but de Morville flung the strap round his neck.

As Palmer grasped at it with both hands, de Morville tightened the coil in a savage twist.

"No." Theodosia raised a hand, as if it would stop him.

"You should watch your back, boy," said de Morville. "Too busy fishing her out to see me coming."

She tried to get to her knees but her legs wouldn't respond.

Palmer's face turned a dark, mottled red as he pulled in vain at his constricted throat. He kicked back, but de Morville stepped to one side.

"Not long now." De Morville's tendons strained into bumpy knots on the backs of his scaly hands.

Theodosia stretched out a hand to grab at his ankle, pull him over. But her senseless fingers slipped from his thick boots.

"And don't worry about the girl." De Morville brought his foul mouth as close to Palmer's ear as their unmatched heights would allow. "Fitzurse will get her warmed up in no time. Like I will with my cock. It's good and hard in readiness."

Palmer swung his right hand down. Square on de Morville's privates.

De Morville's grasp broke, and he dropped like a stone on the ground beside Theodosia.

She jerked back with a scream.

As de Morville writhed in helpless pain, hands clutched to his crotch, Palmer flung the coil from his neck.

He coughed and wheezed hard as he pinned de Morville on his back with one boot pressed hard on his chest. "I'll wager it wasn't ready for this." He bent down and grabbed de Morville by the hood of his surcoat. With one strong pull, he brought the skinny knight to the river's edge, next to Theodosia.

"Mercy on me!" De Morville got a shriek out.

*Sir Palmer. Do not do this.* Her lips would not move with her thoughts.

"Doubt me as a fighter, would you?" Palmer flipped de Morville over onto his stomach. He put a large hand on the back of de Morville's grease-slicked hair. Then pushed his head under the water.

The sight wavered before her as if it were not real.

De Morville's skinny arms and legs thrashed and drummed on the bank as he fought for release. A couple of high screams echoed up through the streams of bubbles around his face.

Bent over him, Sir Palmer kept his iron hold. De Morville's movements weakened to mere twitches. Then he was utterly still.

"De Morville?" Fitzurse's angry shout echoed down from beyond the weir.

Palmer released the drowned knight but left him facedown in the uncaring torrent.

Wordless with shock, Theodosia watched as the murdering Sir Palmer turned to her.

Still hunkered down, he shook his head hard as he rested both elbows on his bent knees. "Faith, he nearly had me then." The hoarseness in his voice made it like another's. He brought a hand under her elbow. "Come. Fitzurse won't be far behind."

◆　◆　◆

"Sir Palmer. Sir knight. I insist you allow me some comfort." Theodosia halted in the alleyway and pulled her soaked leather shoes off. For the third time.

Palmer took a quick look back the way they'd come, to check Fitzurse hadn't caught them up. Not yet.

"You'll soon have all the comfort you need, Sister." He bent down and slipped her right shoe back on again.

The narrow, walled passageway they stood in led off one of Knaresborough's cobbled main streets. Thank the Almighty the many shops and houses had still been closed up as he'd hauled the anchoress along. This part of the town had wealth. The hue and cry would definitely have been raised at his and Theodosia's strange appearance. He hooked her other shoe back on as she warbled quietly to herself. But the shops would be opening soon, people would be stirring. He needed to find cover. And warmth.

Palmer straightened up and put a coaxing arm around her shoulders. "Now come with me, and we will seek out that comfort."

"I do not think you should touch me." She gave a simultaneous shake and nod of her head and lurched forward again.

Curse the river, curse the cold. Her woolen clothes soaked right through, her many minutes in the water. She showed all the signs of the dread disease he'd seen many times on winter campaigns. Men near frozen to the bone would lose their senses, pull off what clothing they had, claim to see things that weren't there, hear loved ones who were half a world away.

Theodosia gave his chin a clumsy pat. "Your sins are in you, you know."

She touched him readily. Faith, her wits were truly scrambled. He had to get her warm. It wouldn't be long before she slid into unconsciousness and from there to certain death.

They carried on along the street as he sought out any shelter. He couldn't allow it, she'd saved his life. Twice. If he'd carried on yammering like a knave to Fitzurse, de Morville would've stolen up behind him and carved him in two. Her strike at the coins had ruined that. Then she'd leapt to his defense, same as she had for Becket in the cathedral. Foolhardy again—she could've died. But also very, very brave. And for no reward. Not like him, with his foolish plan of ransom. There'd be no ransom now, even if she did live. By the knights' code he held, her saving him released her. No matter. Her life was what mattered. He couldn't have her die because of him and his fool's judgment.

A sleepy low came from a windowless, thatched stone building that backed onto the quiet alley.

Palmer stopped and put his face to a narrow gap in the moss-covered wall. The heavy odor of animal dung met his nostrils.

"Through here." He led a reluctant Theodosia around to the door of the byre, which led off a small yard. No lights showed in the attached two-story, half-timbered building.

Palmer quietly slid back the well-oiled bolt and pulled the door open. A stocky brown cow stood in the gloom and chewed on a mouthful of hay from a half-full iron rack on one wall. Dry straw piled on the floor, with a couple of fresh cowpats in one corner.

Palmer pulled Theodosia in after him and pulled the door to. The cow chewed on, unbothered.

"Why do we come to my cell? And why is there such a smell?" She swayed as she stared at him, testy as a drunk.

"Hush." He took his knife and eased the bolt shut again through a gap in the door planks. Turning back to Theodosia, he dropped to his haunches and drew her down with him. He tested her skin with the palm of his hand. Still like marble.

His eyes adjusted to the darkness, helped by the open row of bricks under the thatch that let in air and light for the animal.

Theodosia took the darkness as a different signal. She sank to the floor and stretched out on her side in the tumbled heaps of cow bedding. "Jus' want…sleep." Her eyelids slid shut, wet hair plastered against her cheek.

"Theodosia."

"Hmm."

"Wake up." He kept his tone sharp but low.

"Soon."

"Now." He shook her hard. Nothing. He gathered her into his arms and rubbed her body vigorously with his palms, brought his breath to her neck. Still nothing. He rubbed harder. "Come on. Come on."

Theodosia remained still, her breathing shallow. He held her tighter, and her chill seemed to soak into his own bones.

He raised her eyelids with gentle fingers, and her set pupils stared back. His innards lurched. She was in mortal danger. He needed to get her soaked woolen clothing off, get her covered with straw. He laid her back down on the floor. Even as he started to loosen her skirt, he knew it was useless. But he had to try.

The bolt rattled in its barrel, then the door creaked open. Lamplight flooded in.

Palmer's hand went to his dagger as he peered through the cow's brown legs.

"Good morning, Mistress Marigold," said a sharp, matronly voice. A red skirt rustled against the straw as the woman stepped inside. "Mind, no fussing when I take your milk this morn."

Not Fitzurse. But still the threat of discovery. He crouched low, his arms circled around Theodosia.

The light danced across the low-beamed ceiling, with a couple of metallic *tings* as the woman secured the lamp. "There. You won't be able to kick it over, no matter how hard you try." The sound of her palms rubbing together told him her task. With a wooden-pattened shoe, she pushed a three-legged milking stool to the cow's side and sat down. As she tucked her wiry, graying hair under her linen cap, her eyes met Palmer's. She jumped up with a shriek. "Gilbert! A robber!"

She clattered out the door.

They had to get out before the woman returned with help. Palmer went to gather Theodosia into his arms.

The door creaked once again. Whoever Gilbert was, he'd responded quickly. "Show yourself."

A male voice, with the quaver of advanced years. Easy to get past, but not carrying the unconscious Theodosia. Palmer stepped around the cow's hairy haunches. He unsheathed his dagger as a threat.

A thin, white-haired man faced him, tall once, but now stooped with his years. Dressed in neat black jerkin and breeches, he held a rusted curved tanner's knife aloft. The blade was pitted and uneven with age, but his grip rested sure. His wife, square-faced and plain but younger than he, shielded herself a step behind him.

"Lower your weapon, you wastrel," said Gilbert. "Then get out. That is my animal." His watery blue-gray eyes had the mettle of a man quarter his age.

"I don't want your animal, sir," said Palmer. "I only came in here to seek warmth." He gave the cow a firm push, and she stepped away with a low of protest.

Gilbert's look turned to surprise as Theodosia's form was revealed on the floor.

"I was trying to revive my wife," continued Palmer. "We were traveling by the river, and the bank gave way. She fell in, and it was many minutes before I could get her out. I fear the cold has its hold on her and her life's at risk."

The man's look softened, so Palmer pressed on.

"Please, let me keep her in here. Otherwise, she'll die." He dropped his dagger at Gilbert's feet. "Have my weapon. I mean you no harm."

"Don't listen to him, Gilbert," said the woman, her face set in well-worn lines of hostility. "They will both be vagabonds."

To Palmer's huge relief, Gilbert lowered his hefty blade. "Hush, Gwendolyn," he said. "The knight has disarmed. His poor wife is in great peril." He retrieved Palmer's dagger from the floor and handed it back. "Your property, sir knight. Bring your lady inside. 'Tis far warmer there than in here."

Palmer bent to Theodosia and lifted her soaked body into his arms. Her eyes opened and his heart surged in relief.

"Isssit time for dancing?"

"No, my love," he said. "But maybe later."

Gilbert nodded. "She still has hope. Let us make haste."

Palmer followed the couple out of the cowshed and across the yard to the main building. Theodosia's head tipped back over his left arm. She was lost to the world once more. They entered a side door, and Gilbert gestured for him to come through.

Palmer stepped into what appeared to be a shuttered shop. The light of a single candle placed on the narrow counter showed different pelts and skins fastened to wooden shelves and frames, ready to be put on show. The scent of new, good leather hung sweet in the air.

"Gwendolyn, go and put some water on to heat," said Gilbert.

His wife did as he asked, but with a displeased set of her jaw. As she went to mount the narrow staircase, she addressed her husband. "I'm not having these people in my home. We don't know a thing about them." She stamped up the wooden stairs without waiting for an answer.

Gilbert gave a soft sigh. "Good sir, bring your lady through here." He picked up the candle and indicated to a room at the back.

As Palmer carried Theodosia in, he noted whitewashed walls and clean, swept floorboards. Windowless, it contained no furniture but instead stored bales of more pelts and skins.

Gilbert entered behind him and placed the candle on a wooden wall shelf. He bent to one bale. "I'll be as quick as I can." His breath rattled loud in his chest with effort as he untied the twine. "Here." He unrolled a half dozen spotless, combed sheepskins. "Put her in those. I've not tanned for years, only sell 'em. As my wife says, less smell, better money. But I can still tell a good one."

Palmer nodded as he placed the anchoress on the soft cream wool. "Thank you, it'll surely help. But I need to get this wet clothing off her."

Theodosia's eyes opened once more to scan the room, empty of sense. "This place pleases me. No windows to the world."

Gilbert went to the door. "I'll give you your privacy. Call me when you're ready for the water."

"Thank you again, sir," said Palmer. "With all my heart."

"Thank me when she's ready for that dance, eh?" With a brief smile, the older man shut the door.

◆　◆　◆

Gilbert Prudhomme made his breathless way up the stairs to his home above the shop, his heart sobered by the strangers' plight. The young woman looked at death's door, so she did. A plague on that river. But he could never move from this house, not with its memories of Catherine, of Isobel.

His long-drowned little Izzie, her soaked curls stuck to her lifeless forehead. Her tiny hands, still like a babe's, with plump wrists and dimples across the knuckles, but cold as stones as he kissed them and cried and cried. His only consolation had been that Catherine hadn't lived to see that terrible day. He blinked the memory away, as painful now as it had been all those years before. He entered the orderly long room, where his second wife bent to an iron pot over the fire lit in the central hearth.

Gwendolyn straightened up and gave him her sourest look. "Before you ask, it'll be a while. There's nothing to break your fast, neither, not with all this bother."

Gilbert had already noticed the table. Well scrubbed as ever, but empty. "It's no matter this once."

She nodded at the floor. "I suppose you think it's all right to leave that pair down there? With all them furs and skins, ready for market day and worth a pretty penny?"

"I'll go down as soon as the lady's out of her wet clothes," he said. "You can't expect me to stay in there for that." He gave her a little smile, but to no avail.

"I don't know what to think. Two complete strangers turn up in our cowshed at the crack of dawn, and what do you do? Bring them straight in here." His wife's mouth contorted as if she tasted sour milk. "If those two are married, Marigold's a prize bull."

Gilbert laid a placating hand on her arm. "It doesn't matter about that. The young lady's near drowned. We have to try and save her."

Gwendolyn shrugged off his touch. "So that's what this is about. Well, she isn't your Isobel. Your Isobel's dead. Dead and buried for forty year, Gilbert." She rolled her sleeves up with angry movements. "We have this house, this shop. A profitable trade. A comfortable life." She marched to the door. "I'm going to milk the cow. You can be a hero if you want." As she stepped out the doorway, she paused. "But remember: you're forty years too late." She stamped off down the stairs.

Gilbert unhooked an iron ladle from the row hung above the fire. Gwen's words had cut to the quick, as ever. He wasn't trying to be a hero. That was never going to happen, not when his sixtieth Christmas had just passed.

He gave the pot of water a stir. But maybe he could be of some help. And maybe someone else's daughter could be saved.

◆　◆　◆

Here he was again, disrobing Sister Theodosia. Steeling himself for an almighty clamor, Palmer pulled off her sodden long woolen skirt.

But this wasn't like the night at the back of the stables, where she'd wept and wailed as if he were half-killing her. Then she'd been in her senses. Now, she only murmured nonsense words to herself, her gray eyes vacant and staring.

Underneath the skirt, she wore another layer, this one of thin white linen, also soaked and clung to her skin.

As he peeled it from her, his hands met the smoothness of her skin, followed the curve of her hips. His loins surged at the neat triangle of dark blonde hair between her legs. He quickly pulled a sheepskin over her naked lower body. He shouldn't gawp at her like that, not when she didn't even know it.

Next, her long-sleeved top, torn from her time in the water. But it had saved her. He'd scarce believed his eyes when she'd resurfaced the first time. Palmer eased off the cold, wet wool, careful not to tear it more. De Morville, curse his soul, had had the luck of the devil. A long branch had fallen in with him, and he'd clung to it till he'd reached the weir.

Palmer allowed himself a satisfied nod at his dispatching of de Morville. Sometimes even the devil can't protect you.

Theodosia looked at him with sudden intensity. "Tell me when to pray." She frowned hard.

"I will." Another linen layer clung to her. He removed it and exposed her high, taut breasts, nipples hardened from the cold.

His body called harder, and he pulled another fleece over her to cover her completely. She wasn't his. Wasn't any man's. She belonged to the church, with all the sacred vows she'd have made.

Palmer rubbed at her damp hair with his hands, ruffling it hard to get the worst wet from it.

The glint of gold around her neck caught his eye. He bent down to look closer. A fine gold chain lay at the front of her throat. He gave it a gentle pull, and a crucifix slid round from under her hair.

It must have been forced up there by the wild water. He squinted at it in the dim light of the single candle and caught his breath. This was no ordinary rood.

Fashioned of deep yellow gold, it was inset with rubies in a pattern that he supposed represented Christ's wounds. A vow of poverty, eh? You could buy a shire with this.

He couldn't help the knot of regret in his guts as he stared at it. All he had to do was slip it from her neck and put it in his own pocket. Then there would be no more begging, no more shame. No more rattling about this earth, trying to make his living. He'd be able to build high, safe walls to keep poverty, disease, hunger at bay. He sighed. To rob an unconscious woman who was near death— that would make him worse than a pander, fair and square.

A knock came at the door. "I have the water, sir knight," said Gilbert. "Are you ready?"

"Yes, please come in." With a last longing look, Palmer tucked the cross out of sight under the concealing sheepskin.

◆  ◆  ◆

Sir Reginald Fitzurse made his way up the steep roadway to the high gates of Knaresborough Castle, perspiration and river water an unpleasant steady trickle down his back. His legs and shoulders protested under the weight of his unsavory sodden burden: the dead body of Sir Hugh de Morville, lord of Knaresborough. De Morville hadn't been a big man, but the weight of a corpse always came as a surprise.

In the weak winter dawn, he could see the silhouette of a sentry patrolling the high walls.

"You there."

The sentry stopped at Fitzurse's shout.

"Get those gates open," continued Fitzurse, "and find me le Bret and de Tracy. At once!"

The sentry gaped but disappeared to do Fitzurse's bidding.

The door was hauled open as Fitzurse approached. He entered the courtyard as half a dozen castle guards arrived, summoned by the sentry's calls.

A sleepy-looking le Bret and de Tracy emerged from a turret door. "So you've been roused, dogs?" he said.

Le Bret's big stupid face remained mute in reply, while de Tracy's gaze sought out de Morville's slack, soaked body.

"What ails de Morville?" said de Tracy, as he and le Bret hurried over.

"Guess." Fitzurse flung the corpse onto its back on the ground to shocked murmurs from those watching.

De Morville's eyes fixed sightless and glazed. With a blue hue, his thin face was splotched with livid pooled blood where Fitzurse had carried him over his shoulder. Cream foam mixed with pink blood leaked from his mouth and nose.

"Dead," said le Bret, mystified but unquestioning.

"How?" De Tracy's amber eyes bulged like a squeezed frog's.

Fitzurse wiped the sweat from his forehead with his forearm. "Palmer."

"But Palmer was with us..." De Tracy stopped, realizing his mistake.

"Was. Until?" The question hung in the air.

"Not there now." Le Bret kept his gaze on the body.

"No." Fitzurse pulled off his leather gauntlets and struck him hard across the face.

Le Bret didn't even blink.

De Tracy remained transfixed at the dead de Morville. "But my lord Fitzurse, why did Palmer kill him?"

"The answer lies in the dungeon," said Fitzurse.

De Tracy didn't look any more comprehending. "The anchoress?"

"No," said Fitzurse. "The oaf of a guard de Morville found in there."

De Tracy paled. "You mean—"

"Yes." Fitzurse cut across him. "Palmer's freed the girl and murdered our companion in the process."

"Why?" said de Tracy. "He hasn't a bean to his name. He was following you for the money like you had twine tied round his balls."

"He hadn't the stomach for real men's work," said Fitzurse. "Instead, he plans to ransom her back to the church. Get his sordid little pile by those means."

"But he has ruined us!" De Tracy struck an angry fist into his other, open palm. "May the devil piss on his soul for all eternity."

"Quite." Fitzurse raised his voice to address the guards, who stood in silence, staring at their dead lord. "Put the word out through the town that this heinous crime has taken place. There is a reward of fifty gold crowns for the man that secures the woman prisoner, Theodosia Bertrand." A murmur of delighted appreciation at such riches met his words. "She's pale, slim, short dark-blonde hair. Dressed in rags. But she is not to be killed, do you hear me? I want her alive."

"What about Palmer, my lord?" asked one of the guards.

"Palmer's tall, dark; his surcoat's got a garish cross." Fitzurse slid his gauntlets back on and noted the stains from de Morville's bloody effusions with deep irritation. Palmer wanted to be worth his weight in gold, did he? That was a wish he, Fitzurse, could still grant. "The reward for him is a gold crown for each piece of him. No limit."

With a roar of anticipation, the guards set off for the gates.

De Tracy looked at Fitzurse. "Us too?"

"Of course not. You're the pox-brains that let them run off in the first place. But I'm not unduly worried. Palmer can't have got far." He went to walk back inside.

"Uh, my lord?"

Fitzurse turned at le Bret's voice. "What now, idiot?"

Le Bret pointed at de Morville's body. "What about Sir Hugh?"

"What about him?" said Fitzurse.

Le Bret exchanged an unsure glance with de Tracy. "We need a priest. Bury him proper."

Fitzurse gave an impatient wave of his hand and continued on his way indoors. "Feed him to the pigs, for all I care. The saphead deserves no better."

Le Bret's shocked grunt stopped him once more. "But, but, he should be in the ground…" He trailed off.

Fitzurse sighed. *Too bone-headed to continue a coherent argument.* "Then pay someone to make the necessary arrangements. I'm far too busy. I have important business to attend to before we set off."

"What business would that be, my lord?" De Tracy kept his enquiry properly polite.

Fitzurse rolled his eyes and held up his blood- and mucus-stained gauntlets to his companions. "These, of course. If I don't get some clean water and salt soon, my favorite gauntlets will be ruined. That would upset me greatly."

De Tracy kept his expression neutral, but le Bret stared at him like the simpleton he was, scarred mouth slack and open.

"Now, do not delay me any longer." Fitzurse went inside with all haste, his irritation ready for the first servant he found.

# CHAPTER 9

Palmer knelt by Theodosia on the floor of the storeroom. She lay cocooned in the sheep pelts but had not yet recovered.

The furrier, Gilbert, knelt opposite him, bowl of hot water in hand. "I'm sorry this took a while, sir knight."

"We wouldn't have it at all if it weren't for you, sir." Palmer put a hand to the back of Theodosia's head. He tilted her chin forward and supported her as Gilbert brought a metal ladle full of warm water to her mouth.

"Drink this, my lady. It will put you right," said Gilbert.

"It's not poison?" She gave Palmer an anxious look, her imagined fear real to her.

"No." He nodded to her to go along with the old man's request, and she took a first cautious sip, then several more.

"That's it." Gilbert refilled the ladle for her.

The first minor flickers of her skin stirred against Palmer's hand. *Come on.* Then her teeth rattled against the ladle as she began to shiver in earnest. Relief allowed him several deep breaths.

"Methinks she will come round." Firm satisfaction showed in Gilbert's wrinkled face, and his rheumy eyes lit with hope.

"I agree, sir," said Palmer, laying her carefully back down again. "And thank you for your aid."

Gilbert stood up with a click of his stooped knees. "No need for thanks. I'm only glad I could do summat. If you ask me, what you need now, sir knight, is a good kip. You look all in. What with the worry for your wife and everything." His careful words showed Palmer he suspected more than he'd been told.

"I was worried, but not anymore." Palmer closed off the unspoken question.

"Then I'll leave you to rest awhile." Gilbert picked up Theodosia's wet clothing. "I'll get Gwendolyn to dry these. You'll be on your way after?"

"We will," said Palmer.

"Then sleep well, stranger."

As Gilbert left them alone once more, Palmer looked at the shaking Theodosia.

Her eyes were tight shut, and her teeth clattered so hard he feared they'd break.

He brought one hand to her cheek, and her eyes opened.

"I'm so cold," she whispered.

"That's a good thing," he replied. "You couldn't feel it before, and that's a time of great danger."

Her forehead creased in a deep frown. "But it hurts so."

Palmer knew it would. The return of feeling to limbs dead with cold had a cruel, sharp edge, as if the skin would burst open and bones shatter. "Can you feel your hands and feet?"

She shook her head. "My boots are too tight."

Her senses were still scattered. She needed more warmth. He pulled off his surcoat and loosed his chain mail. As he removed it, his muscles relaxed into the familiar sudden weariness that came when they no longer had to carry its weight.

Dressed in his woolen breeches and undershirt, he climbed under the top pelt next to Theodosia, careful to keep her covered.

She paid him no heed, lost once again in her wandering mind.

"I mean you no harm, Sister." He said it aloud, though he doubted she'd hear. He drew her close to him. Faith, her skin was like stone. He took her in his arms, wrapped his legs around hers, brought her head close to his chest, willing her body to take the life-giving warmth from his.

Shivering still, she clung to him. It was as if her instincts took over and her body knew what it had to have.

Trouble was, so did his. Her naked breasts firm against his chest, her soft, damp hair against his chin. He kept his palms tight on her shuddering back. If he moved them lower, touched the smooth swell of her behind, then he'd lose control.

With a soft, agonized moan, she tightened her grip on him. His lips brushed her ear as she shifted in his hold.

"I keep my soul safe, Benedict," she murmured.

Her words knocked at his conscience, and he lifted his head away. He was trying to warm her, not bed her. His body needed distraction. Now. "Benedict? You usually call me Sir Palmer."

Theodosia tipped her head back to look at him with pain-clouded, vacant eyes. "You are Benedict. It means *blessed.*"

"I don't feel very blessed. But you must be." He moved one hand up to her neck. "Your cross is of great value, and yet you didn't lose it in the water."

"The water was dark...c-cold." Her eyes widened as another spasm went through her.

"I know." He rubbed her between her shoulder blades to calm her. "But you were very brave."

"Cold is good. Hot is bad."

Did her shivering ease? Her skin beneath his hand seemed a mite warmer. "Cold can be bad too, Theodosia."

"N-n-noo." She ground out the word through chattering teeth. "Cold is good. Keep your food cold. Your heart cold. Keep your life cold. Cold is pure. Pure. And I have my cross."

"You do." Faith, she was truly scattered. She might not come back from this. He carried on rubbing, kneading her skin.

"Good. Mama gave it to me. My mama was pure. Said keep it, so I wouldn't forget her. When she went away."

*Mama.* The woman Fitzurse would roast Theodosia alive to find. His heart tripped fast. "Where did she go?" Faster as he waited for the answer.

"Got...jewels on. I cried."

Palmer kept his tone low, calm, though he wanted to pull the answers from her. "I'm sure you cried. Did she go a long way?"

"Mmm." She drifted toward sleep, her flesh warmer under his hands, her shivering almost stopped. "Becket took her."

"Really? Took her where?"

"Posewore." She yawned again.

"Where on God's green earth is that?"

"It's secret."

"But you can tell me."

"No. Don't know." She nestled back to his chest again. The rise and fall of her shoulders told him she'd slipped into her dreams.

Heart racing, Palmer watched the candle sputter to its end in a puddle of wax. He'd found the information Fitzurse had been so desperate to get from Theodosia. What it meant, he didn't know. But it mattered more than Becket's life, Theodosia's life. Faith, his own life too. He had to find out, find out where Posewore was and find Theodosia's mother. It was the only way to end this. Fitzurse might not know where he and Theodosia were right now, but he would never give up.

For a start, Palmer had to get the anchoress out of Knaresborough. They would have to wait until darkness fell again. And then what? Escape as fast as possible. That would take a horse. You needed money to buy a horse. Lots of it.

Palmer lowered the top of the sheepskin to reveal the cross again. It wasn't money, but it was a start. His fingers went to Theodosia's neck, and he fumbled for the catch. It sprang open, and he slid it off. She didn't stir.

He held it up in the dim light. It swung gently, the rubies' glow like blood in the dying candlelight. He should wait until she came to her senses. It was worth a fortune. More than that: it was a mother's gift. *Stop prating like a fool.* A mother's gift it might be, but it didn't have four swift legs and a broad back.

After tucking the cross into his own folded chain mail, he settled back down. The warmth of the sheepswool seeped through him, and the sleeping Theodosia fitted perfectly in his hold. Gilbert was right. He needed to rest, no matter how much he wanted to act. The candle flared, puttered, flared again, then died.

Palmer looked into the sudden dark and waited for sleep to take him.

◆　◆　◆

The monastery bells rang out the call to the midday office as the market-day crowds thronged past Gilbert Prudhomme's skin-and-pelt shop. The crisp winter sunshine dazzled but had little warmth, as he stood outside to catch trade. He blew on his raw hands and looked over at Gwendolyn, busy with what she did best.

"That's my final offer. Take it or leave it." Gwendolyn eyeballed the male customer and folded her arms across her chest.

The man shot a glance at Gilbert, obviously hoping that he would intervene. Gilbert gave a slight shake of his head to indicate the futility of trying to outbargain her.

The customer caved in and opened up his leather belt-bag.

Gwendolyn shot out her right hand, palm up, for fear the money wouldn't materialize. Once the coins were counted out into her hand, she pushed the sheepskin bundle to the man with her foot.

He picked it up and slung it over his shoulder. "Drives a hard bargain," he said to Gilbert as he went on his way.

"Thanking you." She sounded in great good cheer as she clinked the coins into a cloth bag under the wide wooden window shelf.

Money was the only thing that brought such color to her pinched cheeks, that brought a glint to her eye. She was already back on the street, calling her wares and stopping people for custom.

Catherine had never been like that. Funny how he could think of her now, even after all these years. He'd had her for only ten months, till giving birth to Isobel had killed her. If she'd lived, maybe she would have been like Gwen. A woman of advanced years is often not similar to how she was at twenty. He winced as Gwen tested a suspect coin with her long teeth. No, Catherine would never have been Gwen, no matter how many years might pass.

Gwendolyn came over to him. "Are you just going to stand there and let me do all the work, as usual?"

Gilbert drew breath to reply that in his years as the tanner, he'd prepared hundreds of items like those on sale, with hours of back-breaking and foul-smelling work—he was entitled to go easy.

Gwen's expression changed his mind.

He let the breath out again. "It's past dinnertime. Let's have some food. We'll need plenty." He nodded toward the back room, where the young strangers still slept.

"What?" A bubble of spit flew from her mouth, such was the strength of her response. "You don't expect me to feed them too, do you?"

"They need so—"

Gwen peered past him. "What's going on?"

A group of apprentice lads assembled at the end of the main street, shouting and calling amongst themselves. Two or three broke off from the group and headed off down the side alleys, still shouting.

The hubbub spread from them like a wave, with people stopping and gathering to exclaim and chatter.

"Oi," Gilbert called to a shoemaker he knew, whose stall was close to the fuss. "Tell us the tale."

The man hurried up, apron wound round his large belly, leather-cutting knife still in hand. "Unbelievable, Gilbert," he said. "De Morville's dead, slain by a strange knight, tall fellow by the name of Palmer. Some girl helped him with the crime, can't recall her name. Teresa or summat, ragged-looking, she is. The guards are going round the whole town. There's fifty crowns going for her, and the reward for the knight is to be by the pound."

Gwendolyn gasped and fixed her gaze on Gilbert. She opened her mouth, but Gilbert interrupted. "Why did he kill de Morville?" he asked.

"No idea," said the man. "But I tell you, that knight's done this place a favor. Fingers crossed we'll get a lord who doesn't beggar us all with taxes, eh, mate?" With a wave, the shoemaker returned to his shop.

Gwendolyn squared up to Gilbert, her fury barely contained in her low, vicious tone. "Oh, well done, Gilbert. You've only gone and dragged us into a murder. Not just any old murder, neither. Only the murder of the lord and master of Knaresborough."

"Hold." Gilbert looked around to make sure no one could overhear them. "No one knows they are with us. We need to keep it that way, at least for the time being."

"Have you taken leave of what little sense you have? We need to report them. Now."

"Suppose there's more to it? De Morville has bled this place for years. Think of all the money he's had from us."

Gwendolyn stared at him for a long moment, then leaned close to him, her eyes flitting from one stranger to another as they passed by. "Very well, I'll give you that one."

Gilbert congratulated himself on his appeal to her mercenary side; it had worked a treat.

"Come, husband. Let's wake them and tell them what's occurred. We need to make sure they stay hidden."

◆  ◆  ◆

Theodosia surfaced from a deep sleep on soft, warm wool. But she couldn't move. She hated these awakenings, where a Satan-sent homunculus would keep her paralyzed from her dreams, keep his hold on her even though she woke. She opened her eyes. It was no demon that held her in the dim light, but thick sheepskins piled over her. She stirred, and dull pains throbbed from every part of her body. Her hands found her woolen underwear, no habit. She put a hand to her face. No veil.

But Palmer had taken her habit, her veil. The man called Fitzurse had ordered him.

Head spinning, she half rose, the covers a dead weight. Where was this place? Light framed a closed door directly in front of her.

"You're back to health, Sister. Good."

She turned her head, and it swam as she made out Sir Palmer, standing by a tall pile of pelts.

He stood fastening his leather belt over his surcoat and mail.

She pushed herself upright. "There's no light. No windows." *The gold. The riverbank. Fitzurse.* "You've locked me up again." Her head whirled as she tried to rise.

Palmer dropped to his haunches and took her shoulders in his powerful hands. "You're not locked anywhere. You're safe. We're still in Knaresborough, but not in the castle. A man called Gilbert and his wife, they've given us shelter here in their shop."

An image of an old man hovered at the very edge of her memory, a snippet of a middle-aged woman's voice. No more. She shook her head. "I cannot recall it."

"You're still addled from your time in the water."

*The water?*

"You fell in the river. With de Morville," he said quietly.

Her hand flew to her mouth. "Oh, Iesus Christus, have mercy on his soul." A violent trembling seized her as it all came back. "You killed him. Killed him in front of me, with your bare hands, when I pleaded with you to show mercy." She pushed him off. "Don't touch me." She clambered from the pelts and rose to her unsteady feet.

Palmer muttered an oath. "I'd have shown him mercy if he deserved it. But I had to kill him. He was trying to kill me." He stood too and glared at her. "And Fitzurse wants to kill you. I'm trying to protect you."

"Like you protected me when Fitzurse threw a bag of gold to you?"

The knight flushed deep red beneath his weather-beaten skin. "He fooled me, Sister. Thank the Almighty he didn't fool you. Otherwise I'd be dead and you would be soon."

"At least you can admit that much."

"Just because I made a mistake doesn't mean I'm not trying to keep you safe. I've risked my life to get you out of the castle, remember?"

"What I remember is I am worth a lot of money to you alive. As far as you are concerned, I could have a large red *R* for *ransom* branded onto my forehead." Anger steadied her head's whirl. "That is all you care about."

"You're free from that. You aren't worth anything to me now."

He made no sense. "Why? What else has happened that I cannot remember?"

"You, Sister Theodosia Bertrand, saved my life when de Morville would surely have killed me. My code demands release from ransom for such a deed." He gave a slight smile. "Usually it applies to knights, not nuns."

An urgent knock came at the door. "It's me, Gilbert. Sir, I need to speak to you at once."

"Hold one moment!" Palmer got to his feet and gave her a sheepish look. "There's one thing you should know. The tanner and his wife think we're married. You'll have to call me Benedict." He went to the door without meeting her eye.

*Married to him?* She put a hand to her neck. Then gasped, "No."

Palmer paused. "It won't be for long."

"Not that. My cross, it's gone."

"You must've lost it in the water."

Another knock, harder this time. "Sir! It's urgent!"

"Benedict," he mouthed as he opened the door.

An old man with a kindly face and a middle-aged woman whose demeanor matched her sharp features waited in a spacious shop.

"What if someone sees them, Gilbert?" said the woman.

"Don't fret, Gwendolyn," said her husband. "I've closed up the shutters and locked the front door. No one can enter."

Gwendolyn's eyebrows arched in displeasure. "Good rest in our skins?"

Theodosia inclined her head but would not dignify this odious woman with a reply. She addressed the husband directly. "Thank you for everything you have done for us. I believe you have helped to save my life."

"'Twas nothing, my dear."

"We'll be leaving once night falls. You'll not need to bother with us after that," said Palmer.

*Benedict*, she reminded herself. But leaving to where?

"Glad to hear that much," said Gwendolyn. "Gilbert, it won't take the two of us to tell them what's going on. I'm going to go and fetch a pie and a jug of ale. Some of us have been working all day and need sustenance." She jingled coins in her pocket.

"That would be champion, Gwen," said Gilbert. "Can you get a bite for all of us?"

Her lips pursed. "I'll see what I can do. I'll be a while," said Gwendolyn. "Everywhere will be ten deep because it's market day." She walked out without a backward glance, her wooden pattens rapping hard on the floor.

Gilbert went to see her out the front door. The sounds of a stout lock engaging echoed through the quiet shop. He returned with an odd look on his face.

Theodosia glanced at Benedict. The knight had seen the look too. "Is there something amiss, Gilbert?" he said.

"No." The man's breath came fast. "No, there isn't, Sir Palmer."

She looked at Benedict in horror as the knight straightened and his big hands closed into fists. "How do you know my name?" he said.

"I'll tell you, and more besides, if you tell me the truth about you and that lady you call your wife."

"I still have my dagger, sir." Benedict's action matched his words.

E. M. POWELL

The old man blanched but held his ground. "If you kill me, you won't know what I know. That could be fatal. For you both."

Theodosia spoke up. "Benedict, you are not to hurt this man. He has helped us, saved my life."

Benedict still held his dagger.

She pushed his arm down. "There will be no more bloodshed. Do you hear me? Your soul is already halfway to hell."

Benedict muttered another of his oaths but replaced his dagger on his belt.

She addressed the furrier. "Kind sir, your shop has crucifixes on the walls, and you have a well-kept altar to Saint James in the corner. You are a man of God?"

He nodded.

She looked at Benedict. "Then tell him. Tell him what has happened to us." She crossed herself. "To Archbishop Becket."

◆　◆　◆

Gwendolyn marched along the crowded streets of Knaresborough, cursing people silently and aloud as they blocked her path.

"Excuse me, mistress." A youth stepped in front of her, legs and back bent under a basket of muddy turnips. She was tempted to dash them to the ground, but she didn't want to be delayed by the ensuing commotion.

She waved him past, pulling her woolen cloak tight on her shoulders. All round her, the air buzzed with one topic: the murder and the knight who'd done it.

"Chewets! Coffin pie!" A huckster stood on a corner with a tray of steaming pastries that made her empty stomach growl. Never mind. Plenty of time for that later.

Her path clearer, she set off again, scanning the crowds for the uniformed castle guards. She wanted to bring her information right to the horse's mouth. Otherwise some scoundrel was bound to present her information as his own, and rob her of her fifty crowns for that strumpet and whatever she'd get for the knight. She smirked at the memory of the mail-clad Sir Palmer. He'd be worth more than a stud stallion.

At last. She spotted the dull-gray conical metal of a castle guard's helmet. She pushed her way through the knots of people who gawked at stalls like they'd never seen an eel or a set of pins in their lives.

"Guard."

The man turned with reluctance from whomever he spoke to, to see who it was had interrupted so rudely. When his eyes lit on Gwendolyn, they glazed with the utter disinterest of a young man for a middle-aged woman. He returned to his conversation.

Gwendolyn tapped him sharply on the shoulder.

The guard stepped back to view her with some ire. "I'm busy, mistress. Very busy."

The man to whom he spoke also viewed her with considerable irritation. A knight in full chain mail and immaculate surcoat, he had the noble features of an ancient statue and eyes bluer than the winter sky.

"Begging your pardon to interrupt," she said. Something about the knight made her dip in a quick curtsey. "But I have news about Sir Palmer."

The guard rolled his eyes. "In your closet too, madam?" He winked at the knight. "That'll be four so far."

The knight didn't respond to the guard but focused his attention on Gwendolyn. "Go on."

"The girl is with him."

The knight hissed in a sharp breath.

"Short, dark-blonde hair. Skinny. Pale. Soaked to the skin when I found her." Gwendolyn allowed herself a little preen. "But they have duped my blockheaded husband, got him to do their will. They're still with him at our shop."

The knight muttered a set of instructions to the stunned-looking guard. "Now, mistress." An angelic smile played on his fine lips. "Take us there. With all due haste, if you please."

# CHAPTER 10

As Benedict finished his rapid account of the Archbishop's murder and their pursuit by the murderous knights, Gilbert crossed himself.

"I can't believe there's such evil in the world," he said. "To think a man so holy would be struck down. In his own church." His faded eyes met Theodosia's. "To think a knight like Reginald Fitzurse would inflict such an end on a holy woman." He shook his head.

"Now, sir," said Benedict. "You said you had information that could save our lives?"

"Aye." The old man looked from Theodosia to Benedict. "Everyone is looking for you. Word has come from the castle that there's a price on your heads."

"How much?" said Benedict.

"Fifty crowns for Sister Theodosia. He's not said she's a sister, though."

She caught her breath. People would hunt her to the ends of the earth for such a huge sum. "I hope you are not tempted by that reward, Benedict." She gave him a knowing look.

He flushed, but Gilbert gaped at her, aghast.

"Sister Theodosia, it's hardly my place to say it, but how can you make such a cruel jest about Sir Palmer?"

Benedict raised a hand to him. "Ignore it, Gilbert. I deserve it."

"No, you do not, Sir Palmer," said the furrier. "Sister, if you'd seen the state Sir Palmer was in when I found him in my byre. With

you in his arms, him that beside himself with worry, 'twas no wonder I believed you were married."

"Gilbert," said Benedict. "Pay it no mind."

But Gilbert carried on. "Half the night tending to you, caring
for you, willing you back to life. The look on his face when you were
out of danger."

Now it was her turn to blush, caught by surprise at the furrier's account. "It appears I should not have made light of Benedict's
actions."

The knight would not meet her eye. "Is the fifty crowns for the
sister alive?"

The old man nodded. "Aye."

Alive. *Of course*, she thought. So Fitzurse could roast her to
death for his pleasure. She asked, "You said there is a price on both
our heads. What has been said about Benedict?"

Gilbert paled. "A crown…" He swallowed hard. "For each piece
of him."

Stifling her cry of disgust, Theodosia looked to Benedict,
still embarrassed by her clumsy barb. "That will have come from
Fitzurse, won't it?"

His face remained composed. "Of course. Having me chopped
to mincemeat would bring him great joy."

"You can hide here as long as you like." Gilbert squared his bent
shoulders as best he could. "'Tis too late to save the Archbishop's life,
but I can stop any more evil being committed. I'll not turn you out.
Stay here, then leave under cover of darkness, as you'd planned."

The knight shook his head. "Make no mistake, I'm truly grateful for your offer." He cast his eyes up with an oath. "But I don't
think the cover of night will help much now. Folk are out hunting,
with us as a wealthy prize. They won't give up just because the sun
sets." He paced the floor of the shop.

"Then we hide for longer," said Theodosia, a deep urge within her for him to agree. "It's safe here, Gilbert has promised us. We'll lock the doors, stay in here. No one will know."

"Exactly, sir knight," said Gilbert. "This storeroom will be your sanctuary. For as long as you need it."

Benedict frowned as he stopped his pacing and gestured around him. "A sanctuary, until someone decides to search the houses. Anyone comes, there's no windows in the storeroom, no way out. We're here for the taking."

"I'll hide you better than that," said Gilbert. He indicated to his stored piles of skins. "I can make a space in those. No one would think to look."

The old man's tremulous hope touched Theodosia to her soul, though she knew his suggestion was useless. "I think, kind sir, they would," she said, as gently as she could.

"Then we'll have to make a run for it. Darkness will be better, but not much. And we still have to stay hidden till then." Benedict unsheathed his dagger and turned it over in his palm. His dark eyes met Theodosia's. "This is all that stands between us and death."

She nodded, finding no words with the turmoil in her chest. That he'd held her, a rough man like him, she could understand. But worried for her? Cared for her?

"Gilbert, what weapons do you have?" said Benedict.

"There's me tanner's knife," said Gilbert. "You should have that, because your young hands shake less than mine. Though the blade's not what it was. A bit like me. There's a mallet on a shelf in the cowshed. Nothing else."

"That's better than nothing," said Palmer. "Can you fetch them, please? We need to be as ready as we can be." He stared at his knife, as if willing the short blade to become a sword.

"Aye, sir knight." The old man gave a small smile as he went to leave. "Lord knows, I wish I had a sorcerer's wand and could make you both invisible."

"That would be a miracle, sir. Would it not?" Theodosia looked at Benedict.

The knight stood stock-still and stared at Gilbert. "What did you say?"

"I said I would make you both invisible."

Benedict broke into a broad smile. "You, sir, are a man of the finest intellect."

◆　◆　◆

Gwendolyn trotted along beside the blue-eyed knight, head held high. So many of her neighbors pointed her out, spoke to each other with great excitement as she passed by.

The blue-eyed one, Fitzurse, had been joined by another two. A great hulk of a fellow called le Bret and a loud-voiced, red-bearded one named de Tracy.

Oh, she was someone now. Walking through the center of Knaresborough, with three high-ranking knights, if you please, not to mind four castle guards.

Her thoughts went to the reward again. Fifty crowns definite, plus at least a hundred for Palmer. They'd have a horse, fur cloaks. She'd have new silk dresses. She brought a hand to her throat. A pearl necklace.

"How much further, mistress?" Fitzurse had the refined tones of a real nobleman, tones that dripped with wealth.

Gwen thrilled to her toes. "Another three alleyways, my lord."

"Make ready, men," said Fitzurse.

The group drew their swords in one movement.

Those who watched from the pavements gasped and moved back with somber murmurs.

Gwen held her head even higher. Oh, she was someone now.

◆　◆　◆

Theodosia stood in the privacy of the storeroom in Gilbert's shop, a clean embroidered linen shift of Gwen's strange against her skin. Clumsy in her haste, she laced up the front of a soft wool corset with fingers that shook.

She scooped up her ruined woolen underclothing from the floor and went out to the shuttered shop. "Do you really think this is going to work?"

"We'll soon find out if it doesn't." Benedict's reply came through a set jaw. Bent over a bowl of soapy water on the countertop, he shaved his stubble with rapid strokes of a razor.

*When you are pulled apart in front of me and I am dragged off to Fitzurse.* "I do not know how you can make light of this." Palms damp with fear, she placed her old clothes on the free space on the counter. "What is more, you still have not told me where we are going."

Careful footsteps came from the stairwell.

"I'll tell you when we're alone," said Benedict quickly.

Gilbert arrived with an armful of clothing. "I've found what I can. Here, Sister."

Theodosia took the proffered dress from him, its rich red-brown hue like the autumn chestnuts she had seen on the altar at harvest thanksgiving. The finely spun soft wool rested light in her hands. "My goodness. Gwen likes to display finery." She pulled it over her head.

"Aye, she does," said Gilbert. "Dresses always make her happy—the finer, the better."

"I'm ready, Gilbert." Benedict wiped his newly shaven face clean with a cloth, and Gilbert handed him his clothing. The knight went through to the storeroom.

The front of Gwen's dress closed by means of supple leather lacing, with the loose material gathered in. Its neckline sat far lower on her chest than Theodosia had ever worn in her life. She touched her exposed skin, the skin where her cross had lain. She was naked twice over now, her body exposed and her cross gone. A thin leather belt, fastened tight, made the dress sit even lower. How could she parade in public like this? She eased the dress up as far as it would go, then adjusted its short sleeves and straightened out the long sleeves of the linen shift beneath.

Gilbert handed her two tubes of light-green fabric heavily embroidered with cream silk. "Pin-on sleeves," he said. "All the townswomen have them."

"It is a pity there is no pin-on cover for my bodice." She took them and went to affix them to the dress. The small metal pins slipped in her sweat-coated fingers.

"Permit me." Gilbert's gnarled digits were far more deft than hers.

With her linen shift covered by the patterned sleeves, she picked up a spotless pale green linen head wrap. She slipped it on and pushed her hair beneath with rapid tucks. "Is it all under? I hate my hair showing."

"You look champion, Sister." The old man busied himself wrapping up Benedict's mail in his surcoat to make a neat bundle.

"Gilbert, I need your help or I'll be here forever." Benedict emerged from the storeroom, chin lowered in his task. Already clad in dark red woolen hose and knee-length black boots, the knight held the two edges of a brown woolen doublet that he strained to bring together across his linen-covered chest. "I don't think this will go on." He looked up, and his eyes lit on Theodosia.

"Looks quite the lady, doesn't she?" said Gilbert, with clear satisfaction.

Benedict's swift glance traveled down, then up, her body. "You could say that."

His appraisal brought a flush to the exposed skin on her chest and neck. "Hopefully not for long." She went to the counter and folded her skirt and chemise into a tight bundle, fighting down her shame.

Pants of effort came from Gilbert as he helped the knight with his clothing.

"We need your help, Lady Theodosia," said Benedict.

"Do not mock me." She knotted off her bundle with a furious twist. "It is not seemly, and certainly not at a time like this."

Gilbert moved to one side of Benedict and pulled one edge of the doublet with both hands. "This is going to be a tight fit. I was close on your height when I was young, sir knight, but never as broad. Come on, pull hard. Sister, pray give us a hand."

Leaving her tied bundle, Theodosia went over to them. She stopped in front of Benedict and tightened the laces of the doublet, working them up through the eyeholes with swift twists of her fingers.

"Don't think I'd want this performance every time I got dressed." Benedict held his chin up out of the way. "Give me chain mail and a surcoat any day."

"Do not speak," said Theodosia. "It makes it twice as hard to do this up, and we have little time." She had to stand on tiptoe to reach the top two. When the ends were secure in a double knot, she stepped back as Gilbert loosed his hold with a long breath.

"Will I do?" Benedict screwed up his face as he shifted in discomfort in the tight doublet.

"I suppose so. But I am more accustomed to men concealed in the modesty of robes." *Not parading every muscle.* She stepped to one side and bent over to put her shoes on. The unwanted flush was back—she'd cut her throat if she thought she could stop it.

"It's the fashion, Sister," said Gilbert. "Most folk would near kill for a well-cut shirt and hose."

"Well, more fool them." Shoes buckled, she straightened up.

A heavy brown wool, fur-trimmed cloak was now fastened across Benedict's shoulders. He pulled a loose black velvet cap onto his head with gray-gloved hands. "Come, stand next to me."

Theodosia picked up a mustard-colored woolen cloak and placed it over her shoulders, then moved to Benedict's side. "What do you think?" he asked Gilbert.

The old man shook his head in disbelief. "Who'd have thought it? The whole town is looking for a knight and a ragged girl. No one is looking for a visiting townsman and his lady wife. Besides, it's market day; the whole town is full of strangers." He smiled. "Maybe not all as fine-looking, but certainly as well-dressed."

"Then it's time to go." Benedict went and picked up the bundles of their old clothing.

Theodosia took hers from him, mouth dry. This was like being back in Canterbury again. Safe within walls, but forced to go out, to leave the peace of enclosure for a wild, dangerous world.

She followed Gilbert and Benedict to the door.

As the old tanner unlocked it, Benedict extended a hand. "Our most grateful thanks to you and your wife, sir. We owe you our lives."

Gilbert shook his hand. "'Twas nowt. Anyone would have done the same." He pulled the door open.

Bright winter sunlight flooded in, along with the sound of dozens of voices, of footsteps on the street. The voices and footsteps of people who sought her and Benedict, who would claim them for the huge prize in a heartbeat.

"Godspeed, my friends," said Gilbert.

"May God keep you," whispered Theodosia. "You're a good, good man."

Benedict stepped out into the street and looked up and down. "Come, my dear." He crooked his free arm for Theodosia to take.

"Is that necessary?" she asked.

"It's what real people do," he said.

Theodosia stepped out and took his embrace, her bundle clutched in her other hand. The pale sunlight fell sharp on her eyes after so long indoors, and she scarce dared to breathe. Surely someone would guess, someone would shout? But no. Like Benedict had predicted they were invisible. They set off down the street with the same measured pace as the other market shoppers. Underfoot, rubbish cast aside by stallholders and shoppers crunched beneath her shoes and stirred against her skirts.

Lines of shops and stalls stretched on either side along the street. A shoemaker's, with the scent of leather on the air and the steady blow of his hammer on the awl. Candle stalls, with rows of fine beeswax tapers hanging high out of reach, and piles of smelly tallow lights in baskets at the front. Dried flowers and lavender at one, the scent not as pure as fresh blooms, but still welcome sweetness from the displayed posies. A heavy-armed woman stood holding out handfuls, others arranged in her apron pocket. "Sweet your air! Sweet your air!"

Theodosia breathed more easily as they made their way along. It was so easy, so simple. It was working. *Praise God.* "Now tell me. Where are we going?"

"It's not a place—" He broke off. "Forcurse it." His gloved hand tightened on her wrist.

"What are you doing?" She tried to shake him off.

He propelled her to look at a stall hung with dozens of woven straw bonnets.

The stallholder was busy with two young women who were making each other shriek with laughter by pulling faces as they tried hats for size.

"Explain yourself," she hissed.

He put down his bundle of clothing and picked up a ribboned hat. Bringing it close to both their faces, he said, "Keep your back to the street. Gilbert's wife is on her way back."

"Then we should say good-bye to her, thank her."

Benedict's dark eyes bored into hers. "For what, precisely? She brings the knights with her."

"No." Her whole body tensed to run.

Benedict's hand went to her shoulder. "Invisible, remember?" he murmured.

Shouts came from behind her. She wanted to turn, every inch of her screamed to face the terror, to know when a sword would let fly at Benedict, when hands would grab her. She clutched her roll of clothing tight in both hands.

He kept his gaze locked on hers. "Now, let's see." His voice was normal, steady. He lined up the straw hat and placed it on her head at a deep angle, arranging the ribbons under her chin. "Perhaps?" He bent his head to one side. To a casual observer, he perused his wife's new bonnet.

The shouts grew louder, more voices joined. The stallholder and the girls stopped their banter and stared up the street at the source of the noise.

Benedict glanced around. "They're almost level."

Metal spurs tramped hard, and the familiar rap of wooden pattens echoed with them. Voices raised in question, encouragement, conjecture echoed round her.

Out of the corner of her eye, she saw them pass. Feet away. The knights and guards with swords ready. Fitzurse, his face purposeful and eager. Gwendolyn, her skirts held high to allow her swift steps. The woman's gaze flicked across her and Benedict, but no recognition sparked there. It was clear she eyed the whole crowd, the better to check that everyone noted her passing. High color showed in her cheeks as she strode along.

The color of triumph, triumph that she'd get the huge reward. Theodosia had to bite back a cry of anger, had to clutch her bundle not to fly at the woman for her betrayal.

"They'll be at Gilbert's in a few minutes." Benedict's voice was only for her again. "When I put the hat down, we go."

A horrified realization swept over her. "What will Fitzurse do to him?" she whispered.

"We can't help him," said Benedict. "We have to move on."

"But we cannot just abandon him." She cast a furious look up the road as the search party moved along. "Not when he has been betrayed by his own wife, the sinful—"

"It's the rules of war. He'd understand."

"Well, I do not follow such rules and I have no such comprehension. He did not abandon us, so we should not abandon him." She set her shoulders. "He is a furrier, not a knight. I am not moving. We have to try."

Benedict swore softly. "Then I'll go. If I'm not back in a few minutes, you have to leave this place."

"I want to come with you."

He swore again. "Theodosia, you have to calm yourself. Gilbert was appalled by Becket's murder. He's a good man who wants to do good. Your rushing right back into Fitzurse's clutches won't help him any. Stay here and look after these." As he thrust his bundle of clothes at her, an odd half smile flickered on his lips for a moment. He said something as he walked off.

She stared after him. *Foolhardy?* What did that mean?

◆  ◆  ◆

Alone in his storeroom, Gilbert folded away the pelts that had saved the anchoress's life, his breath unsteady in his chest with the effort. Well, unsteady with excitement too: he'd had such a time of it.

He went back out into the shop and wondered if he should reopen. Probably, even though it was getting late on. Gwen would have something to say if he didn't.

Pity she hadn't been there to help the knight and the sister on their way. She was taking an awfully long time to get the food. Not that he'd even try to criticize her for it. Some things weren't worth the trouble.

He went to open the wooden shutters. The door crashed open and sent him staggering to one side.

A huge knight with a scarred face burst in, sword at the ready. He pointed it at Gilbert. "Where are they?"

Gilbert raised his hands. "I'm sorry, sir knight. I-I don't know who you mean."

"Don't be such a donkey, Gilbert."

The familiar voice cut him to the quick. "Gwen?"

His wife strode in, along with a tall knight who had the bluest eyes he'd ever seen. Sir Reginald Fitzurse. It had to be, from Sir Palmer's description. Gilbert looked from him to Gwen, appalled. "What have you done?" he asked.

"I've done what you should have done," she said. "I've told the knights who we have here." She dug him hard on the arm. "The reward?"

Gilbert's strength disappeared from his limbs, and he sagged against the counter. "I have nothing to say."

Gwen pointed a triumphant finger at the storeroom. "In there."

Fitzurse nodded to the big knight, who yanked open the door. He peered in, but his voice rumbled in surprise. "Empty."

Fitzurse grasped Gwen's arm. "If you have been lying to me—"

"No!" She was shriller than ever. "I left them here."

Fitzurse loosed his hold on her. He leveled his sword at Gilbert's face, unblinking eyes like sapphire as he looked along the blade. "Where. Are. They."

Gilbert waited for the terror, but he felt none. Only a wave of calm. "Gone from here." His heart beat fast, then slow, in his chest, but he cared not.

Gwen flew at him, slapping at his face. "You idiot! Tell them! Tell them so I can have my money!"

Gilbert shook his head. His chest suddenly had no air. Funny, that.

Fitzurse transferred his gaze to Gwen. "I will give your husband a count of ten, then I will chop his fingers off."

"Wait." Gwen ceased her onslaught. "The woman. In the street." She turned to Fitzurse. "I saw a woman. In a dress. Exactly the same as mine: chestnut, with a yellow shawl. Down this street. I thought nothing at the time. But it was made special for me." She wheeled back to Gilbert. "They're wearing our clothes, aren't they? Tell Sir Fitzurse. Where are they gone?"

Gilbert watched her expression change to surprise as he sank to the floor. The stone was cold against his cheek, but so very, very soft.

Gwen's shrieks, Fitzurse's threats, all faded together until there was only silence.

"Dad-dad?"

He moved his eyes to the door. There stood his Isobel, in her primrose-yellow linen frock. She waved her special wave, her little fingers making a twinkling star. He scrambled up and ran to her, his old limbs moving as they had as a young man.

"Izzie!" He grabbed her and swung her into his arms.

Her hands went tight around his neck, and he buried his nose in her soft, sweet curls.

"Gilbert?"

He looked up at the sound of the young woman's voice. One he had not heard in a long, long time.

Framed in the light, waiting at the door, was Catherine.

"It's time to come home, love," she said.

Palmer retraced his recent path, every sense alert for a call he'd been seen.

The furrier's house and shop came into view. A noisy crowd surged around it, all the shops and stalls abandoned as people tried to see inside.

Near to Palmer, a couple of cooked-meat stalls stood empty. Beneath the metal cooking griddles, bright orange embers glowed and sputtered from drips of melted fat. Maybe he could set a fire, cause a distraction.

Hat low over his face, he moved to the back of the crowd, careful to keep out of the line of sight of the shop.

Rumor and opinion about what might be happening in there buzzed around him.

"I saw a sword behind the counter earlier, I swear on my mother's life," said a fat man.

A horse-toothed woman jabbered to a group of two or three others. "That knight, the one that killed de Morville, I'll wager he's killed in these parts before. Jane's cousin said the man who murdered her husband had black hair." They shrieked.

"I'll bet Gwen charges them to search the house," said a large man who held a tankard of ale, much to the mirth of his friends.

Palmer wanted to shout at them, pummel some sense into their heads. A man could be being tortured, killed in there, and they cared not a whit. He craned his neck to catch a glimpse, catch the slightest sound.

Nothing. The crowd filled the place with their noise.

Desperation began to take hold. If he were to act, he'd have to do so blind. And in full view of all here.

Should he be recognized, Fitzurse's order would have him torn to shreds by the crowd's bare hands. "*A crown for every piece of him.*" It would be only a matter of minutes before Theodosia was found. Then Fitzurse would have her to torture to death at his leisure. The nightmare of her smooth, delicate skin, roasting and melting like the meat on the griddles nearby, flashed before him. But unlike the animals cooked on there, Theodosia would still be alive. He couldn't do it. Whatever Fitzurse might do to Gilbert, it would be swift. Fitzurse needed his information urgently.

*Gilbert, my man. The bed of heaven to you for your courage. Forgive me for abandoning you. Your death is on my soul.* The old battle prayer gave Palmer no comfort. He turned to leave, sick to his heart though he knew it was the right decision.

"Excuse me, mate." A stocky man in a shoemaker's apron bumped against him as he too made his way out of the crowd.

He fell into step beside Palmer and gave a loud sniff. He rubbed his eyes with the back of his hand. "Look at me, blubbing fool."

Palmer nodded a response.

"A disgrace, that's what it was." The man continued as if Palmer had replied. "Kicking their way into Gilbert's home like that, frightening the daylights out of him. I couldn't hear nothing clear, not with all the yelling. But when he fell down, and him an old man, no one went to help him." He sniffed richly again.

"Was he all right?" asked Palmer.

"Naw. Went down like a tree. Didn't move. I know a dead man when I sees one. My granddad went the same way." The man palmed at his watery cheeks. "God save us all from such a fate. Good day, stranger." He peeled off from Palmer's side and went to a nearby shop piled with neatly paired boots and shoes.

Palmer carried on, desperate to hurry and frustrated he couldn't. Yet his spirit soared for Gilbert, for the valiant, brave man who'd answered his battle prayer from the gates of heaven itself. And with any luck, Saint Peter had readied the knighthood.

# CHAPTER 11

Theodosia stood near the back of the hat stall, a tall basket filled with peacock feathers shielding her from plain sight of the street. She pretended to examine them with deep interest, lest the stallholder wonder why she stayed for so long. She risked a peep through the bright fronds back up the street. No sign of Benedict. The pattern on the feathers mocked her, for all the world like eyes accusing her of stupid rashness, of quickness of mood. She'd no right to force Benedict's hand the way she had, to send him back into mortal danger. What if he were being torn apart right now? A terrible end, and one that she had caused. The blue feathers shimmered in her trembling touch. Brother Edward had chastised her over and over for her impetuousness, her inability to keep herself contained. Gwen's betrayal had brought her own sinful anger forth in a heartbeat, with Benedict paying the price.

Still no sign. Fitzurse must have him. Her stomach turned over. Then it would be her next. Should she go, go now, while she still had a chance? That's what Benedict had told her. Her stomach turned harder at her base cowardice. She'd no right to flee her own death if she'd sent Benedict to his.

There he was. Her knees weakened with relief, to the point she might drop. He made his way through the crowd at a measured pace, calm as the day. But only him. She stepped out from behind the feathers to meet him, damp hands locked on her two packages of their old clothes.

She looked past him to check if anyone followed. "Gilbert?" she whispered as she handed him his bundle.

He shook his head. "He's dead."

With a soft gasp, Theodosia crossed herself. "May God have mercy on his poor soul. Who performed this foul deed? Fitzurse?"

"No, he went with the strain. His heart stopped."

She scanned his face, looking for his lie. "You are humoring me."

"It's the truth, I swear," he said. "One of his neighbors was a witness. I left quick as I could."

She crossed herself again. "His virtue was rewarded with his merciful release. He will have even greater reward in the next life, bless his soul."

"Bless Gilbert indeed. Thanks to him, we're still alive." Palmer took his package of clothes from her. "And his sacrifice will be for nothing if we don't get away from here." He offered her his arm.

She took it, her knees still like water. "I should not have sent you back. It was a decision based in anger. I am sorry."

"You didn't send me; I went."

*Not exactly.* Theodosia prepared to argue but fought it down. *Containment.* "Then I stand corrected. Where are we going to go?" She kept her voice low, but it mattered little. The crowds were louder and denser than ever as the street ahead opened out into a wide square, surrounded by tall half-timbered inns and shops. Canvas-topped traveling stalls and wagons filled the central area, with people thronging around them.

"You're going to tell me," said Benedict.

Music echoed in the air: a fast hurdy-gurdy, the pipe of tin whistles.

She glanced up at him, bewildered. "I don't understand."

"Posewore."

She stopped dead to an impatient tut from someone behind her. "What did you say?"

"You heard."

A cheer came from one area, and a man in a jester's hat appeared on a wobbling ladder, then collapsed back down again to howls of laughter and loud applause.

Her heart raced in her chest. How could he conjure up a name from her past, a name she'd never breathed to anyone?

"I'm waiting." His dark eyes did not leave her face.

She drew herself up and tightened her hands on her bundle. "Unless you tell me where you heard tell of this place, you can wait until the crack of doom." She gave him her fiercest look. "For only a spy or a traitor would know."

The suspicion of a smile twitched at the corner of his mouth. "Oh, believe me, I heard it from you."

She opened her mouth to deny his ridiculous assertion, but he cut across her.

"Heard it while your mind was addled from the cold. Now spit it out—every moment is a risk."

She'd no memory of what she'd said, done, while the cold had gripped her, no way of testing if he told the truth. She had to trust him; she had no choice. "The only time I heard it mentioned was the day Mama left Canterbury."

*She was ten years old, had been for just over a month. She was still Laeticia, her baptized name, her name of childhood, of innocence. The early-summer sun warmed her arms, her face, as she sat in the bright cloister garden at Canterbury, Mama next to her on a low bench. She had an open manuscript of verses from the Bible on her lap, reading quietly. Mama sat with her lips moving wordlessly as she held her own tiny Book of Hours.*

E. M. POWELL

"Sister Amélie."

Laeticia looked to the source of the serious-sounding male voice. A tall, dark-haired man stood in the shade of the cloisters. His deep blue robes were far, far finer than any of those she had seen the monks wear. Next to him stood a black-robed monk, her Brother Edward, though she didn't know it then.

"Chancellor Becket." Mama's questioning gaze was locked on his.

He gave a rueful grin. "Not chancellor anymore. Archbishop."

Mama gasped. "You mean?"

He nodded. "Of Canterbury."

"Oh, my dear Thomas." Mama tucked her little book away in her pocket, got to her feet, and hurried to him. She fell before him on her knees and kissed the ring on his left hand with deep reverence.

His straightly featured face showed some discomfiture. "Please rise, Sister A-Amélie."

Laeticia wondered at the little trip he gave over his words.

Becket nodded in her direction. "We need to talk," he said to Mama.

"Of course, my lord." Mama raised a warning finger. "Leave us be, Laeticia."

Becket turned to the strange monk. "Brother Edward. Why don't you converse with little Laeticia?"

"Yes, my lord." Brother Edward made his way over to her as Mama and Archbishop Becket set off at a slow walk down the east cloister, engaged in low-voiced conversation. Brother Edward took Mama's place on the bench. He was tall too, not as tall as Becket, with shiny black tonsured hair and eyes as green as the early-summer leaves.

He gestured to the manuscript. "You like the pictures?"

She gave a copy of the short sigh Mama would give when her childish ways exasperated her.

"No?" The monk's eyebrows rose in surprise.

144

"I prefer the words, Brother."

"Goodness." His eyebrows remained up. "A little bird that can read. How remarkable."

She curled her bottom lip in. She shouldn't have prattled so. Mama had always told her it wasn't very ladylike to read.

But the monk didn't seem to mind. He gave a disbelieving frown and shake of his head. "I think you tell me a tale."

She couldn't tell a lie. "I do not, Brother Edward." Laeticia pointed to the words on the open page and read them to him steadily.

"My, my." He gave her an astonished look.

A muffled cry came from the cloisters. She looked over to see Mama, face in her hands.

She shoved the book into Brother Edward's hands and jumped from the seat.

"Stop, child."

She took no notice of the monk, made for the shaded cloister. Briefly blinded from its contrast with the brilliant sunshine, she cried out, "Mama, what's wrong?" Her vision adjusted to see her mother drop her hands, face deathly pale.

"Theodosia." Her tone was sharp. "I told you to leave us be."

"I am sorry, my lord." Brother Edward had followed after and went to take her hand.

"No, leave her." Thomas sounded kind as he addressed Mama. "You have to tell her, Amélie. Now."

Mama knelt before her and took her by the shoulders. "Thomas is a very important man. He has had to bring me some very important news."

"Amélie, you must be brief," said the important man.

Laeticia shot him a look. His eyes looked sad.

"My dear girl, Mama has to go away."

Terror clutched her heart at Mama's words. Away? "Where?"

"I'm afraid I can't tell you where, because it's a secret. Somewhere very special."

"But it's special here in Canterbury. You've told me so. Lots of times."

"I know, I know. But I cannot stay here."

"Can I come too?"

Mama glanced up at Becket, then back at her. "No, my dearest." Her tone was firm, the tone that Laeticia knew would never budge or shift.

Tears pooled in her eyes as the terror clutched harder.

"You must stay here, with Archbishop Becket and Brother Edward," said Mama.

Laeticia cast a doubtful glance at these two tall strangers as her tears spilled over. "But they are not my family. Only you. Papa's in heaven. There's no one else."

Mama took her face in her hands and gripped it tightly. "But they will be your family soon, my dearest. For I am gifting you to Canterbury, to learn the ways of a woman of God."

The tears came faster. "I am not a woman, Mama."

"But you will be. You will be a great woman of God: noble, contained, pure. It is a terrible, terrible sacrifice for me, yet I give you as an act of gratitude to God, for He is our Savior, giving His life for us."

Laeticia shook her head, Mama's words far above her ten-year-old understanding. "Stay here, Mama."

"It is time, Amélie." Becket was gentle but firm.

Mama reached behind her neck to undo her crucifix. She held it out to her. "You see this, Laeticia?"

She nodded, still without speech. She'd admired the beautiful golden cross, with the rich glow from the little red stones, so many times.

"I give this to you to mark this special day." Mama placed it round her neck and adjusted it against the lace bib of her dress. "Whenever you get lonely, touch it and ask God to comfort you." She stood up and bent once more to kiss her cheek. "And He will, my love, He will, because you are my gift from Him. I return that gift, with all the grace you have and will acquire."

"Mama. You can't go." She reached out, but Mama already walked away, head down. Becket went with her and spoke to her in low tones as they made their way down the cloister.

Brother Edward stood with her and laid a hand on her shoulder. "An oblate, eh?" he said. "God be praised for you and the talents you will bring to the office. And your mama is Sister Amélie. It's most important you call her that. The Archbishop himself says so."

"She's not, she's not. She's my mama." She shook him off, to a displeased exclamation from him. She raced after Mama, her calf-skinned feet silent from years of practice on the smooth stone. They all called her special, holy. But she couldn't be—Mama was leaving her. She must have done something very wrong, have sinned very greatly. Be so very, very bad. As she almost caught up, she heard Becket's words.

"Polesworth Abbey is Benedictine, a place of great devotion." He opened a heavy door that led outside and ushered Mama through.

As he did so, he saw Theodosia. He shook his head sadly, and the door thudded closed to prevent her coming too.

Its echo mirrored that of a loud drum, beaten by the jester back up on the ladder.

"Are you all right?" said Benedict. "You've lost your color."

A roar of laughter came from the crowd as the jester began a lewd song about the joys of a woman with no teeth.

Theodosia looked back at Benedict. "It wasn't Posewore," she said. "It was Polesworth. Polesworth Abbey. That's where my mother went." *When she left me.*

"Then that is where we're going."

She caught her breath. "We cannot. I was never supposed to go with her. My lord Becket, Brother Edward. Mama herself. They were absolutely clear I could not. I cannot disobey them."

Benedict started to walk her along, faster this time. He bent his neck to bring his mouth close to Theodosia's ear. "Could not. But everything's changed. Archbishop Becket's dead because of your mother. I've drowned de Morville in his own river, that poor furrier has lost his life, the knights have tried to kill me. All this, because of you and your precious mama. Fitzurse wants to roast you over an open fire to find out where she is. Our only chance to stop this is to find her first."

To find Mama. After all this time. "Do you know where it is?" The feeble question masked the huge longing, painful as deep hunger, that surged within her.

"No. But I'll find out." He craned his neck over the crowds. "First, we need a horse."

◆  ◆  ◆

Sir Reginald Fitzurse listened to the thumps and clatters from the furrier's home above the shop and sighed in frustration. "How much longer is she going to be?" he asked de Tracy.

De Tracy shrugged in return. "I say we set off after them. I don't think the woman's much use to us after what's happened." He nodded to the furrier lying dead on the floor.

"Quite." Fitzurse eyed the corpse with deep irritation. If the old fool's heart hadn't given out, he would have been a far better source of information about the girl and Palmer.

"You want him moved?" asked le Bret.

Fitzurse looked at the huge knight, shoulders hunched to ensure he didn't bump his head on the shop's low beams. "No. We haven't time."

Rapid footsteps came from the stairwell, and the old man's wife appeared, her sharp face set rigid with shock but not dampened with tears. Averting her gaze, she stepped around her husband's body and addressed Fitzurse. "I have been through Gilbert's things. What's missing is a pair of dark red hose and a blue doublet, a brown woolen cloak and a dark hat. You already know what the young woman wears." She swallowed hard and drew herself to her fullest height. "Now, I realize I haven't delivered them to you, but I have given you vital information. If it pleases your lordship, what's my reward to be?"

"Reward? Who in creation do you think you are?" De Tracy's bellow in such confined quarters buffeted Fitzurse's ears.

To her credit, the woman didn't flinch but kept her gaze on him. "My reward?"

He saw a repeat of the look she had given him in the market, the look that suggested she was a kindred spirit, that they shared common goals in life.

How wrong she was. "Your reward is that you are free to flee with your life when the guards burn this place to the ground."

"You can't." A whisper of defiance, but still no tears. "It's all I have now."

Fitzurse clicked his fingers to le Bret. "Tell the guards to act immediately. De Tracy, come. We have work to do."

The woman fled over to the shuttered window and pulled out a bag of coins from a shelf beneath. Her hands shook with haste as she went to attach it to her belt.

"Mistress?"

She looked up.

"I'll thank you for that," he said. "I can make good use of it."

She passed it to him, a low moan of despair escaping her lips as he took it from her.

He threw the bag to de Tracy, who caught it in a deft movement. "Share it out amongst the guards. My thanks for ensuring the traitorous furrier's entire property will be naught but ashes." He gave the woman a final glance as he left. Ah, now the tears came. Good.

# CHAPTER 12

The sun lowered in the sky in a red fireball over one side of the town square's tall roofs. Dark clouds gathered around it and fueled a biting wind.

Theodosia shivered in the strong breeze and pulled Gwen's yellow shawl tighter around her, scanning the crowds for any sign of the knights. A short way off to her left, Benedict stood at the entrance to a dark, narrow alleyway in intense discussion with an odd-looking man. The knight had ordered her to stay here, with a curtness that allowed no argument.

The man was older than Benedict, and well dressed. But he had a difference about him that seemed familiar. His pale skin, his heavy features. A reddish beard. Something passed between them, then the man turned and disappeared back down the alley.

Benedict gestured for her to join him as he set off at a pace for the other side of the square.

"What have you been doing?" she asked.

A scream pierced the noise surrounding them.

She clutched at Benedict's arm.

"Fire! Fire!"

The scream was taken up with shouts, roars, a surge of people moving toward the shouts as still others ran from it.

"I'll wager it's Gilbert's, it's over that way." Benedict pulled her along. "But thank the Almighty for the distraction."

She clung to him in the confused mass of yelling, shouting people as the smell of smoke floated on the breeze.

"Fitzurse?" she whispered.

Benedict nodded, shielding her in his steady hold.

"Make way!"

The crowd pressed back as a small cart rumbled past, pulled by two men and loaded with water-filled barrels. People fell in behind it as it raced along, headed for the source of the spectacle.

Benedict led the way to where a fenced-off area held a group of horses, the animals shifting nervously, eyes rolling at the commotion and smell of burning.

"Benedict. You have not answered me about that stranger you spoke to."

He paid no heed. "Fellow," Benedict called to one of the men who watched them.

The man came over.

"I've my eye on that gelding," said Benedict.

The man nodded and went to fetch the horse.

She tugged at his sleeve. "We have no money for a horse. Please do not tell me you are going to steal one."

He shook his head and reached beneath his cloak. "We've got money." He pulled out a small leather bag and selected a few coins. "I'll sort the animal," he said quickly. "You go and buy food for our journey."

She stared at the money in her hand. Of course. The man. Why he seemed familiar. The pictures in her manuscripts. She glared at Benedict. "That man. He was a Jew, was he not? You have borrowed from a moneylender."

"If you say so." Benedict gave an impatient pat to her shoulder as the horse trader brought the animal before him. "Now, be quick. Food, all right? It's a simple task. Just get it done."

*Containment.* Theodosia bit down a reply at this fresh order as he turned to the horse trader. She walked rapidly back to where she'd seen food stalls. The coins she held might as well be burning through her palm, hot with the sin of usury. A sin that did not appear to bother the knight a whit.

Stallholders were closing up with haste, keen to leave with the threat of fire. The smell of smoke came stronger now, and men and boys rushed to and fro with leather buckets.

Her eye lit upon a barrow where two squat women packed away a selection of raw meat. Would that do? She looked back to where Benedict and the horse trader had an arm each on the animal's side, deep in studied argument.

Obviously far more important than her simple task. Jaw set in irritation, she approached the women. Food was food. He could figure out how to cook it, and unless she hurried, they'd have nothing.

"Afraid we're closed, mistress," said one, with a kick out at a thin dog skulking at her skirts. "We have to be off."

Her friend nodded, hurling gobbets into a wooden pail.

"Could I not have what's left, then you wouldn't have to pack it away?" Theodosia held out her coins. "See, I have my money ready."

The first woman raised her eyebrows to her companion. "Good idea. I'll even put it in a cloth for you, mistress." Her swift actions matched her words. "Cockscombs, sheep's lights." She tossed in a frightful jellied lump. "Lovely bit of pig's liver."

Theodosia kept her expression polite. It all appeared a gristly, blood-soaked mess to her. The smell of it was none too fresh either, and her stomach rebelled. She nodded at her money on her open palm. "Will this be enough?"

"That'll cover it." The woman scooped the coins into her own hand and shoved the bundle at Theodosia. "I'm afraid we're closed now. We have to be off."

Her friend's smirk told Theodosia of her own naiveté.

Theodosia went to object, but the woman started to push her loaded barrow away. "I wouldn't hang around if I were you, mistress. This whole place could go up."

Seething at their dishonesty, Theodosia started to make her way back toward Benedict. She could hardly make a fuss. What's more, neither could he. His money was tainted, so serve him right. She stepped aside to let yet another cart hasten past with more water.

A couple of streets away, the flames now licked high enough to show in the sky. Gathered outside the inns were their large numbers of customers, as people had run outside to point and exclaim at the sight. She saw the knight shake hands with the horse dealer and increased her pace, squeezing past three portly male pilgrims. "I beg your pardon, good sirs."

They looked at her, eyes flicking over her.

"No need to beg anything, chicken," said one, a leer on his fat face and a full jug of ale in one hand. "D'you need aught? You look a bit lost."

Her mouth tightened in disapproval. Holy men should not behave so. She went to move on. *Wait.* They might know. If Polesworth Abbey was a holy place, they may well have been there.

"As a matter a fact, I do," she said. "I have an enquiry from my husband." She emphasized the word and indicated Benedict. The men followed her pointing finger. Benedict would stand head and shoulders over them.

Backs straightening, they became instantly polite.

"We have heard of a place called Polesworth Abbey," she said. "Have you been there on your blessed travels?"

One man preened. "'Course we have, mistress. It's near Warwick. A very holy place."

An innkeeper came to the door. "Sirs! Your meal is ready."

They tipped their hats with a cautious look at a glowering Benedict.

Theodosia went back to him as he adjusted the stirrups on their newly purchased mount.

"I told you to hurry," he said. "We need food, not idle gossip."

"I did not waste my time in gossip. I used my wits to get the information we needed." She thrust the bundle of raw meat at him with a triumphant look. "Here's your precious food. But I've also found out where Polesworth is."

Benedict did not share her triumph, casting around the crowd instead with an uneasy air. "In future, ask me before you use your wits. Do you hear me?"

A great shout of many voices rose up, followed by a heavy crash that shuddered through the cobbles beneath them.

"Let's be off. Every minute here is a minute we could be seen." He boosted her up into the saddle before she could reply.

◆　◆　◆

The first tiny snowflakes stung like sand as the strengthening wind flung them into Theodosia's face. She rode atop the heavy-boned bay gelding, Benedict behind her in control of the reins. Astride a horse once more, she found her body moved in time with the animal, her muscles knowing how to balance in its rhythm.

The night sky had no moon, and the weak starlight was banished by the arrival of the snow clouds. *Oh, the cold, the cold.* She buried her cheeks in her shawl and tried to contain her teeth's relentless chatter. She and Benedict had ridden across barren open scrubland for the last couple of hours, and the stiff breeze had found its way into every gap and opening of her clothing. Now the snow brought with it a new level of discomfort.

Frigid too was the atmosphere between them. They'd not spoken except for a terse exchange in which she relayed where the pilgrims had said Polesworth was.

"You see those?" His voice came as a surprise as he pointed ahead to where the dark outline of trees showed through the sheets of powdery snowflakes. "From here on, there'll be many miles of dense forests."

"Won't that slow us down?" she said, her words muffled by her shawl.

"Yes," came his short reply, "but it should protect us from the worst of the weather."

"Do not seek protection on my account."

"I'm not. We have to stop on Quercus's account. I don't want to wear the animal out and have him die on us."

The gelding too had his head lowered against the onslaught of the weather, but he walked on, bearing his heavy load without hesitation.

"Better that than Fitzurse and his knights catch us up."

"That's not likely."

She half turned in the saddle to catch his eye. "Then you admit I did the right thing by talking to those pilgrims?"

"Fools like that, wasting their lives parading around the country, looking for pieces of dead saints to pray to?"

She pushed her advantage home. "Of course you'd see pilgrims as fools. But you haven't answered me. They knew where Polesworth Abbey was, so I did the right thing."

"I'd rather you did as you were told. It was a risk. And I suppose it paid off," he added ungraciously.

"I am glad you acknowledge my quick thinking."

"More like mine, Sister. The knights are scouring Knaresborough for a chain-mailed knight and an anchoress in cream wool clothing." He patted their bundle of clothing behind him. "They'll find neither us nor our clothes, and this noble animal takes us well beyond their reach."

"Noble except he was bought with tainted money?"

An odd look came across his face. "A gelding like this can eat up the miles." He began to talk of horses, of distances.

Theodosia faced forward once more. Doubt nipped at her, but she could not voice why. Something was not right with Sir Benedict Palmer. Every time she mentioned the moneylender, he changed the subject, made her busy. Distracted her. What was he up to? She needed to think, to concentrate, to try and figure it out. If he thought she could be easily fooled, he'd be wrong.

◆　◆　◆

Fitzurse crossed the cobbled town square of Knaresborough with care, the stones beneath his boots covered in a slick of freshly fallen snow.

"Any sign of them?" said de Tracy.

Fitzurse scanned the homebound crowds, noisy still after the excitement of the fire. "No. We'll start to ask in there." He set off for the brightly lit inns. "Le Bret, you stay out here, ask around."

Le Bret gave a nod of acknowledgment and set about his task.

Fitzurse pushed open the first inn's door and was met with a wave of warmth that carried with it a loud clamor of voices and the smell of boiled mutton and onions. Long wooden benches and tables were crammed with travelers and pilgrims who supped ale and tucked into bowls of steaming food. He wrinkled his nose in disgust. "They might as well set a big trough down in the middle of this room," he murmured to de Tracy as a sweating, harassed-looking innkeeper bore down on them, pots of ale in each hand.

"Oh, I don't know," said de Tracy. "Looks all right to me."

"What can I get you, sir knights?" The innkeeper set the ale down in front of a group of weather-beaten farmers and their dreadful women.

"Only some information, my good man," said Fitzurse. "Have you seen a townsman and his wife come in here?"

The innkeeper took an exaggerated look around the heaving room and returned his gaze to Fitzurse. "Only half a dozen, my lord."

Fitzurse itched to strike the buffoon's face, but he didn't want to draw unnecessary attention to his presence, in case Palmer was within. "I wasn't clear enough. The man's around his twenty-third year. Tall, broad. The woman's younger and very fair." He went on to describe their clothing.

The man considered the request for a moment. "Not staying here. But there's that many through here," he said with a shake of his head.

"Think, man."

The innkeeper looked askance at Fitzurse's sharp tone, but it got his full attention. "A woman who might be the one was outside earlier. Very bonny."

Fitzurse scanned the room as if his gaze could summon his quarry there. "And the man?"

"Never saw her with anyone. Only with them three over there." The man pointed out three middle-aged men dressed in long woolen sclaveins, with their broad-brimmed felt hats discarded on the tabletop.

"Pilgrims?" said de Tracy.

"Aye," said the innkeeper. He picked up empty beer mugs. "I'm sorry, sirs, but I can't stand here yapping all night."

De Tracy drew breath to admonish him, but Fitzurse stayed him with a warning hand. "Thank you, my man." With a nod to de Tracy, Fitzurse led the way to where the three pilgrims sat at the end of a bench. They were clearly the worse for wear. One looked ready for sleep and swayed where he sat, while the other two argued with the loudness of the truly drunk.

"Gentlemen." Fitzurse stood before them and gave them a tight smile.

They nodded at him without recognition, clearly annoyed at having their row interrupted. Then one came to his senses. "Yes, sir knight?" he asked.

"I'm trying to catch up with a friend of mine," said Fitzurse. "A goodwife. Her name is Theodosia Bertrand."

"Never heard of her, sir," said the second, drunker one.

"You may not know her by name, but the innkeeper says you had a conversation with her this very evening."

All three looked at him blankly.

"Small-built," said Fitzurse. "Plenty of means, expensively dressed. Very comely."

The foggy expression cleared on the second man's face. "I recall 'er." He dug his friend hard on the arm. "Gorgeous titties."

The third one's eyes slid closed and flew open again.

"'Course. I remember her now," said the first. "She asked about Polesworth Abbey, of all places. We was only there last Easter."

"Polesworth, did you say?" said Fitzurse.

The man nodded. "Aye. Near Warwick."

"Was she going there?" De Tracy's voice had a barely concealed tremble of excitement.

"Far's I know," said the man. "She left awful quick. Shame. But we didn't want to tangle with her husband. Big bloke, he was. Had a big gelding."

His friend snorted a laugh. "Bet he does."

"Quite." Fitzurse inclined his head. "I thank you, good sirs." He shot a glance at the third pilgrim, who was now asleep on his friend's shoulder. "Godspeed for your pilgrimage."

The two who were still awake gave solemn bows. "We'll need it," said the first. "Canterbury is a long way."

Fitzurse exchanged a glance with de Tracy. "Why Canterbury?" he asked carefully.

"An't you 'eard?" said the second. "T'Archbishop hisself's been murdered. Miracles have already started. Got to get in quick if you want one." He brought a finger to the side of his nose and near poked his eye out.

"Perhaps the dead Archbishop will cure your sight. Good evening, gentlemen." Fitzurse led the way outside without any need for further time on these fools.

"Cure their hangover, more like," muttered de Tracy.

Fitzurse was having trouble controlling his breathing. "Palmer and the girl can't be that far ahead, de Tracy." He raised his chain mail hood against the large, soft snowflakes.

His companion nodded, with eyes that gleamed in anticipation. "Not with one horse between them, no."

"Then let us get ours and make all haste." A couple of snowflakes settled on his lashes, and he flicked them away with a short laugh.

"What amuses you?" said de Tracy.

"Becket's pilgrims. So even a traitor can have devotion once he's dead." He summoned le Bret with a shout. "Who knows? If we find the anchoress, we might even have to go back to Canterbury to give thanks for our own little miracle."

"Let's find her first, eh?" said de Tracy.

"Oh, we will," said Fitzurse. He licked a snowflake from his top lip and savored its cold purity. "We will."

# CHAPTER 13

"This looks as good a place as any." Benedict brought Quercus to a halt in a clearing surrounded by dense stands of leafless trees and the occasional thick evergreen. To Theodosia, his voice sounded oddly deadened by the trees and the thickly falling snow. Huge, dry flakes replaced the earlier powdery fall, descending in a multitude of tiny rustles that whitened the whole world.

The horse blew out a heavy snort from his efforts and put a hopeful nose to the ground to search for food.

"Stay where you are and I'll get you down." Benedict dismounted from behind her and came into view at the horse's head. Snow plastered his black hat and the shoulders of his woolen cloak.

Ignoring his offer, she slid down herself from the animal. She could not bear his touch on her. On the long ride, as she'd turned things over and over in her mind, the suspicions that had been whispering at its corners had become a deafening chorus of certainty. Now it was time to bring her challenge to him. As she stamped her feet hard to return sensation to them, clumps of dry snow fell from her shawl and skirt.

Benedict led the horse to a nearby fallen tree and tethered him there, then removed their bundle of clothing from behind the saddle.

Theodosia huddled into her shawl, tensed for her task.

"You'll get covered if you don't move." Benedict came over to her, his dark lashes pale with stuck snowflakes as he looked down to rummage beneath his cloak.

"That is of no consequence."

Her sharp tone made him raise his gaze to her as he drew out a flint and fire steel. "It is if you're buried in a snowdrift." His words jested, but his look was careful, alert.

"How did you persuade that Jew to lend you the money for Quercus?"

He stiffened. "It's part of being in the world, Sister. People deal in money all the time." He walked away to the base of a sheltering evergreen.

She followed him. "Do not dismiss me. You have not answered my question."

He squatted down to gather small twigs and dried leaves together. "I have."

"You have not. I remember from my manuscripts that Jews will only lend if you have means to pay them back."

"Then you've a good memory, Sister." Benedict hunched over the pile he'd created, busying himself with hard strikes of the flint against the steel.

"But you had nothing with you to pay him back. Neither had you anything to give him in exchange."

A tiny orange flame flared from the leaves, and he sheltered it with one hand as he placed a couple of twigs on it. "If you say so." He didn't look round at her.

"You gave him something, Benedict."

He said nothing, just piled the fire higher as the flames took hold.

"Something that was worth a great deal. At least have the honesty to tell me, and not have me drag it from you."

"All right, then." He got to his feet, watching her face.

She clutched her fists tight as she waited for his answer.

"I took your cross. At Gilbert's. And then I sold it. Are you satisfied?"

*I was right.* "You stole my crucifix? Sold it to a...to a Jew?" Her outraged cry, pent up for many miles, tore through the trees.

"Yes. And it doesn't matter, it doesn't matter who I sold it to. We got the money, we got the horse." His voice climbed too.

"No, you got the money. You got the horse. To do that, you stole my most treasured possession from me. My symbol of Christ's suffering, and you traded it with one of the people who had put him there. Does your heartlessness know no bounds?"

He snorted in disgust. "I could say the same for your stupidity. No one but the Jews can lend, thanks to your precious church's rules. That man in Knaresborough is no better or worse than you or me. And I would say better. He traded with me, without fuss or bother, when he could have called on the constable. A rood of that value was suspicious, but he let it pass."

"How very convenient for you: the moneylender and the thief, gentlemen both."

"I'm not proud of what I did. But I had to do it. We had to get out of Knaresborough, and we have to find your mother. And that will take money." The suspicion of shame flickered in his eyes. "I had nothing. Nothing. But you had."

Cold no longer with the anger that pulsed through her, she nodded slowly. "Well, now I know you for what you really are."

"Like I know you for what you really are." Anger quickened his words. "Listen to yourself! You care more for a piece of metal than you do for your life, for my life."

"You have no idea what I care for."

"Oh, but I do—you never stop telling me. Your habits, your veils, your cross, your cell." The fire crackled high and bright behind him. "Anything you can surround yourself with to keep the world at bay."

His words stung. "Such a fool's description means you know nothing of my calling." Well, she could sting back. "Foolish like you were on the riverbank, dancing for Fitzurse's gold. At least I'm not a thief."

His face was like stone. "So now you judge me for a thief, what are you going to do about it?"

"I would that I would leave you here to rot," she replied through clenched teeth. "But I cannot."

"You cannot because...?"

"Because, God help me, I depend on you to get me back to the church."

"Exactly. And, God help me, I'm stuck with you." He rummaged in his bag and pulled out a stone bottle. "Unless you want to prate on at me some more, leave me to get on feeding and watering us. I need to melt snow so we can drink."

She grabbed it from him. "I will do it. It saves me looking at you a minute longer than I have to."

"Please yourself, Sister."

She stormed off into the quiet of the trees, where the drifts were deeper. The snow rustled down, a quiet backdrop to the banging of her furious heart. How could he have done this to her, how could he, how could he? She hunkered down next to a smoothly curved drift, and her fingers quickly deadened as she tried to push snow into the bottleneck. She shook it hard, as if it were the knight himself. The snow melted to give a few drops in the bottom. This would take an age.

She pushed a palm across her face in frustration. Frustration at the stubborn snow. Frustration at her own stupidity in trusting a man of the world. Gilbert's account of Benedict's care had touched her, confused her, but she should never have let it. At bottom, Sir Benedict Palmer was a grasping ruffian.

As she shoved more snow in the bottleneck, the trickle of running water sounded through the quiet. If that was a stream, it would be ten times easier to fill her bottle. She followed the sound as it became louder, then the snow was carved in twain by a deep stream that flowed gently over scattered rocks and reeds.

Theodosia went to the low bank and crouched down carefully. The sooner she got this filled, the sooner they could be on their way, and she would be one step nearer to being rid of Sir Palmer. Careful to keep her numb fingers' hold on the bottle, she tipped it on its side. It filled rapidly and she brought it upright to cork it.

As she raised her gaze to it, her eyes met another's across the stream.

A huge wolf stood there, head lowered, with eyes that glowed orange against its gray-brown fur. It drew its lips back and bared long, pointed fangs. Its deep, deep growl vibrated through her bones.

The bottle fell from her paralyzed grasp with a splash into the stream. She didn't care. She couldn't take her eyes from this animal. Could it swim? Or jump across? She was sure it could. She'd heard tales of these beasts. Satan himself was said to take one of his bodily forms through them.

The growl changed to a snarl, the wolf's long muzzle in a deep wrinkle. Still it watched her.

She rose to her feet, hardly able to breathe. "Benedict?" It was barely a whisper.

As she backed away, the animal lurched forward. She screamed in anticipation of its pounce. But it stopped short of the water's edge and snarled even louder.

It didn't want to go in the water. That was enough.

Theodosia turned and fled back the way she had come. "Bene-dict! Benedict!" The snow whirled round her, struck her face as she ran. She didn't even know if she ran the right way anymore. Any second, the animal would find her, be on her, tear her to pieces. "Where are you?" Her scream pierced the woods, but she couldn't see him.

Something brushed her shoulder. The wolf. "No!" She reacted with her fists, her feet.

"Stop it." Strong hands grabbed hers. "It's me." Through the driving snow crystals, Benedict looked down at her with ill temper. "What are carrying on for?"

"By the stream." She took huge, heaving breaths and pulled from his tight hold to point. "There was a wolf."

His expression changed. "A wolf? Are you sure?"

A long howl echoed through the woods, echoed by several more.

Her heartbeat soared, and she clutched for the knight.

A terrified whinny came from Quercus.

"Back to the fire." Benedict set off at a run through the woods, pulling her along with him.

The howls became louder, closer. The lying snow dragged at her skirts, clogged her shoes. She half-fell onto one knee, but he steadied her and dragged her with him. Falling snow drove into her face, heavier than ever. She couldn't see the fire. Growls came from a thicket. "We're lost." She choked on a sob.

"Not yet." He kept going, kept her with him.

Then she saw it. Bright flames beneath a tree. The crackle of burning sticks. A plume of smoke.

A shadow skulked through the trees to their left. Then another, and another. The howls again.

With speed fed by terror, she ran with Benedict to the fire.

He yanked a stout burning branch from it and thrust it to her. "Keep it before you." He pulled out a second for himself.

The shadows emerged from the woods, emboldened that their quarry had stopped. Four. Five. Seven. They prowled forward with low growls that reverberated in one awful sound.

"There's so many, they keep coming." Theodosia held out her branch and waved it from one side to another, frantic to keep count.

"Just keep the flames moving."

The animals paused about six feet away. They continued to thread in and out amongst each other.

Quercus whinnied in terror, eyes rolling and straining at his tied reins.

The biggest wolf's head whipped round to the source of the noise. It broke from the pack and jumped toward Quercus.

*Not their horse.*

Quercus spun and kicked out hard with his hind legs. With a loud *crack*, the wolf soared through the air and landed with a yelp in a shower of drifted snow. The pack grumbled loud and long, turning their snarling muzzles back to face Theodosia and Benedict.

A second, smaller wolf surged forward with a savage snarl. It leapt for Benedict as Theodosia screamed, but the knight slashed it away with a sweep of flame.

"Have it, you devil!"

The animal fell to one side and whimpered, the acrid stench of burning fur wafting in the air. The wolf retreated back to its pack, and another licked its burned face.

The others settled into a regular rhythm of passing one another, back and forth, in and out.

Transfixed with fright, Theodosia didn't dare shift her gaze, the scene livid, hellish through her branch's flare. "What are they doing?"

"Waiting," came Benedict's terse reply.

"Waiting? For what?"

"They've tried Quercus. Tried us. Both of us are a bit too much to handle at the moment. So they'll wait. Wait for one of us to weaken."

Her voice cracked. "And then?"

"Then they'll move in for the kill."

Gray-brown fur gleamed in the light as the wolves continued to circle. "What are we going to do?"

"We have to try and make for Quercus. Get on him and outride the beasts."

He couldn't mean it. "But he's on the other side of them." Her quick glance at his set jaw told her he could.

A sudden hiss. "Forcurse it."

She looked again. Benedict's flames were dying, losing their battle with the snow. He shook his torch hard, but it fizzled out.

Theodosia prayed, willed hers to keep alight, holding it out before her as Benedict grabbed at another.

"How many are left alight?"

Branches snapped from the undergrowth stopped his answer. The wolves turned as one to look.

With a terrific snarl, the burned one took off toward the source of the noise. The bushes moved in abrupt movement, then a wheezing thump ended in a whine.

The dense growth parted. The monstrous form of le Bret emerged, a dead wolf impaled on his huge broadsword, Fitzurse and de Tracy close behind.

"You look like you need our aid, Sir Palmer," said Fitzurse.

Theodosia's breath stalled. How? *How?*

Le Bret heaved the dead wolf off his blade, and it thudded into the fallen snow and rolled over, blood seeping from its side.

The pack converged on the strangers. Their snarls and howls of rage echoed through the woods.

Le Bret swung his sword again and caught another wolf's ear. With a yelp it scuttled backward, the others close around it.

"Forgive the delay. We won't be long." Fitzurse's blue gaze locked on hers through the curtain of falling snow, worse, far worse, than the wolves' orange eyes.

She looked to Benedict.

He wasn't there.

"Hey!" De Tracy's yell told her he'd found him.

She looked in the direction of his pointed sword. *Dear God, no.*

Benedict ran for Quercus, the distraction of the wolves momentary but enough. He leapt into the saddle and yanked the reins free. With a shake of his head to Theodosia, he kicked hard at the horse's sides. Quercus took off through the trees.

*He'd left her to them.* She swayed on her feet, sounds blurred. She fought her faint, clinging to her branch.

"Leave him!"

She turned, stumbling, at Fitzurse's clipped order to the knights. They stopped, watching their leader.

He raised his weapon to the leading wolf. "I'm sorry, my beauty," he said, "but you leave me no choice." He raised his sword in both hands and sideswiped. With a sickening crunch, he sliced through the animal's neck and took its head clean off.

# CHAPTER 14

"God's eyes, what a strike!" De Tracy's roar echoed out as Theodosia ducked away with a cry.

Blood sprayed from the animal's severed neck, and its head bounced and rolled through the snow in a slash of scarlet.

Her faint increased, darkening her vision, numbing all sound.

Fitzurse advanced toward the pack with his stained sword up, boots ploughing through the lividly stained snow, as uncaring of the carnage as he had been in the cathedral. "I'm ready." His voice was soft, measured.

Far away.

The animals turned and fled to guttural calls and hoots from the other two knights.

Theodosia gulped in deep breaths, struggled to keep hold of the branch in hands that seemed to weigh a ton.

Fitzurse turned to her. "Sister."

She held her branch out and waved it, her last feeble defense. "Stay away from me."

He clicked his fingers, and his companions stepped to him.

"Or what?" Fitzurse stepped toward her through the blood-soaked snow, flanked by the other two monsters. He gestured to the dense trees. "You'll run in there? Oh, no, you can't. You'll get eaten." He stepped closer.

Theodosia raised the branch.

His sword flashed out and struck it from her hands, the wood grazing her palms with the strength of his blow.

"No!" She jerked back, fighting for balance. She fell to her knees, hands grasped before her, urging a blow that would take her head from her shoulders too. Take it, and with it her secret of where her mother was. With her gaze defiantly fixed on Fitzurse, she summoned her act of contrition, ready for her end. "*Deus meus, ex toto corde p-paenitet—*"

Fitzurse's clout to her cheek sent her sprawling into the snow. "Shut up."

Her skull hammered from his strike, the sight of the three knights' boots swam before her. She struggled to draw breath, to carry on with her prayer, but a sob of pain and shock choked her.

"Get her on her feet, le Bret. De Tracy, keep an eye out for those animals."

The huge knight's hand grabbed her shoulder and hauled her upright.

Fitzurse regarded her with complete, icy calm. "You are shockingly uncooperative." He stuck his sword point-first into the snowy ground. "But even you've got more virility than Palmer." He removed a couple of coils of rope from his belt. "Running away, like a yellow-breeched knave, just like I accused him on the riverbank." He gave a tight smile. "Not able to see a job through, remember?"

A job. That's what she'd been to that coward, that renegade Benedict Palmer. It was what she was to them all, what Mama was. A job that had to be finished. She'd not help them in their foul work, any of them.

"You'd have done well to listen to me, then," continued Fitzurse, uncoiling the rope with swift movements. "Carried on running yourself, instead of stopping the noble Hugh de Morville ending the dog." He nodded to le Bret. "Put her hands behind her back."

Le Bret shifted his iron grip to wrench back one of her wrists. Pain sparked up her arms as he crossed it with the other.

"Let go of me!" She struggled uselessly in his hold as Fitzurse coiled the coarse rope tight around her wrists, then bit into her skin as he secured it with firm knots.

Benedict had said Fitzurse wanted her bound before he burned her to find out what she knew. The fire behind them. Damped down by the snow but still hot. She pulled all her weight against them, tried to kick out with her feet, to sink her teeth into le Bret's chain-mailed arm.

"You see what I mean about lack of cooperation, le Bret?" Fitzurse sounded amused as he passed the rope around her body, looping it across her chest.

She gasped in pain as he pulled it cruelly tight to knot it at the back. Her arms were now completely pinned behind her, the rope cutting into her breasts if she tried to move her hands. Still she kicked.

"De Tracy," came Fitzurse's clipped command. "We need another pair of hands for the sister."

De Tracy complied, coming to stand before her as she struggled.

"Bend her over," said Fitzurse.

De Tracy gave a wide leer. "This should warm us up."

Her stomach lurched. Dear God, they couldn't. Not her virginity, her chastity. "Stop it, please, stop it!"

De Tracy grabbed her by the neck and forced her down until she was bent double.

A noose went round her neck and panic overtook her. She thrashed in the knights' grasp, screaming for someone, anyone, to help her.

Fitzurse crouched behind at her ankles and tied them as tightly together as he had her arms. Then his hands were busy at the front of her neck.

"Let her go," he said.

The red-bearded knight stepped away as le Bret loosed her. Fitzurse stood before her.

"Stand up," he said.

Theodosia staggered upright. The noose squeezed tight around her throat, pulled by the cord attached to her ankles, stopping her breath, her voice. Blood pounded in her face, her head. She tried to scream. None came.

Fitzurse nodded. "That will suffice." He grasped the back of her neck and forced her over again.

The rope around her throat loosened, and she pulled in fast, frantic gasps of air.

He brought his face close to hers with blue eyes that shone with an unnatural pleasure. "You need to keep very, very still, or you will throttle yourself. Do you hear me?"

She returned Fitzurse's gaze, though her heart seemed to want to break from her chest. "I hear you." Her voice came thick with her own spittle. His warning had given her a tiny hope. Thrown on the fire, she'd struggle like a dervish. Fitzurse's ropes would take her more mercifully than the burning embers; she would die without revealing Mama's location.

Fitzurse clicked his fingers to the waiting le Bret. "Bring her back to the horses."

*The horses?*

Le Bret's enormous arm went around her waist, and he flung her over his shoulder.

The huge knight's odious smell caught the back of her throat. Worse, he steadied his hold on her with one huge hand wedged

173

between her thighs. But she kept completely still. Fitzurse's hideous snare might well prove her salvation, but only if certain death was the only alternative. Horses were not fire, not death, at least not yet. The snow-covered forest floor swayed beneath her in time with le Bret's giant strides, purest white now they'd left the blood-ravaged clearing. The hoofprints of a single horse were rapidly filling in with the relentless snow. Quercus's tracks, from when that betrayer Benedict had fled when he could. Fled to save himself. Abandoning her, throwing her to the savage dog that was Fitzurse.

"Put her on mine." Fitzurse again.

Le Bret swung her up and over the horse's back. She landed smack on her stomach on the saddle, and her breath gasped out.

Fitzurse appeared next to her at his mount's neck, one hand on the reins. "Secure her, le Bret." Another rope was lashed across her back, tightening her as hard against the saddle as Benedict had tied their bundle of clothes.

Fitzurse raised a gauntlet-clad hand and grasped her jaw, forcing her to look at him. "I had such delightful plans for you. Thanks to that knave Palmer, they've been thwarted."

"Good." She forced the word out.

"Thwarted. Not stopped." He tightened his grip. "When I get to Polesworth Abbey, I will have double the pleasure. Your mother first, then you."

*He knew.* She stared at him, stomach contracted. "Who betrayed us?" she whispered.

"You did, you clever girl." He let go her jaw and tapped her playfully on the nose. "Clever and pretty, so those idiot pilgrims remembered you."

It was her fault. Her stupid, sinful pride in her wits. She wanted to scream out as Fitzurse gathered the reins and mounted the stallion beside her.

She'd led Fitzurse to Mama, led death to Mama's door like she'd sworn she never would.

Settling in the saddle, he crushed her ribs against the saddle horn to her right. He patted the back of her neck. "But I'm not sure just how I will dispatch you both. The Bull's only one option, and I have many, many others. It'll pass the time to Polesworth if I tell you about them." He clicked to his horse, and it set off. "But I promise you, Sister. For all the trouble you have caused me, I will make sure you get something very, very special."

◆   ◆   ◆

Palmer sat astride Quercus in a thicket of concealing evergreens, watching out for the party of knights. And Theodosia. What could be taking them so long?

He had no guarantees they'd come this way, but it was the only route through this thick-grown woodland, a rough path with the signs of few travelers on it.

He peered ahead through the darkness. Still no sign. His guess might be wrong, Fitzurse might have taken a different direction. No. This was the quickest route to Polesworth. And Polesworth would be where he was headed. Another guess, but Palmer had no other choice.

The snow had near stopped, with only a few lazy flakes drifting down. With the clouds clearing fast, weak starlight and the sliver of moon gave some light, made many times stronger by the reflection of the bright fallen snow. He cursed it quietly. The cover of darkness would've been better. At least it gave him an early warning on the wolves. They still patrolled the night, and their distant howls sent fear right through him. But he needed the beasts. They were his only chance to secure Theodosia's freedom. If she was still alive. Doubt knotted his guts.

A horse snorted in the distance.

Palmer went rigid in the saddle. This could be they.

A male voice, not taking any care to lower or hide it. De Tracy. It had to be.

He kept his gaze fixed on the direction of the sound.

Another grunt of a voice. Le Bret. Surely.

Then he saw them, the three knights on their fine mounts, riding in single file. And before Fitzurse, slung across the saddle, Theodosia's still form, her wrists and ankles secured like a prize hog's at a fair.

Palmer's fists clenched to hold back his rage. They'd killed her, the bloody, bloody, damnable cowards. It was all his fault. He'd abandoned her, the woman who'd had the rash, foolish courage to stay and fight for him against de Morville.

But he'd had to. He'd had a split second to make a decision when the knights had stepped from the bushes, and he had made it. His battle sense, he called it. It had never failed him before. Now it had. And how.

Palmer's hand went to his dagger. He was going to make them pay. He'd take at least one out, maybe even two if luck fell his way. If he was killed, so be it. He'd no right to walk this earth while she rotted cold in the ground.

The group passed by, unaware that he watched. Their voices echoed over to him, full of cheer at their devilry.

Palmer caught a familiar word. *Polesworth.* So they knew. He looked at Theodosia's body, trussed so carelessly to Fitzurse's horse. What had they done to her to make her tell? He should do for them now, the bastards. But he held back.

He needed to see if his plan worked. If it did, there'd be no need for his weapon. No mind. Either way, he was going to avenge the woman who'd fought so bravely for him. Fought, but lost.

◆　◆　◆

Theodosia's head throbbed from being tipped half upside-down. Fitzurse's bonds, tight when he first made them, tortured her more with each stride of the animal beneath her. Her arms cramped right down to her fingers, and her bound breasts bumped hard against the saddle with each step the horse took.

Fighting down the pain, Theodosia asked God in her soul for mercy. Asked, asked, asked. Begged. Not for release from this awful journey slung on Fitzurse's horse, but for her mother's escape. But God wasn't listening.

One of Thomas's sayings came back to her. "*He always listens, my child. It's just that we don't always get the answer we want.*"

But why wouldn't God listen about Mama? True to his dreadful promise, Fitzurse had told her the first of his depraved options, describing it in minute detail, with the unspeakable agony that could be inflicted on a woman's body. The Pear of Anguish. Sickness roiled through her stomach at the hideous pictures Fitzurse had planted in her mind, and she swallowed hard. If it were her fate only, she could understand. She'd sinned so badly, disregarded her vows. Mama had given her to God, and she'd spurned that generosity. Instead of passing on the gift of holiness, she'd squandered her gifts in wild, foolish actions. She deserved God's abandonment. But Mama? Her pure, noble Mama. Why should she be rent apart by these men? She had to keep praying. She focused on the monotonous snowy ground that Fitzurse's horse traveled over. She would ask Our Lady, a woman and mother who might intercede if offered up a sacred rosary.

Theodosia blinked hard. Now her vision played tricks, with dark red blobs appearing on the virgin snow. She opened and closed her eyes several times, but they remained, some tiny, others large as a spoon.

She turned her head to the right as much as she dared. De Tracy rode directly in front. A corner of his canvas saddlebag had a dark stain. As she watched, it dripped onto the snow to form another blob. It looked like—

Another followed.

It looked like blood.

♦  ♦  ♦

Palmer tracked the group, tensed for action, staying well hidden by the trees. His plan had failed. The woods were silent again. The wolves must have moved on, forcurse them. What bad fortune had led them to him and Theodosia? No doubt the same bad fortune that had led the knights. There was no point in blaming fortune. His own poor judgment had finished Theodosia.

He caught sight of her lifeless body before Fitzurse again. Regret lumped in his throat. Cursing himself for carrying on like a maid, he set his will and prepared to make his attack. A shadow flicked at the edge of his sight. He turned to look and caught his breath.

One wolf, then another, and another, ran down the trail of blood that dripped from de Tracy's saddlebag. Noses to the ground, they ran faster toward the unaware knight.

"Come on, Quercus." Palmer urged his horse forward. Some of his plan could still work. Just not the part that could have saved his brave Theodosia.

♦  ♦  ♦

"Pick up the pace, men." Fitzurse's order sounded above Theodosia, interrupting her rosary.

A faster pace would be even more painful. But she would endure, lose herself in prayer. She gritted her teeth as she tried to start again.

A dark blur shot past on the snow below, then another.

"Wolves!" Fitzurse's warning echoed through the trees.

Snarls came from ahead, then de Tracy's shout.

"Get off, you bastards!"

Theodosia twisted in her bonds, frantic that the animals would try and grab for her as she dangled from Fitzurse's horse.

"Stay still, or you'll have us over." Fitzurse's hand clamped a warning hand on the back of her neck. His stallion skittered beneath them with terrified whinnies and tried his best to bolt, flinging her harder against the ropes that held her. "Use your sword, de Tracy!"

"I'll lose my hold! I need to—"

Yowls and snarls drowned his calls.

Theodosia wrenched her head to one side in Fitzurse's grasp.

Wolves surrounded de Tracy as his horse spun to try and escape leaps, jaws, teeth, claws.

Fitzurse's stallion bucked, and the ground tipped up to her. She cried out. If the ropes gave, she'd be on the ground.

"Back him, le Bret," said Fitzurse.

The huge knight urged his powerful animal toward the stricken de Tracy, but the horse would have none of it. It backed away with rolling eyes and flared nostrils.

With a grunted oath, le Bret swung himself from the saddle, stained broadsword in hand. His animal jerked from his grasp on the reins and took off through the trees.

"You oaf!" shouted Fitzurse.

"Sorry, my lord." Le Bret waded in with his broadsword to slash at the group. He connected with one, and it fled with a howl.

Another clamped its jaws on de Tracy's bloodstained saddlebag. The bag gave with a loud rip and spewed its contents onto de Tracy's leg.

"What the devil's in there?" said Fitzurse.

The wolves howled afresh. Most fell on the bloody chunks that scattered on the snow. But a couple, crazed by the scent of fresh meat, leapt for de Tracy's leg.

An agonized scream came from de Tracy.

Theodosia cringed in horror. One of the wolves had bitten on his ankle, swung off its paws as the beleaguered knight tried to pull away.

The rest of the pack regrouped, surrounded le Bret, closed him in.

"My leg! It's got my bastard leg!" De Tracy hung on to his horse by the mane, stirrups lost, as the wolf held tight, pulling, snarling.

"Help us, my lord." Le Bret wheeled left, then right, as the pack circled closer.

With an exclamation of disgust, Fitzurse jumped from his horse and tethered it in one movement. He made for the group with a yell, brandishing his sword.

Theodosia wriggled frantically atop Fitzurse's panicked stallion. The wolf pack was consumed with bloodlust, could easily turn on this horse, her ankles. Her face.

A fresh shriek came from de Tracy. The wolf pulled him to the ground, his riderless horse kicking out in terror as it fled after le Bret's.

The wolf released the knight's leg, then fell on his throat, tearing out a mouthful of red beard and wet flesh.

Theodosia looked away as bile rose in her throat. Noises from a nightmare filled her ears: the wolves' snarls, the rip of live flesh, the pitiful screams of the dying de Tracy and le Bret, and Fitzurse's shouts and oaths.

An animal snorted near to her left. With a start, she moved her gaze to its source, braced for what she knew not.

Screened by a couple of huge fallen tree trunks, Sir Benedict Palmer sat astride an anxious-looking Quercus.

She blinked in case she dreamed. No. He was still there.

He put his fingers to his lips and brought Quercus to her horse's side. With a neat slash of his dagger, he loosed the stallion's reins.

A roar of recognition came from Fitzurse, but Benedict didn't pause. He grasped the stallion's reins in one hand and jerked Quercus's reins with the other. Neither horse needed encouragement. With a rapid canter, they set off through the woods, snow erupting from their hooves as they took flight from the murdering pack.

# CHAPTER 15

Fitzurse's stallion surged beneath Theodosia, its long strides tossing her body in the vicious straps that held her. Snow flew up from its rushing hooves and struck her face, her chest. The noose tightened, then loosened, with every step. "Stop! I'm choking."

"Soon."

The stallion stumbled on a stride and went to its knees. Theodosia's weight flung full against her bonds. They held tight, tighter around her neck. She couldn't breathe. Blood roared in her ears.

"Hold." Benedict was off his animal, floundering through the deep snow to the stallion's neck. He held the horse steady with one hand, then pulled his dagger from beneath his cape.

With a nip of cold metal against her throat, the noose fell away. She dragged in a breath, then another.

Benedict urged the stallion back to its feet and palmed the side of its quivering neck. He looked up at her, his dark complexion shades lighter than normal. "I thought they'd done for you."

"Get me off this animal." She strained to free herself from the saddle. "Now." She struggled harder, and the stallion jerked in fright.

"Steady there, boy, steady." Benedict kept hold of the reins. "Keep still, or you'll fright him. I'll get you off, but we need to get out of sight."

"Then do it and get me down."

Calling to Quercus to follow, Benedict guided the stallion toward a thick grove of pine trees. Steam rose from the stallion's coat, matching her own skin, sweat-coated from pain and terror.

Her arms, her legs, screamed for release as Benedict threaded their way through the dense trees, snow sliding off the green needled branches.

She couldn't stand it any longer. "Enough! Do you hear me?"

"Quiet." Benedict secured the stallion to a tree. Knife in hand once more, he sliced through the thick hemp that secured her to the horse. He slid her from the saddle, one arm behind her shoulders and one underneath her knees, as he gathered her to him.

Theodosia stiffened in his hold. He carried her a few steps from the horse's side to the shelter of a large pine tree, the ground dry with heaps of dried pine needles. He set her down into a seated position, staying hunkered down before her as he severed the ropes across her chest.

"Faith, that devil Fitzurse has you tied like a carcass for market." He leaned behind her to free her wrists.

She brought them before her painfully, wincing as the blood returned.

He bent to her bound ankles. "There." He sat back. "You're free."

"No thanks to you." Theodosia ripped the cut ropes from round her body and whipped them across his face.

He jerked back. "What are—"

"It's a pity Gilbert didn't have a yellow suit for you. It would match your cowardice well." She lashed out at him again, but he ducked to one side with an oath.

"Me, a caitiff?"

"Yes. A yellow-breeched page, Fitzurse called you. He was right." She scrambled to her feet on the soft ground.

Benedict rose to his feet too, a deep frown carved into his brow. "You're a convert to Fitzurse now?"

"How dare you!" She launched herself at him in fury, ropes whipping as she tried to land a blow. "You betrayed me, you traitor, you coward. You're as bad as he!"

He grabbed at her weapons and yanked them from her grasp, flinging them to the ground in a scatter of dried needles. "Then why am I back?"

"Because you saw an opportunity. Sneaking, following, not willing to lift a finger. Waiting until you could grab Fitzurse's animal, worth ten times the beast you sold my precious cross for." Shame lit his eyes, and she knew she'd hit true.

She pressed on, anger a wrongful, sinful, delicious hot urge as it tore through her, burning away her self-control. "You left me, to die without hope and, worse, to bring death to my mother too. But what do you care? You saved your shameful skin, turned a profit from stealing my cross. You'll boil in oil in hell for your avarice, Benedict Palmer. I shall take the greatest pleasure in watching for all eternity."

"Boil in oil? Are you sure you're not Fitzurse's disciple?"

She pointed to her neck, the noose's welt a painful lump on her skin. "Does this look like I am?" she hissed.

"And neither am I a coward, or a thief." He reached beneath his cloak and thrust a leather pouch into her hand. "That's the rest of the money. It's yours. So will the horses be, once we get to Polesworth." His dark brows drew together in disdain. "I'd never have traded your cross, but I had to. I told you that."

"Oh, easy, easy words." She shook the pouch at him. "Along with your most generous gift—a gift that is mine by rights anyway." She shoved the pouch into her skirt pocket with a shake of her head. "You abandoned me when the danger got too great, simple as that."

"Of course I did." He nodded hard. "You're right, Sister, as always." He folded his arms and put his head to one side, as if pondering a weighty question. "Then answer me this. Why did the wolves attack de Tracy?"

"His own foulness. Whatever spoil he had in his saddlebag."

"And what if the spoil was the meat you bought at the market?" His gaze bored into hers.

Theodosia brought a hand to her mouth. "You mean—"

"Yes. When those devils found us in the forest, I was outnumbered and outarmed. I had to act—I'd no time to think more."

Her anger dissolved into a flush of shame. "Oh, may God forgive me for such harsh, wicked words."

He snorted and opened his arms wide. "And me? The yellowshirt?"

"Of course you also. I cannot believe I let my sinful anger take me over." Mortified at his accusing stare, she felt her flush grow worse. "It all happened so quickly, and all I saw was the knights, then you were gone..." She trailed off helplessly. "I am so sorry. I have accused you of a great wrong."

He shrugged. "Then apology accepted." He strode over to Quercus, the gelding nosing the weedless ground a safe distance from the tethered stallion.

"Yet you still look angry," she said, following him.

Benedict straightened the horse's reins, gathering them into his hands. "Not at you. At myself." His jaw tightened. "I don't know how they found us. I thought I'd left no clue. But they did, God rot them."

If she could cut her tongue out, she would happily do it there and then. But she had to confess her dreadful error. "It was my fault."

"What?" Quercus shied at his sharp question.

185

"Fitzurse told me. He found the pilgrims I spoke to in Knaresborough."

Holding the horse steady, he muttered a long string of oaths. "That's how they knew about Polesworth. I heard them talk of it."

"I know now how foolish my actions were. You told me so at the time. Well, I paid for that foolishness, did I not?"

His look hardened. "As you could have. With your life? Can't you see that?"

"I do now. But at the time, I thought it was a clever move. I wanted to show you I have quick wits too."

"You're a nun, an anchoress. You have wits that can pray, can read. Fine for a life locked away in the church. Not the kind of wits that you need out in the world."

"I know of the world." She kept her tone measured though he mocked her vocation. "People came to pray at my window all the time, would tell me of every sin and trouble imaginable."

"Sister, I've had to live off my wits since I was sent away to become a fighter."

"You chose your own sinful path as a man. But it does not make you sharper than me."

"A man?" He looked as if he pitied her. "I was seven years old. And poor folk have no choice. With my father dead and my mother not able to feed herself or my four sisters, she begged the lord of our estate to take me as a page. I was that small—I could hardly reach the stomachs of the squires, let alone land a blow, as they beat me, time and again. I had to rely on what's between my ears to get by. For years and years, until I became big enough and strong enough to do the beating. There were some hard lessons, but I've learned them and you haven't. And certainly not from listening to the prating of knaves and fools in church." He drew a deep breath. "From now on, you don't act unless I say. Will you at least promise me that much?"

His eyes shone oddly bright, like his flood of words had made him ill. She'd no desire to add to it. "I will."

"Good." He handed her Quercus's reins. "You take him. You'll manage on your own?"

She was not at all sure, but she nodded, not wanting to inflame Benedict's anger any further. She put a hand to Quercus's neck. "He's steady."

Benedict boosted her up into the saddle. She found the stirrups, apprehensive to be in control of the animal alone.

"I'll stay at a safe distance," he said.

She looked over. Benedict was already astride the heavily muscled black stallion, Harcos.

With a click from Benedict, both animals set off, Theodosia mindful to keep a couple of lengths behind. "How long before we get to Polesworth?"

"We can make twice the progress now," said Benedict over his shoulder. "So I reckon maybe three days." Guided by the knight's skilled hands, Harcos trotted smoothly ahead of her.

Impossible to believe she'd been buffeted so when she'd been tied to the animal. Tied, helpless, listening to Fitzurse's sadistic, depraved account of how he'd used the dreadful device called the Pear of Anguish. How he would take a bulb fashioned from closed metal plates, force it between a woman's legs. Then turn the screw of the device, until it opened out, farther, then farther, then... Her question pressed on her, and she had to ask it.

"Benedict."

He looked around again.

"Are they all dead? Did Fitzurse and le Bret go the way of de Tracy?"

He faced forward again. "My wits tell me yes. But we still have to ride as fast as we can."

187

Her wits remembered that Benedict had made her hide, be quiet in the woods. Theodosia tightened her hold on the reins. You did not hide from ghosts, keep quiet from corpses, hasten from spirits. The knight feared just as she did. But she kept her silence. Her loose tongue would do no more harm.

# CHAPTER 16

"We seek an audience with the Abbess." Benedict spoke through a small metal grille set in the closed wooden doors of the gatehouse to Polesworth Abbey.

Theodosia scanned the tall, square tower, fashioned of huge blocks of moss-coated gray stone soaring into the blue winter sky. They were finally here. Clustered around the tower, the pitched roofs and high walls promised their journey's end. Mama would be safe in there, safe with the answers she and Benedict sought. The exhaustion of the last days and nights threatened to overwhelm her. They'd stopped only for the horses' sake, but even then she could tell Benedict stayed fully alert, watching out, listening out for any pursuers. That Fitzurse might find her while she slept had meant she'd not dared to. But no one had disturbed their travels.

With a long, shuddering sigh of relief, she turned her attention back to Benedict. He was locked in argument with whomever was within.

"No, she isn't expecting me," he said, his exasperation clear.

Another softly spoken question, inaudible to Theodosia's ears.

"I could give you my name," he said. "But it would mean nothing to her."

A reply.

"Look," he said, his tone ever more forceful. "If you could let me speak with her, then I could explain everything. But I can't explain unless I see her. Can't you understand?"

The response this time was the snap of the shutter behind the grille.

Benedict turned to her, face ruddy at being so thwarted. "She shut it. Can you believe it?"

She took in his broad frame, his mud-spattered clothes, his unshaven skin. "Unfortunately, I can. The sister who refused you entry judged you as parlous."

He spread his hands in disbelief. "How could I look risky? You told me I looked like a respectable townsman."

"That was a few days ago. It didn't last long; you can't help looking like a knight. Now are you going to allow me to try?"

Before he could disagree, she stepped past him to tap on the door and bring back whomever guarded the entrance. As she waited for an answer, she met his annoyed glance. "I am not doing anything rash," she said. "I am of the church, I have a far better chance of gaining our admittance. Whereas you are something that makes the sisters instantly suspicious."

"A knight?"

"A man."

The shutter slid open, and a shadowy veiled figure appeared behind the close-knit metal mesh.

"Yes?" came the nun's cool tone, ready for Benedict again.

"God and Mary be with you, Sister," said Theodosia.

"To you too, my lady." Recognition of a holy greeting slightly warmed the voice from within. "What can I help you with this day?"

"My husband and I need to speak with the Abbess. On an urgent and private matter."

"Your husband is the man I spoke to?"

"Indeed, Sister. He's overcome with fatigue, so my apologies if he came across as rude." She shot him a glance.

"Rude?" he mouthed, out of sight of the little window.

"I can speak with her and convey your message," said the nun. "She is, however, extremely busy, and it might well be tomorrow when she has time."

Aghast, Theodosia pressed on. "It really is very, very urgent."

"I will pass on your message." A hand came up to close the shutter again.

"Please! It concerns Amélie," said Theodosia, her palms pressed to the grille.

The hand paused, then slid the shutter closed.

Theodosia faced the blank barrier, sealed against the world. Against her too, though she was not of the world.

"Good to see your plan worked so well," said Benedict.

The *clack* of a key turning in the lock was accompanied by a turn of the cast-iron handle. With a low creak, the door swung open and a stooped, elderly nun, clothed in the black robes of the Benedictines, stood there. "Amélie, you say?"

"Yes, Sister."

"Those are your animals?" The nun pointed to their mounts, tethered to nearby hitching posts.

"They are, Sister."

The nun nodded. "I'll send word for them to be brought round to the stables." She stood to one side and beckoned. "You had both better come in."

"Thank you, Sister." Theodosia shot Benedict a victorious glance and led the way inside.

◆　◆　◆

Hat in hand, Palmer walked behind Theodosia as the Polesworth sister led them through the gatehouse and down a lengthy stone-flagged passageway that was open to the sky. The nun's age and limp meant they had to walk slowly. No mind. He'd never been in these private places before, and it was like another world.

He'd expected silence, and had a childish picture in his head of rows of praying nuns, eyes aloft. He couldn't have been more wrong.

A cheery nun hurried past, arms piled high with clean linen.

"One of our infirmary sisters," said the nun to Theodosia. "We are very proud of our healing here."

The anchoress nodded. "Healing for the body as well as the soul."

With her head bowed and hands linked, she matched the set of the old nun. Her voice too: low, barely above a murmur. Like the thin, dried snakeskins he used to find on compost heaps as a boy, she'd cast off her worldly self at the gate. The change didn't suit her. He'd become used to her gray eyes raised and challenging, her tread as definite as his. No mind again. This was her world, where she belonged. He'd pulled her from it, and it was right he delivered her back. He should be glad to be rid of her, with her chiding of him, her arguing, her foolhardiness. But he wasn't. For he also lost her bravery, her loyalty. She turned to the old nun again, and he caught the curve of her cheek, her pale, fine skin. Her beauty too.

Keen to turn his heavy thoughts aside, he looked to where an anvil rang steady under a hammer. Through a series of archways, the forge was in full use, with the glow of piled embers and the smell of hot iron. Nothing unusual, except a gaunt, tall sister worked it. Her face shone with sweat, and her sleeves were rolled up and secured in linen bands. Her powerful hammer blows looked expert to his eye.

"I'm surprised you have no lay brothers to perform such heavy tasks," said Theodosia.

The nun tutted. "No lay brothers here. No brothers at all. Nothing they can do that we can't."

The smell of freshly baked bread wafted from a side building across a small courtyard and called to Palmer's stomach.

"A bakery as well? You must have no time for praying." He said it as a jest, trying to raise his spirits.

Theodosia shot him her fierce look of old. He smiled inside. Maybe she wasn't quite lost to the world yet.

The old nun pretended she hadn't heard him. Instead, she pointed to a broad, high doorway far at the end of the corridor, its carved-wood double doors closed tight. "The cloisters are through there," she said to Theodosia. "Private, of course. The Abbess's lodge is on the next floor."

He walked behind them to where a stone vestibule led off the corridor. Yet another sister swept the floor hard with a broom of long twigs. She made room for them to pass, then went back to her task with the same vigor.

Their guide led them up a stone stairwell, which ended on a small landing. An iron-hinged oak door, aged by time and use, stood open.

"Please make yourselves comfortable. I will fetch the Abbess," said the nun.

"Bless you, Sister," said Theodosia. She led the way into the room, Palmer close behind.

The oak floor shone from beeswax and many hours of polishing. Arranged around an inlaid pale wood table were straight-backed chairs with fine-turned legs and decorated with painted green bands. Each chair had a gold velvet cushion and a tapestry footstool. A folding table with a sloped desktop stood in the huge leaded window, the better to catch the light. Painted wood panels covered the walls, each a scene from the Bible in costly colors and gold leaf. A stone fireplace threw out heat from a couple of large logs. No wonder Theodosia was so keen to get back to this life.

"I see the Abbess likes her comforts," he said dryly.

"This room is to help her serve the Lord." Theodosia went to stand before the fire and rubbed her hands. "Not for comfort."

Palmer didn't reply as he joined her at the welcome warmth. Religious folk had a different view on comfort, it seemed.

"Oh, where can she be?" Theodosia's impatient question was to the flames, with no mind to him.

Rapid footsteps sounded on the stairs.

Palmer and Theodosia turned from the hearth as a small, slight woman walked in, dressed in the familiar black robes and white wimple. He guessed she was of advanced years, but she had a keen, sharp look and moved like a much younger woman.

"May God be with you." She nodded first to Theodosia, who dropped in a deep curtsey, then Palmer. "I am Mother Ursula, the Abbess of Polesworth. I believe you wanted to speak to me, mistress…?"

"Theodosia Palmer." Palmer answered for her.

"You are Mr. Palmer?" The nun lifted her eyebrows.

"Sir Palmer," he said.

"Then you will be Lady Palmer?" said the Abbess to Theodosia.

Her shrewd look reminded Palmer of his squire master: years of experience of sorting out truth from lies.

Theodosia walked from her place before the fire to address the Abbess. She gave a deep bow, hands clasped, before she spoke. "He is not my husband, Reverend Mother."

"Have you sought me out to play games?"

"No, Reverend Mother." Theodosia bowed her head again and crossed herself. "We had to tell some untruths to get past the gatehouse. Please forgive us."

"That depends." Ursula folded her arms and shot a glance at Palmer. "I note this man does not ask for my pardon."

Theodosia urged him with a glare and a nod.

Palmer gave a slight bow. "Forgive me, also," he said through clenched teeth.

To his surprise, Ursula gave a rasp of laughter. "You're doing well, madam," she said. "I can't imagine he's easy to control, but you're part there."

"She doesn't control—" began Palmer.

The Abbess cut across him. "I received a message to say you wanted to see me regarding Amélie." She looked from one to the other. "So, what is it?"

"Sir Palmer and I believe you have a sister within these walls by the name of Amélie," said Theodosia. "She would have come here about ten years ago. She'd be well into her third decade by now."

"Why do you enquire about her?" said Ursula.

"Because we have an important message to give her," said Theodosia.

"We have no Amélie here," said the Abbess, polite.

Too polite.

"But you did have?" Palmer challenged with his question.

Ursula hesitated for a heartbeat. "No." A tiny muscle quivered at the edge of her jaw.

"You're lying to us, Mother Abbess," he said.

"Benedict!" Theodosia cringed at his rudeness. "Mother, please forgive him, he's a ruffian, he knows no manners—"

Palmer carried on. "Like you will lie to us if we ask you if Thomas Becket brought Amélie here."

Red circles appeared on Ursula's cheekbones. "You are no longer welcome under this roof. Good day, sir knight, and take your lady with you." She waited for them to leave.

"But we cannot go. We have to find her." Theodosia's anguish broke from her, and she appealed to the Abbess. "Please, please tell us if you know of Amélie."

"I have already given you my answer," said Ursula. "Now, good day. To you both."

"Oh, please don't send us away," said Theodosia. "We seek Amélie to warn her of great danger."

Ursula frowned. "Danger? What danger?"

"That is for us to tell her," said Theodosia.

The elderly nun looked from Theodosia to Palmer. "And who, with the greatest of respect, do you pair think you are? You land from the sky at my door and demand—"

"I am her daughter."

The Abbess stiffened but still didn't relent. "Easy words. Like Saint Thomas the Doubter, I like to have proof."

Theodosia shot a desperate glance at Palmer. "Do we have anything?"

The cross might have done it. But he'd sold it. He gave a helpless gesture with his hands. "Only you."

Theodosia faced the nun again. "Mother Ursula, listen to what I say, I implore you. If you still do not believe me, then we will respect your wishes and leave."

The Abbess hesitated for a long moment, then folded her hands beneath her sleeves. "Go on."

"I was brought up at Canterbury. Mama was a vowess there," said Theodosia. "She went away with Archbishop Becket one day, a summer's day. I was ten years old. She told me she was giving me to the church. I overheard him say Mama would come here."

"You do well to convince me," said Ursula. "Except that your name is Theodosia. No daughter of Amélie's has that name."

Theodosia shook her head. "My christened name is Laeticia, Mother. Laeticia Bertrand."

Ursula's stony look broke with a huge smile. "Laeticia? Can this be true?"

"It is, oh, it is," said Theodosia.

To Palmer's relief, Ursula held out her hands. "Oh, praise God and His blessed Mother."

Theodosia stepped to her, and the nun hugged her hard. "Oh, my dear girl. Your mother spoke of you to me many, many times." She loosed her hold and went to an embroidered linen bell pull next to the fireplace. "I'll order us some dinner; we have much to discuss. Come, come." Ursula went to the table and sat on one of the chairs, gesturing for Theodosia and Palmer to do the same. "I take it, then, that you are not Sir and Lady Palmer?" She rasped a husky laugh again. "Though from your warring ways, you might as well be wed."

"No, Mother." Theodosia gave her a shamed glance. "I am Sister Theodosia Bertrand. I wear these lay clothes for a reason, which I will be glad to explain to you."

A respectful knock came from the open door.

Palmer looked over. A plump young lay postulant waited there, quivering at her task of serving the Abbess's guests. The poor girl couldn't have been more than fifteen, and it was probably just as well she'd chosen the religious life. Her face might have been pleasing enough, save for a terrible scar from a wound that had lost her an eye and reddened the skin down one side of her face.

"Wilfreda, bring in our dinner," said the Abbess. "Make sure you're prompt."

The girl's mouth turned down in worry. "P-prompt? Wh-what's that, Mother?"

"Quick, girl. Quick."

"Yes, Reverend Mother." The girl ducked into a curtsey and fled like a mouse down a cornstalk.

Ursula sighed. "Lord, give me strength. I think she lost more than an eye when she fell in her mother's lye bucket." She turned her attention to Theodosia. "Now, what do you want to know?"

"Is my mother here?"

Palmer shared the desperation in her gray eyes. Amélie was the key to everything.

"No. I may have bent the truth earlier, but told no outright lie," said Ursula.

Theodosia looked fearfully to Benedict. "Then we are still in danger—"

"Child, child." The Abbess interrupted her with a raised hand. "Patience is a virtue. You need to hear me out."

"Sorry, Mother." Theodosia folded her hands, her pale cheeks pink.

Ursula went on. "She was here. Becket himself brought her here, many years ago. He had only recently been made archbishop then."

"Like you remembered." Palmer met Theodosia's gaze, and she nodded.

"It was a great sadness to her to have left you behind," said Ursula. "As to why, she said she was sworn to secrecy. The Archbishop said it was for the best of reasons, but none he could tell either."

"And you accepted that?" said Palmer.

"My life, the very life of the church, is based on vows of obedience," said Ursula. "Unquestioning obedience. A notion some people struggle with." She raised her eyebrows at Theodosia, who colored again. "Yet while your loss gave her great sadness, it also gave her great, great comfort that she had gifted you to the church, to be a great woman of God."

A clatter came from the doorway.

"Ah, here's our food," said the Abbess. "We can talk as we eat—it won't delay my mouth any."

The unlucky postulant came in bearing a large platter that held spoons, three hefty bowls of ground pork and bread crumbs in rich gravy, a round creamy cheese, and a tall earthenware jug of ale with matching tankards.

As she set it down on the table, the Abbess spoke on. "All was as ever here, with Sister Amélie living in our community. Then, only a matter of days ago, the messenger who carries the monastic posts told me he had a letter for her."

Wilfreda placed a dish, spoon, and tankard before the Abbess, then Palmer, and finally Theodosia. She put the cheese in the center, then cast an anxious glance at the Abbess.

"Drinks next, Wilfreda, remember?"

Wilfreda picked up the jug and poured a full tankard for the Abbess. She next went to Theodosia.

Theodosia placed her hand over the top of the drinking vessel. "No ale for me, thank you. May I please have some water?"

"No ale?" Surprise met disapproval in the Abbess's voice.

"No, Mother. I took it as one of my vows, as an anchoress," said Theodosia.

"Ah." Mother Ursula's expression cleared. "That explains it. Not much call for ale if you're in one of those cells." She gave her infectious rasp of a laugh again. "I've been digging turnips all morn, so I need to keep my strength up. Wilfreda, when you've served Sir Palmer, please fetch some well water also."

"Yes, Mother." The girl moved around the table to fill Palmer's tankard. She poured too fast, and a couple of mouthfuls slopped over the top.

Ursula made an impatient click with her tongue.

"Oh, I'm s-sorry, s-sir." Wilfreda's hands shook more than ever.

"It's naught," said Palmer. "I've spilt a lot more than that in my time. I was one of the most cack-handed pages in the country."

Her hand flew to the ruined side of her face at being spoken to by him.

"Fetch a cloth along with the water," said Ursula.

Wilfreda gave her bob of a curtsey again and fled.

The Abbess bowed her head, joined by Theodosia. Palmer did likewise.

"Let us give thanks for what the Lord has provided." The older woman finished with a rapid sign of the cross. "Now, where was I?"

"The letter?" Palmer spooned a mouthful of hot, herbed pork into his mouth.

"Yes. The letter." Ursula also tucked into her food.

A glance at Theodosia confirmed she had little appetite yet.

"I gave it to Amélie," said Ursula. "She read it, became highly agitated. Then told me she had to leave at once."

"Only days ago. After so many years." Theodosia's face showed her torment. "Where did she go?"

"I don't know." Ursula took a long draught of ale.

"You must know," said Palmer. "All you had to do was look at the letter."

"It had the seal of Canterbury on it, sir." The Abbess's stern reply had him realize why poor Wilfreda shook like she did.

"But as I have said, Canterbury is where we have come from, Mother," said Theodosia. "That's where I have been, all these years. I never left."

The Abbess put down her spoon in her bowl with a sharp *clink*. "Then what do you know of poor Archbishop Becket's murder?"

"We witnessed it," said Theodosia. "A group of fi—four knights."

"Oh, my child." The Abbess reached for Theodosia's hand and squeezed it hard.

"They killed him because they wanted to find Theodosia," said Palmer. "And Amélie."

"But why?" Ursula shook her head in incomprehension as she looked from one to another.

"We don't know," said Palmer.

"Just how have you come to be embroiled in all of this?" Ursula pinned him with her look.

"It matters not," said Theodosia. "He has saved my life. Many times." The corners of her mouth lifted in spite of her troubled expression.

"Noble indeed. But not an answer."

"The truth?" said Palmer.

"The truth," said Ursula.

"I was the fifth knight."

"You sit here, a murderer, accepting the hospitality of the church—"

"No, Mother," said Theodosia. "Benedict was ensnared by their falsehoods. Once he realized their foul intents, he has done everything within his power to keep me from harm."

The Abbess focused on Theodosia. "You trust him?"

*A thief, a coward.* He tensed for the words.

"With my very life, Mother," came her quiet reply, though she did not meet his eye.

Palmer kept his smile in. He'd finally won her trust. Her respect. But his happiness died inside him. He'd still lose her.

Silence settled on the sun-filled room, then the Abbess finally nodded. "Very well."

The scuttle of footsteps sounded from the landing, and Wilfreda came in, cloth in one hand, stone jar in another. "I've brought what you asked, Mother."

"Good. Now, give Sister Theodosia her water and mop up that mess." The Abbess released her hold on Theodosia's hand and gestured to her and Palmer. "Eat up. Waste is a dreadful sin."

As they both acted on the Abbess's instruction, Wilfreda poured Theodosia's water.

"Mother Ursula," said Theodosia, "have you still got the letter?"

"Yes, I do. It's in that chest, behind my desk." She pointed over to the window.

"We have to see it," said Theodosia.

Palmer mopped the last of his meat with a piece of bread, eyebrows raised to himself at Theodosia's firm demand.

"S-sir?"

He picked up his tankard so Wilfreda could clean beneath.

She scrubbed so hard he thought she'd go through the tabletop.

"That's fine, thank you. Leave us now, Wilfreda."

"Yes, Mother. Sorry, Mother."

Off she shot again, poor wretch.

Palmer took a drink as Theodosia pushed her point. "Mother Abbess? The letter?"

He didn't join in. That letter, any letter, would be as much use to him as a straw sword.

"I don't know." For the first time, the Abbess seemed unsure of herself.

"Please allow me to read it," said Theodosia. "It must have a bearing on Becket's death. On the hunt for my mother and me. If it does not, then there is no harm done."

"Very well," said Ursula. "Once you've finished, I'll show it to you." She sighed and pushed her bowl away. "My own appetite has departed. Who are these men that would have carried out such evil acts and want to do yet more?"

"They're led by a Reginald Fitzurse," said Palmer.

"To look at him, you would think he was an angel," said Theodosia. "Eyes as blue as the summer sky, but a heart that belongs to Satan."

"One of them, Hugh de Morville of Knaresborough, is dead." Palmer helped himself to a cut of soft cheese rich with best cream.

"As is de Tracy," said Theodosia. "We believe Fitzurse has joined him, and the fourth one, a great, scar-faced brute called Richard le Bret." Her eyes met Palmer's. "Do we not?"

Palmer knew her well enough that she suspected his doubt. "We've been on our own for days, haven't we?" He washed his cheese down with the last of his ale. "Now, Mother Abbess, can you show Theodosia the letter, please?"

◆　◆　◆

"I'm coming, I'm coming." Sister Agatha hobbled to the gatehouse in response to the loud knocks.

Her painful hips would allow a certain speed and no more.

Another series of knocks, harder this time.

She sucked a piece of meat from her three remaining teeth and chewed it fast in annoyance. It were that busy today, she'd hardly had time to settle, let alone enjoy her lunch.

First the broad young man who needed a shave, with his companion. A woman of God, but with no habit? What was the world coming to?

The knocks were more a pounding now. Did some folk have no manners?

"I said, I'm coming." Agatha entered the gatehouse and undid the shutter. She slid it across.

203

A pair of the bluest eyes she'd ever seen met hers.

"My apologies, good Sister." A male voice, the tones of a cultured man.

"What is your business, sir?"

"I have an injured companion. A bad dog bite. I entreat you to provide him with your excellent ministrations."

Agatha sniffed at such fancy talk. "You mean you want the infirmary?"

"If you please, Sister."

Second time today she'd have to open this big door. With a wince of shoulders that were stiffer than her legs, Agatha turned the key and opened up the door to the strangers.

# CHAPTER 17

Palmer stood by Mother Ursula's desk with Theodosia as the Abbess bent to the small wooden chest under the window. She undid the shiny brass clasp that held it shut, then reached in and took out a tightly rolled piece of manuscript.

Palmer's flesh prickled. It indeed bore the seal of Canterbury.

"There you are, my child." She laid it on Theodosia's outstretched palms.

Theodosia opened it out and scanned it, eyes moving along the many lines of shapes, swirls, and forms. "Oh, Brother Edward." It came out as a near sob. "What do you think?" She turned to Palmer.

"I don't know what it says," he said. "I can't read."

The two women exchanged glances.

"I've used my wits for fighting, not letters. Just read it to me."

"Do you want me to leave?" asked the Abbess.

"Please stay," said Theodosia. "My mother was in your exemplary protection for many years. It is from Brother Edward Grim," said Theodosia. "A good, holy monk, Mother. He was Thomas's aide for as long as I can remember. He was injured trying to protect the Archbishop from the knights' attack."

The tall monk, with his surprising valor for an unarmed man of the cloth. Palmer had noticed it on that night. The night he'd been with the murderers, serving Fitzurse. What a wrong choice he'd made.

Theodosia looked to the jumbled squiggles again.

In a steady voice, with not a stop or a stutter, she made them speak.

"My dear Amélie,

I hope and trust with all of my faith that this message finds you safe and well. I came across your location in Archbishop Becket's private papers. It was my sorry task to have to go through them, for, Amélie, terrible events have taken place.

Our beloved Thomas Becket is dead, murdered defending you and your secret. I, useless creature, could not defend him in turn, and my failure will be on my soul forever. Grief weighs heavy on my heart, as it does on all who served him here. My only consolation at this time is that he will now be seated in his rightful place in heaven with Almighty God.

His life was taken by a group of five knights, led by one named Sir Reginald Fitzurse. Fitzurse and his men are in pursuit of you, and want to do you the greatest of harm.

I have worse to tell, though I know it will break your heart if it is not broken already to hear of Thomas. They have taken your beloved Laeticia, and I fear for her to the depths of my soul.

I sail to France on the feast of Saint Theodosius, whose name I praise and pray for his special intervention, from the port of Southampton. I go to bear witness in an audience with King Henry, to tell of the terrible crimes that have been committed.

I beg you to come with me. If you remain where you are, I believe you will be in great peril, with your life at risk.

Travel with the monastic posts; they are swift and will offer you protection. I will await your arrival and hide you until our departure.

May Saint Christopher keep you safe on the sinful perils of the road. God bless you.

Brother Edward Grim."

Theodosia lowered the page. Edward's neat script proclaimed his anguish at what had taken place; his holy grief leapt from the paper, burrowed into her heart. "How he blames himself for the sin of others. No one could have stopped that attack. No one."

"I blame myself far more than Brother Edward." Frustration burned in Benedict's dark eyes. "He's only a monk. I'm a knight. I had a sword. Had I not been a fool, I could have done something. And Archbishop Becket might still be alive."

"Thanks to your protection, Sister Theodosia is still alive," said the Abbess, "and Sister Amélie has her guardian angel in Brother Edward Grim. We cannot change the sins or omissions of the past, much as we'd like, Sir Palmer. But what we can do is make amends, make restitution. What do you propose to do?"

Benedict went to the window, broad shoulders framed against the light. "Mother, Theodosia and I have been hounded for our lives by Reginald Fitzurse. Sister Amélie has been in mortal danger too. We know Archbishop Becket was murdered for that secret, whatever that is."

The Abbess shook her head. "I know not."

Benedict gestured to the convent buildings outside. "Theodosia, I know this is your world, a world you're desperate to return to."

Return to order, calm, silence. Peace. Holiness. Her vocation, her life. "I am." So why did her reply sound so weak?

"But?" said Mother Ursula.

"But we still don't know why all of this has happened," said Benedict. "Brother Edward seeks an answer too, by going to bear witness to the King. We, as the other Canterbury witnesses, should go too. It's the only way to finish this."

Go back out into the sinful world again. But a world where she might find Mama. She steeled herself against her longing. She should not let her ten-year-old heart rule. Benedict ran a broad hand through his dark hair as he looked out the window again. Nor her nineteen-year-old one. Her place was in here, not with him. Nor any man. "You can go, Benedict. You do not need me."

He turned back to her and Mother Ursula. "As far as Edward knows, I'm one of the murderers, one of your abductors. If he sees me alone in Southampton, he'll run a mile. Or, from what I've seen of him, have me arrested and executed as fast as he can. Am I right, Theodosia?"

"Brother Edward has a steely reputation for righteousness," she replied.

Ursula raised her eyebrows. "In a monk, that's a fearsome quality." She laid a hand on Theodosia's arm. "My child, I swear to you, I wouldn't send you or any other soul to harm. But a terrible storm of evil descended on you out of nowhere. Unless you and Sir Palmer find your answers and put an end to this once and for all, who's to say it will not happen again?"

Her words sparked Theodosia's earlier fears back into life. "You think Fitzurse is still alive. Both of you."

"From what you've both said—indeed, from what you've not said—that may be true," said Ursula. "But who's to say he needs to be? You can cut and cut at a serpent's tail. Unless you sever the head, it can still devour you."

"Wise words, Mother," said Benedict.

Ursula released Theodosia's arm with a squeeze. "Then go after Sister Amélie to Southampton. There may still be time to find her before she sails to France."

"When is the feast of Saint Theodosius?" said Benedict.

Theodosia allowed herself a small smile. "I know that at once, for he is one of my patrons. It's in four days' time."

Ursula nodded. "It is indeed. Maybe the blessed saint himself is showing you the way."

Benedict clenched a fist. "Then we can do it. I swear to you."

The Abbess clapped him on the back. "I was a witness to that. Now, to your horses, both of you. Order them saddled up. I'll go and find that serving girl of mine, and she can pack you up enough food for the journey. Clean clothes too."

Theodosia held up Edward's letter. "What should I do with this? Should we take it with us?"

Benedict walked from the window with a shrug. "Throw it away if you like. Doesn't matter now we've read it."

"Not we. I." She smarted at his dismissal of her skill. "Of course it matters. The written word has great power."

"Only if you smother someone with it." He moved to the door. "Now, let's be off. Every second is precious."

Theodosia tightly rolled the letter once more and handed it back to the Abbess. "I think it is safest with you, and not my heathen companion. If anything were to happen to us, to Edward..." She couldn't continue.

Ursula finished for her. "We would still have a robust account with which to bring the murderers to justice." She replaced it carefully in the little chest and patted the closed lid. As she stood up, her look met Theodosia's. "Oh, my child," she said, her voice hoarse with sudden emotion. "I understand your struggle for your vocation, the obstacles in your life that seem too high. God will guide you, I can promise you that."

"Thank you, Mother. I will try and think of your words often."

"Think too of Amélie's joy when she sees you, and yours when you see her," said Ursula. "A glorious reward for your courage, Laeticia." She gave Theodosia a soft pat on the cheek. Composing herself, she returned to her brisk demeanor with a clap of her hands. "Now, come. Let us make all haste."

◆　◆　◆

"Wilfreda!"

The call cut through the hubbub of the busy kitchen.

Wilfreda paused from her scrubbing of a copper pot, wet bran stuck to her fingers.

Stood in the doorway, one of the infirmary sisters beckoned to her across the noisy room. "We have two new arrivals. Bring a pail of hot water. At once!"

Wilfreda looked to the nearby cook for permission.

The cook nodded. "The sooner you're gone, the sooner you're back. Don't dally." She returned to her supervision of a young sister who prepared a pile of sheep's hearts for the evening meal.

With a quick wipe of her hands on the front of her apron, Wilfreda filled a wooden pail from one of the large boiling vats that would cook the peeled and chopped carrots and parsnips. She hurried out to follow the nun across the courtyard, glad to leave the steamy kitchen and its heavy scent of uncooked meat. She liked the infirmary, liked it much better than waiting on tables, where people who didn't know her would stare at her one eye. Sick people were a lot kinder than hungry people. Patients with a fever cared not if you were disfigured. They cared only that you could damp down the raging fire within them.

She could do that. Sit there, by the bedside, as the night stretched long and dark. Put the cloth in the bowl of iced water. Wring it out. Put it on the sweltering brow. Soon as the cold left the cloth, put it back into the water. Wring it out. Back on the brow. Over and over again, till the burning left the sufferer. Time didn't matter when you were with the sick. All that mattered was that they got well.

As Wilfreda entered the infirmary behind the nursing nun, the familiar sight met her.

Neat beds, calm, order, with the settled half a dozen patients. A flurry of activity around the new, as the groans of the injured man drew nosy looks from the rest.

Three sisters attended to a huge knight stretched out on the bed, the sleeves of their black robes rolled up to reveal pale busy arms and hands. A second knight, soiled from battle of some sort, stood over him too.

Wilfreda approached, pail handle secure in both hands, ready for her instructions, ready for the companion's look of mock, of disgust. She cared not. One day, she'd be first round the bed, checking the wound, guessing the rash, judging the strength of the fever. For now, all she could do was watch, learn.

"A dog bite, you say?" The head sister addressed the second knight.

"More serious," he said. "A wolf. We were attacked as we rode through the forest."

This knight must be a high-ranking one. His tones were definitely those of a gentleman.

"Is it only this one at the top of his leg?" said the sister.

"That is the worst," said the knight. "He has a number of scrapes and scratches, as do I, but not anything to cause harm."

The sister bent to make a closer examination.

The big knight gave a muted gasp of pain as his heavy brows drew together and his scarred mouth closed tight.

Wilfreda panged inside. He too bore the cross of a damaged face.

"Make up an onion poultice," said the sister as she straightened up. Her two assistants hurried off at her order. "His breeches need to come off. Wilfreda, I need your help."

Wilfreda stepped forward. "P-pardon me, sir."

The second knight moved back to let her past as she placed her pail next to the bedside.

His fine looks matched his voice. Eyes of startling blue, high cheekbones. His gaze upon her was intent, and the back of her neck warmed. She wasn't used to male attention. With looks like hers, they always moved on quickly.

With a clear view of the injured man on the bed, she admired his restraint in complaint. A large chunk of muscle had been torn from the top of his thigh, the wound deep and open and glistening.

The sister produced a pair of long scissors. "We will be quick, sir knight."

The big man nodded as his large hands formed fists.

"Do we need to restrain him?" asked the sister of the blue-eyed knight.

"Do it." The big knight's voice rumbled deep in his chest.

"You need have no fear of him," said the blue-eyed one.

The sister nodded to Wilfreda, who bent to the knight's torn breeches. She held the thick woolen material as still as possible. With a flash of the scissors, the sister cut around it. Only jagged strips of material remained, stuck to the moist wound.

"I will check on the poultice," said the sister. "Wilfreda, remove those bits of material. Use this." She handed the novice a piece of fresh linen, then made for the small room at the back of the infirmary with quick steps.

Wilfreda sat on the edge of the bed and immersed the cloth in the hot water.

The big knight watched her, silent except for his breath loud through his wide nostrils.

"What are you doing, Wilfreda?"

She looked up at the question, surprised the blue-eyed knight should have remembered her name. So many folk didn't. "I'm going to soak the wool stuck to his wound. It should come away easier."

"Good." He nodded in approval.

She took out the wet linen and placed it carefully over the matted, bloodstained fragments that edged the wound.

The big man held still.

She judged her time and carefully peeled the offending material away.

Her patient stiffened, then relaxed as he realized the delicacy of her actions.

"Well done. You indeed have a skilled pair of hands. It is a pleasure to see you work."

Wilfreda shot a glance up at the second knight. His smile was wide, his expression set in admiration.

"Th-thank you, sir knight." She resumed her task, mortified yet delighted at his praise.

"Do you concur, le Bret?" said her observer.

The patient grunted but seemed content.

"That is praise from my companion, my dear," said the second knight. "He's a man of few words." He bent closer to look at her progress. "My word. You are a miracle worker. An angel of mercy, one might say."

Wilfreda shook her head, a huge lump of pride in her throat.

"Even more remarkable, given your sad affliction." His blue gaze held hers.

He...he didn't mind her eye.

"How many years have you been an infirmary sister?"

She would have laughed, but it would have made her hand shake. "I'm no infirmary sister, sir. I'm only a lay postulant, a servant to the Abbess."

"What? With healing hands like yours?"

"Yes, sir."

"A shocking waste. Do you agree, le Bret?"

The big knight nodded, eyes closed.

Wilfreda's heart soared. She must have this talent, if this grand knight thought so. Maybe this was God's way of showing her true vocation.

"And what did the Abbess have you doing today?"

She dipped another piece of clean linen in the hot water. "S-serving at table."

The knight raised a mocking eyebrow. "The Abbess is too grand to serve herself?"

"N-no." Wilfreda gave a shocked giggle. Fancy her joking about the Abbess with this gentleman. "She has visitors today."

"Of course," he said. "Nuns like to show off to each other."

She shook her head as she picked off some stray strands of wool from the oozing wound, mindful of not touching the agonized flesh. "One was a nun, well, an anchoress. The other was a knight."

"An anchoress and a knight? How odd. Here, let me take those from you." He held out a sheet of clean linen for her to place the bloodied wool within.

"I'm near finished, sir knight." She spoke reassuringly to the injured man. Emboldened by his friendliness, she addressed his companion. "How did the wolf get him?"

"We were traveling at night, through the forests."

"From what I know, sir, that's very dangerous."

"Indeed." To her shock, his blue eyes glistened with sudden tears. "But I've been trying to find my betrothed. She has run off with another man, a knight who has turned her heart against me." He gave her a wry smile. "If only you could heal hearts. I have to find her before she marries, to try and change her mind."

"I will pray for your intentions, sir knight." She placed a last strip of linen on the wound.

"Thank you, Wilfreda. I'm sure God will listen to your intercessions." He sighed. "Just ask him to bring me to my beloved Theodosia."

"Theodosia?" Wilfreda looked up at the knight.

"That is my beloved's name."

"B-but, sir knight, that is the anchoress's name."

"Are you sure?" Bewildered hope lit the knight's eyes.

"Aye." Wilfreda struggled to keep her hope in check, her hope that she, Wilfreda Percy, would answer this noble knight's prayers. "The knight with her was called Sir Palmer."

The knight drew his head up and gave a slow blink. "That is he. The man who turned my dear one's head. They are putting forward some pretense of her being a religious woman? Goodness, the lies."

"But you've found them." She gestured to her patient. "Maybe this poor man's suffering was God's way of leading you to them."

"Indeed." The knight seemed overcome with emotion. "Can you take me to them?"

Wilfreda got to her feet. "Indeed I can, sir. They are with the Abbess in her visitors' parlor."

The knight looked at his companion. "I'll not be long."

Sir le Bret nodded.

"Wilfreda." The knight took her hand in his, the strength of his grip a surprise.

Blood surged to her cheeks. Her bitten nails held grime from the pots, as well as congealed blood from her work on the wound. The blue-eyed gentleman seemed to care not.

"I will be forever in your debt," he said. "Now, shall we make all speed?"

She nodded. "Aye, sir."

He tightened his grip further, and Wilfreda tried not to wince. He smiled. "Indeed, you are an angel."

215

# CHAPTER 18

Mother Ursula hurried along the corridor to her second-floor bedroom, irritation growing with every step.

Bless Wilfreda, she was willing enough, but she was chuckle-headed beyond belief. Every task had to be explained fifty times, shown a hundred. Give her a job, and she'd somehow muddle it up.

Ursula passed one of the novices, sweeping the corridor with the due diligence she'd expect.

"God bless you, my child." Ursula hustled by.

The novice gave the Abbess a quick curtsey and continued with her task.

Ursula opened her bedroom door, hoping Wilfreda worked within. Of course not. The room stood clean, tidy. Empty.

With a frustrated sigh, she made her way back down the corridor.

"Have you seen Wilfreda?" Ursula asked the novice.

The broom didn't stop. "No, Mother."

Ursula went back down the many steep stairs and along to the kitchens. "Is Wilfreda in here?" she called from the doorway.

The cook looked over from her preparations. Her face shone from perspiration and steam. "She was doing the pots, Mother, but was called to the infirmary. Goodness knows what she's doing, but she hasn't returned."

"I'll send her. When I find her." Ursula rolled her eyes. "In the meantime, can you please prepare food for two travelers? Enough for a few days."

"Certainly, Mother." The cook went to task another novice, and Ursula set off in the direction of the infirmary.

She cut through the silent cloisters, then up a back flight of stairs. She was quite out of breath by the time she entered the quiet room. Her eyes lit on the latest admission.

Three of the sisters gathered around the bed, their long black robes masking the occupant. The sweet smell of an onion poultice hung in the air. Clean linen bandages awaited their application.

Ursula walked up to the bed, and her stomach lurched when she saw its occupant.

"Good afternoon, Mother." The sister in charge continued her work.

Ursula forced a calm demeanor. "Good afternoon." She cast a cool, professional eye over the prone man. Inside, her spirit quailed. *A great, scar-faced brute*, Theodosia had said of one of Becket's murderers. That, to a fault, was the knight who lay on one of her infirmary beds. "What ails this poor man?"

"A wolf bite," said one of the other sisters.

The gaping wound on his thigh was covered with the soothing poultice. More was the pity. Ursula would be happy for this monster to suffer all the torments of hell for the wrongs he had committed. She nodded sagely as if she considered his predicament. "A sorry tale, sir," she said. "How did you escape from the ferocious animal?"

"Fought it. So did my lord." The man's thick-tongued voice had the roughness of a rogue.

"Dreadful." Ursula tutted in a parody of sympathy. The sisters began the precise task of bandaging the wound. "And what happened to your lord?"

217

"He's here."

"Ah, God be praised." Ursula could feel that cursed muscle quiver in her jaw. It always happened when she told untruths. Even good ones. She looked around to cover it. "I must congratulate your lord on his valor. Where is he?"

The knight shrugged. "Went with that girl."

"Wilfreda?"

"Think so."

"Sisters, do any of you know where Wilfreda went?" Ursula folded her arms and slid her wide sleeves over her hands, the better to hide her trembling.

"No, Mother," replied one.

"We went to prepare the poultice while she removed the knight's torn clothing from the wound," said the second.

"She did a good job," said the third, the sister in charge. "But when we came back, she'd gone. I'm afraid I don't know where. You know Wilfreda, how absentminded she is." She gave a knowing little smile, then confirmed Ursula's worst fears. "Happen she's lost that poor blue-eyed knight, and he's wandering unaccompanied around the monastery."

The other sisters tittered.

Ursula thought she might be sick there and then. "Then I shall find her. Enough of your unkindness, Sisters." She turned on her heel and made for the door.

◆　◆　◆

"T-the Abbess's parlor is up these stairs, sir."

"You lead the way, Wilfreda."

The novice did so and marveled once again at her newfound authority. She tapped at the closed door. No reply.

She looked around at the sound of metal sliding over metal. The knight had drawn his sword. She gulped.

"Don't be alarmed, my dear." He laid a hand on her arm. "Palmer is a complete ruffian, and I want to be ready for him."

Wilfreda swallowed hard and tapped again at the door. Nothing. She raised her gaze to the knight's. New courage she might have, but that didn't extend to walking into the Abbess's parlor without permission. "They're not answering, sir."

"Or they're gone." He shoved past her, flung the door open, and marched inside, pulling her with him.

He was right. The room, flooded with pale sunlight, was deserted, with the remains of the earlier lunch still scattered on the table.

Wilfreda put her hands to her face, brought them back to her apron, clasped them, unclasped them. "I s-should tidy up, sir. Otherwise the Abbess will be angry—"

The knight booted the door shut with a bang. "She's not the only one," he said.

She took a step back at his controlled yet furious tone. His blue eyes, so kind, she'd thought, blazed with disdain.

"Where could they be?" he said.

"I d-don't know." It came out as a wail.

His nostrils flared as he paced the floor, sword in one hand. It caught the light in a sharp gleam, near blinding her. "Think, girl. Think. You were with them as they ate."

"Not all the time, sir. I was in, I was out. Bringing things, like they asked, and, and, I spilled the water—"

"Oh, spare me the details of your tawdry little life. You are as boring as you are hideous."

"Sorry, sir." She bowed her head and waited.

"Now, think. Think. They may have said something, done something. Anything could be important. Just think, girl."

Wilfreda chewed her lip. "They talked about a letter."

"What letter?"

"I don't know, sir." She raised a shaking hand and pointed toward the chest. "M-mother said it was in there."

He was to it in four strides. He bent down, pulled open the lid, and spilled the contents across the floor. Picking up a rolled paper, he opened it out and read it without saying a word.

Oh, Lord, was this any help? "S-sir?"

He tucked it beneath his surcoat. "Wilfreda." His kind smile was back.

Her knees buckled in relief. "Will this help you find your betrothed, sir?"

The knight's smile broadened even further. "It is more help than you could possibly imagine."

"Oh, g-good."

He held up a finger and beckoned to her. "Now, come over here, my dear. I want to say thank you."

◆　◆　◆

Theodosia sat astride Quercus in the stable yard as Benedict stood holding Harcos's reins.

"How much longer do you think the Abbess will be?" he said. "I want to get a good few miles in before darkness falls."

"Be patient. I'm sure they'll be here soon." Theodosia cared not. She used these last precious moments to savor the atmosphere of the Abbey, with its safety, its security, before she was cast out into the harsh world once more. The world of sin, of danger. She took a deep breath to try and collect herself. As Reverend Mother said, the world where she might find her mother, her one consolation in this terrible quest.

"She's only gone to arrange some food," said Benedict. "What on earth could be keeping her?"

As if conjured by his words, Mother Ursula came through the archway that connected the yard to the abbey. But she bore no bags, no baskets. She hastened to them as if chased by a foam-mouthed dog.

"They're here," gasped the nun.

"Who are?" said Benedict.

"Le Bret. Fitzurse."

Theodosia went rigid. "But how—"

"They asked for sanctuary in the infirmary. Le Bret has a huge wolf bite at the top of his leg," said Ursula. "Ride. Ride for your lives."

Benedict swung himself up into saddle.

Theodosia collected Quercus's reins and felt him respond, ready to set off. "Do they know we're here?"

The nun raised despairing hands. "I fear so. Fitzurse befriended my servant while she tended le Bret for a wolf bite."

The poor one-eyed girl? Theodosia met Benedict's dismayed gaze.

"Then we have no time." He went to kick the stallion's sides.

"Wait!"

He responded to Theodosia's cry.

"The letter," she said. "What if he finds it?"

"It'll be safe for now in my room," said Ursula. "Nobody else knows of its existence. I'll retrieve it and find another hiding place. Now go."

"But, Mother, what about the knights? You and the sisters are at their mercy."

"Don't worry on our account, child. If we're threatened, I might be so afraid that I reveal your plans to follow Amélie to London." Mother Ursula winked.

"Well thought through, Mother," said Benedict.

"But what if they do you harm?" said Theodosia. "They are driven by the devil himself."

"I've spent my whole life fighting the devil," said Ursula. "He's not bested me yet. Theodosia, the holy Thomas Becket wanted to keep you alive. I'm blessed to carry on his wish. Go, child. Now."

Theodosia appealed to Benedict with a look, but he shook his head. "Then God bless you, Mother." She reached a hand down to the small-boned nun, and their fingertips brushed.

"Come, Theodosia."

She pulled Quercus's head round and cantered after Harcos out of the stable yard.

◆ ◆ ◆

"God be with you both." Ursula held a hand up in farewell. Once they'd cleared the gateway, she retraced her steps, even faster than when she'd run down here. The letter. She needed to get that. Then find Wilfreda.

Ursula took the stairs up to her parlor two at a time. The door at the top stood ajar. A shaft of sunlight shone through and formed a pool of light on the landing.

She slowed her last few strides. Hadn't she closed it? Or had she? Impossible to remember, she'd left with such haste with Theodosia and Benedict.

Prepared for an encounter, she entered the room. "Wilfreda?"

Silence.

The table, littered from the lunch she had shared earlier, appeared untouched. Cautious relief replaced her anxiety. Wherever Wilfreda wandered with Fitzurse, it wasn't here.

She hastened over to her desk. Pristine as ever. The chest sat in its usual place. *Praise be.* She'd got here in time. She squatted down and opened the lid. Her horn books. A couple of quills. Blank paper, a section of thin vellum. Two seals. Lumps of red sealing wax.

No letter. Impossible. She ran her hands over the inside of the chest, pulled the blank sheets of paper apart in case somehow it had got wedged between them.

"Looking for something, Mother?"

The male voice came from the doorway.

She shot to her feet to see the door swing slowly shut. A knight stood there, had been hidden behind the open door.

*Eyes blue as the summer sky*, Theodosia had said. "But with a heart like Satan." Ursula said it aloud.

Fitzurse merely inclined his head and held up his drawn sword. Livid red stained its gleaming blade.

Ursula's horrified glance went to the floor. Slumped at his feet was the body of Wilfreda, the poor creature's one good eye taken out by the sword that had pierced her skull, a pool of blood beneath her.

Ursula's hand flew in a blessing for the girl. "You monster." She returned her look to Fitzurse. "You didn't need to kill her."

"Oh, but I did." He stepped over Wilfreda's body. His careless boot crushed one of her plump hands as he did so.

Lifeless as she was, she would have felt nothing, but his utter disrespect enraged Ursula to a new depth.

"Like I have to kill you." He advanced with steady steps toward her, sword aloft. "Then Brother Edward's little note remains a secret." He moved between her and the door.

"What a noble warrior you are." She scanned the room as she backed away. "A half-sighted simple girl and an old nun." She spat the words in contempt. The fireplace. She made the few steps, flung herself to her knees, and grabbed for the iron poker.

Her hand closed around it. She went to swing it at him. A blow thudded into her shoulder. Like being kicked by a cow. She tried to shout, but no sound would come out.

She felt warm. The fire. No. This was from within. The warmth seeped across her chest. She clutched at it. Her hand came away smeared with bright red, with an unmistakable metallic scent.

*Forgive me, Lord. I know I could have done better.*

She half-turned onto one hip.

Fitzurse stood over her and watched her bleed out onto the floor with a calm that conveyed his pleasure.

With her last strength, she took a breath and liquid bubbled in her lungs.

"You, sir, will burn in a hell of your own making."

His lips formed words.

But Ursula couldn't hear them. Couldn't hear them, because the light that poured through the window started singing.

# CHAPTER 19

Theodosia's wayworn concentration had reached its limit. The latest leg of their journey had taken them through an exposed, featureless landscape that climbed in a long incline of many miles. With rocks and stones half-hidden under thin soil and patchy snow, the horses stumbled frequently and had to be ridden with extreme caution. Heavy clouds brought ice on the wind and scudded over the moonless sky to shift the night into deeper darkness, making the going even more treacherous.

She carried with her too the added burden of her worry for Mother Ursula and the nuns of Polesworth Abbey. The Abbess had been ready to face Fitzurse with huge courage. But with such a man, courage might not be enough.

"Looks as good a place as any to stop." Benedict's voice made her start; he'd been quiet for many miles.

He pointed ahead with his whip.

She peered into the gloom and took her shawl from her face. "Where do you mean?"

"That small outbuilding, looks like a lambing shelter."

She picked it out with difficulty. A short way up the slope ahead, a single-story stone building huddled against the desolate land. With a roughly thatched roof, it had no windows and a small door. A few gray-wooled sheep wandered nearby, oblivious to the cold in their thick coats as they fed on clumps of coarse grass.

"Should we not keep going?" she said as they neared it.

"We have to rest the horses." Benedict dismounted and tethered Harcos in the shelter of the building. "Bring Quercus around the corner so they can't see each other."

She did as he instructed. With a quick pat to Quercus's neck, she made her way back to Benedict.

As he pushed at the damp-warped crude door, the clouds broke and the stars cast a poor light on the stark hillside. At its summit, a huge regular mound soared heavenward, topped with a high stone wall.

"Look," she said. "A fortification. We could ask for shelter there, send help back to the abbey."

Benedict glanced up, shaking the door by one twisted panel. "We could. If anyone lived there. I've seen a fair few of those forts in my time, always abandoned." The door squeaked in protest but gave a little. He shoved at it again. "Folk like to say they were built by King Arthur. But I think that's so they can sleep nights. I've heard such places were built by the ancients, a race of giants who roamed the land before Christ, some with a huge eye in their heads, others with the legs of animals."

The starlight disappeared once more behind the clouds, and the wind brought a fresh icy blast from the hilltop.

Theodosia shivered as if the wind came straight from that pagan world, a world without her Savior. "Then we still have no way of knowing what has happened to the Polesworth nuns."

The door finally gave beneath Benedict's powerful shoves. He reached in and removed an armful of straw. "The Abbess's fake story would keep the monastery from harm. Us too, sending Fitzurse off to London." He placed the pile on the ground, and Harcos dipped his head to eat.

"It should never have happened. I led him there, with my fool's pride."

Benedict picked up another pile of straw. "What's done is done. And the Abbess was ready for him, remember?" Calling to Quercus, he went round the corner of the shelter.

Theodosia took a dubious look inside. A few heaps of straw backed up against the far wall. No floor had been laid, with the hillside's whitish rock exposed. "I will not have peace of mind until I know they are all safe," she said as Benedict returned.

"Then when we find your Brother Edward, you can ask him to help you with one of his letters."

The scent of old animal waste filled her nostrils as she ducked her head below the low lintel to enter the shelter. "If we find him."

"We will. And your mother." Benedict came in behind her and pushed the door closed again. Its swollen wood yielded a squealing challenge as he kicked it flush with the lintel.

In the gloom of the hut, she fumbled for the pile of prickly straw and lowered herself into it. "God willing."

Benedict settled himself next to her and gave a deep yawn. "The dawn's on its way soon, and we need to set off then." His hip pressed close to hers as he lay down. "We'll get a short kip. Small mercies, eh?"

She ached to lie back too, let the straw take her tired limbs into sleep. But she could not allow it. "You can sleep. I will be staying awake."

"What on earth for?"

"I cannot sleep beside you."

"What do you think I'll do?" His features were a blur in the darkness, but his voice held the edge of one insulted.

"It would not be your fault. But when you are asleep, you are open to Satan and sin. My body would be against yours, sinful and unchaste of me. The devil would call forth lechery in you as you lie defenseless."

"I've never heard such cultch." With a rustle of straw, he sat up beside her. His face close to hers, she could make out his deep frown.

"I would not expect you to understand. You are not learned in the ways which sin could find you."

"No, I'm not. But I know my own actions and how to control them."

"You only think you do. That is how Satan collects souls for hell. Brother Edward explained it to me many times."

He snorted. "Then explain to me where Satan was the night at Gilbert's."

"You know I cannot remember that night."

"Then I'll tell you. I held you, all night. While you weren't in your senses. For much of that night I slept. With you in my arms. And believe me, I controlled my actions where many men wouldn't have."

A hard knot gathered in her stomach. "What are you saying?"

"You were naked."

His words stopped her breath. Naked? With a man? *With Benedict Palmer?*

"And no, Satan wasn't there. Only me, holding you to try and will warmth back into your body. I didn't lay a wrong hand on you."

His ignorance knew no bounds. "Of course it was wrong." She clutched her bent knees as she fought for breath. "How could you? I trusted you; I even told Mother Ursula I trusted you with my life. Now you tell me this?"

"Faith, I should never have said a word. I got you dressed again before you woke, left your bed. You would've been none the wiser."

"Then thank the Almighty I have found out. This sin, this terrible breaking of my chastity, has been on my soul for days, and I have not known a thing about it. If anything had happened to me, I would have gone straight to hell."

"I don't know how saving a life is a sin. But you know far more about sin than I do." The straw crackled as he flung himself onto his back once more. "I'm going to sleep. Wake me if you see anyone with horns and a tail." He turned over, his back to her, his anger tangible.

Theodosia remained sitting upright, hands rigid on her bent knees. Unclothed, like a wanton. Presenting an occasion of sin to him. She could not sleep now if she tried. Penance, she had to beg God's forgiveness for what Benedict had told her. She shuddered at the mortal danger she had been in, danger she'd known nothing about. Benedict Palmer might pride himself on saving her life, but his pride was an empty, foolish one. He could have lost her immortal soul.

◆  ◆  ◆

"Saint Michael's." The monastic post rider pulled his mount to a stop outside the fine Southampton church. "I can't take you no further, mistress."

Amélie Bertrand appraised the church's high stone tower and gave silent thanks. King Henry himself had granted this chapel, along with three others in this town, to the priory of Saint Denys. This was surely a link to her and her vocation.

"If you'll permit me, mistress." The post rider had dismounted and now awaited by Amélie's horse, arm outstretched.

"I thank you." Amélie unlocked her cramped hands from their grip on the front of the saddle and eased herself from the animal's back, her limbs stiff from her many undignified hours upon it.

The post rider steadied her as she dropped to the ground, exclaiming to herself at having to perform such a graceless action. He untied her bag from the saddle as she looked around, the dawn light still harsh and gray. They stood at the side of the church, in a yard edged with a row of stables. Grooms and stable boys and other rough men went about their business but paid her arrival little heed.

The post rider handed over her bag with a respectful bow. "Good day to you, mistress." He led the horses away.

Amélie drew breath to ask him for further directions but contained herself. Brother Edward had said he would find her. She would not seek the judgment of a man with the post over a holy, ordained one. Clasping her bag close to her, she walked back out onto the main street, where she joined a steady stream of people. They all seemed to be going in the same direction. Why, they must all be heading to the church, of course. Even at such an early hour, on such a cold morn. She relaxed. What a godly place indeed it was. Brother Edward would surely be among them.

But the chattering strangers walked past the high doors of Saint Michael's as they drew level. She saw for herself the doors were still closed. Mystified, she stayed with the flow of people and turned to the right again, which brought her to the other side of the church, showing her the reason for the crowds.

A fish market, set out beneath the shadow of the looming church. That was where the folk of the port of Southampton hurried to, hurried to in their droves. The sights and sounds of its business at dawn's break assailed her senses. Men's coarse shouts as they unloaded the cram of carts. Raucous cries from hardened women as they squabbled over the price of slick silver fish. Charcoal fires that hissed with steam from boiling pots. A group of mangy dogs that snarled over a discarded rotten fish.

Yet she had no choice but to thread through the dreadful throng, to try and catch sight of Brother Edward, or he of her.

While the din was bad enough, the chaos and disorder were worse. She stepped through suspicious-looking puddles, slick and brown with clumps that squelched under her feet. A gap-toothed man, dressed in foul rags and reeking of ale, staggered into her and bumped her hard.

"Sorry, dolly." He leered openly at her.

Amélie shuddered inside, drew her cloak tighter round her, and hurried on. She detested these lay clothes. Without her wimple and veil, her head felt chilly beneath the simple linen wrap. The cloak was a nuisance, slipping this way and that. Worst of all, she felt exposed, nay, almost naked, without her sacred black habit.

She craned her neck and looked to see if she could catch sight of Brother Edward. Nothing, only hordes of strangers. She took a deep breath but stopped it, revolted by the smells of fish and frying bacon that overwhelmed the fresh dawn air.

Amélie set her mouth to avoid its turndown in disappointment. She would have to remain here until the church opened its doors. That would give her a refuge in which to wait. The thought that Edward might not come, that she might be amongst these hardened folk as night fell again, panicked her to the core.

"Mistress."

A powerful hand landed on her shoulder.

She turned with a suppressed cry.

A tall man stood before her, shrouded in a dark brown cowl and cloak.

As she parted her lips to challenge his rudeness, he brought both hands to his hood and lowered it to his shoulders.

She could have wept with relief. "Brother Edward. Oh, thank the Lord."

"Sister Amélie." His green eyes shone with his success at finding her. "God be praised for your safe arrival."

"The years have hardly changed you, Brother," she said, permitting herself a smile of chaste welcome.

"If only that were the case, Sister. I don't move as fast as I did. And it's well I have my tonsure, as I'm sure I'm half bald."

She eyed his thick black hair with its few silver threads. "Oh, do not belittle yourself so, not with such a fine head of hair for a man."

"Let me take your bag." Edward gave the nearby crowds a quick perusal. "We are completely anonymous here, which gladdens my soul. I have arranged a couple of rooms. Saint Michael's has a fine maison-dieu where we can await our sailing to France. It's this way." As they made their way out of the market, he paused by a woman selling a hot milky drink. "Two, please." He handed over a small coin for two steaming cupfuls.

Amélie held up a finger to him as he proffered one. "It does not have alcohol?"

He shook his head. "Honey only. I wouldn't insult you with such baseness, Sister. I remember your virtues well."

"Bless you, Brother." She took the steaming cup and sipped with relish at its wholesomeness.

"I hope it revives you a little," he said.

"Indeed it does," she said. "The journey with the monastery post horses was swift, for which I was grateful. But I feel my bones are rattled to pieces, as well as my dignity." The delicious warmth spread through her limbs. "Are you still planning for us to sail the night after next?"

"Our passages are booked." He cast her an inquiring glance and lowered his voice. "Have you had any word of Laeticia?"

"No. I do not know anything more than your letter." Her voice trembled. "Who knows what may have befallen her by now at the hands of those terrible knights? Robbed of her virtue, her chastity. Carried off by death without a proper confession." She trembled harder. "Her soul might be crying out to me now from hell, but I cannot hear her."

He raised a hand in sympathy. "Sister Amélie, you cannot torture yourself with such grave fears."

"But without a confession—"

"If she has departed this world, her soul will be receiving its eternal reward in heaven, united with our beloved Thomas." Edward took her empty cup from her and returned it to the stallholder. "I have been her confessor for many years, and have offered up absolution every day for her since we lost her."

Amélie let out a long breath. "Oh, God be praised for you and your care, Brother."

"Now you need to come with me so you can rest at the hostel. You must recover your strength for the journey to France."

She fell into step beside Edward as they left the market to join a busy street. "It will be hard to rest while I do not know my daughter's fate."

"Then if you cannot rest, use the time to pray."

Her voice cracked. "But what should I pray for? I am so afraid for her."

His green eyes softened in sympathy. "Pray for her deliverance," he said. "If God is good, that will mean her safe return to you."

# CHAPTER 20

Theodosia began the second of the glorious mysteries, the regular rhythm of her rosary bringing comfort and peace to her soul. The weak light of the winter dawn showed Benedict asleep beside her, his breath measured and even. Soothed by her prayers, her heart softened for the sleeping knight. She should pray for him next, with his soul so far away from the protection of the church. He needed to realize the wrongness of his ways.

A low murmur came from outside. In this inhospitable place? Prayer abandoned, she strained to listen. The wind moaned from the hilltop fort like a disturbed spirit, as if the ancients questioned her and Benedict's presence. Was that the sound? An abrupt bleat made her start, then almost laugh aloud. Of course. The sheep that roamed outside. She settled back into her sacred call to Mary.

There it was again. A voice. Male. Definitely. Kept low. A whinny of recognition from Harcos. Dear God. Fitzurse. *Oh, Mother Ursula. What did he do to you?*

She grabbed for Benedict, put her mouth close to his ear. "Wake up, wake up. Fitzurse has found us."

He shook off sleep in an instant. "Are you sure?" he whispered.

"Harcos knows his master," she whispered back. "Listen."

The muted sounds repeated, along with the low rumble that could only be le Bret.

She tightened her grip. They were stuck here, like beasts at slaughter. The door, wedged shut as it was, would open with a few hard pushes.

"The roof." Benedict's lips formed the words against her temple. "How?"

"Thatch. I'll cut through and get you out. Then run. Make for the fort. It's the only cover."

A stifled cough from outside brought them both to their feet.

Benedict stretched to the sagging fibers of the roof. Loose pieces snapped off onto Theodosia's face and shoulders as he cut furiously and quietly with his dagger.

The door squealed, sealed for now against whoever gave it a cautious push.

"They're coming in, Benedict."

"Almost there."

Another protest from the door's damp wood.

Benedict hauled at the thatch as he slashed harder. It came away in a shower of dust and dried, dead insects. A circle of pale dawn sky appeared above them.

"Palmer. I know you're in there." Fitzurse's voice. "You make more noise than a herd of swine. You know what I want. Come out if you know what's good for you."

"Quickly." Benedict crouched to form a step with his hands.

Theodosia raised her right foot onto them and grasped his shoulders. She looked into his dark eyes, ashamed at her earlier anger. "You save me again." It sounded so weak.

"Go." He boosted her up.

Her upper body squeezed through the gap in the thatch. She looked down. Their two horses grazed on. Le Bret and Fitzurse crouched before the door. Le Bret's spiky-haired head crammed against it to listen for sounds within. Fitzurse had his sword drawn and ready. All it would take was for one of them to glance up. Pushing steadily with her arms, she eased herself out. She beckoned to Benedict.

He gestured for her to run.

"I'll count to three, Palmer." Fitzurse's voice, so clear in the open air.

She nodded, her heart torn. She slid across the roof to the side opposite the waiting knights, terrified the small snaps and rustles she made would be heard.

"One."

The thatch moved beneath as Benedict tried to jump up. But there was no one to help him.

She got to the edge. The ground was double her height below. Rough rocks poked through the thin layer of grass. What if she landed wrong? Broke her leg? Fitzurse and his sword would be on her in a moment.

"Two."

The thatch bounced again. She looked back. Benedict's hands clawed for purchase at the opening, then fell back. Theodosia focused back on the ground. She had to do this. If she failed, his selfless bravery would've been in vain. She launched herself off. The ground came up to meet her. Sharp stone stung her outstretched hands, and fire shot up one knee. She scrambled to her feet and set off toward the fort at a run, a complaint from her knee with every stride.

An oath came from Benedict.

She glanced over her shoulder, and her heart leapt. Benedict had levered himself up through the roof, his chest and shoulders clear.

"Three!"

She slowed. He had to make it.

He was out. He threw himself across the roof and rolled off.

Le Bret's roar of murderous intent echoed across the barren slopes as Benedict hit the ground.

The crash of the door was followed by another shout, this time of surprise.

Benedict rose and sprinted toward her.

Fitzurse appeared round the side of the shelter. "They're here, le Bret!"

Theodosia turned and ran up the steep hillside, Benedict's rapid steps behind her.

"Keep going." He caught her up and grabbed her hand.

"We're done for. We can't outpace horses."

He stumbled on a loose rock. "They won't use them to chase us on this. Too risky."

"You're on a fool's errand, Palmer!" said Fitzurse.

"Not as foolish as yours, Fitzurse."

Tendrils of mist draped around the fort's forbidding silhouette as they raced toward it. With fast, shallow breaths, they neared the top of the slope. Then the ground fell away beneath them in a great dry moat, three times the height of a man and twice as wide. The other side rose even higher.

Theodosia glanced behind her, Benedict too. Their pursuers closed the gap with every purposeful step.

"What do we do?" she said.

"We slide." He yanked her down with him as she screamed, flat on her back. Wet with dew, the grassy sides were like oil. Bumped and jarred by stones, she landed, winded, at the bottom of the huge ditch.

Benedict splashed beside her into a slime-filled puddle. He got to his feet at once and pulled her with him in a swift movement. "We have to climb. Now." He propelled her to the final slope.

Close up against it, she could see it rose to ten times Benedict's height, topped off with the high stone wall.

"A section of the wall's collapsed." He pointed. "Make for that." He bent to grab her around the hips and boosted her up to give her a start.

She grasped at the coarse long grass with both hands. It held her weight. Just. She reached for another one. It barely held.

Benedict was already past her. He climbed with swift movements, hand over hand, never letting the grass bear his weight for more than a second.

With gritted teeth, she tried to follow suit. But her arms wouldn't do it. She pushed with both feet. Better. Another handful. And another.

"Hurry, Theodosia."

She tipped her head back.

Benedict stood atop the fort's wall, hands on both hips, breathing hard. The mist had closed in; he looked like he stood in a cloud.

A thump and splash sounded beneath her, then another.

Le Bret and Fitzurse had made it to the bottom of the ditch.

Dear God, she couldn't fall now. She grabbed another slippery handful. Stronger-looking heather bloomed to her left. She took hold of the sharp little branches.

"Not that!"

Benedict's cry came too late. The plant's delicate roots lifted right into her hand.

She slipped with a scream and slid back down the slick moat side. Somehow she halted. She looked down past her skirt.

Le Bret was closest. He stretched to his fullest height to grab for her ankle.

"Use your sword, man." Fitzurse.

A shadow flicked over her, and a grunt of pain came from le Bret. The rock that struck him dropped to the ground with a soggy *thud* into the wet ground.

Another rock flew past her head and clipped Fitzurse's sword.

"Thank you, Palmer, it needs sharpening. It's blunted from that Abbess. She was a tough old bird."

*He's killed Ursula.* Grief and rage flooded Theodosia's arms with fresh strength, and she clambered on. As she neared the dry stone wall at the top, Benedict leaned down to her from the gap.

"I've got you."

He hauled her up beside him, and she stood up. Her legs shook from fear and effort and would hardly support her. The driving mist cloyed her face, dampened her hair.

"Where can we go?" She scanned the fort top, but all it consisted of was the dry stone wall and a smooth green circle of grass inside it.

"I'll hold them off." Benedict didn't take his eyes off le Bret and Fitzurse far below. He bent to pick up another couple of black and gray rocks from the fallen area of the wall.

She gasped. "They're climbing up here."

Benedict flung a rock down, and it caught le Bret on the shoulder.

"You're dead, Palmer."

"Go along the wall to the other side," Benedict said to her. "Stay on the top, it's quicker than cutting across the middle." He threw another stone, this time at Fitzurse.

But the element of surprise was lost. The knight swiveled to one side, and it bounced past him without harm.

Benedict continued his rapid orders. "Once you're as far across as you can go, climb down and double back for the horses. Take Quercus. And go."

"I'm not leaving you." Theodosia grabbed at a stone and cast it down at le Bret. Her aim was true and caught him on the arm, but had no effect.

"My, my," said Fitzurse. "Throwing pebbles, Sister? How unbecoming."

Le Bret grunted with laughter as he made swift progress.

"Go, Theodosia." Benedict's look allowed no argument.

She clambered up onto the high ridge of intact wall. To her left, a drop of fifty feet, to her right, twenty, both veiled in swirling wet fog. Her head spun. She concentrated on the narrow gray path beneath her shoes as she took fast but cautious steps.

"Le Bret! The wench is making a run for it!" came Fitzurse's shout.

Theodosia increased her pace as much as she dared, then slithered to a halt. The wall hadn't crumbled only where Benedict stood. It had collapsed here too, in a wide gap of fallen stone. What else could she do? She turned to call to Benedict. In time to see le Bret haul his monstrous bulk up onto the wall between her and her knight. She was trapped.

"Theodosia, don't stop!" yelled Palmer, as le Bret steadied himself, sword ready.

The mist shifted in a gust of cold wind. *Forcurse it.* A gap in the wall. She could go no further.

"You're mine, Sister." Le Bret closed in on her along the top of the narrow wall.

"Get away from her." Palmer aimed a couple of rocks at him. He may as well have thrown a daisy at a bear.

Theodosia backed away from the sword tip, feet inches from the edge of the long drop. "Never."

"Need a hand up there?"

Palmer looked down. Fitzurse had changed course to le Bret's path and made steady progress toward the big knight and a rigid Theodosia.

Palmer bent and grabbed two of the largest chunks of flint he could see. "I said leave her, le Bret." He jumped up onto the wall and bolted to where le Bret loomed over Theodosia.

The huge knight adjusted his sword in both hands. He raised it up, preparing to smash it through her skull as he had done with Becket's.

"Le Bret! Your back!" Fitzurse's warning came close below.

Le Bret paused and turned at his lord's warning. When his eyes lit on Palmer, he grinned with the unscarred side of his mouth. "Come for a closer look, Palmer?"

Benedict threw a flint at him. It caught him on one temple, and blood exploded from the blow.

Theodosia's hands flew to her face.

Le Bret roared in pain and teetered on his feet but steadied himself. "I get you after the girl, Palmer." Le Bret readjusted his grip before he turned back to Theodosia.

Palmer's fist closed around his last, heavy stone, Mother Ursula's words sharp in his mind: *Le Bret has a huge wolf bite at the top of his leg.* He aimed at the bandage on Le Bret's thigh. Then he threw.

Le Bret's scream of agony echoed through the fort of the ancients as he doubled over. His heavy sword overbalanced him, and he fell into the collapsed section of wall. His massive frame struck the pile of loose rocks. They shifted under the impact and began to roll.

Fitzurse flung himself to one side as a screaming le Bret and the pile of knocking rubble surged toward him. It was of no help. He too was swept down in the bruising, suffocating flood of rock.

The avalanche settled in the bottom of the moat, and silence returned to the hillside, save for the moan of the wind.

Theodosia's stricken look met Palmer's. She staggered to him as he came for her.

She reached for him, clung to him as if in fear she too would be carried over. "You've saved me again. I don't deserve it, with doubting you over and over. Please forgive me. Please."

Palmer held her tight, heart still racing, the picture of le Bret and his raised sword seared in his memory. "Like I doubted you. You stayed awake to watch for Satan, which I put down as foolish prating." He brought a hand to her cold cheek as the wind circled round them. "Yet your watching out for evil saved us both." Unseen by her, he brushed his lips against the top of her hair and thanked his own God silently in his heart. *And may those two bastards rot in the hell of their own making.*

# CHAPTER 21

Palmer led the way through the crowds on Southampton's busy quayside, Theodosia close behind him.

"I fear we will not be able to find her in time, Benedict," she said.

Though the port was at the edge of a tidal estuary, there was still enough salt on the wind to make his skin prickle. The ocean, his old enemy. The one that had taken him from his family, set him adrift in the world. The one that would force him to deliver Theodosia back to the church. "We're not looking for her," he said.

"What do you mean?" She grabbed his arm hard enough to stop him and pull him round to face her. "Don't be so foolish. We have to. People have lost their lives through looking for my mother. We cannot stop. Do you hear me?"

Palmer drew breath to match her sharp reply, but guilt stabbed at him. Her gray eyes, haunted by things she shouldn't have seen, heard. Her pale skin, her clothes, spattered with the mud and dirt of the hundreds of miles they'd traveled. She must be at her limit.

"What I meant was," he said, "it could take days to find two people here. Especially as Edward will be wary of being seen. And we don't have days." He squinted up at the sun's position over the town's castle. "We're not much later than midday, and from the monk's letter, tomorrow is the day they sail. That's why I'm not looking for your mother, I'm looking for the reeve's office."

She frowned. "A reeve?"

"A reeve's an official of the king. They control the foreign trade that comes into and out of ports. They've the power to raise taxes from foreign merchants and goods that come in from other lands."

"That's no help. My mother and Edward are not coming in from abroad."

"Such a man will know all of the ships that come and go. Including the one your mother will be on."

"Then why are we wasting time?"

Limit or no, she could fair try his patience. Palmer set off again along the quay, Theodosia alongside him.

Ships of different size and age took every space at the dockside. Men loaded some, unloaded others. Some vessels sat full in the water, some empty. Between them, choked with seaweed, spoil, and rotten wood, the ocean lapped still and dirty. Men carried out repairs with hammers, saws, mallets, quick to get back to sea.

Ahead, a group of men with heavy muscles unloaded a large cog. Each man carried an oak barrel on his bent shoulders along the sagging wooden planks of the gangway. They carried their loads across the dock, then up through one of the arches set into the high defensive banks surrounding the town.

"These men will know," said Palmer to Theodosia. "Those are wine barrels."

As one of the dockers returned to collect another load, Palmer stopped him. "A word, fellow."

The man looked from Palmer to Theodosia. Sweat dripped from his face, and his leather jerkin moved in and out from his toil. "What is it? I'm in a hurry."

"Where are the harbor reeve's rooms?" said Palmer.

The man jerked his thumb over his shoulder. "Fifty yards along," he said. "Goes by the name of Rodger Oswin." He spat on the ground in contempt. "Hope you're not bringing aught in. He'd tax the shite dropping into a privy, that one."

"My thanks." Palmer put his arm around Theodosia's shoulder and drew her away with him.

With a wave, the man continued on his way to the cog.

"How ill he speaks of Mr. Oswin," said Theodosia, eyes rounded at the man's response.

A wood-and-stone building, battered from storms and the elements, caught Palmer's eye. "Look. That's it." It stood at the end of a row built leaning against the town's defenses, each one between an open brick archway.

A large wooden board, painted with a crown, hung from a metal bracket above the open door. The building's contents spread out across where people walked. Bags piled up, barrels stacked one on another. A chair. Earthenware pots. A bale of straw. Piles of mangy animal pelts.

Palmer went to the doorway and looked inside. Here, the jumble was worse. Huge metal weighing scales sat on the wooden counter with piles of parchments and papers, a songbird in a rusted cage, and one old leather boot.

Palmer met Theodosia's glance, and she pulled an unimpressed face. "Hello?" he said, unsure if anyone was there.

A man rose from behind the counter, wiping his mouth with the back of his hand. He wouldn't be much more than Palmer's age but was not a man of action. His stained clothing stretched tight over rolls of soft flesh. Greasy hair clung at either side of his pale, puffy face.

"Yes? What?" For a heavy man, his voice didn't match: high-pitched and close to a woman's.

"I'm looking for Rodger Oswin," said Palmer.

"I am he. Who might you be?"

"My name is Sir Benedict Palmer."

"What is your business? Jewels? Wine?" He gave Theodosia a pointed look. "Silk?"

"None of these, sir," said Palmer. "We're trying to find my companion's mother. She is due to sail to France in the next two days."

Oswin rolled his eyes aloft. "You expect me to know who this woman is." He addressed Theodosia. "Is your mother a merchant?"

"No, Mr. Oswin. She is not. But her companion is a Brother Edward Grim. Perhaps he arranged the sailing?"

Oswin sighed long and hard. "Is he a merchant?"

"No. He's a holy brother," she said.

"Then they'll be nothing to do with me." He waved a filthy hand to his papers. "My only concern is to get the rightful taxes owing from foreign merchants and our own good countrymen who bring in any kind of goods from abroad. A monk and a matron traveling to France are of no concern to me." Sudden interest weaseled across his shiny face. "Unless they're going to buy something valuable and bring it back?"

"Oh, please, sir." Theodosia clasped her hands together. "Could you not check the sailings and see if you could tell us which vessel they might be on?"

"I could. But I won't." Oswin smirked at Theodosia's beg. "I'm far too busy on the Crown's business. Good day to you both."

"Couldn't you just—"

"No, missy. I could not. Who do you think you are, plaguing me with questions, a tattered baggage like you? Now, clear off before I have you arrested for endangering an officer of His Grace."

"Come, Theodosia." Palmer brought her outside before he punched the oaf in the face.

"Oh, why couldn't he look at the sailings?" She flung her hands up. "It would not have taken him long."

246

"Because he was in too much of a hurry to get back to his flagon of wine under the counter." Palmer's steps treaded hard on the wooden dock. "Seized no doubt because someone couldn't pay the toll. Like everything else he had piled around him, curse him. We'll have to keep looking, asking."

Theodosia stopped to pull the money pouch from her pocket. "There is another way to find what we need from Mr. Oswin."

"Bribery? No luck with that. There's only a couple of coins left. I had to leave almost everything at that tavern to secure the horses."

She eyed the crowd. "Not bribery." She darted from his side.

He tried to catch her up as she bent toward a filthy small lad.

"You look hungry, my sweet," she said. "Have you eaten today?"

"No, mistress."

"Would you like to earn this coin?" She held it up and his eyes lit.

"Yes, mistress." A wary look. "How, mistress?"

"All I want you to do is go into Reeve Oswin's office and tell him you saw a Saracen steal off that ship, carrying a large sack."

"Which ship?" The lad stuck his head around her muddy skirts to get a better view.

"Theodosia, don't annoy the reeve any more," said Palmer. "He wouldn't think twice about having us arrested."

She ignored him. "The one where the barrels are being unloaded," she said to the boy.

"That's all?" said the boy.

"That's all," she said.

The lad gave her a huge grin, pocketed the coin, and sped off.

"Didn't you heed a word I said?" said Palmer.

"Of course," she said. "Hurry, we do not have a lot of time." She led the way back to Oswin's rooms, but with a hand to Palmer's arm, hung back in the shelter of the crowd.

The boy went inside, and within seconds, Oswin waddled out, face dark with outrage. He hurried down the quay toward the unloading vessel, deep huffs with every step.

The boy came out, gave Theodosia a confirming nod, then lost himself in the crowd.

"Wait here." She raised a finger to Palmer. "Whistle if you see Oswin return." She went into the reeve's office.

Forcurse it, she'd done it now. Oswin would have her carted off if he caught her. Palmer watched the crowd for any sign of the reeve. What could she be doing in there? He hoped to his boots she wasn't stealing something. The man was a leech, but a leech with the King's authority.

He caught the bob of a greasy head on its return journey through the crowd. With two fingers between his lips, he blew a sharp whistle.

She didn't come out.

Oswin pushed his way through, a sheen of sweat on his angry face.

Palmer took a quick look over his shoulder. Still no sign of Theodosia. He squared his shoulders. She'd left him with no choice. Avoiding Oswin's line of sight, he made straight for him.

"Oof!"

Oswin's stomach bounced against his elbow. "I beg your pardon, sir." Palmer turned to the breathless reeve.

Oswin's eyes opened wider as he recognized who'd thumped into him. "Clumsy fool! Can't you look where you're going?"

"I beg your humble pardon, sir. My companion's got lost. I'm worried she'll come to harm in this rough place."

"Then you're blind as well as a fool. She's right behind you."

Palmer turned to see Theodosia, breath quick but with a pleased look. "Ah, you're there," he said through set teeth.

"Get yourselves out of my sight, the pair of you. Ragged ruffians like you can be up to no good. Now clear off before I have you arrested. This is your last warning." The reeve headed back to his shop, rubbing his stomach.

"What have you done to him?" she whispered to Palmer.

"I thwacked into him to stop him. He's not hurt—he's lined with his own blubber."

To his surprise, she caught back a giggle. "Let's do as he says. We do not want to make him any more suspicious."

"No. I can't believe you just did that. If he'd caught you, it could've been the end of everything. What did I tell you about doing as I say?"

"But he did not." She raised her clear gray eyes to his, cheeks flushed in pride as they walked away from the reeve's office. "I think I have discovered the name of the boat."

"How?" he asked in surprise. "Was there someone else in there?"

"Oswin has a full record of all the sailings," she said. "Either he was too lazy to check them or he thought we were too lowly to bother with. I simply read them for myself."

"But the record wouldn't have listed your mother or Edward as passengers. He told you that."

"No. But I looked for boats traveling to France in the next week without a taxable cargo. I found two: the *Seintespirit* and the *Stella Maris*."

"Then it could be either of those."

She shook her head. "The *Seintespirit* doesn't sail for a full seven days. But the *Stella Maris* goes tomorrow night. A Jacob Donne is the captain. To Cherbourg. What do you think?"

He forced down his envy that he couldn't have done what she had, even if he sat in front of the documents for the rest of his life. "That reading and writing can be useful once in a while?"

"Oh, shame on you, Benedict Palmer. They are useful all the time, the key to freedom. Where is your acknowledgment of my quick wits?"

"Not too bad, for a nun."

Frown at the ready, Theodosia drew a breath to reply.

He held his hands up. "I'm only teasing. I'm full of admiration."

Her frown eased.

"But," he continued, "we still need to find this vessel, and there's scores here."

"That's easy." She pointed to the nearest ships. "*Trinité, Grace de Dieu, Katrene, Constance.* I can read them as fast as we can walk."

"Then God bless those wits of yours. Let's go."

She was as good as her word. She reeled off names quickly and quietly as they made their way along. How she did it, he didn't know. His squire master used to pride himself as a man of letters. But each word used to be a battle in itself, with Lullworth holding a finger beneath each letter, making a comedy of sounds till he got its meaning. For Theodosia, the marks on the ships' sterns could've been calling their names out to her, she was that quick.

"That's it." She stopped with a caught breath. "*Stella Maris.* The star of the sea. Another name for Our Lady herself. It must be a sign, a blessing."

Stacked high with planks of wood on the decks, the small, high-sided boat bobbed peacefully at the dockside. Its curved sides gave it a rounded appearance, and its furled sail sat neat on the single mast.

"Hallo?" Benedict gave a loud call. "Captain Donne?"

A slack-jawed member of the crew appeared, his head and shoulders visible as he looked down on them. "Not 'ere at the minute. Who's asking?"

Theodosia let her breath out. "Oh, still nothing," she murmured to Benedict.

"My name is Sir Benedict Palmer, and my companion is Theodosia Bertrand." He looked at the sailor for any sign he knew her name, the same name as one of the next passengers. None came.

"I'll tell him you came by when I seen him," said the sailor.

"When will that be?" said Palmer.

The sailor shrugged. "Dunno, mate." He disappeared from sight behind the side of the ship.

"Oh, how can this be?" Theodosia balled her hands into fists. "We are close, yet not close enough."

"We are," said Palmer. "We'll just have to wait here."

"But what if Brother Edward spies you first?" She gestured to the crammed quayside. "He could easily do that, and we would have no chance to tell him of your innocence. He'd raise the hue and cry, have you arrested. The reeve has already marked us as suspicious." She swallowed. "You might be hurt, or even worse."

The sailor reappeared, a wooden pail in both hands. "Still 'ere?" He emptied its contents of stinking liquid into the ocean.

"Yes," said Benedict. "We need to speak with Captain Donne. It's urgent."

"Oh. Why din't you say?"

As Palmer's arm muscles engaged, Theodosia put a hand on his arm. "Steady," she whispered. "God forgive me, I want to strike him too."

"He's gone to Saint Michael's maison-dieu. Feller who booked the passage wanted to see him."

"And who was that?" said Benedict.

"A monk. Brother Edmund, Edwards. Summat like that."

Her gasp of joy. "Oh, Benedict. We've found them."

"And where's this hostel?" said Benedict.

"Back through the defenses, French Street, then up High Street. Saint Michael's has the tallest tower, hostel's behind it. You can't miss it." He gave a lopsided nod. "Follow yer nose if you get lost. Stinks o' the fish mart."

Theodosia didn't wait, and Palmer matched his fast steps to her own.

# CHAPTER 22

"Sister Theodosia! God in his blessed goodness be praised." In the narrow ground-floor vestibule of Saint Michael's maison-dieu, Brother Edward Grim stepped from the bottom of the flight of wooden stairs.

"Brother Edward!" Hands clasped, Theodosia bowed to him for a blessing. He smelled so familiar: clean, soapy, the sweetness of frankincense.

His depth of emotion showed in his tone as he held his hands over her head and thanked the Lord.

When he finished, she raised her head once more.

"My child. I can't believe you're here," he said. "It is indeed a miracle, though your roughened appearance troubles my soul." His green eyes scanned her face. "I could not believe it when Brother Paulus here came to me with the message you were downstairs."

Brother Paulus, thin, sparse-haired, and elderly, and in charge of the hostel, kept a polite expression fixed on his face. His question of what relationship Brother Edward would have with a young woman showed clear as day, yet he kept his counsel.

"Neither could I believe I'd finally found you," she said.

"But those murdering knights had you in their clutches," said Edward. "That evening in the cathedral when they put their foul hands on you, abducted you so roughly. How in heaven's name did you get away?"

"I had the best of help, Brother." She raised her voice. "You can come in now."

Benedict entered through the door from the street, a cautious look on his face.

Edward's brows drew together. "You." His tone reverberated low and furious.

"Sir Palmer helped me—"

With a swish of his black robes, Edward was across the vestibule in three strides. "You have the nerve, the gall, to present your shameful visage to mine." He struck Benedict hard in the face. "Brother Paulus, fetch the authorities."

Benedict clutched his jaw with one hand, the other on his dagger. "Don't even try."

The old man gaped. "I'm not going past him. He's a ruffian, Brother."

"Then I'll go past." Edward advanced instead, but Benedict drew his knife.

"No!" Theodosia placed herself between them. "Stop this, stop it now."

"I beg your pardon, Sister Theodosia," said Edward. "Since when have you issued orders to me?"

"She's saving your life, Brother," said Benedict through gritted teeth. "And given her bravery of the past few days, I'll wager she can give orders with the best of them."

Pride fluttered in her chest but died away at Edward's look of disapproval. "My apologies, Brother." She bowed her head as of old. "But listen, I implore you. Sir Palmer was with the murderers in the cathedral, no one knows that better than I. He saw the error of his ways almost immediately. Fitzurse had recruited him under false pretenses. Once Sir Palmer realized I too would come to harm, he sacrificed everything, almost his life, to protect me from harm. He has fought with such valor; the four murderers are dead, thanks to him."

"Is this the truth, Palmer?" said Edward.

Theodosia noted he didn't give Benedict the dignity of a "Sir." She could tell by Benedict's rigid expression he'd noted it too.

"It is."

No title or politeness in return. Benedict's dark brown gaze, lit with the passion of fury. Brother Edward's steely green, with the fire of the righteous. It was like she stood between two thunderclouds that would collide at any moment.

She raised joined hands in pleading. "I beseech you both, now is not the time for strife. You have both been my protectors at different times of my life. You have no quarrel with each other."

Edward moved first. He swallowed hard and extended his right hand to Benedict. "Sister Theodosia is right. I lost my control when I saw you, which I will be confessing. Please also forgive me for my assault. It was born of rage, which taints my soul."

Benedict sheathed his dagger and shook Edward's hand. "Apology accepted, Brother. You weren't to know the truth." He let go of Edward and raised a hand to test his jaw. "Faith, you're a brawler for a man of the cloth. I think you've knocked a tooth loose."

Brother Paulus continued to gape. "Should I fetch the authorities or not, Brother Edward?"

"No, Brother. But please arrange a room for Sir Palmer for tonight." Edward gave Benedict an approving nod. "It's the least I can do to thank him for the sister's safe delivery." He turned to Theodosia. "Now, would you like to come upstairs? There's someone waiting who yearns for you without end."

Theodosia caught her breath in delighted anticipation. "Benedict can come too?"

"Certainly," said Edward. "He's one of us now."

◆ ◆ ◆

Brother Edward advanced up the narrow wooden stairs, each step creaking underfoot, Theodosia eager behind him. Palmer climbed up last, leaving Brother Paulus to mutter and click his tongue about the preparation of another room.

She glanced back at Palmer, her excitement almost touchable in the air.

He was glad for her, he truly was. To find someone you loved when you believed she was lost would be the greatest joy. But he was the one who was losing a loved one. He'd seen it the second Theodosia laid eyes on Edward. Like at Polesworth Abbey, she had snapped back into her old behaviors of shyness, silence, obedience. The behaviors that showed she chose God, not him.

Edward led the way along a corridor, then knocked at a closed door. "Amélie, it is I, Edward."

"Come in," said a woman's voice.

Edward opened the door and ushered Theodosia and Palmer through. Palmer took in a square, plainly furnished room: two beds along one wall, a high wooden settle, a couple of wooden stools, a small oblong table.

"Laeticia?"

He heard Theodosia's tiny gasp as he looked over to where a middle-aged woman in a dark red dress stood by the tall, narrow window.

Her look fixed only on Theodosia. "Laeticia? Is it really you?"

"Oh, Mama." Theodosia ran to her. "It is, it is."

Light-boned like her daughter, Amélie put her small hands on Theodosia's face, cradled it. "Oh, my dearest, blessed one. Look at you. How you must have suffered." She broke into sobs. "Those men, those dreadful, sinful men."

"I am not hurt, Mama." Theodosia sobbed as hard as her mother, and held her in return. "I'm not, I'm not."

Palmer understood now why the Abbess had taken convincing that Theodosia was Amélie's daughter. Though their build was similar, their coloring didn't match. Theodosia had those gray eyes and dark-blonde hair, while Amélie had deep-blue eyes and the hair under her linen cap was brown. Theodosia's features were small, delicate. Her mother's mouth and nose were fuller.

"You see, Amélie?" said Edward. "God has answered our prayers." The monk had a quiet, satisfied smile on his face.

"Then let Him be praised without end." Amélie gave a light stroke to her daughter's cheek, tucked a wisp of hair behind her ear. "For when I saw you in the doorway, looking so disheveled, so, so rough, I feared…" She shook her head. "It's God's own miracle you're here."

"God was on my side, as always," said Theodosia. She turned from her mother's embrace to smile at Palmer. "But Benedict here was my protector, saving me from certain death."

"Benedict?" Amélie brought him forward with a gesture.

"Sir Benedict Palmer," said Theodosia in quick correction.

He bowed in formal courtesy. "Yes, Sister Amélie."

"Then I thank you from the bottom of my heart for my daughter's safe deliverance," said Amélie. "There will be a place for you in Paradise."

"Once you've finished in purgatory," came Edward's swift comment.

Amélie appeared not to notice as she turned her attention to Theodosia again. "I believe, Laeticia, that you took another name at Holy Orders."

"Yes, Mama. Theodosia."

"How wonderful. My gift from God." Amélie sighed. "I made the right choice." Her voice wavered.

"You did, Mama," said Theodosia. "My vocation has been my life, though I have yet to achieve my full holiness."

"Oh?" Amélie dropped her hold, tears suddenly dry.

Theodosia hung her head and clasped her hands. "I still have to take my final vows."

"A short while away, I can assure you, Amélie," said Brother Edward smoothly.

"I am most relieved to hear that," said Amélie.

Palmer stiffened at the coldness in her voice. The woman should be rejoicing her daughter was safe and well, not prating on about vows. Not now.

Theodosia didn't appear to notice, giving Edward a grateful look for his intervention.

"Now, Amélie," said the monk. "You have something to discuss with Theodosia."

Amélie grew somber. "Indeed I do." She took her daughter's hand. "It is not bad news, my blessed. But it is a little...delicate."

"It's the reason you were the knights' quarry, Theodosia," said Edward quietly.

"Is this true, Benedict?" Theodosia addressed her frightened question to him.

"I don't know any more than you," said Palmer. "My mission was never about you and your mother. All Fitzurse ever told me was that we were to deliver a message from the monarch to Archbishop Becket, one he wouldn't like. Arrest him if we had to. It was no surprise. The whole kingdom knows he and King Henry fought like dogs these past few years."

"Ah." Edward exchanged glances with Amélie. "Then I think you need to stay and listen to Amélie's account." He picked up a heavy outdoor cloak and swung it round his shoulders. "I've heard it, so I can better use the time to secure a passage to France for you and Palmer, Sister Theodosia." He fastened the front of his cloak. "We need to bear witness to His Grace the King."

"Of course." Theodosia squeezed her mother's hand.

Palmer gave a definite nod.

The monk closed the door behind him, and Amélie gestured to the wooden settle and one of the stools. "Sit with me," she said to Theodosia. "Sir Palmer, take your ease on the stool." She placed Theodosia's hand in her lap. "This will take some time."

# CHAPTER 23

Theodosia scanned her mother's face, unsettled by the seriousness of her tone. "Speak, Mama," she said. "Whatever it is you have to tell me, I can bear it. After all, I am a grown woman now."

"So you are, my blessed one." Amélie squeezed her hand tight. "Although I never wanted to have to tell you, or anyone else, of this." She put her head to one side and drew in a long breath. "Have you ever wondered about your papa?"

"A little," said Theodosia. "But whenever I asked about him, you would only say he had been in heaven for a long time."

Her mother's steely look reminded her of her response.

She went on. "So to pray for his soul, world without end, amen."

Amélie repeated the old words with her, then sighed. "I could never speak of your papa to you. How I longed to, during those short years you and I were together."

"Can you tell me now?" said Theodosia, heart a little faster at this change in Mama.

"I can, and, God help me, I should." She sighed again. "The very first thing he did was frighten me out of my wits." Amélie's memory brought a radiance to her face. "I was returning from a day's cherry picking, near my home village in Anjou. Oh, it seems so far away now."

"It is," said Benedict. "I've fought there. Over the sea, in the other part of King Henry's great kingdom."

"Then you know how beautiful it is," said Amélie with a wistful smile. "It was midsummer, and everyone in the village helped through the day, for the cherry season is short and the fruit will spoil if it's not brought in quickly. It was a hot, hot day, with the sun on our backs, the sweet smell of the fruit in the warm sunshine. My hands were stained dark pink with juice, and I'm sure the scent from crushed fruit made me fuddled, for I set off for home at sunset with my companions, but without my water jar."

*Father was a farmer?* Theodosia waited for her to continue.

"I went back to get it, for I didn't want to be without it the following day," said Amélie. "It took me a while, but I found it. I was making my way home through the lanes, high bushes on both sides and crowded with roses. I don't know what it is with roses, but when the evening comes, they seem to send out ten times their scent. Then, suddenly, from the bushes, out steps this strange man. I screamed with fright, as I was only your age, my blessed." She arched her eyebrows and pursed her lips.

"Your daughter has seen sights more frightening than that," said Benedict.

Amélie's hand went to her mouth. "Please, do not remind me." She shook her head. "I went to run, but the stranger grabbed my wrist and pleaded with me for help. While his appearance was rough, with his pale skin burned and lips cracked from the sun, his thick red hair matted with sweat, his voice was that of a nobleman and his face was the strongest I had ever, ever seen. I took a better look at his clothing. Though it was without decoration and torn in many places, I could tell it was the finest cloth and beautifully tailored."

"Then was he a lord?" said Theodosia.

"Hold, Theodosia." Benedict gestured to her. "A nobleman wouldn't be roaming the land on foot, he should have been mounted."

"Why should I hold? It's my father—"

"Theodosia, your manners. Sir Palmer asks a perceptive question."

Mama's tone that allowed no argument—she remembered it well.

With a gracious nod to Benedict, Amélie continued. "A hunting accident, poor soul. He'd gone out on his own, his horse had thrown him. Oh, but in spite of his hours in the heat, he was still furious. He dug into one of his pockets and waved a horseshoe at me. 'Look, look,' he said, 'some'—and I cannot repeat the word—'used the wrong-size nails.' He was not familiar with the countryside, so had wandered for hours in the boiling sun. He railed about his accident, his farrier." Amélie gave her inward-looking smile again. "I feared he would drive himself into a paroxysm."

Theodosia did not dare to comment.

"The heat can drive a man mad," said Benedict.

Amélie nodded. "That was what worried me. I handed him my water jar and told him to drink what was left. I do not think I have ever seen a man so grateful for a few mouthfuls of spring water warmed through from a day in the sun. As he drank, I took my straw hat and fanned him with it as best I could, took my own kerchief and mopped his brow. He smiled at me as he drained the bottle. Oh, the way that smile lit his eyes: piercing gray, they were, as sharp as an eagle's, and such huge life in them." With a sigh, she shook her head once more. "I offered to take him home."

Theodosia dared not give voice to her disapproval, but she doubted if it mattered. Though her mother spoke of her father, Amélie seemed far more focused on Benedict.

"I know what you must be thinking, Sir Palmer." Amélie had a delicate flush to her cheek. "But I was not a nun then. I lived with my parents, respectable, God-fearing free tenants with ten virgates of their own. I had to offer him shelter, somewhere to eat, drink. My poor offering of water would not have been enough to sustain him for long."

"A noble offer." Benedict gave a slight nod as Theodosia stayed silent.

Her mother didn't seem to notice any undercurrent in Benedict's remark. "As we walked along the lanes, he appeared restored to great good cheer. He told me I'd been sent from heaven by the Almighty to save his life, plucked rose petals from the bushes, and strew them where I walked, said such a woman should not have to tread upon this earth." She smiled again at her own recollections. "I laughed at first at such absurdity, but he would have none of it, kept calling out my virtues. Darkness was falling as we approached my father's farm. I could see lights moving about, and I knew folk would be looking for me. I turned to him to point them out to him." Her voice dropped to a whisper. "As I did so, he fell to his knees and promised himself to me."

Theodosia matched Benedict's look of surprise. For a terrible second, she thought she might laugh, as much at her late father's wild actions as at the idea of Benedict behaving so. She coughed. "Did you take him seriously, Mama?"

Amélie considered her for a moment. "Of course I did. His behavior was unorthodox, but there was no wrong in it. Are you saying otherwise?"

Benedict rescued her. "Pray go on, Sister Amélie. I think Theodosia relives your own surprise."

"I brought my young man home," said Amélie. "My parents were greatly relieved to see me and, once they had heard his story, my young man too. Mama had the servants prepare him a room so he could be brought back to health. Our house wasn't a grand hall, only a farmhouse, but it was very spacious and well appointed. My stranger left after a couple of days, with a borrowed horse."

"Then I was born out of wedlock?" Theodosia could scarce get the words out.

High spots of color pinked her mother's cheeks. "How dare you suggest that I would commit such a sin? Have you lost your reason, Laeticia?"

Theodosia clamped her hands together. "Theodosia."

Amélie's nostrils flared. "Well, now I see why your vocation eludes you, with sinful thoughts ready in your mind." Straight on the settle before, she sat even straighter. "My virtue was never in question. Unlike yours has been, over the last couple of weeks, with you in the company of sinful men."

Now it was Theodosia's turn to color. She couldn't meet Benedict's eye.

"My young man came back, time after time," continued Amélie. "Always seeking my hand, pressing me to take him, begging my father to influence me. I grew to love him and his noble love. So eventually, I told him yes. When we were promised to each other before God, it was the happiest day of my life. Then you, Laeticia, were born the next time the harvests came round. We named you as joy, happiness, for that was what we had: noble, blessed love."

An odd expression formed on Benedict's face. "How long were you together, Sister Amélie?"

"Only a year." Amélie's eyes filled with sudden tears. "Then he had to go."

"He died," said Theodosia, keen for the truth.

"No." Slow tears rolled down her mother's face. "He had to go. For as a nobleman, he was pressed to other duties."

"I think I see," said Benedict.

"I do not," said Theodosia, bewildered, looking from one to another. "You are a widow, Mama."

Amélie brought a hand to her brow. "Oh, this is so hard."

"You're a widow now, but only since the close of the year," said Benedict. "Your husband was a nobleman. Called to another duty. Couldn't give his name to his family." He met Theodosia's eyes with a look of triumph before he addressed Amélie once more. "He was Thomas Becket, wasn't he, Sister?"

Theodosia grasped her mother's hands as if in a vise. "Oh, Mama. Is it true? My own dear Thomas, kindness himself to me always." Her own tears threatened. "Laying his life down for both of us, just like a loving father would do."

Amélie pulled her hands away, shaking her head. "No, no, you are both wrong."

Benedict persisted. "That's why Becket had you both hidden away. That's what Fitzurse wanted, to seek you both out on behalf of the monarch. The discovery of a wife and daughter would cause Becket to lose his position as Archbishop of Canterbury. The King would be rid of his meddlesome priest once and for all."

"I said no."

Benedict stiffened, caught by Mama's displeased tone for the first time.

"Your father wasn't Thomas, although he kept us safe for many years."

"Then who was he, Mama?"

Amélie drew herself up again, cheeks still wet. "I found that out when you were eight weeks old."

◆ ◆ ◆

*Amélie relaxed into the high-backed chair pulled before the fireplace in her bedroom, her baby cradled in both arms. "Shush, shush." The padded tapestry cushions of the nursing chair were bliss to her tired limbs. Baby Laeticia had kept her from her rest for many hours last night.*

Laeticia continued to mewl and grizzle, then buffeted her small face against Amélie's woolen-clad bosom.

"Not so impatient. It's coming." Oh, this baby had her father's strength of will, his enormous appetite too. Amélie undid the fastening at the front of her dress, moved her linen shift to one side, and released one full breast. Her tiny infant sought it out with her pink gums and settled in an instant.

Amélie gazed down at the little downy head, one baby fist tight against a baby cheek as if to guard against a milk thief. The wood fire crackled bright and heated the room through from the cold of the windy autumn day. Outside, her parents busied themselves as always, Mother supervising a servant as she swept red and orange leaves from their yard, Father overseeing the repair of a barn door in preparation for the winter to come. The rhythm of brush and mallet, along with the baby's steady nursing and the warmth of the room, pulled her to a near doze.

But one thing was absent. Or, rather, one person. As if her thoughts called him there, she heard hooves in the yard and Geoffrey's deep voice salute her parents.

She smiled to herself. Now the day was perfect.

Firm footsteps sounded from the stairwell, and the door opened to a waft of cold air. Geoffrey came in, a fur-edged dark green cloak slung around his wide, powerful chest and shoulders. Smooth calfskin hose and polished leather boots emphasized his strongly muscled legs. He pulled off his rolled-edge fur cap and smoothed his red hair.

"Husband." She smiled her love at him as she savored his familiar face. Familiar it might be, but still with the power to arouse every inch of her body.

"Amélie." He came over and pulled up a stool next to her. "My, my, our girl has a fierce appetite." He raised a gauntleted hand and touched the top of Laeticia's head. The baby suckled on, oblivious to her father's presence.

*Amélie sighed at her daughter's intent purpose and looked to Geoffrey. Her insides contracted. His face was set in a mask of sadness.*

*"Geoffrey, what's the matter?" she said.*

*He rested his elbows on both knees and clasped both hands. "I'm afraid I have some bad news, Amélie."*

*"Are you ill? Injured?"*

*"More complicated than that, I'm afraid." He got up and paced the clean rushes on the floor before the fire.*

*"Then what?" She wanted to jump up and grab hold of him, shake him into speech, but the greedy bundle in her lap would not allow it.*

*He paused. "You know I love you, don't you?"*

*"Yes."*

*"And our daughter?"*

*"Yes."*

*"Please remember that when you hear what I have to say." Geoffrey resumed his slow tread before the fire, back and forth, back and forth, as if his steps helped him to find words. "When we first met, I told you I was a nobleman. Part of such a life is about duty, and you understand that?"*

*Amélie nodded. "With all my soul."*

*"Last week, I discovered I have a new obligation to fulfill." He closed his eyes and wouldn't look at her. "I am to be married."*

*A chill enveloped her, like the fire threw ice, not flames. "But you cannot. You are already married to me."*

*He opened his eyes and cast her a shamed glance. "I know. But it's more complicated than that."*

*"Oh, is it, noble sir?" Laeticia stirred in her lap, her feed disturbed by her mother's raised voice. "I cannot see how. You stood next to me before the priest and swore your vows before God himself. How can that be undone?"*

"It can't, it can't." Geoffrey dropped to his knees before her and held her face. Grief clouded his gray eyes. "Which is why I've put you in a terrible situation."

"You talk in riddles. All I can glean is you want to marry another."

"I don't, Amélie. But my duty insists on it." He let go of her and raked his spread fingers through his thick hair.

"How can duty, nobility, be more important than a promise before God?"

"I'm not saying they're more important. Only that I have to fulfill them. As God is my witness, Amélie, I wish I didn't have to. I still love you, I'll never stop loving you."

"But you will go through the lie, the sin, of marrying another." Amélie bit her lip to hold in her fury. "How could you do this, Geoffrey?"

He looked at her for a long moment. "Not Geoffrey. That's my father's name. My real name is Henry. And as a prince, I have to."

❖  ❖  ❖

Amélie fixed Theodosia with a calm gaze. "Your father is King Henry himself. My handsome stranger was a prince, and I did not know it when I married him and bore his child."

Theodosia's lungs wouldn't fill. Words wouldn't come. Benedict's astonished exclamation sounded as if it were underwater.

"Help me, Benedict." Her mother's voice too, at a great, great distance.

The room lost color, faded to black and white.

Strong arms slipped across her shoulders. "Put your head down," said Benedict, his deep voice near.

Theodosia did so, and the room whirled back into focus. She raised her head and looked from her mother to Benedict. He too had paled with the enormity of this revelation.

Amélie seemed sad yet utterly composed. "You can only imagine my shock at his words. I was sure I was to be put to death, and you, my blessed baby, along with me."

"Why were we spared?" said Theodosia.

"His Grace was adamant he loved me from the moment he saw me, always would. That his marriage to Eleanor of Aquitaine was for political gain and no other reason." Her lips puckered in bitterness. "She's senior to him by eleven years, so I could believe him. Soiled goods, as well, cast aside by a king of France. Oh, he could persuade a stone to turn to gold, could your father. By the end of his visit, I had agreed to stay with my parents, and he would come and see you and me as often as he dared."

"And he did?" said Benedict.

Amélie nodded. "Things changed suddenly after a couple of years, when Henry and Eleanor succeeded to the throne. For a prince to travel anonymously is difficult enough. He had barely managed it by behaving oddly and changing his plans at short notice. For a king, especially with a watchful queen, it was almost impossible. That was where our dear Thomas Becket came in."

The door opened.

Theodosia gave a dreadful start, as if a ghost had entered.

Brother Edward Grim greeted them as he shut the door carefully and removed his cloak. "The sailing passages are booked," he said. "Have you told them your story, Amélie?" He placed a flagon of wine, a jar of water, and a loaf of bread on the small table.

"I am almost finished, Brother," she said. "Becket was serving as an archdeacon in Canterbury. Due to his brilliance and compassion, he was recommended as chancellor to Henry. They hit it off straight away and became the closest friends. Henry confided his secret to

Becket, as not seeing Laeticia and me was breaking his heart. It was Becket's suggestion to move us to Canterbury Cathedral."

"I never saw the King there," said Theodosia.

"You couldn't," said Amélie. "As you grew up, your coloring, your looks, became more and more like your father's." Her brows drew in a fleeting frown. "Not to mention your demeanor. We could not risk people seeing you and me with him and wondering about our ties."

"It worked," said Edward with a nod. "You were under my nose all along, and I never guessed."

"That was why I had to go to Polesworth Abbey," said Amélie. "But God consoled me. I made you as my gift to God, Laeticia."

"Theodosia," said Edward.

"Of course, Brother," said her mother.

Theodosia had no words. It did not console her. She'd been ten years old, her mother's place had been with her.

Benedict got to his feet. "Then my mission with the knights would have been ordered because the King and Becket had fallen out. Becket held Henry's darkest secret. If it had got out, everything would have been ruined: the King's marriage, his sons illegitimate."

"Indeed," said Edward. "Henry sent them to arrest Becket and find Sisters Amélie and Theodosia. He must have wanted to contain his secret once more."

A deep sorrow and even deeper guilt tore through Theodosia. Bad enough that Thomas had died to save her, that had plagued her enough. But to have been cut down for a sinful lie—the lie was she and her false vocation. She might as well have landed a blow on the altar at Canterbury herself. Her stomach convulsed, and she put a hand to her mouth. How could she ever have thought she was a woman of God?

Around her, they talked on.

"Is it safe for Sisters Amélie and Theodosia to travel to France to see the King, Brother Edward?" said Benedict.

"I believe so." The monk lit the wick of the open-dished oil lamp. "Come." He gestured for all to sit round at table as he too sat. "Sister Theodosia?" His prompt allowed no delay.

Theodosia complied with weakened limbs, joining her mother.

"Thank you, Brother," said Amélie. "I hadn't noted the time slip away. Why, the darkness is almost complete outside."

"Palmer, sit down," said Edward.

The knight hung back from the table, standing with his big hands awkwardly at his side. "I don't think I am fit to share this table, now that I know the truth." He bowed to Amélie.

"Oh, dear boy." Amélie gave him a sweet little smile. "I have lived humbly for so many years. It is very important that I am treated as a vowess." She patted the free stool. "Things must be as before."

"That's very important," said Edward, addressing Theodosia also. "Not a word of this can come out."

"You have my word." Benedict sat as directed. "Faith, it's a shock to have heard it. I'm not sure my mind can make sense of it all." He bowed his head with the others as Edward said grace, then poured out goblets of wine for himself and Edward. "Indeed, it was a shock to me also," said Edward, "but a good lesson in finding out that people may not always be who they seem." He poured water for the women.

Theodosia stared at her piece of bread, appetite gone. How could they all carry on as normal? Talk. Smile. Exchange pleasantries. When her sinful lie of a life had brought death to Canterbury. A liar's death for Thomas. The words beat like a drum in her head.

"Tell me, Edward," said Benedict, mouth full as he chewed, "why do you think Theodosia and Sister Amélie are safe to come with us to see the King?"

Edward took a thoughtful sip of his wine. "We have heard Amélie's story. It's corroborated by items I found in Archbishop Becket's papers. Add to that our eyewitness account. You, Sister Theodosia, and I were all there, Palmer. His Grace needs to know that the arrest went wrong, that murder was committed in his name by brutal knights who'd lost control." He looked round the table. "This is our chance to set the record of history straight and to ensure the King's name is cleared. That is our God-given duty, isn't that so?"

Amélie and Benedict murmured their agreement.

"Sister Theodosia?" Brother Edward's searching green gaze rested on her.

Duty it might be. But no longer God-given. Only by sinful man.

Amélie's gaze rested on her too, drawn by her silence.

She couldn't form words, not now, not to them. To anyone. "Of course." She managed a whisper.

Satisfied, they turned their attention from her and began to talk through the whole wretched story once again.

# CHAPTER 24

Theodosia lay abed in the shadowed, quiet room and watched the pattern of stars change slowly in the small window. Every muscle in her exhausted body ached for sleep, for oblivion. But it would not come. Not like all the times she'd lost her battle against sleep in her cell, slumped forward over her Psalter in the early hours. Her regret afterward, the knowledge of her weakness. Now, when she would welcome sleep's dark forgetfulness, it would not come, and she knew why.

She'd been taught to look on her bed in the same way as she did her grave, as if she were entering it for burial. A clean, washed body. She had done that earlier. A clear conscience also, to grant her scared rest.

Her conscience had never been so disturbed. Her mother's account of her birth whirled through her mind over and over. All she thought she'd been had been broken to pieces. Her life, based on truth, on holiness, had been revealed as one gigantic lie. A lie of which she hadn't even been aware.

She turned over yet one more time, willing her body to relax into unconsciousness. Her sore limbs refused, tensed as if they had life of their own. Across the room, her mother slept in the second bed, her slow breaths a reflection of her deep, peaceful slumber.

The sleep of the just. With a sudden wave of fury that sickened her to her stomach, Theodosia sat upright. How on earth could

Mama rest so? Mama's calling to the holy life had been a lie, a lie to conceal a wrong passion and to continue it while her husband became betrothed to another. Mama's gift of her, Theodosia, as an oblate: another falsehood. Worse, a falsehood that had cast her away as if she were of no importance, her child's heart broken in the process.

She bent up her knees and hugged them, willing her rage, her grief, to subside. But it did not. Her mother slept on, her form still beneath neatly tucked sheets.

Her mother had given her life, the most precious gift there was, but through her selfish desires had brought death knocking, calling to her daughter, over and over again during the past, terrible weeks. Theodosia tightened her grip. Not only to her. To innocents like Becket, Gilbert, the nuns.

And Benedict. The man who had faced death with her, had shielded her over and over again from its hideous embrace. His thanks had been her constant rejection of him, her desire to be rid of him, so she could reclaim her calling as an anchoress. A good, good man put aside so she could follow a calling as empty and false as the painted lands on the stage of a miracle play.

Her limbs trembled with the tightness of her own angry embrace. She had to lose some of this wrong emotion or it would consume her. She slipped out of bed, the bare wood floor chilly beneath her feet. Arms crossed, she walked the short distance from bed to door and back, over and over. If she had to pace all night, she'd do it.

The small table with the remains of their simple meal caught her eye. The few scraps of bread didn't appeal. A half-full stone wine bottle did. Benedict had told her once he favored alcohol to help him sleep, to take the pains from his battle-weary limbs, to make him forget the terrible sights he'd seen. Perhaps it would help her pain in the same way.

Theodosia went over to the table and picked up the bottle. A sniff to the open top had her wrinkle her nose. It smelled like the stuff he'd made her sip, had splashed over her in the kitchen at Knaresborough. Wine might be made from grapes, but it had a peculiar sharp scent. Further, it was a sinful potion that robbed men and women of their senses, made them fight. Lust. She went to replace it, then halted.

So if it did cause sin? Why should she care anymore? Her days of virtue and purity had been for naught. She could achieve no rest, she was marked with evil. Now, if she chose to indulge as the rest of the world did, it would not matter. With hands that shook, she picked up a goblet and poured a full measure.

She put the bottle down and brought the goblet to her lips. Again, the heavy scent of the wine prickled the inside of her nose. She took a sip. Bitterness flooded into her mouth, a soil-like taste and scent mingled together. Her tongue curled.

As she wondered how anyone could tolerate such a thing, the liquid hit her stomach. Strange warmth began to grow there, as if she had a low fire within. She took another mouthful. The bitterness was less this time, and the subtlest taste of fruit broke through. The heat brought by the first mouthful increased and spread along her arms, her legs. This was what Benedict must have meant. She drank again, and it tasted almost palatable. A final mouthful emptied the goblet, and she replaced it on the table. A slight wooziness in her head should have prevented her from having any more. *Should have.* She filled another goblet and drank it down in one untasted draught. She wiped her mouth with her fingers. Now perhaps she'd sleep—her head spun as if she might faint.

Theodosia considered her narrow, hard bed with its tousled covers and scratchy straw mattress. She'd lain in it for hours already without closing an eye. Hours where she had thought of her mother, the King, Thomas. She clenched her fists in frustration. Here they came again, the same thoughts, the same pictures in her head. The wretched wine hadn't worked, whatever Benedict might claim. She needed to get out of this room, try somehow to break this horrible repeated wheel in her mind.

She made her way out the door and onto the deserted corridor. A large window stood at one end, secured with iron bars rather than the rare, expensive glass of the church. It faced the open sky to light one end of the corridor. Through it, she could see the small moon hang in the starlit sky. She went toward it to get a better view. Funny how the chill night air seeping from it seemed to bother her little, even though she was dressed only in her thin shift and underskirts.

As she stepped up to the barred window, she caught her breath. On the quayside, the sea had lapped dirty against the dock, hidden by the jam of boats and humanity. But from this high window, the water glistered with starlight and the mirrored moon, opening out before her, promising her a world of wonder, of possibility. She had a sudden desire to leave the hostel, to go out and get on the first boat to leave, put this life and its heartbreaking history behind her. She put a hand to the bars as if they might part before her touch. Of course they didn't. They stayed resolute, cold, hard, like all the barriers in her short existence. Barriers put up by her mother. By Edward. By the church. Even by her beloved Thomas.

"Theodosia?" Benedict's voice made her start.

She turned from the window.

The knight stood at the door of his room in woolen breeches and half-open shirt, his dark hair rumpled from bed. "What are you doing?"

"Nothing," she said. "I could not sleep."

"Waiting for Satan again?" His sleep-filled tone was kind, but she shook her head in a terse reply.

He came up to her and put a wide palm on her arm. "You're shivering. You need to go back to bed and get warm."

"I'm not cold. I'm upset. Sickened. Angry."

"About what?"

"Not what. Who." She shook him off and paced again, eyes fixed on the stretch of open water beyond the window. "Everyone. Mama. My fa—the King. Edward, the whole church. Even Becket."

Benedict took a sharp breath. "Theodosia. Think of what you say. Becket laid down his life, paid the highest price. For you."

She halted and looked at him. "What about my life? I was disposed of as neatly as a set of soiled rags. Buried alive on the pretense of serving God."

Frowning, he bent toward her, his face inches from her mouth. "Have you been drinking wine?"

"What if I have? It's only my stupid, silly naiveté that listens to the teaching that says it's a sin, that keeps my head covered because loose hair is a sin, that keeps me from sight because that's a sin, that, that—"

"Hush." Benedict raised his hands as he glanced around uneasily. "You'll wake the whole house."

"And if I do?" Theodosia glared at him for his interruption.

She got a stern look in return. "If Brother Edward or your mother finds us here, alone, half-dressed, in the dead of night, they'll have my manhood lopped off. Lord knows what they'd do to you. Please, go back to bed. I am, before someone hears us."

He went to return to his own room, but Theodosia didn't budge.

Instead, she turned back to the window, folded her arms, and looked out once more.

"Oh, forcurse it." He came up behind her and put his hand on her shoulder. "You can't stay here," he said, tone low and forceful.

"You'll freeze, your skin's already like ice. You don't feel it right now because of the wine."

"Like ice." She raised her eyes to his. "Like the night I fell in the river?"

He shook his head with a half-smile. "No. Not as cold as that."

She didn't drop her gaze. "Like when you found me in that cell in Knaresborough? Like when we rode all those miles in the snow? All you've done for me, the number of times you've saved me, and all for a stupid lie. You've been made as big a fool as I."

"You talk in riddles. There is no lie to you, to who you are."

"Not riddles. The truth. For once. Everything about me was a lie. My calling. My life. My religion. Even my name. I'm no gift from God. I'm just a worthless woman."

Benedict brought his other hand to her shoulder and pulled her none too gently from the window. "My room. No arguments."

"Take your hands off me." She squirmed in his hold.

"As soon as no one can hear you."

Benedict hustled her through to his room and pushed the door shut behind him with one foot. He sat her down on the hard bed and hunkered down with his back to the wall opposite her. It was far less fine than her and her mother's room; their knees almost touched in the narrow space.

"I'm not staying in here, Benedict." She went to rise, breath fast in her chest.

"Yes, you are." Reaching forward with one long arm, he pulled the rumpled rough cover from his bed and wrapped it around her shoulders. "Keep that on. You need it." He pinned her with his dark gaze. "Out with it."

"Out with what?"

"My squire master used to say it to me. He'd say it to any of the lads who fumed and raged. It'll eat you up, he'd say, if you keep it in. And not only are you angrier than a she-bear who's had her cub stolen, you're drinking wine, telling me you're worthless. So out with it."

Theodosia's lips tightened. "Do you presume to be my new confessor?"

"I never said I was here to grant forgiveness." He raised his eyebrows. "Worthless?"

Her own word tore into her soul. "Yes." Her anger was twisting her so hard, she felt tears build.

"Why?"

"I told you. I've only lived a lie." Realization bit. "Because...I'm not chosen. I'm not picked by God." Her tears spilled over, running hot and unchecked down her cheek.

Benedict said nothing, did nothing. Only sat in silence as she cried quietly, painfully.

Then his hands covered hers. "Can I tell you what I think?"

"Please don't. I know what your opinions are about my religious calling, the religious life. I don't need you to gloat, to tell me you were right all along."

"That's not what I was about to say." His grip tightened, held her hands fast within his. "I want to tell you that you are the furthest thing possible from worthless. You're brave. Headstrong. Resourceful. Clever. Quick-witted." He let go of one of her hands and gently brushed away her tears. "You have courage that makes you foolhardy. But I admire it to the soles of my boots, and that's not worthless."

"It is good of you to say such things." She collected herself, brought her sobs to a stop with a shuddering breath. "You have said them before, I've not forgotten." She tried to smile. "Even though they make me sound more of a knight than a woman."

"Believe me, you're a woman. I've seen you, remember?" He gave a sheepish smile. "In my sinful way."

"I can't have looked much. You lay beside me and didn't touch me wrongly." Her cheeks flamed. "Remember?"

His dark eyes held hers with a sudden intensity. He let go of her, raised his hands to her. "Believe me, I almost had to cut these off. But I couldn't do anything, you weren't in your senses." He lowered his hands again, and a corner of his mouth lifted. "You might say Satan was there. I'd say I lay with a desirable, beautiful woman."

"Not I." She wished her voice didn't shake.

"Yes, you, Sister Theodosia Bertrand."

"Sister Theodosia Bertrand used to eat cold food to keep a pure heart. Sister Theodosia Bertrand used to dream of men in that cold, horrible cell, dream of them as any young woman would, and be repenting it for days after. Sister Theodosia Bertrand was horrified that you'd held her in your bed." She trembled with where her words were taking her, but she couldn't stop them if she tried. "Sister Theodosia Bertrand was a lie. I want to stop lying, be a woman, a real woman. The woman Laeticia never got to be." She wrenched the bedcover off, exposing her shoulders, the curve of her breasts in her thin shift. "So is Satan here now?"

Benedict ran his hands through his hair. "You can't—"

Her fingers fumbled for the thin ribbon that laced the front. Gaze locked on Benedict's, she slipped open the knots, loosed the top. "Now?" Softer.

"Faith, I don't care if he is." He brought his hands to either side of her face, drew her to him. His lips brushed her cheek, the side of her mouth. His unshaved face was a scrape on her skin that almost hurt, yet pulled a heat from deep inside her. It was the feeling from those dreams again, the feeling she'd fought down, pushed away, scrubbed away in her confession. Now she could let it loose, now she could savor every second of it.

"Nor I." Her arms went round his neck as she pulled him yet closer to her. Her mouth found his, and his lips pressed hard, demanding, upon hers.

His wide hands went to her hips, pulled them to him as he lowered her onto the bed.

Theodosia parted her lips, let his mouth press harder, deeper, on hers as his sweetness brought an ache to her breasts, a warmth between her legs. Her breath came in a long, low moan.

Benedict broke from her.

Pulse hammering, Theodosia forced herself to look into his eyes. If she saw disinterest, disappointment there, she'd flee. Not a bit of it. He scanned her face as if she were made of pure gold. He traced the line of her face with his fingers, then her neck, the top of her breasts. "I wanted this so much the night at Gilbert's," he murmured. "Your body called to mine the first night I saw you." The glide of his rough, callused skin over her smooth, untouched flesh made her gasp. With a deep sigh, he brought his hand back to her face, stroked her cheek. "But it would be wrong for me to carry on. Wrong as it would have been those other times."

"Let me decide what's wrong. Wrong was me fighting these feelings for years. A wrong, foolish battle. But you don't want me, so—"

"Forcurse it, woman." He grasped for her hand, brought her hand to his chest, to the wide opening of his woolen shirt. "What does this tell you?" Beneath his coarse black hair, his hard muscles, his heart raced in a rapid thud that matched hers.

He did want her, he really did.

He went on. "I know full well what it's like to keep fighting when you're weary of carrying heavy weapons. All you want to do is stop, even if that means the enemy besting you." He gripped her hand tight, kissed it hard. "But that's not you. You never surrender. And neither do the best warriors until the day is done." His arms closed around her, held her tight against him.

*The King, her father. His falsehoods, Mama's falsehoods. Her, Theodosia's, vocation, a lie. Her fresh, raw anger tonight. Anger that had awakened desire, desire for Benedict Palmer. Sinful desire, no matter how much she ached for it. For him.* "The day's not done, is it?"

"No."

She tipped back her head to look at him. His steadfast dark gaze soothed her anger, her pain. But not her desire, not yet. "Then at least let me have my truce." She squirmed hard to burrow down against his chest.

"Theodosia, you should go back to your own bed." His voice came deep, low, as she lay in his warm hold. "We can't risk your being discovered here."

She shook her head, the quiet joy of being held by him enveloping her. "My truce," she said with a yawn, the edges of sleep relaxing her limbs. "A little while."

"I'll wake you soon."

Theodosia yawned again. Then knew no more.

◆  ◆  ◆

Palmer brought his lips to Theodosia's bare shoulder and brushed it once, twice. She slept already, curled against him in his hold. Her ribs rose and fell in a steady, peaceful rhythm as he stroked the curve of her hip with one hand. He'd imagined this, thought about it, hoped for it. And more. Yet he'd passed up the chance at more, like a witless fool. Not a fool. He was used to women of the world, not a nun with vows of virginity. And not one beside herself with anger, with grief. And drink. Taking her while she was in that state would've made him low. He sighed to himself. He probably shouldn't have done any of it, should've packed her back to her own bed. But when she'd sat there, gray eyes raised to his, the pale skin of her naked arms, shoulders. Then the pull of her shift open, with the swell of her smooth white breasts, inviting him, asking him…

He shifted his position to ease the strain in his breeches. He had to stop thinking of her like this. Specially with her the daughter of the King. Did that make her a princess? And if so, was he now first in line for beheading?

He rolled his eyes to himself at his knave's prating. All that mattered was he held the woman he loved. Loved more than any other he'd met. Ever. His Theodosia. With need still hammering in him, he stroked her soft blonde hair away from her smooth cheek. She could never, ever be Laeticia to him, no matter how much she railed at him about it. She would always be Theodosia, his gift from God. But he couldn't allow her to sleep here much longer. She needed to be in her room before her mother woke up. A long journey lay before them tomorrow, when they would set off for France for an audience with King Henry. Her father.

Henry would be bound to send his real wife and daughter away, hide them again from the world. What claim would he, Benedict Palmer, ever have over her?

He knew the answer as well as his own name. None. He was a jobbing knight, a lowborn cur with no power, no influence. Unlike the woman he held in his arms. Fate mocked him, as always. Why couldn't she have been the daughter of a swineherd or a farmer? Then he might have had a chance. But had she been out in the world, a woman as beautiful as she would have been taken years before.

She stirred and muttered in her sleep.

No matter how much he wanted to hold her here, stay here forever, he had to wake her. He kissed the back of her neck, caressed her hip harder, and brought her slowly to wakefulness.

"Mmm." She stirred in his arms. "Let me go, Benedict. I can hardly breathe."

He loosed his hold, though his heart felt it would break. "Time to go back to your room." Let her go? He'd have to. Of course he would. It was his duty. For king and country.

# CHAPTER 25

"You have more color in your cheeks this morning, Sister Theodosia." Brother Edward entered their room and gave an approving nod to Amélie. "Sleep has refreshed her."

"Indeed, Brother," said Amélie from her seat by the window.

Theodosia carried on with tidying her bed. The bed she'd crept back into a few short hours ago. Fearful that Edward might read her embarrassment at her wanton behavior, she was grateful that the distraction helped her to hide her face.

"I too feel the better of it," said Amélie. "I think my soul could finally rest knowing you were safe from those men, my blessed."

Task finished, Theodosia stood up.

Her mother smiled at her with satisfaction.

She smiled in return, but guilt gnawed at her conscience. She doubted if her mother would view her behavior last night as safe. At all.

Edward joined her mother to stand at the window. "God be praised for this morn. We may have no sunlight, but such high, dense clouds calm the seas. We are blessed for our passage to France tonight. It should be easy and swift. The Lord smiles on us, does he not, Sister Theodosia?"

"Yes, Brother."

"Methinks Sir Palmer intends to sleep the day out." Edward's words, pleasant in their delivery, were accompanied by a shrewd glance at Theodosia.

Oh, dear God, he knew. He always knew when she'd sinned, even in her thoughts.

Footsteps sounded from the corridor, and Benedict came in fully dressed, his dark hair silvery-damp with droplets of water. "Morning, all."

His glance didn't linger upon her, for which she was profoundly grateful. If it had, she'd have reddened worse than if she'd spent a day in the fierce summer sun.

"I've wronged you, Palmer," said Edward. "I've just accused you of being a slugabed, yet your appearance tells you've been out and about."

"I went to see if there might be any problems with our sailing tonight," said Benedict. "None. The sea's like a millpond." He rubbed his hands together and blew on them. "Still powerful cold, mind. A bit of sleet fell for a time, but an old sailor told me it wouldn't be for long. He says clear skies and no wind tonight."

Edward grinned broadly. "My thoughts too. Now, Palmer, I suggest we leave these ladies to prepare for our journey and our visit. You, sir, need to come with me to buy you and Sister Theodosia a set of new clothing. You cannot appear before His Grace looking like ragbags."

Benedict's mouth tightened. "I'm afraid I've no means to buy any, Brother Edward. Neither has Theodosia." He gave Theodosia the first eye contact he'd made since he entered.

"No need to worry about such things," said Edward.

"No, indeed," said Amélie. "Brother Edward and I are well looked after by Mother Church. It is only fitting we should provide for you."

"Thank you, Mama, Brother Edward," said Theodosia. "But I am sure this dress can be cleaned and repaired." She looked down at Gwen's chestnut dress, ragged and stained but the only thing she possessed.

"Indeed it can, for there will be no waste." said Amélie. "But you still need something more fitting."

"I agree." Edward picked up his cloak. "Come, Palmer. The sooner we're gone, the sooner we're back."

Benedict followed with no look to Theodosia as he closed the door on his way out.

Her mother gestured to her. "Let me see that dress."

She walked over to her mother and stood in front of her.

Amélie tutted as she leaned forward to examine it in the window's light. "Turn, slowly, so I can see how much there is to do."

As Theodosia did so, she tutted again. "What have you been doing?"

Running. Riding. Climbing. Fighting. How could she explain to Mama what she'd done? "Our journey was at times a great trial, Mama, with many hardships."

Amélie looked up at her daughter's somber tone, and the disapproving lines of her face softened in sympathy. "Of course, my blessed. It must have been dreadful for you. You will be keen to be restored to a godly life."

Theodosia opened her mouth to concur, then closed it again. She merely nodded, which seemed to satisfy her mother.

Amélie rummaged in her pocket and drew out a spool of thread speared through with a long sewing needle. "I only pray I have enough thread."

*Dreadful.* There were many, many times over the last weeks when Theodosia would have agreed wholeheartedly. The terrible deaths she'd witnessed. The sheer, awful terror of being at the hands of Fitzurse and his monstrous companions. But there had been other times that had not been dreadful at all, when being out in the world had been exciting, exhilarating. Riding through snow-topped forests, so beautiful they made her heart ache. The scent of dawn air, unspoiled by humankind. The feel of Quercus's power beneath her as she learned to control him.

And Benedict. The way he moved, the way he ran. The effortless strength of his broad shoulders. The force of his kisses, the gentleness of his caresses, last night…

A knock sounded at the closed door.

"Come in!" said Amélie. "Why, Lae—Theodosia, you started so then. You see? You are still shaken by your suffering."

"I am fine, Mama." Theodosia went to the door, cheeks warm at her straying thoughts. She opened it to Brother Paulus.

The monk held two metal buckets, breathless with his burden. "Excuse me, ladies. I've near finished doing the floors. Your room is the last."

"I'm afraid you will have to excuse us a while longer," called Amélie. "We have sewing to do, and I do not want to lose the daylight. Pray leave us."

The monk's thin lips set in irritation, but he turned to make his way back down the landing to the long flight of stairs. Lines stood out his scrawny hands with the weight of the buckets.

"Why not leave those, Brother?" said Theodosia. "Then you will not have to carry them all the way back up again."

He turned back and came in through the door with slow steps.

Her mother wore the dawn of a frown that neither he nor Theodosia had followed her instructions, but Theodosia paid her no heed. One of the buckets was half full of coarse sand, the other with an amber liquid. She was sure she could not have carried such a burden up the flights of narrow stairs, let alone the slight, elderly brother.

Brother Paulus made for the far corner next to the window.

Her mother could no longer contain herself. "Just leave them, Brother. They will not be in the way."

The monk carried on till he reached the corner, then plunked the buckets down on the floor with a grunt. Hands free of the weight, he rubbed them together. "That one's lye." He nodded to the liquid. "I'm not leaving that anywhere folk could trip on it." He stamped out without waiting for a reply, closing the door with an extravagant slam.

"How rude." Amélie raised her eyebrows as she concentrated on threading her needle. "Men of the church are supposed to recognize what a privilege it is to serve one's fellow man."

"Perhaps it is women he doesn't like to serve, Mama," said Theodosia.

Her mother sniffed. "Most impious." She stood up from her seat. "Now come, please. I shall start with tacking up the hem."

Theodosia went to stand before her, pushing a loose strand of her hair behind her ear as she did so. She caught Benedict's scent from her hand and cast her mother a guilty glance. Mama must surely be able to pick up on it. But no. Her mother bent to her work at the dress hem, exclaiming at the state of it all.

A brisk knock came at the door.

Amélie straightened up with a tut. "Oh, what does that Paulus want now?"

Moving to the door, Theodosia tried to placate her. "I am sure he has good reason." Prepared with a patient smile, she raised the stiff metal hasp and opened the door.

Sir Reginald Fitzurse stood there, drawn sword in hand. "Good day, Sister."

◆　◆　◆

"I've seen a number of shops and stalls that sell clothing." Brother Edward cut a path in front of Palmer through the bustling streets, with people quick to defer to his status as a man of God. "It shouldn't take us long to get there, and they will have wide choice."

"I'm not bothered for myself," said Palmer. "I only need to look passable. But I want to get something special for Theodosia."

"Don't you mean Sister Theodosia?" Edward's question carried disapproval.

"Of course, yes. It's hard to go back to calling her that after weeks of using her name only."

"Then get used to it, Palmer. For a sister is what she is. I must say, it gave me quite a shock to see her in a laywoman's clothes. I hardly recognized her. They made her appear something else, did they not? More worldly, I would say, which worries me greatly."

"God bless you, Brother." A toothless, filthy woman limped up to Edward and pressed something into his hand.

Palmer offered up his own thanks for the woman's interruption. The time he'd spent with Theodosia last night had been a marvel for him, but Brother Edward would have a very different view. It wasn't a view Palmer would want to debate, given the still-tender bruise on his jaw.

Edward raised his hand in a quick blessing, and the woman crossed herself with a deep bow.

As she hurried on her way, Palmer drew alongside Edward. "What was that about?"

"Alms," replied the monk. He opened up his palm to show a tiny, bent coin. "It happens all the time in public. People see my robes, remember their sins, then give for the poor in the hopes it'll help." He put the coin in a leather pouch attached to his belt. "It breaks my heart to take it."

"Then why didn't you give it back?"

"Do you jest, Palmer?"

"No," said Palmer.

"Ah. Then your answer comes from pure ignorance, not rudeness."

Who did this man of the cloth think he was? "With respect to you, Brother—"

"Oh, keep your high horse for going into battle, Palmer. You're a fighting sinner. How could you know?" He stopped Palmer's words with a raised hand. "If I refused that woman's offering, she would be cut to the quick. By giving me what little she has to help the poor, she has absolute faith that her reward will be in Paradise. She is, in effect, paying for eternal life. Who am I to refuse that?"

Palmer gave a shrug of his shoulders. "I'd let the poor have the money. Or let that poor wretch keep hers. Either way, let God decide their eternal fate."

"With such unholy thoughts, I'm sure he's deciding yours, Palmer. Well, here we are." Edward gave a wide gesture to the street before them. "I'm sure we can find what we need without too much trouble."

Shops and stalls, crowded with hats, cloaks, skirts, breeches. Some luxurious, some new. Some that had seen better days but were still serviceable. Palmer would make a quick choice for himself.

Then take his time to choose something beautiful for his beautiful Theodosia.

◆　◆　◆

Theodosia opened her mouth to scream.

The metal sword point bit against her throat in one swift movement.

"One sound," Fitzurse's blue eyes bored into hers, "and I will carve you in twain. Understood?"

She backed into the room, chin tilted back so far she thought her neck might break.

Fitzurse pressed harder with the point of his steel. Any second now, he'd carve through her skin.

"You ruffian. Unhand my daughter!"

She couldn't turn her head to see her mother. "Mama, hush. Please." It came out as a croak from her half-shut lips.

Fitzurse eased the door closed with his free hand and slid the bolt home. "I'd advise you to listen to your daughter, madam. Otherwise I will slay her where she stands."

"He means it, Mama. I promise you."

Terrified whimpers came from Amélie.

"Stay where you are, woman." He flicked his gaze to Amélie, then back to Theodosia again. "Make your way over to your mother. Slowly, and facing me."

She did as he ordered, eyes transfixed on the brutal weapon pushing against her throat. One push, one swing, and her head would be off, just like the wolf's. Or would he crush her skull like Becket's, grind her brains into the floor as Mama watched, then take her too?

He released the sword from her flesh as Amélie grabbed her hand.

"Oh, my blessed."

She met her mother's petrified gaze out of the corner of her eye as they huddled together, as if the closeness of their bodies could provide protection.

"Finally," he said. "The two I seek."

"Leave us be," said Theodosia, mouth dry. "Any minute now, Sir Palmer will be back here. With Brother Edward."

"No, they won't," said Fitzurse. "They're headed off to the opposite end of the docks. I saw them go myself." His lips drew into a smile. "My, my, you're very pale, Sister Theodosia. In fact, you look like you've seen a ghost."

"You could not have survived that rock fall," she said. "I saw you go under."

"The fall le Bret set off?"

She nodded.

He took a step forward and grabbed a handful of her hair. She screamed as he gave it a savage twist.

"You mean the fall that killed le Bret?" His voice didn't match his furious actions. He sounded calm, in control.

"No one would have died if you'd left us in—"

Another vicious twist stopped her words as she screamed again. "I said to be quiet, Theodosia." His blade was back to her throat.

"I'm sorry," she whispered. "I'll be quiet, I promise."

"Good girl." He removed his sword once more and pulled his hand from her hair so roughly that some of the roots pinged out.

Theodosia's quick glance showed Amélie so colorless as to be ready to pass out in terror.

"Now, as I was saying before you so rudely interrupted me, le Bret was killed by the rocks. Most unfortunate. One of them caved his head right in." He turned his sword over and brought the handle to Theodosia's temple. "Right in." He rapped it against her head. Hard.

She caught back a cry with a bite of her lips but would not drop her gaze from his blue-eyed one.

"Very good." Fitzurse nodded in approval. "But the unfortunate le Bret, head cracked like an egg, but no matter, fell in such a way that his lifeless body provided a shield for me from the worst of the fall. Yes, it took me an age to force my way out. Yes, I was badly bruised. But I was very much alive. Now here I am, come to finish my mission."

His words presented a ray of hope. "Your mission? My mother and I know something that bears on your mission. You do not have

E. M. POWELL

all the facts, don't know something of the greatest importance. Listen, please, listen. I beg you." Her words stumbled over each other in her haste to get them out.

"Theodosia, we cannot tell this man what we spoke of earlier." Amélie's voice had the edge of panic.

"We can, of course we can." She clasped her hands, the better to implore Fitzurse. "The murder of Thomas Becket was a terrible act. But we all understand. You were on a mission from King Henry himself to silence the Archbishop because of the secret he held about my mother and me."

"Go on." Fitzurse appeared curious. Interested.

"But that silence, it shouldn't have been murder, it should have been an arrest. Things went wrong, badly wrong, and Thomas died. King Henry has always been our protector, but he'd put faith in Thomas to aid in that protection. It had always worked, hadn't it, Mama?"

"Theodosia. Stop. Now."

She ignored her mother and carried on, Fitzurse still rapt. Still with his sword ready.

"But when Thomas and the King quarreled, Henry wanted us back under his supervision, and control over Thomas to keep his secret."

"What secret would that be?" said Fitzurse.

"Us!" Theodosia burst out. "Mama is Henry's true wife, and I am his daughter. All he wanted was to keep us safe. By a terrible, terrible sequence of events, Thomas is dead, and three of your companions. Can you not see, Sir Fitzurse? We are all on the side of the King."

"Indeed I see," said Fitzurse with a slow nod.

She'd done it. Theodosia took a rasping breath.

"I see," continued Fitzurse, with a cold, suppressed smile, "that you have absolutely no idea what mission my knights and I are on."

"What?" Theodosia's gasp was echoed by her mother.

His look hardened. "You think it's to keep you safe? You, my dear, can think again."

# CHAPTER 26

Palmer hitched his own bundle of newly bought clothing onto one shoulder as he went with Edward through the market. The rough woolen black jerkin and breeches, and white linen undershirt, hadn't cost Edward much, for which Palmer was thankful. He hated to be in debt to anybody, let alone this superior monk. What's more, Edward may well have handed over that woman's coin as part of the payment. Palmer vowed to himself to repay the monk, no matter how long it might take.

Edward stopped before a stall hung with women's clothing and gave them a displeased frown. "Why is it that women have such a desire to dress so brazenly?" he said.

Palmer looked at the items on offer. A couple of green skirts. An embroidered head cover. Yellow woolen stockings. Kirtles in red and orange. "They're not brazen, Brother. They're the usual choices for women."

"Precisely." Edward sniffed. "The usual choice to turn against nature and disport themselves as elaborately as possible. Present as an occasion of sin."

"It's not against nature," said Palmer, annoyed by the monk's ideas. "God creates color and finery wherever you look."

"Such as?"

"Birds. Like peacocks. Colors far brighter and richer than anything we see here."

"Yet which sex has the colors, Palmer? The male. The female is a modest brown, remember. She draws no attention to herself whatsoever." He raised a finger to emphasize his point. "God's message to us is consistent. It's a shame that so many fools and ignorant lost souls refuse to listen to it. You have a lot to learn, my boy."

The last time Palmer had been spoken to like this, his voice had been a lot higher. He itched to put the monk on the floor, but if they didn't move on, they'd be here all day. "We need to press on with Th—Sister Theodosia's clothing."

Edward looked at the stall again and sighed. "If only we had time to get her a new habit made up. But our boat sails tonight. We'll have to make do with something from here."

Palmer looked around at nearby stalls. His eye lit upon a cream overdress, with a matching embroidered belt. Its fine hue reminded him of her pale, pure skin. Perfect. He nudged Edward. "What about that one?"

Edward followed the line of his pointed finger and frowned. "Have you gone mad, Palmer?"

Palmer dropped his hand. "Of course not. But if we can't get her a habit, the least we can do is make sure she looks like the daughter of a king."

"She *is* the daughter of a king," said Edward sternly. "The daughter of the king of heaven, Jesus Christ himself. We will find her something that reflects that status. Now, come. There is nothing suitable here."

Humiliation chewed at Palmer's innards as he followed Edward. The monk had absolute control over this decision because he had the money. All he, Palmer, could do was follow like the penniless churl he was.

Edward stopped before a dank cave of a shop. "Ah. This is more like it."

Palmer's heart sank. A couple of drab, grayish kirtles hung from a hook.

A grimy woman came out from the gloom inside. "Help you, Brother?" she asked rudely.

"May I see that one, mistress?" Edward took the offered dress from the woman and held it up to examine it. "A good choice. It will keep the sister's modesty."

Palmer raised a hand to feel the quality. Made of the roughest cheap wool, it scraped under his touch. "I think we could find better."

"I disagree. Remember, I am paying, not you. This will suit our purposes exactly. How much is it, goodwife?"

The woman looked surprised at such a quick decision and named a sum way over what the ugly thing was worth.

Edward didn't question it, but counted out the correct amount from his coin purse.

The woman pocketed the money, wrapped the kirtle into a bundle, and secured it with some hairy string.

"Good day to you, mistress." Edward took it from her and tucked it under one arm. "Let's be on our way, Palmer." As he walked off through the press of people, the crush parted like he had a mystical power.

"Come back again, Brother." The woman's call rang out as Edward walked away. She jingled the coins in her pocket and gave Palmer a bold stare as he went after Edward.

The old jealousy seethed within Palmer. The monk had status, money, while he, Palmer, his life in jeopardy countless times over these last weeks, had been cast aside like the lowest beggar. He had nothing to give Theodosia—everything would come from the monk.

"The women will wonder where we've got to," said Edward as Palmer joined him. "But I'm sure Sister Theodosia will forgive us when she sees our worthy replacement for her habit."

Palmer doubted that a lot. The habit he'd shredded that first night at the back of the inn had been the finest quality.

Palmer bumped into someone, paused, as Edward walked on. "My pardon."

"God bless you, sir," said a young, tired-sounding voice.

Palmer looked down.

A starved-looking girl held out an armful of simple wooden crucifixes, hung from thin leather loops. Hope lit her dull eyes. "Buy one, sir? They're from the Holy Land itself, made from pieces of the one true cross."

*And I'm John the Baptist.* He took in her rags, her filth. Nearly seventeen years since he'd been in the same state, begging for a crust, a brownish apple. Anything to try and feed his starving mother and sisters, anything to try and keep his dying father alive. "I'm sorry," he said, "but I have no money."

The girl's thin white fingers played over the little crosses as her face crumpled in disappointment. "Oh. I'm sorry to have troubled you, sir."

A faint wail came from beneath her clothing. His heart lurched as a baby's small head burrowed out and bumped against the girl's chest in the vain hope she'd suckle it.

"Hush," she begged it, distracted from Palmer.

A child with a child, living their lives starving on the dockside. That he had Edward's deep purse. But the monk strode many yards ahead on his way back to the hostel.

"No trouble." Palmer rummaged beneath his torn cloak and pulled out his dagger.

He wouldn't have thought it possible, but her face whitened even more.

"Don't fret," he said. He held it out to her, handle first. "Take this for one of your crosses."

She took it from him and examined it closely. "This is a fine weapon, sir." She held it out to give it back to him. "It's worth far more than what I'm selling."

He pushed it to her. "I don't think so. Aren't your crosses made from the one true cross?"

Her mouth lifted in the trace of a smile, dried skin stretched across her peaked cheekbones. "Then God will bless you, sir." She handed him a crucifix. "He truly, truly will."

Palmer gave her a nod and set off on his way. If he stayed here one more moment, he'd give her his new clothes too. He looked at the crudely carved wooden cross in his hand.

Well, he could at least replace Theodosia's cross. But it was the poorest of replacements, a reminder to her that she was a king's daughter and he was a cotter's son. He sighed and tucked the cheap trinket away in his pocket. He was fooling no one, not even himself.

Palmer picked up his pace at Edward's wave and shout. At least he'd see her again soon.

❖  ❖  ❖

Fitzurse's words shot through Theodosia. There was no mix-up, no error. She and Mama were still the quarry.

"Then what foul mission are you on, sir," said Amélie, "that you would threaten the lives of the King's real wife and his daughter?"

Fitzurse ran his fingers along the edge of his sword to test its sharpness.

"At least have the decency to give us a reason before you take our lives," said Theodosia, desperate to waste time, to give Benedict and Edward a chance to return.

Fitzurse adjusted his sword in his grasp. "Very well. To carry out the wishes of the monarch, of course."

Amélie's mouth rounded in shock. "After all these years, Henry has changed his mind—"

"Oh, spare me your ignorance." He gave her a pitying look. "Not Henry, a useless windbag who couldn't organize a group of privy cleaners. I mean Eleanor, the real monarch, who would burn in hell rather than see her four boys bastards. So she sent four knights to do the killing. Four in place of her four sons, and a fifth knight to be her champion."

Theodosia met her mother's stunned expression. The Queen, not the King. An unseen enemy who'd been hunting, circling, hiding her evil intent whilst bringing death to the righteous and poisoning the name of the good. The ground no longer felt solid beneath her feet as a worse fear took hold. "Then Benedict knows all this?"

"Palmer?" Fitzurse's nostrils flared in disdain. "The dog knows nothing."

The room steadied, but Theodosia still couldn't speak.

"I recruited him for his skill with a sword," continued Fitzurse. "He was stupid and greedy enough to follow the money, without asking any awkward questions. Or I thought he was. I need to deal with him once and for all."

Then she would be the cause of Benedict's death too. "You cannot."

Fitzurse gave her a pitying look. "Of course I can. You don't need to worry—the pair of you are first."

"But we've never done the Queen any harm, never claimed our rightful place." Amélie's voice trembled. "Never would. Can't she leave us in peace?"

"Believe me, you'd have been dealt with long ago had she known of your existence," said Fitzurse.

"Then who told her?" said Theodosia, anger pushing aside her fear. "Who betrayed us?"

"Becket's strife with Henry meant a lot of things were said in the heat of the moment." Fitzurse gave his usual smile, which showed his teeth but left his blue eyes glacial pools. "My Eleanor, my queen, told me all about it as we lay abed together."

Two livid spots of color appeared in Amélie's cheeks. "It seems she gets you to do her bidding in more ways than one. You are cuckolding a king, sir."

Fitzurse shrugged. "It won't be for long. The whole country is against Henry, thanks to the murder of Becket in his name. My queen has plenty more surprises waiting for him. By the time she's finished, Henry will lose his head and I will take my rightful place beside her." He brought his sword to Amélie's neck.

*Not Mama, not like this.* "Fitzurse, stop, I beg you!"

Amélie choked out a terrified sob. "I love you with all my heart, my darling girl."

His smile again. "I'm going to name this blade Slayer of the Brides of Christ. First Polesworth, now the pair of you."

*Polesworth. The servant Wilfreda. Her eye.*

Fitzurse drew his sword back, but Theodosia ducked for the bucket next to her in the corner.

He went into his final, murderous swing.

She shot to her feet, flung the amber lye into Fitzurse's face.

His strike tilted up, missed Amélie. He staggered, swept his free hand across his eyes, his face. "Oil?" Then he screamed. The sword flew from his grasp and bounced away on the floor. He pitched to his knees, still screaming, a high-pitched sound from hell itself. "My eyes, my eyes!" His hands covered them, but the skin around them blistered red, as from fire.

Theodosia gestured frantically, silently, to her mother to follow her to the door, but Fitzurse blocked Amélie's path.

He wrenched his hands from his face. Both eyes were blister-filled sockets, watery blood a thick stream from them, skin loose from his nose and mouth. He lashed out with his arms, wild, vicious swipes. "I'll get you, you bitches, I'll get you."

"Run, Mama!"

His hand caught the hem of her mother's dress as she tried to get past.

"No!"

He yanked Amélie to the ground with a powerful pull, hands groping at her, tearing at her clothes. "I'll snap your neck."

"God help me!"

Another loud rip.

His hands clawed for her throat. Another scream from Mama.

Theodosia grabbed the sword from the floor and grasped it with shaking hands, hardly able to lift its weight. "Fitzurse."

Still on his knees, he turned his hideous visage toward the sound of her call.

Theodosia thrust forward, drove it into his stomach, her own rebelling as his innards caved in. She held it firm as he froze, her mother scrambling away with a cry of horror.

An unbearable choking sound formed in his throat. "You bloody, bloody whore." His hands went to the blade. The keen steel sliced first one palm, then the other, as he tried to wrench it free. "Roasting alive's too good for you." Then he went rigid, head flung back, and he fell to the floor at her feet.

She couldn't hold his dead weight. The handle slipped from her sweat-coated palms.

"Oh, Mama. What have I done?" Theodosia's breath came in uncontrollable gasps.

Amélie hastened over to her and gathered her into her arms. "Oh, my blessed, my blessed." She clung to Theodosia like she'd never let go. "I thought we were done for."

A loud knock came from the door.

Both started and held each other's petrified gaze.

Amélie found her voice first. "Who is it?"

"It is I, Edward, with Sir Palmer. You need to unlock the door."

"A moment, Brother," said Amélie, "and we'll let you in. But be warned. Something terrible has happened."

# CHAPTER 27

"What in God's name has taken place here?" Edward's horrified question stopped him short in the half-open doorway.

Behind the monk, Palmer craned to look over Edward's shoulder to the room beyond. The unmistakable meaty, iron-tinged smell of fresh blood met his nostrils. Terror prickled through him. "Edward, what's happened?"

"See for yourself." The monk stepped into the room with Palmer close behind. "God in heaven," continued Edward. "It's Fitzurse."

"Fitzurse?" Palmer's repeating of the name meant nothing. His only care was for Theodosia.

*Thank the Almighty.* She stood in the room, clung to her mother, both women ashen-faced. At their feet lay the still body of Fitzurse. Flat on his back, with his arms flung out on either side, blood pooled beneath him from his injured hands and abdomen. His face was a blistered mess.

Palmer raised his gaze back to Theodosia's. Her gray eyes held the horror of one who has taken a life for the first time.

"Are you all right?" His own feeble question annoyed him.

Theodosia's colorless lips tried to form words, but none emerged.

Amélie replied instead. "We're not harmed, if that's what you mean."

"Thank the Lord for something," said Edward. "But how has Fitzurse come to this terrible end?" He addressed Theodosia. "You told me he'd died."

"I was there, too, Brother," said Palmer. "I would have sworn on my own life he'd been killed."

Theodosia swallowed and managed a low whisper. "He said le Bret's body had protected him in the rock fall. Then he tracked us down, and I murdered him with his sword." Her voice broke, and silent tears streamed down her cheeks.

"But his face?" Edward's mouth drew down in disgust.

Theodosia swallowed again. "He was about to…to cut Mama's head off. I had to stop him. Br-brother Paulus had left a bucket of lye for the floor."

Palmer could kiss her for her quick wits, quick as his—nay, quicker—in this deed. And what a great deed.

But Edward crossed himself, his green eyes stern. "You have committed a mortal sin, Sister. Your soul is in terrible peril. It's vital you make your confession. At once."

She nodded but still held her mother tight. "He was trying to kill us. I had to act."

"Couldn't you have tried to reason with him?" said Edward.

"Even if it meant revealing your secret?" Palmer asked his question of Amélie.

Amélie's mouth hardened into a thin line. "Theodosia tried. Told him all about Henry. But he knew already. He wasn't sent by my Henry. He was sent by that she-wolf he's supposedly married to."

"Eleanor?" said Edward.

"She'd only recently found out about my daughter and me," said Amélie. She locked her gaze on Palmer. "Four knights to act on her behalf, and the fifth as her champion."

Edward gave an angry exclamation and turned to Palmer.

Heat rose in Palmer's face. "You don't think I—"

"No, we don't," said Theodosia. "Fitzurse told us you knew nothing of the true mission."

"What else did he reveal?" said Edward, his eye still on Palmer.

"Only that Eleanor plots against the King," said Amélie, "and is using Becket's murder to turn the whole country against him."

Edward let out a long, long breath. "Then the Lord be praised we'll be with the King soon, and can tell him the truth about the sins and crimes committed in his name." He wrinkled his nose at Fitzurse's corpse. "I'll fetch Brother Paulus. We need this dealt with, and dealt with swiftly." He hurried out to the landing. "Paulus! Get up here at once!"

"Theodosia, you did what had to be done," said Palmer, keen to give her some scrap of comfort. "No one could blame you for your actions."

Theodosia looked down at the body and shuddered in revulsion. "God will. Brother Edward's right. I have committed a mortal sin. I have condemned my soul to eternal damnation." She wrung her hands in anguish. "I am the worst kind of sinner. I have to confess. At once. And penance, I have to do penance. For months. No, years."

"You didn't set out to kill anybody," said Palmer. "You were trying to save your life, your mother's life."

"Sir knight, while my daughter showed great fortitude in defending our lives, she has nonetheless put the gravest of marks on her soul," said Amélie. "She must make her confession as a matter of urgency. Otherwise she runs the risk of condemning her soul to hell for all eternity."

"The only one going to hell is him," said Palmer. The woman's refusal to comfort Theodosia with reason enraged him.

Voices came from the door, cutting him off. He looked around to see Edward enter with Brother Paulus.

The elderly hostel monk stopped dead and crossed himself with determined vigor. "Who is that poor wretch?"

"A violent vagabond," said Edward. "He attacked the two sisters here when Palmer and I were at the market, and during his attack, he fell on his own sword."

Brother Paulus looked over the scene and turned to Edward with raised eyebrows. "I can't see how that happened." He sniffed the air. "For a start, his face is burned to naught with my lye. Moreover, his hands are cut. From trying to pull the sword out." His lips pursed and made his thin face even sharper. "I think you need to call the constable, Brother Edward. I'm not sure the women's account is true."

Palmer read Theodosia and Amélie's panic. He shared their fear. Bringing in the law could cost them their freedom, maybe even their lives.

"There will be no constable, Brother Paulus," said Edward.

"I'm in charge of this establishment," said Paulus, "and I'm saying it's necessary."

Palmer's look went to Edward. Any inquiry, even if they walked free, would mean missing their sailing. They couldn't afford that, now they knew the ferocious Eleanor was behind this terrible chain of events. They needed to get to Henry, and fast. "Let the brother know a bit more," he urged.

"Brother Paulus, under normal circumstances I would agree with you," said Edward. "But believe me, there is more to this than you can possibly imagine." He gestured to Fitzurse. "What you see here is a man who was involved in the murder of the Archbishop of Canterbury."

"Never." Brother Paulus gave the corpse a look of open loathing.

"Indeed he was," said Edward. "I'm afraid I can tell you no more. As you'll appreciate, it's a matter of great delicacy."

"Then I'll see to him," said Paulus, "and he won't be receiving the blessing of hallowed ground neither."

"Thank you, Brother." Edward's relieved glance met Palmer's. "Now, Sir Palmer, can you help the good brother here?"

Palmer nodded. Disposing of Fitzurse for good would be no sorry task for him.

"Sister Theodosia, while they do that, I believe you have a confession to make?" Edward extended a hand to usher her to his room.

"Go, my blessed." Amélie kissed her on the cheek and loosed her hold.

As Palmer bent to assist Paulus in lifting the corpse, Theodosia walked past him to follow Edward, head bowed.

"You acted bravely, Theodosia," said Palmer. "Like a knight."

But she didn't acknowledge him. Instead, she walked out after Edward, shoulders bowed in sorrow, without a backward glance.

◆ ◆ ◆

"*In nomine Patris et Filii et Spiritus Sancti.* Amen." Sat on the side of his bed in his room, Brother Edward crossed himself with the familiar gesture.

Knelt before him on the hard wooden floor, Theodosia also made the sign of the cross. The familiar gesture felt so odd in the strangeness of this place. She joined her hands and bent her head to them. "Bless me, Father, for I have sinned. It has been..." She paused to work it out. So much had happened, it felt like a thousand years. "It has been...been..." Dear God, she didn't know. For the first time ever. "A long time since my last confession."

"What sins have you committed in that time?"

"I have committed mortal sin." She knotted her fingers tightly together.

"Tell me, my child."

May the Lord bless Brother Edward. It mattered not that they held this sacrament in a strange room, away from the church, that she was a sinner. He was there for her useless, sinful soul, to bring her back to God, to everything she was promised to. "I have killed a man. Taken his life from him."

"The gravest of sins, Sister." His voice was steady, measured.

"I know, I know. I'm so sorry, so very, very sorry. I will never, ever commit such a deed again, even if my life were to depend on it."

"Did you intend to commit that sin?"

"No, I did not. It was the only way to protect those I love."

"Those?"

What had she said? A flush stole across her face and neck. Edward would have a perfect view of her embarrassment as she knelt before him in this immodest dress. "My mother."

"And?"

The flush grew warmer.

"Remember, you are talking to God. He sees what's in your heart."

"And Sir Palmer," she whispered.

"You have love for a man? A fighting man, a godless murderer?"

God knew her heart. So did Edward, it seemed. "Yes." She swallowed hard. "And I have another mortal sin to confess."

"Another?" Surprise tinged his voice. "Go on."

"I broke my vow of chastity. With Sir Palmer. Last night."

She tensed, waiting for his livid reaction.

Instead, Edward gave a long sigh. "Oh, my child, my child. You really did turn away from God, didn't you?"

Theodosia risked a glance up.

Edward's face held no anger, only a deep disappointment. "Yes, I did."

"As soon as you did, you allowed the serpent of evil to whisper in your ear, just as he did to Eve in God's own garden."

She nodded, unable to speak with the lump of tears and regret gathered in her throat.

"Tempted you with lust, with Palmer a willing companion in that sin." He sighed once more. "The taking of a man's life the next day, again with wickedness learned from Palmer and his murdering ways. Mortal sin followed by mortal sin." Edward thumped his fist on his knee for emphasis. "Do you not see?"

"I do, Brother, I do. I beg the Almighty for His forgiveness, though I deserve to burn for all eternity through my sinfulness."

"The climb back to holiness will be a steep, rocky one. Your penance has to be severe."

Punishment meant at least hope of redemption—she wasn't completely damned. *Praise God.* "I deserve it. I will atone for what I have done."

Edward sat in silence for a few moments. "Then your penance is this. You will not eat or drink for one entire day a week, from Lauds of one day to Lauds of the next. For the night in between, you will not sleep. You will instead pray the rosary all night. That is for taking the life of Sir Reginald Fitzurse."

"I will try with all my heart, Brother."

"You will do more than try, Sister." His tone hardened. "You will succeed. If there are any failures, you will start afresh the next night, or the next day, until you do succeed. This will be your path from now till the day you die. Do I make myself clear?"

She risked a glance up. Edward's green eyes held no warmth or compassion. But who was she to think she could deserve any? She dropped her head once more, with her resolve to do a perfect penance set like stone.

"And for your fornication with Sir Palmer, for your breaking of one of your sacred vows." Edward bent down to reach for a leather satchel stowed under the bed. "This first."

She looked up to see him stood over her with a flat-bladed razor in his right hand. Her mouth dried. She knew what was coming.

"Your hair," he said. "A reminder of the day you took your vows. When the razor of God removed your unsightly hair, that you would be more pleasing in his presence. Hold still."

Theodosia closed her eyes as she felt the pressure of the metal against her skull. This shouldn't matter, shouldn't matter at all. Her head would soon be concealed beneath her wimple and veil again. But tears pooled in her eyes, streamed down her face.

"Your sorrow reveals your soul's repentance, as it should." Edward worked fast and sure, with each slide of the blade chopping a hefty clump from her skull.

Her shorn hair tickled her face and shoulders, the dry shave a painful rasp. But it was what she deserved. It had to be. Fornication. That's what she'd done. Benedict's strong hands, his lips, his touch…Oh, dear God, here came the impure thoughts again. *Oh, please, Lord. Forgive me.*

"Done," said the monk.

She opened her eyes, the dark-blonde tendrils of her hair fallen around her.

"And the rest of the penance for Sir Palmer."

Her spirit quailed as she met Edward's gaze. There was more?

The monk patted a string-tied bundle. "This will have to suffice before you get your new habit." He sliced open the string with the razor, then held a hand up and murmured a blessing over the folded garment. "This is at least a holy garment now." His mouth turned down in disapproval. "Unlike that immodest frock you wear. Get rid of it, cast it off as you do your sin."

"Yes, Brother," she whispered.

He went to step outside. "All of it, do you hear me? You will wear only the coarse wool I have provided. Your nakedness beneath will be a constant reminder of your lustful use of your body."

Theodosia opened her mouth to appeal her judgment, but Edward cut across her.

"By all that's holy, still you argue. Do as you are told. When you are back with the church, you shall have a fresh habit."

A new sacred garment, one to replace the one Benedict had torn from her. A new beginning.

But Edward went on. "Your new habit will have barbs sewn inside. It will be a constant torment against your flesh, flesh that has sinned so abominably. Lust is the scorpion with the tail of poisonous lechery, so you should suffer its constant sting for the rest of your days."

*No.* She dropped her head into her hands.

"I'm glad to see you start to realize your wrongs. Now get changed." He went out of the door and closed it behind him.

With hands that shook, Theodosia ran her palms over her newly shaven scalp. The prickly sensation sickened her enough; at least she couldn't see how dreadful she must look. Not that it mattered. At all.

She took off Gwen's torn dress with an unexpected grief. Then the shift, the shift she'd undone for Benedict's touch, the petticoats. Her heart wept—she had to stop it.

She unfolded the dress Edward had blessed. Made of wiry wool the color of charcoal, it had the stale, horrid smell of another's unwashed flesh. She took a deep breath and pulled it over her head. It slid down her body, a shapeless, malodorous, uncomfortable sack.

No matter. Her physical adornment, her joy in her body, was in the past. "I am ready, Brother Edward."

The monk reentered and looked her up and down with a nod of unsmiling satisfaction. "Your first step on the journey to redemption." He made his way over to the bed and picked up the discarded linen underskirts. He removed a length with a cut of his razor. "Come here."

She stood before him and he placed the white cloth across her forehead, then looped it round the back of her head. He made quick work of wrapping her head, leaving her face exposed. Her neck followed, with the material tighter and tighter as he secured each layer.

"Can you loosen it a little, Brother?" she said.

He shook his head. "Looseness is what brought you to this sorry state. You need to be brought back, mind, body, and soul." He picked up the length of string from the bed and brought it round her waist. With a low grunt of effort, he secured it tight. "Discipline is never pleasant and at the time may seem painful. But for those trained by it, it yields a harvest of peace."

Theodosia bit her lip. The tight makeshift belt made the wool of her dress dig right into her skin.

Edward picked up the last section of linen and arranged it atop her wimple as a makeshift veil. He took a step back from her to consider his handiwork and smiled at the result. "You are returned as an anchoress, at least to the eye. We have redeemed your body as we will redeem your soul. Now kneel to make your act of contrition and to receive absolution."

Theodosia did as Edward instructed. The discomfort of her garments became even more apparent if she had to move. Her neck had been wrapped so tightly, she could hardly breathe when she tried to bow her head. The wool scraped against the soft skin of her breasts, and she could imagine the sensation when her new habit enfolded her, sewn through with a hundred sharps. But worse than the physical discomfort was the sense of humiliation in how she was dressed, although she was perfectly modest to an outside observer. Oh, Brother Edward had taught her well of the foolishness of bodies and bodily things.

Edward raised his right hand to make the sign of the cross. "One more thing. From now until he leaves us for good, Sir Palmer is to be addressed as Sir Palmer. No more Benedict or any other sinful familiarity. The slide to ruin is speedy, as you have experienced firsthand. There is no other remedy but flight from temptation. And believe me, Palmer is the devil's own instrument of that temptation. He must be dead to you. Do I make myself clear?"

"Yes, Brother."

He began the words of absolution, a sign to Theodosia that God had forgiven her sins.

*No more Benedict.* Of course Brother Edward was right. She'd been wrong. But it didn't stop her heart from breaking.

Edward concluded and nodded for her to start her act of contrition.

"Oh my God, I am heartily sorry..." Sobs broke over her words, and she wept her way through the prayer.

"That's it, my child. Repent before God."

But she wasn't crying to God. She cried for her foolish, impossible, stupid love for a sinful, misguided man. A man that forevermore would have to be a distant stranger to her. She would save her soul, do whatever she had to. Though her heart would shatter as she did so.

# CHAPTER 28

Palmer stood on the dockside in a deserted part of the harbor, keen to dispose of the unsavory load he'd carried with Brother Paulus.

In the pale blue of the dusk sky, the red ball of the sun would soon dip from sight. With the finish of daylight came a chill deep enough to freeze a man to death. Unless they were already dead.

"On three," said Paulus, his thin cheeks ruddy from cold and effort.

"One moment." Palmer adjusted his hold on the body of Reginald Fitzurse, wrapped tight in an old sack. He carried the heavier, shoulder end, while Paulus staggered under the weight of the feet. "Whenever you're ready."

"One, two, three."

Palmer flung the packaged corpse with all his might while Paulus added his strength too.

It broke the surface of the water with a smaller splash than he'd imagined, then started to sink from sight.

"That should see the end of him," said Paulus, "and good riddance, I say."

The object sank from view, with only a few ripples on the quiet surface of the calm black ocean. But on flooded, waterlogged battlefields, the half-rotten bodies of fallen knights would resurface as if rejected by Satan from hell. "What if he floats back up?" said Palmer.

"Not with the stones I secured in there," said Paulus. "They'll keep him on the seafloor for all eternity, while the crabs pick over his every bone."

"No wonder he weighed so much," said Palmer. "I'm guessing the stones were at my end?"

"'Course. What do you take me for?" Paulus set off back along the dockside, and Palmer fell into step beside him.

"Happen you've done this before, eh?" said Palmer.

"What makes you say that?" said Paulus.

"This is a very quiet spot, looks like it hasn't been used for years. And you knew to weigh a body down in water."

"Let's just say you come across all sorts when you're running a dockside hostel," said the monk. "Not all of it good. You have to have ways of dealing with things."

"What kinds of things?" said Palmer, his interest captured by this elderly monk.

Paulus obliged him with a couple of astonishing tales that passed the time of their journey back to the hostel. Night had closed in, and lamps and lanterns lit every window they passed.

Once they arrived, Paulus excused himself on hostel business.

Palmer climbed the stairs to their rooms, a warm glow within him. Eleanor's knights were defeated. The boat was due to sail in an hour or two, and he still had a couple of days left with Theodosia; she'd be finished with Brother Edward by now. He wouldn't let anything spoil this last time—it was far too precious. He knocked on the bedroom door, and Edward's voice replied.

"Come in."

"Good evening, one and all…" Palmer's greeting died on his lips.

Edward, Amélie, and Theodosia knelt in a circle, rosaries in hand. But Theodosia was robed as a nun once more. The gray woolen dress served as a habit, and she wore a linen wimple and veil.

"Have you come to join us in prayer, Palmer?" said Edward, with an irritated frown at being interrupted.

Amélie continued with her quiet recitation of prayer, eyes closed, fingers swift from bead to bead.

Palmer's gaze locked on Theodosia, who dropped her glance in an instant. "No," he said.

"Hardly a surprise," said Edward.

The monk's superior attitude riled him. "I came to ask if you wanted any food. Theodosia?"

She shook her head but didn't look up.

"Come on," he said. "You must have an appetite by now."

"Appetite is no longer an issue," said Edward. "The sister is reining back her consumption. Certainly she will have no more meat."

"I wasn't asking you," said Palmer with force. "I asked her. Now, Theodosia—"

"No, thank you, Sir Palmer."

Her subdued reply brought him up short. "Benedict," he said.

"Sir Palmer, as I am Sister Theodosia," she repeated. "It is proper we should address each other correctly." Her face showed as pale as the confining wimple that enclosed it and her neck. Her red-rimmed eyes showed recent, many tears.

From the corner of his eye, he noted Edward's smug expression.

"I don't know what nonsense Edward's been filling your head with," he said. "But we don't need formal names." He waited for a rebuff from Edward, but none came. Instead, it came from Theodosia.

"True repentance is not nonsense, Sir Palmer," she said. "At least I can say I am a sinner, and can spend my life seeking forgiveness. You too need to do the same, or your soul will be damned for all eternity."

Not a spark of recognition for their time together. None of the last days and nights, where they'd fought so hard for each other. When he'd held her, kissed her, when she'd slept in his arms. "Then I'm just a poor sinner, am I?" he said.

"You are." Cold as ice.

Amélie prayed on, lost in her devotion.

Edward cleared his throat and clinked his metal rosary beads.

"If you're not going to join us, Sir Palmer," said Theodosia, "then perhaps you could leave us in peace until the boat sails."

"Whatever you say, Sister," he said, his voice a low growl of fury. "You can all pray. I need to drink."

He stormed out, with a slam of the door that echoed through the whole building.

◆　◆　◆

Palmer strode down the first narrow alleyway he came to, the lights and noise of an alehouse at its end calling to him. He entered the crowded house, thirst for ale, and lots of it, on his tongue.

The server at the counter filled flagon after flagon, while another man carried them to the packed benches.

Palmer nodded to the server, who filled a vessel in readiness. He put his hand in his pocket to take out his payment. Forcurse it. He hadn't a bean. His pocket held only the little wooden cross he'd traded his dagger for earlier. He turned quickly on his heel and left again. The ale server would be either annoyed or pitying, or both, once he saw Palmer had no money. Palmer couldn't face either reaction, he'd seen too much of it as a boy. He'd rather walk the streets while he waited for the boat, cold as the night was.

His angry pace would keep his blood moving, if nothing else. He made his way along, Theodosia's rejection of him an ache in his chest. Though the hour was late, people still walked here and there, some talking in tongues he didn't recognize, and with faces he'd only ever seen on distant campaigns. Carts rumbled past him, while workers filled and emptied open warehouses by the light of lamps and candles. The world carried on as before, but for him without Theodosia, it might as well have stopped.

As he turned yet another corner, he saw Edward and Amélie pass by, bundles in hand. They must be headed for the boat. He gave a curt wave, but they didn't see him.

Palmer filled his lungs but stopped his call. If they'd set off, Theodosia may well be at the hostel still. It was his last chance to try and speak to her alone.

He soon climbed the stairs of Saint Michael's hostel. The door to the room in which Edward had heard Theodosia's confession stood open, lit with meager candlelight.

With quiet steps, he went to the doorway.

Theodosia crouched on the floor, scooping at something with her hand.

"Brother Edward has you cleaning his floors for him now?"

She shot to her feet, hands closed around whatever she'd collected. "Oh, Ben—Sir Palmer. You did startle me."

"I didn't mean to, Theodosia. Can you forgive me, or should I add it to my list of sins?"

She flushed at his heavy sarcasm. "That is entirely up to you and your conscience, sir knight."

"Benedict." He walked in and stood in front of her. "My name is Benedict. You've used it often enough. You don't have to stop."

"Yes, I do. Like I have to stop speaking to you, being with you. It is part of my penance."

"Penance for what?"

"For Fitzurse's death." Her gray eyes wouldn't hold his gaze. "For my fornication with you."

Palmer snorted. "Fitzurse brought his end on himself. It was what he deserved." He gripped her by the shoulders with both hands and forced her to look at him. "He was going to kill you and your mother. Same as he did to Becket, and God knows how many other innocent souls." He tightened his grip. "He was going to cook you alive, Theodosia. So seek all the forgiveness you want. I think I know God's mind on this judgment."

She squirmed in his grasp. "Unhand me, you blasphemer."

He held her with ease. "Not blasphemy—the truth. And the other truth is, we did not fornicate. We had pleasure. Not sin. And it was what you wanted, asked me for, and it was my deepest happiness to share it with you. You said yourself your vocation was a lie. But here you are, back in the clothing of that lie."

"It was Satan telling me it was a lie, trying to get me to stray from the path to heaven. He nearly succeeded, made me believe I was something I am not, and he used you to do it."

"Let me guess: Brother Edward told you that? The smug, arrogant—"

"He did in confession, which means he is the voice of God."

"He's twisted your mind."

"He has shown me the truth." She strained to break his hold again. "It is your soul that is filled with poison, Sir Palmer. I will pray for it, pray that you can be saved. I shall do that to add to my penance."

"I don't want to be saved. I want you to have the life you deserve."

"It is the life of a servant of God, Sir Palmer." Her brow creased in anguish. "Now, I beg you, let me go. Every moment you have your hands on me is another sin for me to repent."

"There's no sin in my touch." He held her tighter, shook her to hammer home his words. "Why can't you listen to me?"

"Benedict, you're hurting me!"

He froze, breathing hard, her cry pulling him back to sense.

"Let me go, Sir Palmer." The extra meaning her words carried was plain as day.

Palmer dropped his hold. Sadness and loss waged war with the anger inside him. "I'll go to my grave swearing you're making the wrong decision. You can repent without burying yourself away in the church for the rest of your life. And it plagues me to think that I'm part of the reason you would want to do that." He rummaged in his pocket and pulled out the little cross. "I know it's a poor swap for the cross I took from you—it was all I could manage. But I give it to you as I gave you my heart: with every good wish, and never to cause you ill, never to be the mark of sin on your soul."

"Then Sir Palmer, I thank you for your gracious gesture." She reached to take it in a quick movement, hand curled over what she already held.

"What's that in your hands?" he said.

"It is nothing." She went bright pink and shoved the cross into her pocket.

He grabbed her other fist and pried it open, ignoring her protests. Clumps of her soft, beautiful hair lay on her open palm.

"What have you done?" He looked at her aghast.

"I said, it is nothing."

"Stop lying, Theodosia. And if you don't tell me the truth, I'll rip that cursed wimple right off your head, so I can see for myself."

Her hands shot to protect her headdress, and her shorn hair scattered. "Brother Edward did it. It is part of my penance. To remind me of my broken vows."

Rage surged in Palmer's chest. "I'll kill him."

322

"You cannot say anything. I should not even be talking to you anymore."

"You said part of your penance. What else?"

"That is between me and my confessor." She bent to the floor once more to pick up her fallen hair.

As she did so, her woolen dress slipped to one side on her right shoulder to reveal soft white skin reddened by the coarse material. The sight hit Palmer like a punch to his guts. "He's got you to mortify your flesh, hasn't he?"

"It is what I deserve." She stood up once more and readjusted her dress without meeting his eye.

"No, it isn't. The man's a bully. This isn't penance. This is an abomination. It has to stop. At once."

"No, Sir Palmer."

Her firm tone took him aback.

"My body, while shared with you for one time of madness, is mine and God's. What I do with it is between me and Him. None of it is your concern. Do I make myself clear?"

"You do. But I refuse to accept it."

Heavy footsteps sounded from the stairwell, and Edward's voice floated up. "Are you ready, Sister?"

Dread showed in her face. "Please do not make it worse. Please."

He couldn't do it. He turned to address Edward as the monk appeared in the doorway.

Edward's glance flew from one to the other. "Sister, I can't believe you consort with this man—"

"Leave her alone, Edward. I came back to meet you here and found you gone. The sister here only told me you'd walked with Sister Amélie to the boat. Nothing untoward has taken place." *Except what you've done to my Theodosia, you filthy devil.* If it wouldn't have made things worse for her, he'd have punched Edward's lights out there and then.

"I'm very relieved to hear it," said Edward. "Now, make haste in gathering your things. We need to leave."

"Yes, Brother." Theodosia kept her head bowed, meek.

Palmer straightened and challenged the monk with his gaze. "I have no need to gather anything. All I have are the clothes that I stand up in. Which I will pay you back for," he added, before Edward could respond.

"Then God be praised for traveling light," said Theodosia.

Edward's attention switched to her. "Indeed. If we're ready, let's set our faces for France."

France. Henry. Palmer vowed to make it his business to advise the King of Edward's sickening treatment of Theodosia. He, Palmer, might have lost her forever to the church. To stomach that was bad enough. But allow another man to use her for his own ends? Never.

# CHAPTER 29

Stood on the rear deck of the heavily laden *Stella Maris*, Theodosia watched the port of Southampton recede into the distance. Its noise and business had faded to a sprinkle of lights against the darkness of the mainland. Above, the crescent moon sat in a sky frosted with a million stars.

A couple of yards away, the captain, Jacob Donne, stood at the tiller, absorbed in steering his craft. The other three crew members had gone below as soon as the ship had caught the tide and was under way.

"You should go below, Sister," said Donne. "It's powerful cold up here after a while."

"I should like to stay for a little while longer if I may." She gestured to the dark water. "I never realized the sea was this big." She felt foolish as she said it, but Donne nodded in acknowledgment.

"Not seen it before?" he said.

"No, and I never will again."

"Then make the most of it. Mind, what you see here might look big, but it's still the harbor. Once we get out onto the open water, 'tis like there's no end to it."

Her mother emerged from the ladder that led below and climbed out with care.

"Oh, my goodness." Amélie tottered to join Theodosia and clutched for the rounded wooden rail. "It's so unsteady."

"It's fine, Mama. There is scarcely a movement."

"Then you must get your sea legs from your father," said Amélie. "Believe me, there's plenty moving."

Theodosia drew in a deep, slow breath through her nostrils. The fresh, salty sea air, so different out here compared with the rank smells of the port, came as sheer delight. It was clean, pure. Like she would be.

"We have a meal waiting below," said Amélie. "Brother Edward sent me up to fetch you."

Theodosia tore her gaze from the ebony ocean and the mirrored moon with reluctance. Were she given a choice, she would stay up here all night. But it wasn't only the appeal of the sea keeping her from her meal. When she went below, she would have to face Benedict, be in his company, yet remain utterly aloof. It seemed an impossible task. When she'd rejected him in the hostel, his dark eyes had blazed with anger. But she'd also seen hurt, pain, bewilderment. If she could have, she would have taken him in her arms, consoled him, comforted him. She could not. She'd chosen her path, made her promises to God. Benedict would have to heal alone, and, Lord help her, so would she.

Her mother staggered and gasped as she crossed the deck. Close behind, the sway of the ship beneath Theodosia's feet felt completely natural. Her body seemed to know how to handle the pitch and roll as if by instinct. Maybe this did come from her father.

She waited as her mother climbed below, then swung around to follow. Her father. The King. She'd see him in a couple of days. Her heart tripped faster. She wasn't sure which made her more nervous, Henry's being her sovereign or being the father she'd never known.

The smell of boiled fish wafted from a small room to her left. Her mother entered first, and she followed.

Benedict and Edward were already seated in heavy silence, elbows propped on the table. An oil lamp suspended from a ceiling hook swung gently above them and sent shadows to and fro across their faces.

"At last. Civil company." Benedict raised a full goblet to them. "Good evening to you, Sisters."

"Good evening," said Amélie with a final lurch for her seat.

Theodosia frowned to herself as she took her place. Both men were drinking, a large stone wine bottle at each of their elbows. But Benedict must have consumed a great deal. His face shone with sweat, and he had a foolish, set look on his face. He glanced at her briefly, then looked away, his expression unaltered.

Edward too had a goblet of wine but seemed well in control of himself.

A large covered pottery dish sat on the table, along with four small bread trenchers. Edward reached forward and removed the lid, releasing a cloud of fishy steam that he savored with a long sniff. "Now let us say our grace, because the Lord needs to be thanked for such a wonderful feast."

Once thanks had been made, he served each person in turn.

Theodosia accepted hers with a bowed head, keen to avoid Benedict's gaze. The plain boiled fillet of mullet sat grayish and plain on the trencher, clear liquid leaking from it. She set to eating the unappetizing repast. While she was hungry, she was also in a state of utter discomfort. She longed to be able to shed her overtight wimple and belt and rid herself of the plaguing wool dress.

"It is indeed godly, plain food," said Edward. "Surprising when you think what an unholy place Southampton is. I've never seen so many strange folk."

"Happen you look strange to them," came Benedict's sharp response.

Theodosia raised her gaze.

Brother Edward's green eyes narrowed at Benedict, and Theodosia tensed for his reply.

"Well, it was certainly strange to us, Sir Palmer," Amélie intervened quickly. "But you must have seen many places like it."

"More than I'd ever want, Sister Amélie."

Theodosia relaxed a mite as Benedict responded to her mother with courtesy.

He took a long drink before he continued. "As a working knight, I've had to go wherever I'd be paid. I've been where the snow and ice could bury a man. Where the sun's so fierce, it's burned the people black."

"You mean like a Saracen?" said her mother, eyes wide.

"No, much, much darker," he said.

She shuddered. "Poor things."

"They seemed happy enough," he said. "But they spoke in strange tongues, so it was impossible to know."

"Then they'll be heathens," said Edward. "Happy in this world, maybe, but in the fires of hell for all eternity." He too took a long drink. "Burned even more, with no end to it."

Benedict smacked his beaker down onto the tabletop. "You know what's in every man's heart, do you? How God will judge them?"

"I know that only the godly can be saved. No one else will." Edward shot him a glance. "Until you mend your ways and repent, that means you too, Palmer."

"Then I'll see out eternity with the Saracens and the savages. I'd prefer their company to yours any day."

Edward looked thoroughly shocked, but Benedict laughed aloud as he took another drink. "Faith, Edward, you're an easy man to rile." His dark eyes crinkled at the edges, as they always did when he smiled, and he pushed back his unruly dark hair. In this light, his teeth glowed white against the shadows of his weathered skin.

A sudden wave of utter longing swept over Theodosia. Benedict was like the sea: wild, untamed. A force of nature. Edward was the direct opposite. Calm, controlled, contained. Like she was once and had to be again. Mortified at her flash of desire, she stabbed at her bland fish with her eating knife. Her choice was made, and she should rejoice in her soul that she'd chosen wisely.

"I'm not even going to answer such fool's talk," said Edward. "How is your food, Sisters?"

"Most welcome," said Amélie. "Well prepared, and a modest amount, with no inflaming herbs."

Theodosia nodded her agreement, though the stuff was foul.

"As we are well prepared," said Edward. "We will be with the King the day after tomorrow. I've already written the account of Becket's murder to present to him."

"I pray it will be kindly received," said Amélie. "But, knowing Henry, there will be no fear of that."

"There's never a fear of truth," said Edward. "God will indeed be on our side." He refilled his goblet and leaned to top up Benedict's once more.

"When did you write it, Brother Edward?" said Theodosia, keen to distract herself from her treacherous thoughts.

"Over the last ten days," said Edward. "I did it as quickly as possible. I think the soul of my lord Becket himself guided my hand."

Theodosia considered his words. "You have given a correct account of Sir Palmer's involvement?"

Edward paused, spoon halfway to his mouth. "Are you questioning my competence with the quill, Sister?"

"No, not at all." All eyes were on her and flustered her. "Only that Sir Palmer's part…changed as events unfolded."

"You don't need to worry on Sir Palmer's account," said Edward with irritation. "I've spent many hours compiling it."

She opened her mouth to question again. "But—"

"Oh, Theodosia, give the man his due," said Benedict, words slurred around the edges from drink. "He might not be able to use a sword, but he's an expert at wielding a quill." He made a crude mime with a cramped hand, eyes in an exaggerated squint.

"Thank you, Palmer. I think." Edward raised a hand. "And remember, she's Sister Theodosia."

"My apologies, Brother." Benedict bowed in exaggerated contrition. "You'll have to forgive me now. You'll be worn out from it."

Edward shook his head. "Your blasphemy knows no bounds. You're lucky you have the likes of me to pray for your soul."

"And you, my friend, are lucky to have sinners like me to pray for. Keeps you busy."

"Never a truer word." Edward raised his goblet to Benedict and sipped.

"I think, gentlemen, we will retire soon. Thank you for this excellent meal," said Amélie. "We will leave you to your wine." Her knowing glance to Theodosia encouraged her to eat up, but she'd already finished.

Theodosia nodded and rose to her feet along with her mother. She couldn't wait to leave the knight's presence.

"Good night, gentlemen." Amélie swayed in the cabin's roll, and Theodosia took her arm to steady her.

"Good night, Sister Amélie." The reply came from both men.

"God's rest to you both." Theodosia escorted her mother from the cabin, with a brief, polite smile for Edward and Benedict.

"And you, Sister Theodosia," replied Edward.

Benedict looked straight ahead, as if he'd heard nothing, seen nothing.

Theodosia helped her mother along, fighting down her anger at his slight, at his crude drunkenness. It shouldn't matter; he would soon be out of her life forever. Then why did she care so much?

◆ ◆ ◆

"Good night, my blessed." Amélie yawned as she settled under the rough cover. "It feels strange to be in a bed that sways, but I know I'll sleep well. My very bones feel tired tonight."

"I know what you mean, Mama." Theodosia bent low to kiss her mother on the cheek. She straightened with care so as not to bump her head on the low roof of their tiny quarters belowdecks. Only a step away in the cramped space, her own hammock beckoned, promising blessed respite from her regret, her sorrow. Suspended just high enough to clear the floor, it too had a single cover. "I'll do the candle now."

"Leave it till you've undressed." Sleep softened Amélie's voice.

"No, I can manage." Theodosia blew out the tiny flame. She didn't want her mother to see her raw flesh and shaven head, have to offer any more explanations. This was between her and God.

The darkness was almost complete and brought the regular movement of the ship under her feet to greater prominence. Though cold and damp, the air smelled stale with the scents of hundreds of voyages and cargoes.

Theodosia raised her hands to her veil and slipped it off. Her wimple proved far more difficult. Her fingers found the tucks, the knots, and eased them loose with difficulty. Finally, it came undone and she pulled it free. She moved her head from side to side and eased out the muscles in her neck and shoulders. When she replaced the wimple in the morning, she doubted if she'd be able to get it as tight as Edward had. Still, she'd have to try.

Now for the belt. Again, she used her fingers to try the knot this way and that. Oh, why wouldn't it loosen? Not being able to see made it impossible. She pulled at it, picked at it, pushed the knot against itself. It wouldn't budge. Perhaps her mother could help. But Amélie had drifted off to sleep, her breaths long and regular.

Theodosia yanked at the rope in frustration, rubbed her fingers and palms raw as she fought to free it. It was no good. Her heart sank at the idea of trying to sleep in this scratchy dress, with its tight cord belt intruding into her flesh all night. That no doubt had been Edward's intention. But she needed rest, at least for now, at least until she met the King. She tugged again. If only she had something to cut it with, but she'd nothing. She brought her hands to the back of her head for a last stretch before she climbed into bed, her shorn hair horrid under her touch. *Hold.* Edward had a razor.

She dropped her hands. Why not borrow that? If the monk and Benedict were still drinking, she could be in and out of Edward's sleeping area in a minute or two. He would never know, and she would get some rest. She turned to make her way back through the dark, damp confines belowdecks.

As they'd come aboard, the captain had directed Edward to the front of the boat. It should be easy enough to find. As she crept out of her sleeping quarters, the narrow passageway held some light from where Edward and Benedict sat. She could hear Edward's authoritative tones as he held forth yet again. Benedict made an incoherent interjection.

They were still safely occupied. She went forward, past the piles of sacks that made up some of the ship's cargo. The full hold was stuffy and airless as she went through, feeling her way in the dim light. A small, closed door showed at the end of one of the high piles of goods. That must be it. She went to it and opened it with care, lest someone else used it. The tiny room was deserted but lit with a covered lamp. It held a narrow bed, with a straw mattress and clean linen. Far finer quarters than those she and her mother had—it must be the captain's. She turned to go, embarrassed at having intruded.

She spotted a neatly folded cloak atop a small chest. Brother Edward's. So he had this fine room to sleep in. Better he should have offered this to Mama. Never mind. She crossed to his bundle of possessions and found his razor tucked into a leather pouch. The tiresome string around her waist fell away in one cut. She winced as she put her hand to her flesh. Relieving the pressure made for a different type of pain. As she put the string in her pocket, her fingers met the little wooden cross Benedict had given her. She pulled it out and looked at it with a fresh pang of regret. For all his faults, he had a good heart, was a good man. The kind of man she would have been blessed to find, had that been her path. Oh, here it came again: the temptation that every thought of Benedict brought. Such thoughts were dangerous—she had to stop. She put the cross back in her pocket, replaced Edward's blade, and tidied his bundle. Now she could go and sleep.

As she turned to go, her eye lit on a rolled scroll, fastened with a length of thin red silk. Edward's account of the murder for the King. Everything neat and in order, as she would expect of him. She thought back to the conversation at dinner. He would have told the truth about Benedict, of course he would. But Benedict was one of the group of knights who carried out the murder. What if Henry were to punish Benedict for the crime, despite his subsequent bravery, despite his saving her life over and over?

She should take a quick look, see how Edward had given his account. If Benedict was going to put himself at risk by appearing before the King, then she should at least warn him. He may have been an occasion of sin to her, but she owed him that much. Then it would be his decision, a decision made with all the facts.

The silk tie slid easily from the new vellum, and the document unrolled in her hands. Edward's neat script lay before her, small and precise as ever, headed with the slightly larger *The Murder of Thomas Becket, Archbishop of Canterbury.*

He must have described every detail, as the lengthy account covered the entirety of the document.

She bent her head to read it.

*The murderers were named Sir Reginald Fitzurse, Sir Hugh de Morville, Sir William de Tracy, and Sir Richard le Bret. They arrived at the holy cathedral of Canterbury and hid their weapons under a sycamore tree beside it.*

Theodosia frowned. Where was Benedict's name? Ignorant of their purpose though he was, he was part of the group. As for hiding their weapons, the knights had come to the door of Canterbury fully armed. She'd seen them, watched as they'd murdered a brother in cold blood. Puzzled, she scanned down the text, the script recording the retrieval of the weapons. Then:

*They broke into the sanctity of Canterbury Cathedral and sought out the lord Becket with rapid pace. Swords drawn, these four brought dread to the holy place as they shouted, "Where is Thomas Becket, traitor of the King?"*

Four? Still no Benedict, who'd made five. It didn't make sense.

*The monks were giving glory to God at Vespers and begged the lord Becket that they would protect him with their lives. Yet he sent them away, like Jesus with his disciples on the eve of His crucifixion. Only one brother stayed to face the four evildoers, Brother Edward Grim, in whose hand this is written. Their cries became louder, but the lord Becket stood firm and steadfast upon the altar, with Brother Edward at his side. When they came through the door, the lord Becket showed no fear, without a drop in gaze or a tremble to his tone. He said, "I am a servant of God. Why do you seek me?"*

*The four rushed to the steps and brandished their hideous weapons aloft. "You have excommunicated the good from the church and sent yet more away. The King demands you return them to the fold."*

Theodosia stared at the words as she willed them to form into something else. She read them again. Of course they didn't alter. Didn't alter to mention Benedict. Or her. Or the truth of what was said and done that evening. Sweat broke out all over her body as she fought down a desire to fling the thing from her grasp and go and find Benedict. Instead, she forced herself to read on. She had to read it all. She had to know the truth.

# CHAPTER 30

Palmer watched Edward pour yet another measure of wine into his drinking vessel. "I don't think I should be having any more, Brother." His words made bare sense as he fought to get them out.

The monk smiled. "What's the harm, Palmer, what's the harm?" He raised his own glass. "God created grapes for a reason, did he not?"

Palmer nodded. It was easier than speech, but not much. This wine kicked like an enraged stallion. He'd had a skinful, but nothing he couldn't normally handle. Yet he could hardly feel his hands and feet, and his mouth and tongue stung in a strange way. He really didn't want any more, but the monk seemed keen to drink on. And talk. Forcurse him, the man could talk.

"Nature is God's own bounty, Palmer, remember that." Edward embarked on a lengthy speech about God's provisions and God's larder.

Palmer fixed his gaze on him, but his eyelids drooped. He must be falling asleep, nay, dreaming.

Edward's features changed shape, his eyes looking big, then small. His face turned pale blue.

With a hard shake of his head, Palmer pulled himself upright in his seat.

Edward's appearance became normal again. A huge yawn broke from Palmer, and he apologized as clearly as the wine would allow.

The monk gave a dismissive wave. "No need for apologies. Now drink up, man." He held up Palmer's bottle. "There's still some more left in this."

◆　◆　◆

*And the lord Becket shall receive his reward amongst the angels and the saints, in the glory of God forever. Amen. This by mine own hand, Brother Edward Grim, Canterbury, the Year of Our Lord 1170.*

Theodosia lowered the scroll with shaking hands. Lies, deception, untruth. Edward had written a fictitious account of the terrible events in the cathedral. One that put the blame for Thomas's murder fairly and squarely at Henry's door. According to this awful fabrication, she and Benedict simply didn't exist. Wiped from history. Which was what Eleanor had sent the knights to do. Remove Theodosia and her mother for good.

Fitzurse's words came back to her with a terrible clarity: "*Eleanor sent four knights to do the killing. Four in place of her four sons, and a fifth knight to be her champion.*"

The fifth knight was Brother Edward Grim. Not Benedict, an honorable man caught up in terrible circumstances.

She folded up the document and shoved it in her pocket. She had to get out of here, get this scroll out of here. Tell Benedict. He'd know what to do. He always did. Sick with fright, she opened the door.

All seemed as before. With a long breath of relief, she started back along the passageway. The wooden planks beneath her feet groaned and squeaked as if demons were in them, with the sway of the craft more pronounced. They must be well out to sea by now. She put a hand out to the pile of sacks to steady herself.

"Then sleep well, Sir Palmer."

337

Terror stabbed her heart. Edward. On his way to his room, with her like a rat in a trap, his scroll in her pocket. She looked around frantically. The only place for concealment was a narrow gap between two piles of sacks. She squeezed right into it, hardly able to breathe. She hoisted her dress up to cover her head and shoulders, and pulled her hands inside it also. She could still see through the coarse fibers of the fabric. Not a second too late.

Edward approached, with a grunt and a stumble from the sea's pitch. His pale hand landed right next to her as he grasped a sack for purchase. His eyes seemed to meet hers through thick weaved cloth. He paused for a moment, and her knees almost gave way. He'd seen her. But no. He fumbled for another handhold and went on his way, unnoticing of her, a shadow amongst shadows.

She had to make haste. He'd see his scroll was gone in a matter of moments. Easing herself from her hiding place, she hurried back to where they'd eaten. Empty. Wine stained the tabletop, red as spilled blood. Edward had wished Benedict goodnight. But she didn't know where Benedict slept. The captain? He could tell her. She made her way to a steep ladder that led up to the decks. With her skirt hoisted out of the way, she started to climb up, her hands slippery with urgent sweat.

A hand closed around her ankle and tried to yank her from the rungs. "Where are you going in such a hurry, Sister?"

She looked down into the blazing green eyes of Edward Grim. One pale hand locked around her right ankle. The other held his razor. He brought it to the flesh of her inner thigh.

"Please. Don't." Her voice wouldn't go beyond a whisper.

"If you do as you're told," he said, "you might survive. Climb up to the deck. Slowly. I'll be right behind you with this efficient blade. We don't want any accidents, do we?"

Theodosia went up, hand over hand. *Please don't let me fall. Please.* The cold night air met her and she hauled herself out onto the bow deck, her breath in rapid gasps. She looked around to see if she could signal to Donne, but the cargo of piles of hewn wood made a high barrier between the fore and aft decks. She was alone. Trapped.

Edward emerged right behind her, his blade a dull gleam in the weak moonlight.

"You can harm me if you want," she said. "But Benedict will find you out, you mark my words."

"Palmer?" Edward gave a snort of laughter. "He's already halfway to hell, if not already there."

Her stomach dropped. "What you mean?"

"I've been filling the fool up with poisoned wine all night. He'll be in a sleep he'll never wake up from."

Shock threatened to rob her of sense. "You....monster."

"Only doing my duty," said Edward. "A lesson you never could learn, you hussy. Now, where is my manuscript?"

◆  ◆  ◆

Palmer leaned over the stern of the ship and vomited his belly empty. Again, he retched. And again. And again.

"Too much wine, sir knight?" Captain Donne's question wasn't overloaded with sympathy.

Palmer shook his head as he wiped his mouth on his sleeve. "A lot of wine, yes. But it's the ocean under my feet. It gets in my head and sends my ears spinning till I'm sick. Always has done." He bent over to retch into the ocean again, then gave the captain a rueful grin. "Always will do, I suppose."

Donne considered him for a moment. "Well, hurling your guts up has done you some good. You were pale as a ghost when you came up here."

"Come to think of it, I do feel better," said Palmer. "I only wish there was an easier way of settling my stomach." He grimaced. "That fish I had for supper didn't taste half as good on the way up as it did on the way down."

"Shame it got wasted," said Donne. "I had to stretch it far enough as it was. Talk about the loaves and the fishes. Maybe the monk worked another miracle."

Palmer looked over the side to where the gentle deep-sea swell moved beneath them. He might be sick again. He hoped not. "How do you mean?" he asked, scarcely listening.

"I only had provisions for two passengers. Not four."

Churning guts forgotten, Palmer focused his full attention on Donne. "Two?"

"Aye," said Donne. "Edward and his usual companion, I take 'em back and forward every now and then, between here and France. They pay well, no trouble, keep themselves to themselves. Wish all folk were like that."

"Who's his companion?"

"Posh bloke, a knight." Donne pulled a sheet in. "Blue eyes, his name'll come to me in a—"

"Fitzurse?"

"That's the one. Instead of him, I get you and two nuns." The captain rolled his eyes. "At least I've been paid well. Oi! Where are you going so quick?"

Palmer paused at the top of the aft ladder. "I need to find Edward. Fast. Where's his cabin?"

◆　◆　◆

Theodosia backed away from Edward until she hit the deck rail.

"I asked you once," he said. "Where is my manuscript?"

"You shall have it when you promise, nay, swear, that you'll not harm my mother." A feeble threat, but all she had.

"Your fates are not in my hands, Sister," he said. "Eleanor herself ordered you both gone. How could I go against her?"

"By being a man of compassion. A man of God."

"A man of God? I've worn this cursed cassock for over two decades, the better to win Becket's trust. He kept his counsel well, I'll give him that. I never understood why he was so protective of you, of Amélie. It was only a few months ago that he finally slipped up, made a mistake. I found reference to you and your mother in an old letter from the King. Becket left it among some other papers he'd been reading as part of his ongoing feud." Edward smiled at the recollection. "As soon as I told my queen what I had found, you were as good as dead. She dispatched Sir Reginald Fitzurse to do his worst."

Theodosia drew her chin up. "But he did not end well, did he?"

Edward was on her in an instant, grabbing a handful of her dress. "Do you think you can get the better of me, like you did with him?" His breath was hot on her cheek as he switched his hold to her neck. "When I met him at the quays, sent him to the hostel, I thought I was rid of you for good."

She tried to choke out a plea.

"But you carried on like that dullard Palmer. Now I have to do it."

"Then you'll never find your manuscript." She rasped her words.

"Of course I will. It's poking out of your pocket. And even if I lost it, it wouldn't be the end of the world. I'd just write another one. Not the best use of my time, but not the worst." His grip tightened. "I'll have plenty of time, once Eleanor gets rid of Henry and makes me her new Archbishop of Canterbury. A far better one than Thomas Becket."

"Let her go, Edward."

The monk wheeled round and gasped in surprise. But he didn't loosen his grip.

Theodosia looked up.

Benedict stood atop the pile of wooden planks that formed the deck cargo.

She tried to call to him, to warn him of the blade. But the monk squeezed her neck tighter.

"Hell too hot for you, Palmer?" said Edward.

"Not a bit," said Benedict. He jumped from the planks and landed a few strides away. "I came to take you with me. Now, I said let her go."

"Don't presume to issue orders to me," said Edward. He raised the blade to Theodosia's eye level. "I shall slit her throat first, then yours. You can watch each other bleed to death." He readjusted his grip on the blade.

"Theodosia!"

Her glance flew to Benedict as the monk paused, distracted.

"Your reading?" said Benedict.

She understood.

"Babbling oaf." Edward pulled his hand back for his slash.

Theodosia's hand went to the thick roll of vellum in her pocket. She whipped it out and parried Edward's razor blow. The sharp metal stuck in the soft animal skin.

With a shout of rage, Edward hauled it free. His grip on her slackened for an instant, and she dropped to the deck, free.

Coughing hard, she clambered toward Benedict as Edward grabbed for her ankle.

The knight flew forward to crash into Edward with all his strength.

Edward loosed his hold on her as he did his weapon. The razor flew from his hand and slid into a darkened corner.

"You peasant!" Edward struck Benedict in the face with a bent elbow.

Benedict grunted in pain but didn't let go of Edward. As both men rolled across the deck, each tried to best the other with a punch, a kick, their strength matched.

Theodosia tried to get to the corner where the weapon lay but couldn't get past their thrashing bodies. She climbed up onto the planks of wood. She stood up and peered toward the stern to see if she could see Donne. "Captain! I need your help! Please!"

No reply.

A roar of pain came from Benedict. To her horror, he stood facing Edward, his hand held to the side of his face. Blood flooded past his palm.

Edward circled him, razor in hand.

"Throw me that rope, Theodosia. Now."

She responded to Benedict's curt order. He caught it in one hand, eyes still on Edward.

"Are you going to try and hang me, fool?" Edward smirked at the looped knot at the end of the rope.

"Not at all." Benedict slipped the loop over one wrist. He pulled it tight as he broke into a run and shoulder-charged Edward. His speeding bulk sent them both over the side and into the blackness of the ocean.

"Man overboard!" She screamed it at the top of her lungs, unable to believe what she'd witnessed. She scrambled across the woodpile, shouting the words over and over.

"Who's over?"

God be praised. A male shout. Donne still stood by the tiller, lamp in hand.

"Benedict and Edward. Edward tried to kill me."

"Saints preserve us." Donne grabbed a short length of rope and rang the ship's bell with all his might.

As if summoned by magic, the other crew members emerged from the hatch, newly disturbed from sleep, pulling shirts over their heads.

"Theodosia? What's happening?" Mama appeared too, her face pale in the moonlight. "And what in the name of the Lord have you done to your hair?"

Ignoring her mother, she climbed across the wood and down the other side to Captain Donne. "Benedict and Edward, they're in the water. We have to save Benedict, we have to."

Donne rapped out a series of orders, and one crewman started to pull in the sail, slow the boat, turn it.

The other peered out over the ocean. "I think I see 'em, Cap'n."

Theodosia looked to where he pointed. The distance made her feel suddenly faint. "How have we come so far?" she said to Donne. "Surely the ship doesn't sail so quickly."

"It goes apace and the tide's under us," he said. He wrenched the tiller round to change course.

Another shout from the crewman. "I've found a rope!"

She wrenched at Donne's sleeve. "Benedict tied himself on before he pushed Edward in. They're still attached. Pull them in!"

"Why would Sir Palmer do such a wicked thing?" said Amélie. "Has he lost his mind?"

"No, Mama," said Theodosia. "Edward's been on the side of Eleanor all along. He's the one who betrayed us."

"The devil." Her mother crossed herself.

"Did you hear me, Captain?" said Theodosia. "We can get them back."

"I did hear you, Sister. But until we slow near to a stop, our speed will continue to pull them along. I'm doing all I can, I promise you."

One of the crewmen gave him a doubtful look. "They won't last long in this cold water. Five, ten minutes. No more. By the time we get them, they'll be blocks of ice."

Theodosia flew at him. "Just get Benedict, get him out of there. You must, you must. Do you hear me?"

"Hey." The captain pulled her off. "You're not helping, Sister. Let us do our job. So why don't you do yours, and start to pray?"

# CHAPTER 31

Barely afloat in the freezing blackness of the ocean, Palmer tried to wrestle the monk from him. The ship, already several yards away, pulled them along on the tightened rope. But Grim clutched his neck in a deadly embrace.

"You madman, Palmer. You've killed us both."

Palmer's breath came in high, fast heaves of his chest—too fast, but the cold wouldn't let him slow. "As long as I've done for you, I don't care." He flexed his shoulders and prepared to break the monk's hold. "Now get off me. I don't want you taking me to hell with you."

"The only one going to hell is you."

The razor appeared inches from Palmer's eyes.

"I'm cutting that rope from your arm, Palmer. I will have it instead." His actions matched his words.

Cut suddenly adrift, Palmer turned over in the water once, twice.

Grim was pulled away, the rope wound round his hands. "You're a fool, Palmer. I thought you should know that."

Screams, shouts, and lights came from the ship.

"A search party already," called Grim. "I'll send them to look for your corpse. While I see to that wanton and her mother."

Palmer flailed his arms, treaded water, a terrible numbness already in his legs. Grim was right. He was a fool. He'd gambled.

And lost. Worse, he'd delivered death to Theodosia and her mother as sure as if he'd landed the blows himself. His shoulders, knees stiffened with cold. Even the small movements of staying afloat became difficult now.

"The ship's stopping. Pity they won't find you!" Grim was now a bobbing form on the surface of the starlit water.

Was it confession time? Probably. He'd already begun to feel drowsy.

"Palmer!" Grim's panicked scream cut through his sleepiness. "Palmer! Come and help me, man. My robes! I'm sinking. Help me, for God's sake!"

Of course. Palmer started to laugh. When the ship had been sailing forward, its momentum had kept Grim afloat. Now that it had stopped, the monk in his heavy wool cassock became a dead weight.

Choking coughs sounded from Grim. "You have to help me! Please!"

Palmer didn't bother to reply. His numbness spread through his whole body, and he felt almost warm.

Final screams and gurgles came from Grim. Then a blessed silence settled over the sea.

Peace. Calm. This was how death should be. He brought Theodosia to his thoughts. That was how he'd leave this world, holding her in his soul. His wonderful, brave Theodosia. His beautiful Theodosia. Beautiful with her foolhardiness, her wits. Her clear gray eyes. He looked up at the stars. Soon he'd be amongst them. If that was where heaven was. His eyes slid closed. Heaven was with her, that was sure enough. One day, she'd come to join him. *Please, God.*

◆　◆　◆

"The rope's gone loose!"

The call that came from the front of the ship pierced Theodosia's heart as well as the night.

"Oh, dear God, Mama. Benedict's not tied on anymore. But I saw him. Why? What's happened?"

"I don't know, my blessed." Mama's voice was fearful.

Hanging over the wooden deck rail, Theodosia squinted at the night ocean as she tried to track the progress of the little rowboat that had put to sea, her last hope now for Benedict. The weak moonlight meant she could see little.

Her mother squeezed the back of her hand but said nothing.

Theodosia knew what the gesture meant. "It's been too long, hasn't it?" Anger built in her throat. "It's too cold. The water will be like melted ice."

The ship, head to wind, sat listlessly in the water, the proud square sail moving in a slow, useless flap.

Dead in the water. Like her Benedict. "What have I done?" Her cry echoed across the silent ocean as she dug her fingernails into the rail. "I let Edward guide me where it should have been Benedict. If I'd made the right choice, Benedict would still be alive."

"No one could have guessed what Edward was really up to," said Amélie. "Remember, I also trusted him. Followed him like a meek little lamb, when all the time he was plotting against Henry."

"But I should have—"

A hullo came from the water.

"That's my crewman," said Donne.

Theodosia gasped as the rowboat emerged from the darkness, low down in the water.

"Any luck?" said Donne.

"We found one," said the first crewman as they pulled alongside.

Theodosia craned over the edge. Her heart leapt. A man lying in the bottom of the boat, long legs clad in breeches. It had to be Benedict. Edward wore robes.

She dared to hope. "Is he all right?"

The crewman looked at her as if she wasn't in her senses.

"I'm afraid not, Sister," said the captain.

"Oh, dear God. No."

Her mother spoke to her, but she didn't hear a word.

The rowboat was hoisted to the side, and the crewmen battled to lift out her dead knight. They laid him on the wet planks of the deck, his eyes closed, dark wet hair plastered to his forehead, a red slash down one cheek from Grim's blade.

She sank to her knees, cradled his cold, cold face in her hands, sobs tearing from her throat.

"We should pray for him, Theodosia," said Amélie, bending to her.

"I don't want to pray for him. I want him. Can't you see that?"

Her mother shook her head slowly and crossed herself.

"He's gone, Sister," said one of the crewmen. "There's no heartbeat, nothing."

She could hardly see through her tears, breathe through her grief, as she stroked and stroked his face.

"He was barely alive when we got to him," said the second crewman. "We was too late."

"Tried to get a word out, though," said the first.

"Aye," said the second. "Made no sense to us."

"What did he say?" said Theodosia. Please let it be a last message of love to her. Please.

"Sounded like 'Knaresborough' to me," replied the second man.

She stared at the man, tears stemmed with hope. Knaresborough. Where she'd almost frozen to death. But Benedict had brought her back, told her how. She shot to her feet. "There might still be a chance," she said. "Take him below to Edward's cabin. Now."

"Oh, Theodosia." Her mother shook her head.

"Sister, he's dead." The captain's face reflected the view of all present that she'd taken leave of her senses.

"Bring him below. At once! Do you hear me? Now, God rot you! Now!"

Madness and rage brought their own authority. Gaping, the men hoisted Benedict's body between them and climbed below.

Theodosia pushed into the crowded cabin as they placed him on Edward's mattress.

Amélie squeezed past the men to the bedside. "We should cover his face." She went to match her words with actions.

"No. Get out, Mama. All of you. Get out!" Theodosia hustled them all out and slammed the door shut behind them. With a hard shove, she barred the door with the small chest.

She hurried over to the bed and ripped Benedict's soaked shirt from his body. His chest remained utterly still. No breath in or out. She put her ear close to his mouth and nose, hoping against hope for a tiny stir of air. Still nothing.

His trousers were next. His male nakedness didn't shock her, it made him seem abandoned, vulnerable. She choked back a sob as she grabbed the bedcover, rubbing him hard all over to dry his skin, warm it somehow. She grabbed Edward's heavy woolen cloak and laid it over him to try and bring some warmth. *Dear God, I'm only a sinner. Hear my prayer. Let him live. Please. Please.*

She brought her ear to his face again. Silence. This couldn't be happening. She brought her hands to his face. She might as well be touching the stone floor of the cathedral. He'd gone. Gone. And it was her stupid, selfish fault.

A brutal, harsh keening seared her throat. As her tears fell, they splashed on his face, made him look as if he wept too, with tears that caused the wound on his poor face to run.

She choked back her sobs, wiping his face dry with the cloak. "You should have let Edward kill me. I deserved it, I'm the one who caused all this death. Not you. But you always knew better, didn't you?"

Pinheads of blood appeared in the wound again, beaded larger and larger.

Her breath stopped.

The beads grew still more, then slid down his cheek.

Dead men didn't bleed.

"Oh, dear God. Benedict." She ripped her dress off over her head and climbed in under the coverlet. Her nakedness was the best warmth, the only warmth she had. She locked her body around his, willing him to take heat, life from her. "Come back to me, please. Come back to me."

Benedict's blue lips parted, then he drew in a shallow breath. Opening his eyes, his gaze found hers and he gave a feeble nod.

◆　◆　◆

Theodosia held her Benedict, rubbed his body, covered him with her own. She did not dare to stop, no matter how much her arms and shoulders ached, no matter how weary she became. At times, the worst, terrifying times, he barely seemed to know her, looked at her as if she were a stranger, muttered words that made no sense. Holding back her desperation, she redoubled her efforts, forcing life back into him.

Time meant nothing. There was only the dim cabin, the roll of the ship, and her own frantic efforts to keep him breathing, living. But it seemed to be working. Praise God, it seemed to be working.

A loud rap came at the door. "Theodosia?"

*Mama.* "Yes?"

"You've been in there for hours, my blessed. You must let him go now. The good Captain Donne will take care of him."

"One moment." Theodosia slipped her dress over her shoulders. She shoved the chest aside and opened the door to her mother.

"Come now," said Amélie, her face drawn in exhaustion. "We shall pray for his soul together. I have already been doing so."

"But, Mama, we don't need to." Theodosia swallowed the lump of overwhelmed tears in her throat. "I've saved him. He's alive." She clutched her mother's hands in joy.

"What?" Amélie thrust her away as if she'd been burned. "You mean to tell me you've been in here all of this time with a man?" She cast a horrified glance past Theodosia. "And please do not tell me that man is naked, for if he is, then you have committed mortal sin."

Theodosia stared at her mother in disbelief. "He's not just a man. He...he's Benedict. He's the man I love, a man who nearly died, and might still, trying to save my life. Your life too."

"If he drags your soul to hell, he has saved nothing." Amélie's nostrils flared in disapproval. "Better he had sunk to the depths of that ocean, or that you had listened to us all when we told you to leave him to—"

"Mother!" Theodosia's yell shocked Amélie to silence. "Stop it. Now. Can't you hear yourself? You never find anything in me except wrongness, sin. Even when we were at Canterbury, when I was too young to want anything other than to please you, to have you love me as a mother should. But you never did. You're so unyielding, so unforgiving, so..." She threw her arms up, dropped them again. "Cold."

Amélie turned white. "How can you speak to me so? All I ever wanted was to protect your soul."

"Because you were so busy concentrating on my soul, you forgot about my heart. Your own heart." Theodosia put a hand to the door. "You're not a mother, not to me. You never were." She slammed it shut before Amélie could say another word.

◆    ◆    ◆

Benedict lay in her arms, in a peaceful, natural sleep. Theodosia stroked his thick dark hair, rejoiced in every strand, drank in every inch of his sleeping features. They'd lain like this for hours, as the ship made its rolling progress. She wished they could stay here forever, cocooned from the world, where it would just be the two of them in warm, sensual bliss.

He stirred and opened his eyes with a smile. "There you are," he murmured.

"I hadn't gone anywhere," she said.

"I dreamt I was being kissed by an angel," he said.

"Then you must be sorely disappointed."

"I'm not disappointed." He raised himself up on one elbow and looked down at her. "Not at all."

"You should be. I must look a fright." She waved a rueful hand at her shaved head.

He cupped her face in one large hand. "The angel couldn't hold a candle to you." Again, a gentle smile. "And waking with you is better than waking in Paradise."

"You were nearly there." She stroked his hand with her own. "I only did what you'd done for me."

"Have you stolen a cross from me too?" He teased her with a kiss on her forehead.

"No. You're a heathen, remember?" she teased back.

"And you're a king's daughter." He lay back down next to her and sighed. "We'll be docking in France soon, won't we?"

His question needed no explanation. Once they saw Henry, their paths would separate. She'd return to the protection of the crown, hidden from the world, under the pretext of a religious calling. He would live out his own life.

"We still have a couple of hours." He kissed her softly.

"Then we have time." She held his gaze, heart fast in her chest. "I want you. Completely."

"But we've spoken of this—"

She stopped his protest with the light press of her fingertips to his lips. "My battle is over, Benedict. The day is done. If I have you, know you, if only this once, then I can bear the lie my life has to be." She lowered her hand. "For I will hold the truth of you, of me, of us, in my heart till the day I die."

He looked at her for a long, long moment. "I don't know what I've done to deserve this."

"You're you, Benedict Palmer."

"And you're my Theodosia, my gift from God." He lowered his mouth to hers.

Theodosia lay sleepless as Benedict again dozed beside her. Her body ached, stiffened, but in a way she'd never known existed. The pleasure Benedict had pulled from her body, over and over. His lips, his hands, his tongue. His hard flesh inside her. She drew in a deep, shuddering breath, utterly spent but utterly at peace. No wonder Grim had hated women who dared to love, to lust, as he'd damned it. It made a woman rejoice in her body, as Benedict had with her.

A faint shout came from abovedecks. "Land ho!"

Theodosia turned to Benedict as he stirred. "In my heart. For-ever."

"Mine too," he murmured. "Mine too." He kissed her softly. "But now we have to face the King. Your father." He kissed her harder, deeper, as if he would devour her.

Then she knew it was the last time.

# CHAPTER 32

"His Grace asks for a few minutes while he washes from his journey." The abbot of Abbaye Saint-Pierre cast a final glance over Theodosia, her mother, and Benedict as they waited outside the abbot's parlor.

They'd arrived at this holy house almost three full days ago, directed by Captain Donne. Her mother had assumed complete control the minute they crossed the threshold, speaking in private with the abbot, sending Benedict to separate quarters. Ordering, fixing. Bringing her daughter back into the fold, with no mention of what had happened on the ship.

Theodosia pulled the sleeves of her new, thankfully barbless, habit straight. She cast a sideways glance at Benedict, whom she'd not seen since they'd arrived.

Dressed in fine dark green wool breeches, a long leather belted tunic, and tailored linen shirt, with his dark hair combed, he could easily pass for gentry. Longing tugged deep inside her, but she pushed it aside. They were here to honor Thomas's memory, to lay the truth before the King. Her father, summoned here in secret by the monastic post.

"Come!" A muffled voice from within.

The abbot opened the door and held it as they filed in.

Theodosia steadied her rapid breathing as she entered the room with her mother. Benedict followed after, silent and respectful.

The abbot closed the door behind them, leaving them in private.

A man stood before the lit fireplace, facing them, arms folded. With his luxuriously clothed stout build, fiery countenance, and keen gray eyes, it could only be the King himself.

"Your Grace." Amélie dropped into a deep curtsey, and Theodosia followed.

Next to Theodosia, Benedict bowed low, though he still soared head and shoulders over the shorter Henry.

"Rise." Henry's voice had a tremulous quality unexpected in such a robust man. Then he looked at Amélie and held out his hands. "My dear one."

Amélie hastened to him and dropped before him in another curtsey. "Not as dear as you are to me, sire."

Henry took her hands in his. "You're not harmed?"

She shook her head. "Frightened only, your Grace."

"Praise God. Now rise. You have no need of such ceremony with me." The King helped Amélie to stand. A smile of great tenderness played on his lips as he loosed his hold on her.

"Thank you." Amélie flushed like a girl as she met his gaze.

Motioning for Amélie to stand next to him, Henry sought out Theodosia. "Our baby, Laeticia?" he said to Amélie, eyebrows raised. "Surely not."

Amélie nodded. "It seems impossible, but yes."

"Impossible until I look in a mirror and see an old man gaping back at me." Henry gave a laugh, which only Amélie joined him in.

Theodosia ventured a smile. A glance at Benedict confirmed him paralyzed with deference.

The King did not seem to notice as he spoke to Amélie. "Inside we might feel as the day we met. The outside world would judge us otherwise."

"Yet I cherish those memories far more than I mourn the loss of my youth," came Amélie's reply.

"Of good spirit, as ever." Henry brushed a hand against her cheek before turning his full attention to Theodosia once again. "Come forward, Laeticia."

Theodosia did as instructed, eyes cast down demurely.

"You're a beautiful young woman," he said. "Yet you chose the cloth?"

"Thank you, your Grace, but the cloth chose me."

Henry's eyebrows arched as he transferred his gaze to Benedict. "And you are?"

"Sir Benedict Palmer, your Grace."

"Duped by Fitzurse and a witness to poor Thomas's demise," said Amélie swiftly. "Neither Th—Laeticia nor I would be here today if he had not come to our aid. Isn't that so, Laeticia?"

Her mother gave Theodosia a gracious smile, as if the harsh exchange on the boat had never taken place.

Theodosia simply nodded.

"Then I will be forever in your debt, Sir Palmer," said Henry. He indicated to two red velvet–padded settles by the fire. "Now please, be seated, all of you. The letter that came to me hinted that there is much to tell, and I need to hear it all."

"It will take some time, sire," said Amélie as they took their places, she next to Henry, Benedict beside Theodosia.

"Then take it," said Henry. "No one will dare disturb us."

It took nigh on two hours to tell Henry the full tale. He listened well but barked short, sharp questions at several points. His interrogation showed a keenly incisive mind, and impressed and terrified

Theodosia in equal measure. Her father he might be, but she could think of him only as the monarch.

Now they'd finished, they sat in silence before the glowing embers of the fire while fat snowflakes rustled against the window.

Henry held Grim's manuscript unrolled on his lap and shook his head slowly, face ruddy with fury. "I always knew Eleanor loved my power and not me. But I never thought she'd stoop to these lows."

"The lust for power makes people do some terrible things," said Amélie. "She will be judged before God, like everyone else."

"If only she were like everyone else." Henry sprang to his feet and rolled up the manuscript.

Theodosia too scrambled to her feet, Benedict quicker than she. Amélie also rose politely.

"No, no." Henry waved for them to sit. "I'm thinking, thinking. Walking helps me think."

As they complied, he paced before the hearth, slapping the roll of vellum hard on his other open palm as he did so. "Knowing Eleanor, she won't worry about the Almighty's judgment. She'd more likely try to oust the Almighty so she could take his place." His face reddened more in his anger. "Curse her!"

His sudden shout made Theodosia jump, and Benedict started beside her.

Pausing before the fireplace, Henry took the manuscript in both hands and struck it against the stone mantel over and over. "Curse her, curse her, curse her!"

Theodosia sat utterly still, not wanting to draw the King's wrath. Now she knew where her own flashes of fury came from. At the edge of her vision, she saw Benedict's actions mirrored hers.

"What am I supposed to do with such scurrilous lies?" Henry wheeled around and waved the manuscript aloft. "Murder in my name! A good man, nay, a great one, slain! Betrayal by my own queen! Devil take her, and devil take those sniveling little curs spawned from her rancid loins. Devil take them all!" Specks of foamed spit flew from his mouth as he shouted.

Did the King need help? His rage was fearsome. Theodosia caught her mother's eye, but Amélie appeared calm, like she had witnessed this behavior before.

Henry flung himself back into his seat beside her mother, his hands trembling violently. "Edward Grim is a lucky, lucky man to have died so easily. He wouldn't have had as swift a passage if I'd got hold of him."

Amélie placed a steady hand over his convulsing ones. "Your passion for truth, for righteousness, shows in your anger, sire. But do not let it make you ill."

The King snorted but seemed a mite calmer. He looked at the manuscript and snorted again, wiping his mouth with the back of one hand. He stared into the fire, lost in his own thoughts.

Amélie patted his hands gently. "You have the truth now. You hold it in your hands." She looked at Theodosia and Benedict and gave a light laugh. "Indeed, sit beside it. For we three are living proof of it."

Henry gave a humph and let out a long breath.

Amélie continued. "But we are not a piece of vellum, with words spelled out along it. We are flesh and blood. Indeed, Laeticia is your royal flesh and blood, conceived in holy matrimony."

Another humph.

"Then what happens to us all, sire?"

Reluctantly admiring of her mother's skillful handling of the King, Theodosia glanced quickly at Benedict. His dark eyes reflected her own trepidation of what might come to pass.

Henry jumped up from his seat to pace once more. "That's what I'm trying to decide." He paused and looked at Amélie. "You know, if I could, I would claim you as my queen?"

Amélie bowed her head graciously. "Sire, you spoke of this many, many years ago. It's not to be, and I accept that. I am happy to live the life of a holy woman. I am content with your blessed patronage."

Henry's mouth creased in a smile. "Few women would ever claim to be content. You're a remarkable woman, Amélie." He set off pacing once more. "Look at this situation from the outside world's view. Eleanor has no proof of your existence." He swept a hand to encompass all three members of his audience. "Her knights are dead. Edward Grim, curse him again, has a solid reputation." He held up the manuscript. "His account tells of a murder that happened due to my poor relationship with my archbishop. No mention of any of you in it." He halted, a triumphant grin on his face. "Then we can return to how we were, except better. Amélie, Laeticia: it will be easy for me to set you up in a new convent, one far from here, where no one will ever suspect your true identities. You will be my secret once more, but completely safe together till the end of your days. I give you my word."

Amélie clasped her hands. "God be praised," she said quietly.

*Return to the lies.* Theodosia plastered a smile on her face, sickened though she was at her fate. But who was she to question a king?

"Sir Palmer," said Henry, "you risked everything, even your life, for my family. I will see to it that you are a wealthy man."

"Thank you, Majesty." Benedict gave a respectful bow.

"But what of you, sire?" said Amélie. "Your plan is most generous, as always. But it means the world will find you to blame for Thomas Becket's death. That would be a great injustice, a great lie."

Theodosia and Benedict murmured their agreement.

Henry waved a hand to dismiss their objections. "To bring Eleanor to justice would be almost impossible. For me to try and do so would tear my kingdom apart. Many, many innocent lives would be lost." He looked at Amélie. "Including yours and Laeticia's, I have no doubt of that. The Queen never, ever gives up, once she has set her mind to something." He took the manuscript in both hands, and his voice lowered. "This is mine to atone for." He stared at it in silence for a long moment, lost in his own thoughts. Then he snapped to, voice strong once more. "Palmer, you can start by having my spare horse, an excellent black gelding. You'll find him in the stables. I have an estate to the south of the country that needs a baron. I'll give you the details later. You might as well set off for there in the morning. No time like the present."

"Thank you again, your Grace."

Theodosia couldn't look at Benedict, couldn't bear to see the joy that would be there. Not just his escape from poverty and shame. Wealth beyond his wildest dreams and a noble title. He would have the pick of noblewomen to take as a wife, to be mother to his children. Her jealousy threatened to overwhelm her, but she forced it down. He deserved it. It didn't matter if it broke her heart. She'd have the rest of her life to grieve.

# CHAPTER 33

Palmer opened the door of the abbey that led onto the courtyard. Though the sky was clear now, the night's fall of thick soft snow came halfway up his boots. At this hour of the dawn, no one else stirred, save for a single blackbird, hopping along in search of food. Only a lone set of footprints marked the snow, showing the path of a groom headed for the stables.

Up in the abbey, Theodosia prayed or slept, he didn't know which. And he'd never know. She would be closed to him forever. He trudged through the snow toward the stables, his heart sick. Last night, he'd not closed an eye, running through his choices over and over. And always coming back to the same one. His mind was made up, and it felt right.

The stable door creaked on its hinges as he opened it. Warm, pungent air met his nostrils as he went along the stalls to look for the gelding. There it was.

"Good morning, handsome fellow." Palmer put a hand out to stroke his new animal. The horse's neck was sleek under his touch, a smoothness that spoke of many hours of combing and grooming.

The saddle waited outside the stall on a rack. Palmer bent to examine it. Made of the finest leather, it was tooled to the highest standard and oiled so it gleamed. This was the kind of wealth the King's reward would command. He shook his head. He'd take the horse, he needed one. As for the rest of Henry's gift, he'd have none of it. The only thing he truly wanted was his beloved anchoress. And because he couldn't have her, everything else meant nothing.

He picked up the ornate saddle and opened the door of the stall. "Definitely made for a king's arse. Not mine," he remarked to the horse.

"What's that about my arse?" Henry's face popped up over the partition between stalls.

Palmer colored redder than he ever had in his life. "Y-your Grace." He bowed deeply and lowered the saddle to the floor. "A thousand apologies, sire. I didn't know you were there."

Henry snorted with laughter. "Obviously." He emerged from the stall, a leather apron tied round his large gut. "Don't worry about it, sir knight. I've heard a lot worse in my time."

Palmer gaped, unable to find words.

Henry looked down and patted his apron. "You're wondering about this, aren't you?"

"Eh, yes, sire."

"I like to get stuck in," said Henry. "Can't abide staying in bed more than an hour or two. Get nothing done. Grooming horses— now, there's a real job. Makes something happen. Gives you time to think." He fixed Palmer with his piercing gray eyes, slightly blood-shot from hard work and the early hour. "Good to see you're not a slugabed. Or are you just keen to see your estate?"

"If I may, I would like to speak with you about that, sire."

"Go on."

"Your Grace, I would be more than grateful to accept this fine horse and saddle."

"But?"

"But if it please your Grace—"

"Oh, spit it out, man. You're stuttering like a simpleton."

"I don't want the estate. Or the title." Palmer swallowed. "Your Grace."

"Hah!" Henry began to pace on the straw-strewn floor.

Palmer winced inside. He'd seen the King's pacing build up to an astonishing rage yesterday. He didn't want to be on the receiving end of another one.

"You interest me, Benedict Palmer. Last evening, I granted you a title. Wealth for life. Privilege. One of the finest steeds in the kingdom. Yet you reacted like I'd asked you to lick a leper. And now, this morn, you don't want it, save for the steed." He narrowed his eyes. "I have to ask myself, what's the matter with you?"

"There's nothing the matter, sire. I'm grateful to you and your generosity. I thought of nothing else last night."

"Flat as a cowpat." Henry stopped dead. "Why?"

"All I ever wanted was to be rich. Build high, fine walls around me. Keep sickness, hunger, death outside the door." Palmer shrugged. "But that was a fool's want. What matters is a place in the world where I can stay put, live out my life with a woman who loves and respects me for who I am, not what I own."

"And what brought about this change of heart?"

"Sister Theodosia. All I want is her, and I can't have her. So now all wealth would do is torture me with a long, comfortable life. More and more days to be plagued by the memory of her." He shook his head. "I'll go back to what I know, to fighting wherever I can. If God is merciful, I won't last long. Then my grief will be over."

"Hah!" Henry clapped him hard on the shoulder and made him jump. "I thought so. Lovesick young men are very easy to spot. Have you told her how you feel?"

"Indeed I have, sire. And she me. But all I've brought her is sin, and a doubting of her calling. And because of who she is, I

365

have to give her up. I've no choice. And that's how things are." He suddenly remembered whom he spoke to. "If you see what I mean, your Grace."

"Indeed I do." To his surprise, Henry extended a hand. "Then I wish you Godspeed, Sir Benedict Palmer."

"Thank you, sire." Palmer shook Henry's firm grasp, then bent to lift the saddle and flung it over the horse's back. He adjusted the stirrups before leading the horse out of the stable.

He hoisted himself into the saddle and looked back to see his king stood in the doorway, his breath clouding in the freezing air.

Henry raised a hand in silent farewell.

"God save you, sire." Palmer clicked to the animal and set off in the snowy dawn.

◆　◆　◆

Theodosia knelt in the chilly, deserted monastery chapel. Fingers tight on the wooden cross around her neck, she desperately called for God in her heart. But he didn't answer. Oh, this was so hard. It had to get easier, it had to. She was gifted to the church afresh, just as she had been all those years before. Gifted by a king, her father. She had to obey his commands, go along with his decisions.

She was alone again, Benedict was gone. From her room high in the abbey, she'd seen him ride out with her own eyes. Gone. Now all she had to do was return to her state of holy solitude. She screwed her eyes shut to try and remember the words of the divine office. But not a word, a phrase, a syllable, would come. Her mind was as empty as the pagans' fort on the hilltop. Not empty, her conscience said, only empty of virtue. Full, though, of thoughts of Benedict, of memories of his voice, his bravery. His touch. His smile. She opened her eyes to banish the image and started.

Henry sat in the pew next to her, dressed outlandishly in groom's clothes, dirt under his fingernails. "Good morning."

"Good morning, sire."

"You looked as if you were praying very hard for something," he said.

"Only to return to how I was. It sore eludes me at the moment. Try as I might, my mind cannot retrieve the words of holiness." She drew in an unsteady breath. "But with God's grace, they will return in time."

"What's stopping you?"

"No one, sire."

"I asked what, not whom." Henry leaned in closer. "I'm your father as well as your king. Tell me the truth."

Theodosia flushed. "Benedict. Sir Palmer."

"What has Sir Palmer done to erase the mind of a nun?"

"Many things. But, worse, I've done them too. I've become something I'm not."

"So he turned you from an anchoress into a…?"

"Someone who rides, who fights, who murders, who…who… uses her body."

To her horror, Henry threw his head back and roared with laughter.

"Sire, please, we're in a chapel."

He snorted. "God doesn't mind if we laugh aloud. He created us in His own image, remember."

"Exactly. Chaste, pure, contained, selfless. All the things I was before I met him."

"Oh, my dear girl. God is so much more than that." Henry put his powerful hand over hers. "Palmer hasn't changed you. He's allowed you to be yourself, allowed you to be like your father, as well as your mother. Yes, you've had to do some hard, hard things.

But so have I. And sometimes we have to ask God for forgiveness for what we've done. The glorious thing is, He grants it. It's what He died for."

"I have to stay with what I was brought up to do." She dared to meet his eye. "What you and Mama decided for me."

"And what would you decide?"

"I already have."

"Which is?"

"To hold Sir Palmer in my heart. Forever."

A distant bell rang, announcing the call to the office of Prime. Then the words came flooding back, crystal as if she read them from her Psalter. "Quicumque vult salvus esse." (Whosoever shall be saved.)

Henry sat in silence as she whispered her way through the prayer, joining with her "amen."

She turned to Henry with a long, soft sigh. "God has comforted me. I pray He forgives my failure too, so I can follow my vocation away from the world."

"You haven't failed." He squeezed her hand. "You have yet to take your final vows as an anchoress. Isn't that correct?"

"It is."

"But one of the tests for an anchoress is to come back out into the world for her final year. To see if she is truly, truly confirmed in her vocation."

She nodded, mouth dry. The test she'd always dreaded, that would keep her locked out of her cell forever if she failed. Now her dread was still the locked cell door, but for it to keep her in.

"Think, Theodosia. Through his terrible death, our beloved Thomas brought you out, gave you your test. Maybe not in the usual way, but by his soul, you've been tested. You haven't failed, my dear girl. Just been shown your true path."

Her heart tripped faster as a tiny, miraculous hope took hold.

Henry smiled sadly. "I didn't follow mine, and my wrong choice has brought nothing but misery. I can't stand aside and let you do the same. I'm your father; go with my blessing."

She gasped. "Oh, sire." King or no king, she didn't care. She flung her arms around his neck and hugged him tight. "Thank you, dearest Father. With all my heart."

He returned the hug, then reached deep into the pocket of his apron. He handed her a small leather bag, weighted with coins. "This should be enough to get you both started with a few virgates. The rest is up to you."

Theodosia clutched the bag, hardly able to speak. "Thank you once more." She looked at Henry. "But why would you do all this for Benedict and me?"

"Because you fought for my crown, for the truth. Even when you thought there was no reward. That is true bravery, true loyalty. Something I value beyond measure."

"I would fight for you again. As would Benedict. In a heartbeat."

Henry smiled and patted her cheek. "I know you would. God willing, you will never have to."

"Then you've just granted me Paradise."

Henry got his feet, as did Theodosia. "Remember that when there are mice in your barn, when your cow stands on your toes, when you're birthing lambs in the middle of the night." He smiled. "When you're holding your babies in your arms." He patted her cheek again. "You're right, it is Paradise. Let's make all haste and get you a mount."

They walked out of the chapel and into the bright, dazzling dawn, headed across the deep snow for the stables.

"Will you say good-bye to Mama for me?" said Theodosia. "I would do it in person, but I fear we would only be harsh with each other. She would hate my choice." She heard the bitterness in her own voice. "For her, virtue and nobility are always first. Not even a child is more important."

Henry said nothing, just reached into his apron pocket again. He handed Theodosia a tiny Book of Hours.

She stopped dead as Henry halted too. It was the one Mama had had all those years ago in Canterbury. Tiny, exquisite: Mama had kept it with her at all times, hadn't even left it behind when she went away to Polesworth.

Her father put a hand over hers and gently guided her to open it at one particular page. On one side was a picture of Our Lady, the Christ child as a baby on her lap. On the facing page, a verse from John: "When a woman is giving birth, she has sorrow because her hour has come, but when she has delivered the baby, she no longer remembers the anguish, for joy that a human being has been born into the world."

The ink was faded, the edges of the page stained with a thousand touches. And marking the page was a baby curl: a dark-blonde feather, secured with a thin strand of white silk.

Sudden tears blurred Theodosia's sight.

"Don't judge her too harshly," said Henry quietly. "She did what she thought was right, which is what all loving parents do. It cost her dear." He closed the book and left it in her hands. "She wants you to have it, with her blessing, and to think of her more fondly when you have children of your own."

Theodosia's tears spilled over.

"Now come," said Henry." "You'll need to be swift if you're to catch Benedict up."

Palmer rode at a steady trot through the snow-covered woods, the gelding easily eating up the miles.

Watery winter sun had turned the sky a washed-out blue. He had a sudden yearning for spring, for warmth, for the sun on his face, for long, sun-filled evenings.

Yet he'd face them alone. His joy would have been to share them with Theodosia, to have her call to him for supper made with her own small hands, for him to bring her flowers from the fields. He could hear her voice now. He shook the imaginary sound from his ears.

But there it was again.

"Benedict! Benedict! Wait! It's me!"

He turned in his saddle. And there she was, galloping after him apace, cloak streaming out behind her. He halted his mount and secured it to a tree as Theodosia raced into the clearing.

She pulled up her mount and flung the reins round a bush.

"What are you doing?" he asked as he dismounted.

She jumped down from her horse and approached him, breathless from her ride. "Are you ready for Paradise?"

"You talk in riddles—"

But she cut off his words with her lips, fastening them on his as she pulled him tight to her.

# CHAPTER 34

*Canterbury, Kent, July 12, 1174*

The streets of Canterbury teemed with people. Henry had known it would be thus.

From his view out a ground-floor window at the Episcopal Palace, they lined the streets, shoved their heads through casements, sat up on walls. All to get a better look. The excited clamor reminded Henry of massed birds in a feeding frenzy, all waiting to get their fill and screaming till they did.

The sight of a king doing public penance was unheard of. Every citizen who could had made the journey so they would witness it for themselves, tell it forever to those who hadn't. But Henry wasn't doing it for them. He did it for his own soul, and as the only way he knew to express his deep, enduring sorrow for the death of his dear friend Thomas Becket.

He turned to the waiting new Archbishop, Becket's successor. "I'm ready."

The Archbishop nodded. "Here is your sackcloth, sire." He held up the rough garment as Henry stripped to his waist.

Successor? Perhaps, but no match for the great Becket. The world would not see his like again. A glance down showed Henry's own corpulent spread, the gift of middle age. How soft his skin had become from his life as king, with the muscle of his vigorous youth softening to useless flesh. It wouldn't be too many years before even that soft flesh gave way to shriveled skin and creaking bones. But at least he still had the gift of life. Because of him, Thomas did not. Henry took the sackcloth and slipped it over his head, glad to embrace his penance.

Next, the Archbishop produced a dish of blessed ashes.

"Do you wish me to apply these, sire?"

"No." Henry dipped his fingers in the nearby holy-water font, then into the dusty softness of the finely ground ash. He smeared his face with the black paste to give himself the mask of the sinner. "Let us proceed."

"Your Grace." The Archbishop moved to the door and bowed as he opened it.

Henry stepped into the broiling sun, and the roar of the crowd swelled in volume and climbed in pitch. His bare feet, delicate as a maid's from years of wearing the finest shoes, hit against every bump of the cobbles in a painful jar.

The line of eighty black-robed monks waited, scourges in hand. Sweat poured down their faces from their wait in the sun.

Henry blessed himself and set off on his slow journey. The first scourge landed across his shoulders and drew a gasp from the watchers. It stung like a serpent, but Henry walked on, praying aloud. Another scourge cracked down, and he continued despite the pain.

The crowd grew more subdued. Many took up the rhythm of his prayer. Others raised their voices in solemn hymns. Still others wept as they saw his suffering, his humiliation on the public streets.

His progress was slow, difficult. The scourges bit, his skin tore. But it was for Thomas, the martyr, the saint. Tonight he, Henry, would spend all night at the ornate shrine in the cathedral, the one built on the very spot where the murdering knights had felled Thomas.

"God bless you, sire. You know He will."

A voice he knew well. A woman's voice.

Henry turned his head to see who spoke. In spite of his pain, he smiled.

Dressed in simple peasant dress, her face tanned from the summer sun, freckles across her nose, was Theodosia. Her belly swelled with a babe who'd be here by autumn.

Next to her stood Benedict Palmer, his shoulders even broader from his near on four years as a farmer.

Palmer nodded his sympathy, and his dark eyes said more than words. Sat on his shoulders, small mouth round in astonishment, was a little red-haired lad of about three. Palmer raised a hand. "The blessings of Saint Thomas Becket upon you, sire."

It was as if his pain had lifted.

Henry smiled in return, squared his shoulders, and continued on his pilgrimage to Canterbury Cathedral.

## THE END

# HISTORICAL NOTE

*The Fifth Knight* is a work of fiction but many of the events and characters in it are based on fact.

The murder of Archbishop Thomas Becket in Canterbury Cathedral in 1170 is one of the most infamous episodes in medieval history. Becket and King Henry II had been close friends and allies, but relations between the two had become increasingly strained from 1165 onwards. Their disputes were power struggles: between church and state, and between canon and secular law.

Matters came to a head at Henry's Christmas court in Normandy in December 1170. Hearing of Becket's excommunication of the King's religious allies, Henry is alleged to have exploded into a rage (for which he was well known) and demanded "Will no one rid me of this troublesome priest?" Other popular versions are "This meddlesome priest" and "This turbulent priest."

Four knights (Sir Reginald Fitzurse, Sir Hugh de Morville, Sir William de Tracy and Sir Richard le Bret) then acted on his words, and left for England to murder the Archbishop. It is interesting that no-one can quite explain why these knights decided to take such action. Various accounts state "They overheard him", or "They took it upon themselves" and "They took Henry at his word." They were not directly ordered by Henry. There are accounts of the four knights fleeing to Knaresborough after the murder, and also to Scotland and Cumbria.

The public outrage that followed Becket's death was intense. The blame for the murder was laid at Henry's door and there were calls for him to be excommunicated from the church. Pope Alexander intervened, instead excommunicating the four knights. Their penance was to be sent to the Holy Land for fourteen years but later accounts of them are vague. Henry conducted a public penance for Becket's death on the streets of Canterbury in July 1174.

Brother Edward Grim's written description of the murder is very detailed. Yet he was the sole person to directly observe Becket's murder (other than the murderers), making his the only eye-witness account. In it, Grim makes sure that his own role is important. He is clear the other monks left, that he was wounded trying to defend Becket and that he stayed to hold the dying Archbishop.

Henry's relationship with his Queen, Eleanor of Aquitaine, was also filled with conflict. When they married in 1154, she was eleven years older than him and had previously been married to King Louis VII of France. She had six children, with four surviving sons. Henry's infidelities were well-known and he may have considered divorce from Eleanor so he could marry a mistress. By 1167, Henry and Eleanor were estranged. Eleanor sided with her sons, all of whom distrusted their father. Eleanor spent several years under house arrest, such was Henry's suspicion of her political intentions and fear of her skill at plotting.

There are many surviving records of anchoress's cells in medieval churches and some cells exist to this day. There is no record of an anchoress's cell in Canterbury, although much of the structure has been destroyed and rebuilt over the centuries.

Thomas Becket was canonized in 1173 and remains a venerated saint. His shrine was destroyed in 1538 on the orders of Henry VIII. Today, a single candle marks the place where it once stood.

# ACKNOWLEDGMENTS

There's only my name on the cover, but it took many special people to get it there. My wonderful husband, Jon and my beautiful daughter, Angela have helped me every step of the way. My literary agent, Josh Getzler and his assistant Maddie Raffel believed in my work and were tireless and relentlessly optimistic champions of it. At Thomas & Mercer, editor Andy Bartlett believed in it too, with the patient Jacque Ben-Zekry providing author support. And for Pat Sider, online angel and keeper of the dream: you know what you did.

# ABOUT THE AUTHOR

E. M. Powell was born and raised in Ireland, a descendant of Irish revolutionary Michael Collins. At University College, Cork, she discovered a love of Anglo-Saxon and medieval English during her study of literature and geography. She is a member of Romance Writers of America, the Historical Novel Society, and International Thriller Writers. A reviewer for the Historical Novel Society, she lives today in Manchester, England, with her husband and daughter. To read more about the world of The Fifth Knight, go to www.empowell.com.

# Kindle *Serials*

This book was originally released in episodes as a Kindle Serial. Kindle Serials launched in 2012 as a new way to experience serialized books. Kindle Serials allow readers to enjoy the story as the author creates it, purchasing once and receiving all existing episodes immediately, followed by future episodes as they are published. To find out more about Kindle Serials and to see the current selection of Serials titles, visit www.amazon.com/kindleserials.